TAKE DOWN

ALSO BY JAMES SWAIN

Jack Carpenter Series:

Midnight Rambler
The Night Stalker
The Night Monster
The Program

Tony Valentine Series:

Grift Sense
Funny Money
Sucker Bet
Loaded Dice
Mr. Lucky
Deadman's Poker
Deadman's Bluff
Wild Card
Jackpot

Peter Warlock Series:

Dark Magic
Shadow People

JAMES SWAIN

THOMAS & MERCER

This is a work of fiction. Names, characters, organizations, places, events, and incidents are either products of the author's imagination or are used fictitiously.

Published by Thomas & Mercer, Seattle

www.apub.com

ISBN-13: 9781477822029
ISBN-10: 147782202X

Cover design by David Drummond, Salamander Hill Design

Library of Congress Control Number: 2014950386

Printed in the United States of America

For Stephen Roberts

ONE

-THE HOT SEAT-

After his arrest at Galaxy's casino, Billy was handcuffed and transported to the Clark County Detention Center, where he sat chained to a chair while a knuckle-dragging deputy two-finger-typed the charges against him into a desktop. He'd been busted before and managed to beat every single rap, but this bust was shaping up to be different. They'd caught him trying to escape, and that was never good. An extended stay at a gated community in the Nevada desert was his next stop if he didn't do something fast.

Saturday was old home day at the jail, and the holding cell was standing room only. He eventually got his one phone call, which he used to call his attorney's answering service, onto which he left a short message explaining the jam he'd gotten himself into.

He spent the night in thought. He and his crew had been made in the employee parking garage before the heist and had probably been photographed. He also had to assume that his crew had been filmed stealing the $8 million inside the casino. Witnesses would tie him to the fire alarm being pulled, and a video of him running away probably existed as well. With that much evidence, a reasonable jury would find him guilty, and his short, happy career as a cheat would come to an end.

It wasn't looking good for the kid, but he wasn't about to call it quits. Like his old man was fond of saying, you can lose every round of a fight, just don't lose the last one.

Around midnight, a female voice called his name. At the cell door, he grabbed bars worn thin by inmates instinctively gripping them at chest height. Across the hall a vision named Maggie Flynn had materialized in the women's holding cell. The orange jumpsuit actually looked good on her.

"You okay?" he asked.

"The gaming board worked me over pretty good. You're next," she said.

"Right now?"

"Tomorrow. They all went home to get their beauty rest."

"How much do they know?"

"Too much. We're going down, Billy."

She sounded defeated, as if the last chapter in the book had been written. He wasn't ready to throw in the towel and brought his face closer to the bars.

"I need you to fill in some holes for me," he said. "There's a bunch of stuff I don't know about your deal with them. I want the whole story."

"You think you can slip out of this one?" she asked.

"Why not?"

She shook her head as if to say, *No way*.

"You betting against me?" he asked incredulously.

"Some people got killed this afternoon at the casino, and the gaming board wants to pin it on us. We're in their crosshairs."

"Screw them. Now tell me about your deal, and don't leave anything out."

"You don't quit, do you?"

"Quitting is for losers. Come on, what else do you have to do?"

She smiled tiredly, and then she started talking.

- - -

The next morning, a pair of deputies removed Billy from the holding cell. Along with smelling pretty rank he had a headache from listening to his cell mates jabber during the night. As he passed the women's holding cell, Mags pressed her face to the bars and mouthed the words *good luck.*

Next stop was the sixth floor, where three grim-faced gaming agents and Billy's lawyer were gathered in a windowless interrogation room. It was said that clothes made the man, and also gave him away. The gaming agents wore designer knockoffs from Jacobi's Men's Fashions, where you could buy three suits, three shirts, three neckties, and three pairs of socks for the ridiculously low price of $399. Many gaming agents shopped at Jacobi's under the mistaken belief that the clothes made them look sharp. Compared to his lawyer's five-thousand-dollar Brioni wool suit, the agents looked like circus clowns that had just piled out of a VW.

Billy pumped his lawyer's hand. Felix Underman was as old as the Rolling Stones and sported a neat part in his shock of silver hair. Back when the mob had run the casinos, Underman had defended every wise guy, hit man, and mobster, and had earned the reputation as the best criminal defense attorney around. That was good, because Billy needed all the help he could get.

"Good morning, Billy. How are you doing?" his lawyer asked.

"I'm doing great," he said, putting on his best front.

"These gentlemen from the gaming board want to talk to you. They think that you had something to do with a heist that happened yesterday afternoon at the Galaxy."

"So that's what this is about. Sure, I'll talk with them."

Introductions were made. The gaming board often hired law enforcement officials from other agencies to fill their top jobs, and it was easy to tell where these jokers came from. John LaBadie, chief, investigations division, sported a flat buzz cut that screamed ex-CIA. Carl Zander, deputy chief, investigations division, was as dull as an accountant, probably ex-FBI. Bill Tricaricco, director of field agents, had bad breath and a cop's big belly. Billy had pulled the wool over Tricaricco at the Hard Rock years ago and wondered if he still held a grudge.

"So you're the infamous Billy Cunningham," LaBadie said. "I've heard your name so many times, I thought there were five of you."

"I get around a lot," Billy admitted.

The room had a rectangular table with an old-fashioned tape recorder and five wooden chairs. Billy sat down at the table with his lawyer, while the gaming agents remained standing.

"For your information, we're going to record this conversation," LaBadie said.

"By all means. My client has nothing to hide," Billy's lawyer said.

LaBadie started the tape recorder. He picked up a microphone and recited the date, time, and location of where the interrogation was taking place, then identified the five individuals in the room. Finished, he placed the mike down and cleared his throat.

"If you don't mind, I'd like to take notes," the lawyer said.

"Go right ahead," LaBadie said.

Underman retrieved an alligator briefcase from the floor and placed it on the table. He lifted the lid so Billy could see the copy of that day's *Las Vegas Review-Journal* resting inside the briefcase, but the gaming agents could not. The screaming headline was impossible to miss.

\- - -

Billy's stomach did a flip-flop. Had one of his crew bought the farm during the heist? There was no TV or Internet in the jail, and he had no way of knowing if they'd gotten out with their skins. His eyes quickly scanned the story. Five people had died violently inside a penthouse office, while another two had been ambushed by the cops Bonnie and Clyde–style on a street behind Galaxy's casino. The names of the dead were included in the article, and he felt the air trapped in his lungs slowly escape. The bad guys had died, and his crew was safe.

But there was more to the article than just a description of the carnage. Several Galaxy patrons had been injured as the gaming board had staged its raid, most notably "a retired businessman who'd come to Las Vegas to marry off his daughter, and been mistakenly shot by a gaming agent." An accompanying photo showed the terrified faces of tourists fleeing the casino with a caption that read, "Can Vegas survive this nightmare?"

Underman removed a yellow legal pad and gold pen and dropped both onto the table. The briefcase was shut and returned to the floor.

Billy rocked back in his chair. Vegas was good about hiding its sins; a lot of bad things that went down here never made the news. But this story had hit the wires, and the town was in serious damage control. Underman had just dealt him a powerful hand; how he played his cards was up to him.

Five bottled waters sat on the table. He picked up one and unscrewed the top. He'd known the seven people who'd died yesterday, and he realized that they were the only ones who really knew what had gone down. Last man standing had its advantages, and by the time the water bottle was empty, he'd come up with a story for the gaming agents that just might keep him from going to prison.

"Let's get started," LaBadie said. "We want you to explain to us what you were doing inside Galaxy's casino yesterday afternoon. Take your time, and don't leave anything out."

"It all started on Wednesday night," Billy said. "That's when I got the phone call."

"You got a phone call on Wednesday night."

"That's right."

"From who?"

"A guy named Captain Crunch. His friends call him Crunchie. If it wasn't for that phone call, I never would have ended up at the Galaxy."

"All right. Start there, and don't leave anything out."

TWO

-WEDNESDAY, THREE DAYS BEFORE THE HEIST-

Vegas was hustler heaven, with over a hundred casinos that never closed. A smart hustler could have five operations going and spend his night making withdrawals like they were ATMs. Two hundred here, another two hundred there—it all added up to a decent night's pay.

Those scores paid the bills, but it was the big takedowns that bought the houses and the fancy toys. Every casino had chinks in the armor that could be exploited. Every casino could be taken down. That was where the crews came in, and the planning.

Billy's crew was in a grind joint on Fremont Street called the Four Queens. Foul cigarette smoke, stinking ashtrays, perfume turned sour on little old ladies sweating out their Social Security checks, combined with flashing slot machines gave the joint its special charm. It was supper time, and they were about to rip the place off for thirty grand.

His crew consisted of seven members, each of whom had a specific job. The big dude shooting the dice was a sleight-of-hand expert named Travis. The luscious brunette and redhead distractions at the far end of the craps table were Misty and Pepper. And the two college-aged boys who'd actually place the bets and take off the game were Morris and Cory.

Billy was the captain and gave the orders. Nothing happened without his say-so.

The casinos knew Billy, so he took precautions. Tonight he wore a sleeveless T-shirt and fake buckteeth that made him look like a country bumpkin. No security guards were sniffing around, and he signaled Travis to start the play. The big man scooped the dice off the table.

"Winner, winner, chicken dinner!" Travis said.

Three casino employees worked the game: a boxman to watch the money, a dealer to supervise bets and make payoffs, and a stickman who moved the dice around the felt with a hook-shaped stick. To keep them distracted, Misty and Pepper wiggled their asses and flashed plenty of cleavage. Before joining Billy's crew, they'd done porno, and were not the bashful type.

Stealing a die off a craps table was a gutsy play, but it could be done. Travis threw one die down the table, while secretly thumb-palming the second in his enormous hand. The human eye could only watch one moving object at a time. As the lone die ricocheted off the wall, Misty and Pepper jumped back, pretending the second die had jumped off the table and grazed them.

"You hit me!" Misty said.

"Me, too," Pepper chorused.

"Die on the floor," the stickman announced.

Resting his arm on the table, Travis dropped the stolen die into Billy's glass of Coke, where it floated to the bottom and disappeared. The boxman shot Travis a suspicious look. Travis turned his hand over, exposing a clean palm.

"Be more careful next time," the boxman scolded.

"I will," Travis said.

Play was halted as the stickman hunted for the lost die. Eventually, the search was called off and the stickman returned to the table. Reaching into the white plastic bowl on the table, the stickman sent a new pair of dice down the felt with his stick.

"Not so hard this time," the stickman said.

"You got it," Travis replied.

Travis scooped up the new pair, and play resumed. Billy watched the three employees to make sure they were cool with the play. No one had felt a breeze, and he headed for the front door with the stolen die.

- - -

He hustled down the sidewalk on the south side of Fremont Street. Old downtown was the pits, the sidewalk filled with nasty-looking hookers and panhandlers. On the corner stood Cory and Morris, having a smoke. Both had curly mops of hair and could have been stand-ins for the actor Daniel Radcliffe. They had aspirations to one day run their own crew and would have scrubbed toilets if Billy told them to.

"Hey, Billy. Everything cool?" Cory asked.

"Everything's cool," Billy said. "You gents ready?"

They both dipped their chins. Billy had to believe they were two of the most innocent-looking thieves in town. It was one of the reasons he'd recruited them.

"Be back in a few," he said.

"We'll be waiting," Morris said.

Billy entered the city parking garage on Fremont and climbed the stairwell to the second level, where the rented stretch limo he used for his jobs was parked. Earlier that evening, he'd picked up his crew from their homes, the limo stocked with cold drinks and deli sandwiches. None of the cheats who'd ever run with him could say he hadn't treated them well.

Leon sat on the limo's hood, plugged into his MP3 player. He was a square john but did not care that Billy was a cheat. Driving Billy's crew around was better than selling dope or pimping, which was how a lot of limo drivers made a buck. Leon unplugged himself.

"Your teeth are funky. Where'd you get 'em?" he asked.

Billy pulled the fake teeth out of his mouth and slipped them into his pocket. "Party City. They've got lots of cool stuff. I need you to call the Golden Steer and make a reservation for eight. Ask for one of the private rooms. We're eating steak tonight."

"What time?"

"Make it an hour from now."

"You got it, boss."

Billy climbed into the backseat of the limo. Gabe, the seventh member of his crew, lay sprawled across the rear seat, watching college basketball on the miniature TV while chowing on a sandwich. Seeing Billy, he sprang to attention.

"How did it go?" Gabe asked.

"Travis was a star tonight. So were the girls."

Billy had discovered Gabe in a mall working at a jewelry kiosk, and had seen a real talent in his chubby hands. Gabe's job was to manufacture the gaffed casino equipment Billy's crew used in their heists, an investment that had paid off handsomely. Fishing the stolen die out of his drink, he dropped it in Gabe's hand. Gabe stole a glance at the game's score before killing the picture.

"How much you have on the game?" Billy asked.

"Who said I had a bet on the game?"

"I did."

Gabe held up two fingers, signifying twenty grand was riding on the game's outcome.

"I thought you were broke."

"I got a line of credit from my bookie."

"Who in this town would lend you that kind of money?"

"Tony G."

"You promised me you'd stay away from that shark. Next time you want to borrow money, come to me instead. Understand?"

"Sure, Billy. Whatever you say."

Gabe had once owned a swanky jewelry store, which he'd lost betting on college sports. His gambling addiction was severe, and Billy was afraid it was going to get Gabe killed.

Removing a jeweler's loupe from his breast pocket, Gabe spent a moment examining the serial numbers and logo imperfections stamped on the stolen die. Every casino in town employed these tricks to thwart cheaters.

"Piece of cake," the jeweler said.

Gabe sprung open a worn leather briefcase resting on the seat. The briefcase contained one hundred pairs of dice stamped with logos from every major casino in Las Vegas. These dice had been acquired through a variety of means, including bribing casino employees. Each die in the briefcase had been loaded with carefully disguised mercury slugs. When thrown on a craps table, winning combinations came up more times than not.

Gabe removed a gaffed pair with the Four Queens logo. Using a portable welding machine plugged into the door's cigarette lighter, he carefully stamped duplicate serial numbers onto the gaffed pair. When the dice had cooled down, a jeweler's engraving tool was used to re-create the tiny imperfections on the logo. Finished, he handed the gaffed dice to Billy.

Billy held the dice up to the light and compared the gaffed dice to the stolen die. The serial numbers looked exactly the same on all three, as did the tiny logo imperfections.

"You haven't lost your touch," Billy said.

"Thanks," Gabe said.

"We need to address this problem of yours. It's going to ruin you."

"You got any ideas?"

"Ever try Gamblers Anonymous?"

"No. I can't talk in front of groups."

"I'll go with you."

"You mean that?"

"Of course I mean it."

Using his Droid, Billy got on the Internet and did a search for a Gamblers Anonymous meeting in Gabe's part of town. He found two daily meetings and showed Gabe the screen.

"Pick one. I'll take you to lunch first. Make an afternoon out of it."

"Can't it wait? I don't think I'm ready for this."

"Pick one, or I'll fire you."

"Don't say that. You're all I've got."

"Then do it right now. That's an order."

"All right. We'll go to the meeting at the Unity Club at one o'clock."

"How much are you into Tony G for, anyway?"

"Too much."

"Are you ever going to learn?"

"I wish I could stop, I really do."

"You know what they say. There's no time like the present."

Billy put the phone away. Back when he was learning how to hustle on the streets of Providence, he'd dreamed of running his own crew. A great idea, only there were times when he felt like he was running a flipping babysitting service.

"Unity Club, one o'clock tomorrow," he said.

"I'm in," Gabe said.

As Billy started to climb out of the limo, Gabe flipped the TV back on with the remote. Billy stopped to glare at the jeweler.

"Didn't you hear a word of what I just said?"

"Come on, man. I've got to see how it ends," Gabe said.

THREE

Coming out of the parking garage stairwell, Billy slipped the fake teeth into his mouth and made sure the gaffed dice were finger-palmed in his hand in a way that could not be seen. There were surveillance cameras everywhere in Vegas, and he could never be too careful.

Hurrying down Fremont Street, he spotted Cory and Morris standing outside the Four Queens and let out a shrill whistle. Tossing away their cigarettes, they followed him inside.

The Four Queens craps pit was by the front doors. It was that way in most joints. The action was loud and frenzied and drew people the way honey draws flies. Travis was still throwing the bones, swigging on a beer bottle filled with water, pretending to be loaded. Billy pressed his body to the table and secretly passed the crooked dice to the big man.

"They're still warm," Travis whispered.

"So blow on them," Billy said without moving his lips.

Cory and Morris came to the table and threw down sizeable cash bets. At the same time, Travis scooped up the casino dice and switched in the gaffed ones in his hand. He wasn't the greatest dice mechanic who'd ever lived, nor did he have to be. The boxman, dealer, and stickman were trained to watch the money. Everything else was secondary, including obnoxious drunks, screaming women, and people flopping dead from heart attacks. An elephant could have stampeded past, and they wouldn't have looked up.

The eye-in-the-sky wasn't watching Travis, either. If the surveillance cameras had been taping Travis, they might have caught the switch. But the cameras weren't watching because Travis had been losing, and that made him a sucker. Surveillance never watched suckers.

"Yo, Eveline, lost her drawers in the men's latrine!" Travis shouted.

Travis sent the crooked dice down the table. Misty and Pepper pounded the railing, urging him on. They had also placed cash bets. The game was locked up.

Eleven, a winner.

The table erupted. Suckers sometimes got lucky, and the boxman, stickman, and dealer displayed no emotion. Travis kept throwing the dice, and their winnings began to add up. Two grand, five grand, then fifteen—the boxman, dealer, and stickman shaking their heads at the sudden turn of events. Like crew hands rearranging deck chairs on the Titanic, they were clueless.

When their winnings hit thirty grand, Billy gave the signal to end the play. He'd done his homework and knew how much the Four Queens would lose before security was sent to the table. Winning too much, too often, had gotten more than one crew in hot water.

Small bets were placed on the table. Travis switched out the gaffed dice for the regular pair and threw them hard.

Two, a loser.

The table groaned. The boxman, dealer, and stickman visibly relaxed, and the losing bets were picked up. Resting his arm on the table, Travis dropped the crooked dice into Billy's hand.

"Where we going for dinner?" Travis whispered.

"Golden Steer," Billy whispered back.

"That's a winner."

- - -

Possession of a crooked gambling device inside a casino was a felony, and Billy headed down Fremont clutching the gaffed dice in his hand until he'd reached a construction site for a new casino. New casinos were always popping up in Vegas, even when the economy sucked. He heaved the gaffed dice over a tall wooden fence plastered with "NO TRESPASSING" signs.

His skin was tingling as he headed for the elevated garage. There was no greater rush than ripping a joint off, and it wouldn't be very long before he'd want to do it again. He'd recently done a walk-through of the Luxor, and decided it was easy pickings. That was what made Vegas so great. There were so many scores and so little time.

His Droid vibrated. Only a handful of people had his number, and he yanked the phone from his pocket. Caller ID said it was an old grifter named Captain Crunch. Crunchie was about as friendly as a coiled rattlesnake, but that was how it was with most of the old-timers.

"Hey, I need to call you back," he answered.

"This can't wait," the old grifter said.

"Everything can wait. I'll call you later."

"You'll talk to me now."

"I'm on a job, man."

"Fuck your job. There's a lady blackjack dealer in the high-roller salon at Galaxy that's flashing every fifth hand, and the dumb shit management hasn't caught on. This might be the single biggest score on the Strip."

High-roller salons catered to whales capable of losing millions of dollars without breaking a sweat. The salons were awash in money, and it was every hustler's dream to take one down. No hustler in town ever had, and Billy would have relished being the first.

"You want me to be a whale?" he asked.

"That's right. Interested?"

"Of course I'm interested. How are you going to get me into Galaxy's salon?"

"It's all been taken care of. Just show up and work your magic. It will be like stealing candy from a baby."

"What's your take?"

"We're straight partners, fifty-fifty."

"Make it eighty-twenty, and you've got yourself a deal."

"Sixty-forty, and that's my final offer. Take it or leave it."

Billy hated to cave but didn't see that he had any other choice. If he said no, Crunchie would call another hustler, and cut him out of the action.

"I'm in," Billy said.

"Meet me at the Peppermill at ten o'clock, and I'll fill you in."

"See you there."

He ended the call and headed up the stairwell. Salons had the highest betting limits around and were known to let whales wager $100,000 a hand. If this lady dealer was flashing every fifth hand, he could steal a hundred grand every five rounds, or roughly seventeen hands per hour, which translated into one point seven million bucks for an hour's work. It got him excited just thinking about it.

But what if he played longer? If he stayed on the tables for several hours, he could cheat Galaxy out of four or five million easy. Normally, casinos cut off a player when he won too much, but the rules were different for whales. The casinos expected whales to occasionally get lucky and take them for a major score, knowing they'd win the money back later on. As a result, whales rarely got cut off.

Whales also got special privileges and were often allowed to play in private rooms, away from the other players, and with employees whom they liked. If a whale was fond of a particular dealer, the whale could request for that dealer to deal his game, and the request would be honored.

Crunchie wasn't kidding when he said it was the best score on the Strip. It was the best score of the last ten years. And all Billy needed to do was pretend he was some superrich asshole, and the money would be his.

FOUR

Billy's head was spinning as he climbed into the backseat of the limo. Every hustler's dream was to scam a Vegas casino for a monster score, and he was about to realize that dream.

He wedged himself between Pepper and Misty. Leon pulled out of the space and drove the limo down the garage's spiral exit with the speed of a carnival ride.

Travis was looking at him funny. Billy chose to ignore it.

"Let's chop up the money before we eat," he suggested.

His crew pulled out their winnings and dropped the money in his lap. He sorted through the bills and separated the denominations into neat piles, then counted the money aloud, starting with the smaller denominations and working his way up, just the way Lou Profaci had taught him during his apprenticeship in Providence. The take came to thirty grand on the nose. He paid his crew a straight percentage off the top. Misty and Pepper got two grand apiece, the same for Cory and Morris, while Gabe and Travis got three grand because they did more of the heavy lifting, while the rest went into his pocket.

The hot dice scam was the sweetest operation he'd ever run. On average, they were taking down three casinos a week. Because the casinos ran three shifts—day, swing, and midnight—they'd robbed several casinos multiple times and had never gotten caught.

Travis cleared his throat. He was drinking two-fisted, a Bud Light in one hand, a Johnnie Walker on the rocks in the other. The funny look on his face that Billy had thought was the booze he now recognized as something troubling.

"You got something you want to tell us, Billy?" the big man asked.

"Not particularly," Billy said.

"You were late."

"So?"

"You're never late. It just bothered us."

"Think I ran out with the money?"

"Did I say that?"

Billy started to steam.

"We were just worried that something happened to you," Travis said. "When you didn't show up, we got nervous. We care about you, man."

Billy didn't hear a word of what Travis had just said. They worked for him—he didn't work for them—and he had half a mind to tell Leon to pull over so he could throw Travis out of the limo and let him go find another crew to work with.

But he didn't do it. He had a temper and he knew that it sometimes got the better of him. Instead, he pulled a Heineken out of the minibar and took a long swig. It calmed him down, and he looked across the seat at Travis and saw the big man cringe. Later in the restaurant he'd corner Travis and straighten him out. If Travis challenged him again, he was history.

No one was smiling anymore, just a bunch of sour faces wondering what to say next. Leon pulled into the Golden Steer parking lot and circled the building. The place was packed, and parking spaces were at a minimum. Misty's hot breath tickled Billy's face.

"Don't be pissed," she said.

"Who said I was pissed?" he said, hearing the anger in his voice.

"We care about you, Billy."

"You're the magic man," Pepper chimed in, snuggling up next to him. "Did something bad happen? You can tell us."

Billy looked down at his sweaty beer bottle. He never should have taken Crunchie's call while he was doing a job. It was the first rule of hustling: no interruptions. Only he'd broken it, and his crew wanted to know why. Trust ran both ways, so he decided to tell them.

"I got a call from an old friend. That's why I was late. Everybody cool with that?"

"She must be a great fuck for you to take her call," Pepper said.

He looked at her. "You think I'm pussy-whipped?"

"All men are pussy-whipped."

"Not me."

"Bullshit. What's her name?"

Pepper's pale green eyes were laughing at him. Pepper had made porno flicks for several years, doing straight fuck films before switching to blow job movies because the pay was better, and she knew everything there was to know about the crazy little brain in a man's dick.

"Crunchie," Billy said.

"Her name's Crunchie?"

"Him. He's an old grifter I used to run with. They used to call him Captain Crunch because he was always good in a tight spot."

"Why were you talking to him?"

"Does it matter?" he said, feeling his anger start to rise.

"You told us no interruptions during a job."

She had him dead to rights. He faced the group.

"Crunchie knows a Strip casino that's primed to get ripped off. He needs someone to play a whale, so he called me. I'm hooking up with him later tonight to go over the details. I would have told you sooner, but I didn't want to jinx it. Is everybody cool with that?"

Their heads bobbed in unison.

"Can you tell us which casino?" Gabe asked.

"Galaxy."

"Have we ever ripped that one off?"

"No. It's only been open a few months."

"How's security?"

He quizzed Cory and Morris with a glance. He'd turned them onto the art of wheel tracking, and they'd visited many of the town's casinos to analyze their roulette games. Roulette wheels sometimes became biased through faulty construction and could produce amazing winnings to a player willing to track a few hundred spins of the wheel with a hidden computer.

"Have you checked out Galaxy yet?" he asked them.

"We got acquainted with Galaxy last week," Cory replied.

"And?"

"Staff is pretty green. I got chummy with a cocktail waitress, and she said that they were having trouble with their systems. It's a candy store."

Billy nodded. The scam was getting sweeter by the minute.

"Can you tell us what the scam is?" Gabe asked.

"We're going to take down the high-roller salon at blackjack," he said.

Misty stiffened, and so did Pepper. The others got real quiet, too.

"Has anyone ever ripped off a high-roller salon?" Gabe asked.

"No. We're going to make history."

Travis leaned forward in his seat, wanting to get back on good footing with the boss. "Billy, this sounds really great. How much do you think we can take them for?"

"Don't ask."

"Why not?"

"Because I'll jinx it if I tell you."

Travis swallowed hard. He'd just bought a four-bedroom, three-bath money pit and needed every spare dime he could get his hands on. "Can you give us a range?"

"Try the stratosphere," he said.

Leon continued to circle the restaurant. All Billy could hear was the fluttering sound of Gabe breathing through his nose. He knew what each one of them was thinking. Was this the big score that would forever change their lives? It was Gabe who braved the silence.

"For the love of Christ, Billy, tell us, before we wet our pants," the jeweler said.

"All right. If this goes as planned, we'll walk away with a few million bucks, maybe more." He paused to let the words sink in, then said, "You'll each get your usual cut."

Everyone got crazy all at once. The girls crawled into Billy's lap and started to unbutton his shirt. He tried to fight them off and ended up kissing Misty instead, wanting more than just a taste of her sweet breath. The slider came down and Leon stuck his head into the back.

"Hey. No orgies in my limo, you hear?"

FIVE

They ran up a two-thousand-dollar tab in one of the Golden Steer's private dining rooms, the booze and champagne flowing like water. Billy sucked down several cups of coffee before taking his crew home, dropping them at their front doors with a promise to call tomorrow and fill them in on the details of Crunchie's big score. Last stop was his pad at Turnberry Towers. He passed $500 to Leon through the open slider.

"I need to ask you a question," his driver said. "Does this score include me?"

"If you want to be in, yeah, it includes you," he said.

"Why wouldn't I want to be in?"

"If we go down, you go down as well. You won't be able to say you didn't know what was going on, you were just hired to drive."

"You're saying I could end up doing time."

"Yeah. You got any priors?"

"A couple."

"Any felonies?"

"A couple."

"Then you'll do hard time if we get caught. Still want in?"

Leon scratched his chin and weighed the risk against the reward. "What's my cut?"

"How does twenty-five grand sound?"

"Are you serious? Just for driving you around?"

"I'm going to be impersonating a whale, and will need a full-time driver at my beck and call. You'll need to get your tuxedo dry-cleaned and wear the hat and do the step-and-fetch-it. You up for that?"

"Shit, I'll wiggle through a pipe for twenty-five grand."

Billy would have enjoyed seeing that. Climbing out, he banged his hand on the roof. The limo pulled away and slowly faded into the night.

Home sweet home was a luxury penthouse condo that he'd won in a rigged poker game from a Dallas oilman. The game had been arranged by the host at a Strip casino with whom Billy had split his winnings and who technically owned half the condo. They talked once a month, the host checking to make sure Billy hadn't pulled a fast one and sold the place. Maybe he'd take his cut from Crunchie's score and pay the host off. It would be nice to get him off his back.

Standing in his bedroom, he peeled off his clothes and tossed them in the trash. Losing your clothes after a heist was an old hustler's trick, designed to keep casino security from remembering you the next time you ripped the place off.

He wanted to look sharp for his meeting, and he entered the closet and picked through the racks. He settled on black Armani slacks and a Louis Vuitton black silk shirt with mother-of-pearl buttons that he'd been saving for a special occasion. When he finished dressing, he appraised himself in the mirror hanging on the closet door. He looked like a player.

What a life. He'd just celebrated his thirtieth birthday, and had made more money and accumulated more sexy stuff than he'd ever dreamed possible. And there was more where that came from. He'd once taken a helicopter ride over Las Vegas. The gaudy casinos and hotels had reminded him of an upturned pirate's treasure chest, just waiting to be plundered.

He called downstairs to the valet and requested that his car be brought up.

- - -

For years, the local hustlers had met at the Denny's on Tropicana Avenue to talk shop. Then several regulars got busted, and word leaked out that the booths were bugged by the gaming board. It had made the Grand Slam special a lot less attractive.

By default, the Peppermill had become the new hangout, so it was natural that Crunchie wanted to meet there. From the street it resembled a retro diner, but in fact was two businesses. The front was a tourist-trap restaurant that served twelve-dollar burgers, the back a cocktail lounge with a circular fireplace and no security cameras. As Billy eased his metallic black Maserati GranTurismo into the narrow parking space in front, his Droid vibrated. Crunchie calling.

"I'm running behind," the old grifter said by way of greeting.

"You're not here?"

"My Vet won't start. I'll call you when I'm on my way."

Billy tapped his fingers on the wheel. Crunchie had called this meeting, and now he wasn't here. This was getting off to a bad start. "How soon will that be?"

"Don't get your diapers in a wad. I'll be over as fast as I can."

"That's not very fast the way you move."

"Fuck you, you little asshole. Sixty minutes. Feel better now?"

"Remember to bring your hearing aid."

There were plenty of ways to kill an hour in Vegas, and he took a stroll up the block to a joint called Slots A Fun. A former crew member named Sal was doing time for sticking a strobe light up a slot machine's coin chute to make it overpay, and Billy had promised to keep tabs on Sal's girlfriend, a Vietnamese blackjack dealer named Ly.

A week after Sal got sent away, Billy had called Ly to see how she was holding up. She'd sounded depressed and had talked him into meeting her at a fleabag motel on North Seventh Street. Pulling into the motel's parking lot, he'd spied Ly's junker parked outside a room. He'd knocked on the door, found it open, and gone in. Burning candles everywhere, and on the bedside table, a bottle of red wine, two glasses, and a pack of Trojans.

Ly stood beside the bed wearing a red satin kimono and a spray of flowers in her hair. As if by magic, the kimono slipped to the floor, revealing erect nipples rubbed with ice cubes, and no pubic hair. The sight of her took his breath away.

"Get in here, and shut the door behind you," she'd said.

Ly meant *lion* in Vietnamese. Billy had started backing up.

"You no like?" she said.

"I don't sleep with my friend's girlfriends," he explained.

"I need money. You gotta help me."

"I'll help you, but I'm not going to fuck you."

"Suit yourself," she said.

- - -

Slots A Fun offered an arcade-like atmosphere created by rows of noisy slot machines. In the back were five purple-felted blackjack tables that were hard on the eyes. Ly's table was empty, and Billy tossed down a wad of cash and sat down. She was as pretty as a doll and wore a tight-fitting purple vest over her uniform. She counted the money with the precision of a bank teller.

"Three hundred," she called out.

A pit boss came over to inspect the money.

"Go ahead," the pit boss declared.

Ly shoved the bills down the cash slot in the table. From her tray, she removed a stack of ten green chips and a stack of ten red chips, which she pushed toward Billy. The greens were worth twenty-five dollars apiece, the reds five dollars.

"You look familiar," the pit boss said. "Haven't I seen you before?"

Billy didn't think there was a pit boss in town he hadn't ripped off at least once.

"*America's Most Wanted*," he replied.

"Hah. That's a good one. Ly will take good care of you."

The pit boss walked over to another table.

"I'm broke," Ly said under her breath.

"You're always broke."

"Come on, help me."

Billy reached into his pocket and finger-palmed a gaffed chip that Gabe had manufactured for him. The gaffed chip had a green Slots A Fun chip on one side, a red Slots A Fun on the other, its edge painted half-red, half-green. He placed his hand on the table edge.

"Good boy," Ly said.

He feigned plucking a green chip from the stack in front of him. In actuality, he pushed the gaffed chip into view. He took a red chip from another stack and placed the two chips into the betting circle. To anyone watching, he'd just bet thirty dollars.

"Good luck," Ly said.

She dealt the round. Billy won, and she paid him thirty dollars. He left his original bet in the betting circle and added the winning chips to his stacks.

She dealt another round. This time, he lost the hand.

"You lose, too bad," she said.

She scooped the losing bet off the felt and flipped the gaffed chip over, pretending to deposit it into her tray with the green chips. In reality, the gaffed chip remained in her hand. As she deposited the red chip into her tray, she left the gaffed chip with it.

To anyone watching, nothing out of the ordinary had happened.

"Change, please." Billy tossed a green chip toward her.

Ly removed the gaffed chip and four normal red chips from her tray and slid them toward him. Billy took the gaffed chip and under cover of his hand, flipped it over. Soon, the gaffed chip was lying in the betting circle with a red chip.

It was one of the sweetest scams ever devised. When he won a hand, the casino paid him thirty dollars; when he lost, the casino made only ten dollars because of the shortchange. On an average night, he could steal $600 without suspicion. Ly's cut was half.

"Where you taking me to dinner?" she asked.

It was how every session with her ended.

"Not tonight," he said.

"You got some other girl you like more than me?"

He knocked over one of his stacks of chips, signaling that she needed to watch her mouth. She continued to talk recklessly, and he rose from his chair. Fear flashed through her eyes.

"Don't go. My rent due," she said.

"That's not my problem."

"I thought you care about me."

She was pushing it. He decided to mess with her and pushed all of his chips into the betting circle. If he lost, Ly lost as well.

"What you doing?" she asked.

"Shut up and deal," he said.

- - -

He walked out of Slots A Fun with twelve hundred bucks of the casino's money. It was more than he normally would have stolen from a joint so small, and he would have to avoid coming here for a while. Ly was becoming a liability. If he wasn't careful, they'd end up getting busted.

Ly parked her junker in the elevated self-park garage across the street at the Riviera. On the fourth floor he found her car and used the spare key she'd given him to pop the trunk. He dropped her cut onto the spare tire and told himself it was time to end the arrangement.

Some things were easier said than done. If he called and broke the bad news, she'd scream at him. If he went and saw her, she'd attack him. He decided to do it subtly and let her figure it out. He placed his cut on top of hers, then took the spare key from his key chain and placed it atop the money, then shut the trunk. Ly wasn't stupid and would understand that they were done.

It was nearly eleven. Time to see the captain and talk business. Stealing a few cool million was at the top of his bucket list, and he hurried from the garage.

SIX

Billy walked back to the Peppermill with a million watts of neon burning his eyes. As he neared the restaurant's parking lot, his cell phone came alive.

"I'm just pulling in," the old grifter said.

"Stop for a haircut?" he asked.

"I got a call right after we hung up that I had to take."

"You couldn't talk and drive? It's the newest thing."

"It's complicated, man. Just leave it alone."

"You're not going to tell me why you're running late?"

"No. Drop it."

Billy felt a breeze. Was the captain trying to set him up? It wouldn't be the first time that another hustler had tried to put him in a bad light. He decided he'd better find out.

"I'm in the bar having a beer. What's your pleasure?" he asked.

"Jack Daniel's, straight up, and a beer chaser," the old grifter said.

"See you in a few."

He ducked behind a light pole plastered with flyers for escorts and watched Crunchie park his vintage '69 Corvette and then get out and stretch. Crunchie had grown up on a ranch in Montana and favored cracked-leather boots and a black Stetson with a rattlesnake band. He was tall and sinewy, his skin rough-hewn. As he crossed the lot and entered the restaurant, Billy noticed that he was limping. Had someone beat him up? It sure looked that way.

A bad feeling settled over Billy. He decided to hang back to see if Crunchie had brought along any unwanted friends. The world being what it was, you could never be too careful.

He'd joined Crunchie's crew soon after arriving in Vegas. Crunchie had run a cooler mob that specialized in switching cards on unsuspecting blackjack dealers. Billy hadn't believed such a thing was possible until they'd ripped off the Mirage. The dealer had shuffled her six decks and placed them on the table to be cut. At the next table, a member of the crew had feigned having a heart attack. As the dealer called for the pit boss, she briefly lifted her fingers from the cards. In that split second, the six decks were switched for six duplicate decks stacked to deal nothing but winning hands. Twenty minutes later, they possessed a hundred grand of the Mirage's money.

Several parties came out of the restaurant, but none went in. He decided it was safe and went inside. The restaurant was packed with tourists eating overpriced food. The hostess flashed a smile but did not offer him a menu. She'd seen him before and knew he was local.

A beaded curtain led to the lounge. Single white candles flickered on tables while a heatless fireplace burned in the room's center like a campfire. A bar with nine stools took up the sidewall. Crunchie sat on a middle stool, pounding brown liquid. Billy took the adjacent stool and got the attention of a cute bartender wearing skintight clothes and her hair tied back.

"Corona, no glass," he said.

"Want a lime with that?" the bartender asked.

"I'm staying away from the fruit. I hear it's bad for you."

She served him. Under his breath, Crunchie said, "Where you been?"

"Outside. How'd you get the limp? You didn't limp when we ran together."

"My arthritis is acting up. I'm getting old."

The cute bartender offered to run a tab. Billy slid her a twenty, told her to keep the change. She flashed a smile that made him want to come back and see her again. Grabbing his beer, he made his way toward a corner table with Crunchie right behind him.

They sat across from each other at a table the size of a dinner plate. Crunchie had once been good looking, with chiseled features and an easy smile. Hard living had taken its toll, and his face looked like freckled rust, his teeth stained so badly that it was hard to tell if he had any.

"What the hell's bothering you?" the old grifter asked.

"You're late. You set a time, you keep it. You taught me that, remember?"

"Did I now."

"Damn straight. And you're limping. You never mentioned having arthritis before."

From the pocket of his jeans Crunchie produced a plastic medicine vial filled with blue capsules, which he placed in the center of the table. "This is the dope I'm taking for my hip. Thirty years ago a security guard at the Dunes threw me down a flight of stairs. My hip's never been the same."

"You never limped when we ran together."

"I hid it, didn't want to look like a gimp. The older I get, the worse the pain."

The story added up. But Billy still needed more convincing. "Who were you talking to?"

"My daughter. She's a real pain in the ass."

"Since when did you have a kid?"

"Back in '91, I had a fling with a sexy little cocktail waitress at the Sands. She wanted to get hitched, I balked, she tied a suitcase to the roof of her car and boogied to LA. Twenty years later my phone rings, and this girl says, 'Hi, my name's Clarissa, and I'm your kid.' Let me tell you, it's been one horror show ever since."

"She hitting you up for money?"

"Every damn time we talk. She's got two little brats, no job, no child support. I send her a check every month, but it's never enough. What are you grinning about? You think this is funny? Fuck you, Billy."

"I'm just trying to imagine you getting hustled, that's all."

"This is different. She's my daughter."

"So you were talking to her, and she made you late, is that the deal?"

A wall of anger rose in the old grifter's face. Producing his cell phone, he showed Billy the recent call memory. In the past twelve hours, he'd gotten three phone calls originating from a 310 area code, which was Southern California.

"Call her, you don't believe me."

Billy nearly did, just to get the old grifter's goat. But he leaned back in his chair instead. There was still a deal on the table, and money made the world go round.

"You and I have known each other a long time," Crunchie said. "You think I'd double-cross you? Hell, I taught you how to rob, kid."

"You taught me a lot of things," Billy said.

"You thought I was setting you up?"

"It crossed my mind."

"Jesus, Billy. I'd never do that. You're the kid I wished I had."

Billy's old man had cheated at cards but had never been willing to teach Billy the ropes, wanting his son to go to college and make something of himself. When Billy had arrived in Vegas, Crunchie had taken him under his wing, and it had been one long joyride ever since.

"You really mean that?" he said.

"Damn straight, I do. I'd never screw you."

"Then I was out of line. Sorry."

"You still want to do this?"

Billy said that he did. Flagging the cute bartender, he pointed across the table.

"Another round. Make my friend's a double this time."

- - -

"So let's hear your deal," Billy said after the bartender served them.

"I've been making a killing off a blackjack dealer at the Rio named Jazzy," Crunchie said. "Jazzy has this bad habit of rocking her hands and flashing her hole card every fifth hand. The other day I found out Jazzy left the Rio and took a job dealing at the high-roller salon at Galaxy. I racked my brain thinking of who I knew could play a whale. Then it hit me. I'll call Billy."

"So how are you going to get me into the joint?"

"There's a fake identity in Galaxy's computer just waiting for you."

"How'd you manage that?"

"I didn't. Skip Johnson did. Remember Skip? He ran with us for a while."

"I remember Skip."

"Skip had a dream. He thought he could walk into a casino, sign a marker for a few hundred grand in credit, get the chips, and cash out without having to pay the casino back."

"Nice dream."

"Skip nearly pulled it off. He hacked into a national credit data system and stole the credit histories of six wealthy guys back east. He set up bank accounts in these guys' names and applied to the casinos for lines of credit, which of course they gave him.

"When Skip visited a casino, he'd show one of his fake IDs to a VIP host. The host gave him twenty grand to play with, which Skip lost playing craps. Skip's brother Ronnie was in the game, betting against him. The money Skip lost, Ronnie won. You familiar with this?"

"Offsetting betting procedures," Billy said.

"Right. Skip did this all over town. When he got home, he paid off the markers, so the casinos jacked up his credit line. In some joints, it reached two hundred grand."

Billy was impressed. Crunchie's big score was sounding better by the minute.

"On New Year's Eve, Skip and Ronnie went for the kill. They checked into hotels where Skip had high credit lines. That night, Skip visited the first casino, signed a marker, and was given two hundred grand in chips. He passed the chips to Ronnie, who cashed them in. Skip was on a roll until he hit the Wynn. A security guard recognized him, and the thing fell apart."

"So how does that get me into the high-roller salon at Galaxy?"

"One of Skip's false identities never got used on New Year's and is still in the casinos' computers," Crunchie explained. "I bought the false identity from Skip so he could post bail. It's for a hedge fund manager named Thomas Pico. He's thirty years old, same as you. You get into Galaxy's salon by pretending to be Pico."

"How can Pico be in Galaxy's computer? The joint just opened."

"The VIP host at Galaxy's salon is named Ed Butler. Butler used to work at Bellagio. When Butler switched jobs, he brought his database with him, including Pico."

"So Butler met Skip when he was impersonating Pico."

"That's right."

"How many times?"

"Skip said he met Butler once. Butler sees a hundred high rollers a month. Trust me, he won't remember meeting Skip."

"So all I have to do is waltz into Galaxy, show them false ID, and rob them blind."

"That's right. So what do you say?"

"I'm in," Billy said.

SEVEN

They went over the terms of their deal and shook hands on it. It was how cheaters did business. No fancy lawyers or contracts, no fine print, just a man's word and the pressing of the flesh. Outside in the parking lot Crunchie said, "You'll need these," and gave Billy a handful of plastic, including a black American Express card, voter registration card, Social Security card, and a Platinum Visa card, all in Thomas Pico's name.

"Skip gave me those as part of our deal," Crunchie said. "All you need is a phony driver's license and you'll be all set."

"I'm going to check out Galaxy tonight, get a lay of the land," Billy said. "I'll call you tomorrow, let you know what I find."

"You don't waste any time, do you?"

"Not when there's money to be made. Later, man."

"I'm looking forward to this, Billy. It's been too long since we've pulled a heist."

"I feel the same way."

Billy drove to Gabe's place in Silverado Ranch with his fingers tapping the wheel. A driver's license would be the first thing that the VIP host at Galaxy's high-roller salon would ask to see. Unlike the good old days when driver's licenses were printed on cheap cardboard with typewriters, today's licenses used special Teslin paper and ID holograms and were difficult to counterfeit. The casinos were constantly seeing phony licenses from underage kids trying to sneak into their clubs, and they'd gotten good at picking out fakes.

It was past midnight when he pounded on Gabe's front door. The porch light came on.

"It's Billy. Lemme in. I've got a job for you."

The door swung in. Gabe stood in the foyer in a bathrobe, his eyes ringed with sleep.

"What's up?"

"I need a fake driver's license so I can go visit the high-roller salon at Galaxy."

"Is the deal on?"

"Yeah. But I want to check the place out first, just to be on the safe side."

"Come on in."

They walked through the downstairs to the spare bedroom in the back of the house that served as Gabe's workshop. Having grown sick of her husband's gambling addiction, Gabe's long-suffering wife had thrown their belongings in a U-Haul and bolted with their kids, taking every stick of furniture, every wall covering, and all the photographs, as if trying to take the memories as well. Gabe's idea of redecorating had been to put packing crates with TV sets into each room. That way, he could watch his beloved college sports anywhere in the house.

They sat in front of Gabe's computer. Billy fished the false ID from his pocket.

"I need a driver's license for this guy," he said.

Gabe put on a pair of cheaters and studied the plastic. "Who's Thomas Pico?"

"Hedge fund manager out of New York. His name's in their database."

"Sweet."

Making a fake driver's license took several steps. To start, Gabe did a search on the Internet and located a blank template for a New York State driver's license, which he copied with Adobe Photoshop into a folder on his Mac. Then he typed Thomas Pico's personal information off the voter registration Billy had given him onto the template, which he and Billy both proofread to make sure the information was correct.

The next step was the head shot. Gabe kept several head shots of Billy stored on his hard drive as JPEG files. He picked a recent photo, copied it from the folder, and inserted it into the template on the screen. Billy shook his head disapprovingly.

"Use another one. I look hungover in that photo."

"I've got to use this one," Gabe said. "The other shots don't have your shoulders in them. Every state in the Union requires that the top of the shoulders be included in a driver's license head shot. It gives the face better proportion."

"Like a mug shot."

"That's right, like a mug shot."

The final step was creating the driver's license number, which was encoded with the driver's name, gender, and date of birth. These numbers were created with special algorithms, and each state used a different one. Gabe owned a software program with all fifty states, plus Puerto Rico and Guam, and using that program, he created a fake New York driver's license number using Pico's personal information. Seconds later, the number appeared on the screen: P09109570426839 2?80.

"What's the question mark for?" Billy asked.

"Good eye," Gabe said. "The question mark indicates an overflow digit, which means there's another guy in the state of New York named Thomas Pico who shares the same birth date. The question mark distinguishes them from each other."

"That's good to know."

"To you it is. To the rest of us, it's just another piece of useless information."

Gabe resumed his task. He inserted the driver's license number into the template, keyed a command into his computer, and watched the inkjet printer on the stand spit out the fake license. They took turns examining it under a bright desk light.

"Like it?" Gabe asked.

"It looks good," Billy said.

Gabe moved to the worktable and glued the fake license to a stiff sheet of Teslin plastic, trimmed the edges, and used a piece of sandpaper to make the card look old and worn. He handed the fake license to Billy, who tucked it away with the rest of the fake IDs.

"Thanks for the quick turnaround," Billy said.

"Anytime, my man. Let me walk you out," Gabe said.

The Maserati was parked in the drive. Keys in hand, Billy said, "I'll see you tomorrow at one. We're going to that Gamblers Anonymous meeting, and don't try to talk your way out of it."

Gabe shuddered from an imaginary chill and tightened the knot in his robe's belt. "Can't it wait? A couple of days won't be the end of the world."

"You're gambling too much. Has Tony G sent his boys around to collect?"

"They came by the other day. I made them scrambled eggs and bacon."

"Did they threaten you?"

"I've got it under control."

Gabe was pretending the money he owned Tony G was no big deal. Nothing could have been further from the truth, and Billy put his hand on Gabe's arm. "You're going to that meeting. I'll drag your sorry ass there if I have to. You've got to kick this habit."

"Whatever you say," the jeweler mumbled.

Billy got into his car and fired up the engine. Gabe was old enough to be his father, and it felt shitty talking to him this way. Gabe stuck his face in the open driver window.

"Don't be mad at me, Billy. It's just making things harder," Gabe said. "I'm trying to help you, man."

"I know you are. Just don't push so hard, okay?"

"You think I'm pushing too hard? I can push you so hard, you won't be able to breathe."

Gabe paused for a few beats, then said what was really on his mind. "Do you really think you can steal all this money off Galaxy?"

"It's sure looking that way."

"What are you going to do with your share?"

"I haven't thought that far ahead. You?"

"What else? Pay off Tony G."

"Good idea."

Gabe was smiling as if all his troubles had disappeared. Slapping his hand on the roof of Billy's car, he walked back into his house without another word.

EIGHT

The houses in Gabe's subdivision looked the same, and Billy drove around until he passed the empty guardhouse and knew he was home free. He connected with Las Vegas Boulevard, the Strip's casinos lighting up the northern horizon with the intensity of a nuclear detonation.

He did the limit, deep in thought. He'd never impersonated a hedge fund manager before, and he needed to find out what their deal was. He pulled into the Fatburger across the street from the Monte Carlo and was soon sitting in the parking lot, eating greasy onion rings while studying photos of hedge fund managers on his Droid that he'd pulled up using Google Images. To a man, it was a boy's club of soft-looking white guys with spiffy haircuts and teeth as white as piano keys. Blazers and gray slacks were the norm, the shirts button-down.

Preppies.

By clicking on the images, he was taken to several online newspaper bios, which he read to get a feel for the lifestyle. Hedge fund managers were übersmart, with MBAs from Wharton, NYU, and Ivy League programs. On a whim, he typed "Thomas Pico" into Google, and discovered there were no photos on the Internet of the man he was impersonating.

Beautiful.

He got out, popped the trunk, and rummaged through his box of disguises containing wigs, glasses, ball caps, and several sports jackets. He tried on a pair of black eyeglasses and a blazer with gold buttons that screamed conservative, combed down his spiked hair with a stiff brush, and had a look in the driver window's reflection.

That worked.

Back in the car, he unlocked the glove compartment and filled his pockets with stacks of hundred-dollar bills that he planned to play with tonight in Galaxy's high-roller salon.

He left the Fatburger lot thinking that only suckers walked around with this much cash, and laughed out loud.

- - -

One a.m. and the Strip was jamming. He drove the Strip whenever possible, the glittering casinos and blinding neon never failing to flip on the pleasure switch in his head. Vegas made Providence feel so small and dirty that he'd never wanted to go back, and if his old man hadn't croaked one dreary Christmas a few years ago, he never would have.

His old man had decided to die at home in his favorite chair, hooked up to an oxygen tank, an unlit cigarette dangling from his parched lips. With each passing hour, his old man's breathing grew more tortured. Knowing the end was near, he'd told his son to get a cardboard box from the closet in the hall. Billy got the box and saw that it was filled with love letters from a woman that was not his mother. Among the letters was a newspaper clipping showing him being presented with an award that he'd gotten during his brief stint at MIT.

Back in the living room, he'd asked his old man what he wanted done with the stuff.

"Burn it," his old man said. "All of it."

The day after his old man croaked, he'd done just that.

Galaxy was in his sights. It was a boxy monstrosity consisting of two mammoth hotel towers and a casino squeezed onto a tiny plot of land. As he navigated the winding entrance, floodlights lit up the night sky as if at a movie premiere. To make it in Vegas, a casino had to be themed, the more outlandish the better. Galaxy's theme was the golden age of Tinseltown, and a medley of popular movie scores played over hidden speakers.

He tossed his keys to the valet and headed inside.

The lobby was designed to resemble the Beverly Hills Hotel, with a circular marble floor, inset ceiling, and cut-glass chandelier. On every table, fresh cut flowers. A man wearing a tux played show tunes on a baby grand piano that made Billy want to dance.

A short hallway led to a casino several football fields in length. Entering, he passed beneath a smoky dome ensconced in the ceiling where an eye-in-the-sky camera recorded his picture and ran it against a facial-recognition program that identified twenty-six points on his face; the profile was then run against a database of known cheaters. To beat the system, all he needed to do was erase three of those points. By wearing glasses, ball caps, changing his hairstyle, or wearing false teeth, he could walk through any casino unchallenged.

There was more to beat than just the cameras. Floor people also studied the customers. Some were ex-cops with a gift for grift. Billy beat them by pretending to be an ignorant tourist and asking dumb questions. Hustlers called this playing the Iggy, and he did it as well as anyone. The high-roller salon was tucked away in the rear of the casino and had a pair of carved white doors at the entrance. As he turned the knob to enter, he reminded himself that his name was Thomas Pico and that he was a hedge fund manager from New York.

- - -

The salon was a cozy space with thick gold carpets and muted lighting. By the entrance, a blond she-devil manned an antique desk. This was the salon's VIP hostess, whose trust he needed to gain before he ripped the place off. Her nameplate said "L. Shazam." It fit her.

"Is Ed Butler here?" he asked politely.

"Ed's off this week," she replied. "Perhaps I can help you."

"Ed comped me at the Bellagio a few years ago. I'd heard he'd moved over here."

"Let me see if you're in our system. Please make yourself comfortable."

He took a chair beside the desk and passed her his fake ID. A cocktail waitress glided toward him carrying a tray with a single flute of champagne. The drink was offered and accepted. "Here you are," the hostess said, tapping her computer screen with her fingernail. "I see that the last time you played at the Bellagio, you were extended a hundred-thousand-dollar line of credit. Were you hoping for that same line of credit with us tonight?"

"I just wanted to say hello to Ed," he said, sipping his drink. "He probably doesn't remember me. It's been a while."

She politely returned his ID. She'd seen enough about him to know that he was worth stealing from whatever casino he was staying at. "Where are you staying in town, Mr. Pico?"

"It's Tom. I'm at the Encore."

"Are they treating you well?"

"Okay, I guess."

"Is there something not to your liking?"

"They usually put me in a suite. Not this time."

"We have some of the most luxurious accommodations in Las Vegas. Some people say we've redefined luxury. I'd be happy to comp you a penthouse suite."

"I'll stay where I am. But thanks anyway."

"Are you a music fan? I can get you front-row seats to the Eagles concert this weekend. It's been sold out for months, but I have tickets left."

She wasn't going to let him go without a fight. Billy tipped his champagne flute, as if to say, *Well done*.

"Just say yes, and they're yours," she added.

Rich people never hurried, and Billy took another sip of champagne before responding.

"Can I bring my friends?" he asked.

She nodded, thinking she had him. "How many are in your party?"

"There are seven of us. I brought my team to Las Vegas to celebrate."

"Your team? Are you in professional sports?"

"I'm a hedge fund manager. They work for me."

"I don't see why not." From her desk drawer she removed a sleeve containing tickets to the upcoming Eagles concert and handed seven front-row seats to him. "Compliments of Galaxy. Would you be interested in staying awhile and playing? Our staff is very accommodating. I can also offer you a ten percent return on any losses you might incur."

Billy tucked the tickets into his jacket. This was great; not only was he going to rob them blind, but they were going to pay for him to go see one of his favorite bands.

"You know, I might just take you up on that," he said.

"Splendid. What's your pleasure?"

"Blackjack."

She rose and came around the desk, her gold evening dress touching the floor. She was tall and statuesque with a body that could have stopped traffic, the kind of ridiculously beautiful woman that Las Vegas had been built around. She touched the sleeve of his blazer and gave it a little tug. He could not remember a casino employee ever making physical contact with him before. It was out of character, and had he not been absorbed with staring at her jaw-dropping breasts, it might have dawned on him that something was not right.

"I didn't catch your name," he said.

"It's Lady. Lady Shazam. Everyone calls me Shaz," she replied.

"That's a cool name. Where you from?"

"Southern Cal. Follow me."

They entered the high-roller salon. The champagne flute was still in Billy's hand, and he took another swallow, having no idea that his life was about to turn horribly upside down.

NINE

The salon's five carved mahogany blackjack tables could have resided in the main palace at Versailles. Each had a well-groomed dealer standing at stiff attention. At the center table stood an attractive African American lady with long bony fingers. This had to be Jazzy, the flashing dealer that was about to make Billy and his crew very rich.

"This lady could use some company. I'll sit here," Billy said.

"Jazzy, make sure you take good care of Mr. Pico. He's a very special customer." To Billy, Shaz said, "Let me know if there's anything else I can do, Mr. Pico."

"I will. Thanks again for the tickets."

"My pleasure."

Shaz returned to her desk to wait for the next well-oiled sucker to step through the salon's doors. Taking a chair, Billy removed two stacks from his blazer and dropped them on the felt. A stern-faced pit boss appeared. Under his watchful eye, Jazzy tore off the wrappers and counted the bills.

"Ten thousand," Jazzy said.

"Go ahead," the pit boss declared.

Jazzy shoved the money down the bill slot in her table. Taking ten thousand in chips from her tray, she slid the stacks toward her only customer.

"Good luck, sir," she said.

Billy's eyes had become fixated on a stack of gold chips in Jazzy's tray. He'd never seen gold chips before, and suspected this was a special promotion for Galaxy's wealthiest customers.

"Are those gold chips something new?" he inquired.

"They are," the pit boss said proudly. "We're the only casino in town that lets its customers play with gold chips. They're worth a hundred thousand dollars apiece."

"Wow. Can I see one?"

"Jazzy, show Mr. Pico a gold chip."

Jazzy took a gold chip from her tray and placed it on the felt for Billy to look at. He'd tried to counterfeit casino chips many times and come up short. Even with the latest and most comprehensive Pantone color chart, it was impossible to find a chip's exact color. Then there was the problem of the microchip under the label that allowed the casino to track the chip's whereabouts. Those two things made counterfeiting chips something you only saw in movies.

"Pretty, isn't it?" the pit boss said.

"It sure is. Unfortunately, it's a little out of my league," Billy said.

"It's out of most people's leagues. Let me know if you need anything."

The pit boss left. Billy placed an orange thousand-dollar chip into the betting circle.

"Deal me a winner," he said.

Jazzy dealt a handheld game. As she sailed the cards to him, her hands rocked slightly. Tilting his head, he peeked her second card's identity before it was tucked away beneath her first card. In blackjack, the dealer's hole card was hidden until the end, which gave the house its edge. By knowing this card's value, the odds shifted dramatically in his favor.

He won the hand, putting him up a grand. Four rounds later, she did it again. Only Billy couldn't keep tilting his head without the pit boss spotting him and throwing him out.

"Where can I find an ashtray?" he asked.

An ashtray was brought to the table. He removed a hard pack of Marlboros from the pocket of his blazer and fired up a cigarette, then placed the pack on the table with the flap pointing at Jazzy. The pack was another of Gabe's creations. Hidden inside was a rectangular mirror resting at a forty-five-degree angle. By gazing down into a slit in the top of the pack, he would be able to see Jazzy's hole card while she flashed.

Soon he was up twenty grand. Had his bets been larger, the amount could have been two hundred grand. Crunchie had been right in his assessment of Jazzy. She was the best score in town. But he wasn't here to steal Galaxy's money. That would come later, after he'd established himself as a sucker with management.

He lost his winnings back through sloppy play while small-talking with Jazzy and learning her upcoming schedule. A new shift worked the weekend, and she'd be back Monday night. That would give him three days to build himself in before pulling his scam.

A cocktail waitress brought him a fresh glass of champagne. He tipped her and gave her a wink. She walked away too quickly, and an alarm went off in his head.

He turned around in his chair. To his surprise, the salon had cleared out. The other dealers and pit boss were gone, and Shaz's desk was empty as well.

The blood drained from his head. Something had been bothering him, and now he realized what it was. No steam. Some steam always accompanied a high roller betting $1,000 a hand, especially when the high roller was a complete stranger who'd just strolled in. But here in Galaxy's salon, there was no steam at all.

He turned back to Jazzy. "Where did everybody go?"

Jazzy glanced around the salon. Its emptiness seemed to surprise her as well.

"Beats me. I guess they went on break," she said.

"At the same time?"

"You're right. It is pretty strange."

It was time to get out of Dodge. He scooped up his chips and the gaffed cigarette pack from the table and rose from his chair. "It's been nice talking to you."

"Have a pleasant evening," she said.

He walked briskly toward the salon's entrance. The fear of getting caught was never far from his thoughts; it was the risk that came with the reward. As he opened the carved doors, he stole a glance over his shoulder. The pit boss had reappeared, and stood in front of Jazzy's table. Their eyes locked. The look on the pit boss's face said it all.

Busted!

He hurried into the main casino. If he could get out the front doors unscathed, he'd run down to the street and melt into the mass of humanity that filled the Strip's sidewalks. Thomas Pico would disappear, never to be heard from again. His car could be dealt with later. He hadn't given the valet his name, and he'd have Leon come by in a few days and claim it.

He sailed through the casino without a problem. His heartbeat was back to normal as he entered the hotel lobby, thinking he'd dodged a bullet. The feeling didn't last long.

Shaz was in the lobby waiting for him. She'd ditched the evening dress for a pair of skintight leather pants and a black zippered jacket straight out of a dominatrix's catalogue. A look of stone-cold hatred filled her eyes.

Flanking her were two of the scariest black dudes Billy had ever seen. They were as big as mountains and were studying him the way a cat sizes up a helpless canary in a cage.

Billy moved backward, having nowhere else to run.

"Get him," Shaz said.

TEN

The scary black dudes knocked Billy's glasses off dragging him across the lobby. He was thrown into a service elevator and taken to the basement, his final destination a claustrophobic room with a single plastic chair and a security camera bolted to the ceiling.

Billy had been back-roomed before and knew the drill. For the next hour, he'd be slapped around and threatened before the police were called, the casino wishing to impress upon him that he should never step foot on the premises again.

The black dudes took a moment to introduce themselves. Their names were Ike Spears and Terrell Bird, T-Bird for short. Both wore lots of gold jewelry and too much cologne. Ike had the larger vocabulary and appeared to be the leader of the two. T-Bird was shorter, with pretty dreadlocks that bounced on his shoulders. They'd both played defensive end for the Pittsburgh Steelers and sported glittering Super Bowl rings.

They took turns smacking Billy around. They were punishers and were paid by the casino to inflict pain upon unwanted guests, just as cocktail waitresses were paid to act nice. Being mean was their job, but they still didn't have to hit Billy as hard as they did.

Soon Billy's ears were ringing. *Somebody answer the phone.* Tasting his own blood, he spit some onto his palm and held his arm out as if directing traffic. The beating stopped.

"Keep hitting him," Shaz ordered them.

"I don't want his blood on me. Little fucker might have AIDS," Ike said.

"Or ebola," T-Bird said.

"You're both pathetic." Looking into the ceiling camera, Shaz raised her arms as if to say, *What now?* Scant seconds later, her cell phone rang.

"Follow me, girls," she said.

She went into the hall to take the call. The punishers dutifully followed.

Billy sank into the plastic chair. He'd taken a few hits to the jaw, and he ran the tip of his finger across his teeth to see if they were still intact. To his surprise, they were all there.

So much for small favors.

Although his body hurt, he wasn't scared. Soon the Metro LVPD would be summoned, and he'd be taken to the Clark County Detention Center and booked. There he'd be allowed to call his lawyer and post bail. He'd be a free man by morning, and he'd go home to his condo to lick his wounds and figure out how he was going to beat this rap.

Cheating cases were hard to prove. Nevada juries would not convict unless there was clear videotape evidence of the crime. Billy was always aware of the cameras when he was making a play, and hid his actions. As a result, the times he'd been busted he'd always plea-bargained out and had to pay fines to the court. It was a small price to pay for all the money he'd stolen from the casinos.

From the hallway came the sound of Shaz talking. He needed to find out how she'd made him for a cheater. His disguises had flown by the best security people in town, and it was going to bug him until he learned how she'd done it.

The unholy trio returned. A smelly towel was thrown in his face. He wiped away the blood, thinking the storm had passed.

A minute later, he learned otherwise.

- - -

They took an elevator to an unfinished fourteenth floor of the hotel's first tower. He felt a hand on his shoulder and followed Shaz down a hallway with no carpet, their feet echoing off harsh concrete. She unlocked a door to a suite with a "Do Not Enter" sign hanging on the knob.

"This is where we bring cheaters," she said.

The suite had colored wires springing from holes in the walls. The dead bolt was thrown and the breath caught in Billy's throat. He was about to die. There was no other reason for them to bring him here. Old-timers called it getting eighty-sixed. Eight miles out in the desert, six feet down in the ground.

"You with us, Billy?" Shaz asked.

"How did you know my name?"

"Haven't figured it out yet? You will. Walk with me."

"Come on. I didn't even steal any money from you," he pleaded.

"Shut up."

A hallway led to the master bedroom. She took a tube of Vicks VapoRub from her pocket and rubbed the ointment beneath each nostril, then passed the tube to the punishers.

"What are you doing?" His voice cracked.

She let out a hideous laugh and entered the bedroom. A violent push sent him stumbling behind her. The stench knocked him sideways; then the visuals took over. Blood splatters on the fancy bedspread, the wallpaper, sprayed across the ceiling like a Jackson Pollock painting and across the carpeted floor. Someone had died here, and had not gone quietly.

Positioned beside the bed was a tripod with a video camera; next to it, a director's chair. It took a moment for the significance to sink in. When it did, he nearly got ill.

The sick bastards had filmed it.

Shaz's fingernails dug into his flesh. She pulled him across the bedroom, the smell growing worse as they neared the closet. Something dead was hanging inside the closet. Bringing his hand to his mouth, he tried not to puke the onion rings he'd eaten earlier.

"Why don't you just get it over with?" he said.

She drew close to him. "What did you say?"

"You heard me. Shoot me, and get it over with."

"Do you want to die?"

"Do I have a choice?"

She pressed herself against his body. She was getting aroused on his fear, and he desperately wanted to get away from her.

"You don't have to die, but you have to look first," she said.

"Why do I have to look?"

"Because I want you to."

She sprung open the closet door. Inside a poor stiff hung from the clothing rack. Death robbed you of life and of dignity as well. The stiff had lost both. Short and skinny, with short dark hair, he was wrapped in plastic and had a thick rope tied around his neck, the other end tied to the rack. The right side of his skull had been shattered, the blow so severe that it had caused his left eye to break free of its orbit. The eye hung loosely on his discolored cheek like a displaced Christmas ornament, his other eye shut in permanent sleep. Something was wrong with his hand, and Billy realized two fingers were missing. Then he noticed the stiff's toes. Someone had worked them over with a hammer until they didn't look like toes anymore.

He asked himself, why? Why beat the poor guy to death, when putting a bullet in his head and plopping him in the ground would accomplish the same thing? Why go to the trouble?

"Recognize him?" she asked.

Billy shook his head. He didn't think the poor guy's mother would recognize him. Shaz picked up the stiff's wallet from the night table. Pulling a California driver's license from the billfold, she shoved it in Billy's face.

"How about now?"

He studied the photograph and name on the license.

"Never heard of him."

"Stop fucking with me."

"I'm not fucking with you. I don't know him."

She turned the license around. A hideous laugh escaped her throat.

"Silly me. I'm showing you the wrong license."

Digging in the billfold, she pulled out a second driver's license.

"How about now?"

He read the information on the second license. Richard "Ricky" Boswell, 1824 Rodale Circle Drive, Sacramento, CA. Age twenty-two, five feet three inches tall, one hundred thirty-two pounds. It took a moment for the name to register. The stiff was a member of the Boswell clan. Descendants from a tribe of Romanian Gypsies, the Boswells had started scamming Vegas in the 1990s and were still going strong. They were so skilled in the art of scamming that other cheaters simply referred to them as the Gypsies. They were the mountain that Billy one day aspired to climb, and he felt bad that one of their group had gone out the hard way.

He handed the license back.

"Yeah, I know him. He's part of a family of cheaters called the Gypsies."

"We know that. We caught him walking around the casino taking pictures on his cell phone. His family sent him here to scope the place out."

"He told you that?"

"Yes. Little Ricky also told us that his family was going to take our casino down, and there wasn't a fucking thing we could do about it."

"He bragged about it?"

"That's right, the little asshole."

Which was why the punishers had tortured the poor kid and eventually murdered him. The picture was getting clearer now, and Billy said, "You want me to figure out what the Gypsies' scam is. That's why you brought me here, isn't it?"

"You catch on fast. Can you do it?"

The Gypsies had fooled the best brains in the business with their intricate casino scams, including the enforcement division of the Nevada Gaming Control Board. Trying to figure out how they planned to rip off Galaxy's casino was a tall order, but he was willing to give it a try, for no other reason than to buy himself precious time.

"I need to look at his personal belongings, see if he took down any notes," he said. "That should point me in the right direction."

"You think you can dope out the scam by looking at his things?" she asked.

"You bet."

She shoved the director's chair in front of him.

"Let's get started," she said.

ELEVEN

The Gypsies' story was known to every cheater in Vegas. They'd immigrated to the Midwest in the 1960s, where they'd made their living boosting furniture from department stores in the Chicago area. Boosting furniture wasn't easy, and the Gypsies had used a ploy called the Dazzle to get the job done.

The family would enter a department store and stand next to the desired item. Dad would give a signal, and the kids would start moving around the floor as if doing a square dance, their movements choreographed to mesmerize any onlookers into looking the wrong way. At the same time, two sons would pick up the item and brazenly walk out the front door.

All scams eventually ran their course. Seeking greener pastures, the Gypsies had moved to Nevada in the 1990s and hit the casinos. Using the same ploys, they'd attacked the blackjack tables and switched the dealing shoes with dealing shoes containing stacked decks of cards. Other scams involving dice, roulette, and rigging slot machines soon followed.

Decades later, they were still going strong.

Billy sat in the director's chair and tried to avoid looking at Ricky's corpse. Shaz handed him three items off the night table: an iPhone, a light meter, and a small notepad.

"Those are his things," she said. "Now tell me what the little fucker was up to."

He examined the iPhone first. There were no text or voice messages, just an e-mail from JetBlue confirming a flight out of town departing Saturday night. He now knew something important: the Gypsies were planning to scam Galaxy's casino on Saturday afternoon. Cheaters always left town a few hours after ripping off a casino.

The notepad was next, its pages filled with cryptic notations and measurements. When he looked up, Shaz was burning a hole in him.

"Explain the notes," she said.

"Ricky was measuring the distances to the exits, in case his family needed to beat an escape. Later, he was going to draw everything out, like a blueprint."

"A blueprint for what?"

"His family practices their scams in a fake casino. They try to duplicate the conditions inside your casino to see what problems might come up."

"How does the light meter play into this?"

"Ricky was measuring the light inside the casino so his family could duplicate it inside the fake casino. The family videotapes their practice sessions, and later critiques the tapes. It lets them see what the surveillance cameras see."

The answer seemed to satisfy her. She pulled up a chair, and sat in it backward so she faced him. "You're a clever guy, aren't you?"

"If I was so clever, you wouldn't have caught me."

"I hear you went to MIT and blew everyone out of the water."

He stiffened, not knowing what to say.

"I also hear you've banged half the beautiful women in Las Vegas. You're a regular love machine, is what I hear."

The punishers laughed under their breath.

"It's why you're so successful," she went on. "The girls you recruit won't give you up, even if they get caught. They're in love with you."

The things she had said only a handful of people knew. No one had ever ratted him out before, and he didn't have a clue who was behind this betrayal.

"So what's the Gypsies' scam? You must have figured it out by now," she said.

She was right. He had figured it out, or at least enough to catch them.

The scam would occur between 3:55 p.m. and 4:05 p.m. Saturday afternoon, right as the day shift ended and the swing shift began. Employees going home, new employees taking over their spots, the casino in a state of flux, no one in surveillance paying attention to the monitors, just the way cheaters liked it.

He also knew what they'd be wearing. Clothes whose colors matched. This was true for every scam the Gypsies had pulled and would be no different come Saturday. Perhaps they'd be posing as a family on vacation, or a group of zany conventioneers who dressed alike.

He also knew that it was an outside job, and that no casino employees would be involved. The Gypsies were a tight-knit group and avoided using outside agents whenever possible.

It was enough information to nail them. But if he told Shaz what he knew, the punishers would ice him. They really didn't have a choice. He'd seen the stiff in the closet and was now a witness. Witnesses talked, so they had to kill him. The best he could do was buy more time.

"I'm waiting," she said impatiently.

"I don't know exactly what the scam is. But I can catch them."

"How are you going to do that?"

"It takes one to know one."

"Instincts, huh?"

"I know how they think."

"You'd better not be fucking with me."

"I'm not fucking with you."

Shaz made a call on her cell phone. "Hey, Marcus. He wants to cut a deal with us." She listened intently before ending the call.

"Marcus wants him to see the film," she told the punishers. "Hold him down."

T-Bird dropped to the floor behind Billy's chair, and put their prisoner into a half nelson. Shaz powered up the room's flat-screen TV. A snuff film of Ricky Boswell began to play. She grabbed Billy by the hair and pulled his head back, forcing his eyes to stay open.

"Watch this. Learn," she said.

Billy didn't think he could learn anything from watching a poor guy get beaten to death, but he was wrong. The punishers were nothing more than bit players, while Shaz was the real star in the horror show. With cold sweat pouring down his face, he watched her break Ricky's toes and snip off his fingers and finally swing the baseball bat that popped Ricky's eye out of his head.

The poor kid was alive for all of it. To his credit, Ricky stuck to the code of never betraying the people he ran with. His family would have been proud of him for doing that.

The beating finally ended. Ricky had taken everything a man could possibly take. He was laid on the bed and started to die, his body a quivering mass of ticks and tremors as his life seeped away. His good eye blinked like the emergency blinker on a car, then grew frozen.

Billy could not help it and started to cry.

"Let him go," Shaz said.

T-Bird released Billy. The young hustler wiped away his tears.

"Get up," she said. "We're going upstairs to see Marcus."

He rose on shaky legs. He was never going to forget this for as long as he lived. He started to follow her out of the bedroom, then froze. On the TV screen, a stranger had entered the picture and moved next to the bed. The stranger brought his hand to his chin, as if trying to decide how to dispose of the body, and offered his profile to the camera.

The breath caught in Billy's throat. It was his old pal Crunchie.

TWELVE

Riding an elevator to the penthouse, Billy thought back to his meeting at the Peppermill with the old grifter. Crunchie had been throwing off bad vibes, which Billy had ignored, too swayed by the lure of a huge score to realize he was being set up.

The doors parted, and they walked down a carpeted hallway to a corner office with a gold nameplate that read, "Marcus Doucette, President & CEO / Galaxy Entertainment." Doucette's name had been in the papers lately. A sleazoid strip-club owner from LA, he'd broken every building code and bribed a building inspector to get his casino built. Money talked in the desert, and the joint had opened on time.

Shaz opened the doors and they entered. The office was sleek and soulless, with as much charm as a terminal at McCarran. Neon bursts from the Strip's casinos danced in the floor-to-ceiling windows, bathing the room in lurid hues. An oversized granite desk sat in the room's center, in front of it, a single chair. Two men stood outside on the balcony, talking.

"Have a seat," Shaz said.

He did as told. A framed wedding photo on the desk caught his eye. In it, Shaz and a handsome devil with burnt-blond hair and soap opera blue eyes stood on a sandy beach, exchanging wedding vows. So she was married to the boss.

The men on the balcony came inside. Doucette sat on the edge of the desk and fired up a cigarette. He favored the movie-studio-executive look and wore a cream-colored Armani suit, an unbuttoned white silk shirt, and crocodile loafers sans socks.

"Crunchie tells me you're the smartest cheater in town," Doucette said.

Crunchie stood by the slider, cowboy hat in hand.

"You're a piece of shit," Billy said.

"Shut up, and listen to Marcus," the old grifter said.

"I want you to tell me what these Gypsies are up to," Doucette said. "Do that, and you'll walk out of here with your skin. Fair enough?"

It was as good as Billy could have hoped for, and he decided to play his hand. "I found some information on Ricky Boswell's cell phone that told me his family's planning to scam your casino on Saturday afternoon during the shift change. They're going to do a little hocus-pocus in the middle of the casino floor and rig one of your games. Your security guards will be watching, and so will the eye-in-the sky, but you still won't see them."

Doucette shifted his gaze to Crunchie. "Is this little prick telling the truth?"

"I think Billy's nailed it," the old grifter said.

"Why didn't you catch that? You saw the cell phone."

"Billy's eyes are a little better than mine."

Doucette shifted his attention back to his guest. "All right, so the play is going down Saturday afternoon. How do I nail them?"

"Do we have a deal?" Billy asked.

"Not until you tell me the rest."

The conversation had taken a bad turn. There was nothing to stop Doucette from snuffing him once he had the information he needed. It was time for Billy to take a stand.

"Get lost," Billy said.

"What did you say to me?"

"You heard me. Take a hike."

Doucette exploded, and searched his desk for something sharp to stick into Billy's chest. He'd been sweating over the Gypsies for days, and the tension inside him had reached a boiling point. Knowing you were going to get ripped off was almost as bad as the crime itself. Shaz came to her husband's side and grabbed him by the arm.

"Calm down. He's nothing but a little street rat," she said.

"Nobody talks to me that way," Doucette said.

She pulled a gold vial from her pocket and cut up three white lines of gutter glitter on the blotter. Doucette snorted them with a small metal straw. It took him to another place, and he tilted his head back and shut his eyes. His wife massaged the tension from his shoulders.

"Feel better?"

"Yeah. Thanks, baby." To Crunchie he said, "Deal with this little asshole."

The old grifter came away from the slider. "Sorry, Billy, but we need to know what the scam is. You're in no position to refuse."

"How long have you been working for these people?" Billy asked him.

"Since they opened. They pay me to keep the place from getting ripped off. I don't have any regrets, if that's what you're thinking."

"Not one?"

"Nope. Not even with you. Your time was running out, the way I see it. You can't rip off as many casinos as you have and not get taken down."

"Is that why you set me up in the salon? So you could film it and blackmail me?"

"You catch on quick. But you always did. Now let's get this over with."

Whatever notion he'd had to save his own skin had just flown out the door. He wasn't going to roll on the Gypsies, even if the punishers hung him over the balcony by the balls and threatened to drop him on his head.

"Fuck you," he said.

"What's that supposed to mean?" Crunchie said, startled.

"It means I'm not telling you."

"Not even if we turn the surveillance tapes over to the police?"

"I'm not ratting the Gypsies out. Not for you, or anyone else."

Crunchie tossed his cowboy hat on the desk and let out an exasperated breath. "We caught a flash of the mirror in the cigarette pack on the tape. The jury sees that along with the fact that you were using a false identity, they'll send you to the federal pen. You'll do hard time, Billy. Do you know what happens to little guys in the pen? They get turned into bitches."

"I'll take my chances in the pen."

"You sure about this?"

"I've never been more sure in my life."

The old grifter looked pissed off, but not defeated, as if he had another card stuck up his sleeve. He took his Stetson off the desk and held it like he was taking a collection.

"Empty your pockets," the old grifter said.

"Fuck you."

"Ike, T-Bird, help our guest here."

Ike yanked Billy out of the chair and held him while T-Bird picked Billy's pockets clean and tossed his personal belongings into the cowboy hat. Wallet, gaffed cigarette case, Droid, and a handful of loose change was the haul. Crunchie went straight for Billy's wallet and was rewarded with a receipt inside the billfold. A smile creased his wrinkled face.

"Look at this. A drink receipt from the Four Queens with a time and date stamped on it. You were there at six thirty last night. What were you doing at the Four Queens, Billy?"

Billy cursed to himself. Normally, he tore up receipts after a job, and he guessed this one had gotten tucked in his change without him realizing it.

"I'll tell you what you were doing there," the old grifter said. "You and your crew were pulling your red hot dice scam. Isn't that right?"

He stared at the floor. A fucking receipt. He'd forgotten to tear up a fucking receipt, and now he was going to pay for it.

"I'll bet that if I called the gaming board and told them to review the surveillance tapes from the Four Queens last night, you'll pop up, along with the rest of your crew. I could help them by pointing out which people at the craps table are involved. I'm guessing you use a couple of hot girls for distraction, a pair of clean-cut college boys as takeoff men, and a mechanic to execute the switch while you direct the action." He paused. "Am I getting warm?"

Crunchie was messing with him. Billy had patterned his crews after the old grifter's, right down to using women from the sex industry as shade.

"Of course, we don't know the names of the people in your crew, or where they live, or anything about them. That's going to make it tough to run them down. Unless we give the gaming board your cell phone."

The old grifter removed Billy's cell phone from the hat. "A Droid. I've got one of these, too. I'd be willing to bet you that your crew's phone numbers are logged into it. Aren't they, Billy?"

"You're a piece of shit," Billy said under his breath.

"The gaming board will use the phone numbers to track your crew down, and haul them in. They'll match their faces to the faces on the Four Queens surveillance tapes, and charge them with conspiracy, and you'll have a real mess on your hands. You know how many years you'll face on a conspiracy rap?"

Billy knew the law. The state's lifeblood came from casino taxes; when you stole from the casinos, you stole from the state, and they didn't take it lightly. Travis, Gabe, Misty, Pepper, Cory, and Morris were in a world of trouble, as was he.

"I still won't tell you," he said.

"That's stupid. You'll do time, and so will your crew. Hard time."

"We'll take our chances."

The office grew deathly still. Crunchie's face turned crimson, embarrassed by his own miscalculation. Out of frustration he tossed Billy's cell phone back into the hat. Something inside the hat caught his eye, and he removed the double-sided Slots A Fun chip.

"My, my, what do we have here?" the old grifter said. "A double-sided chip from Slots A Fun. That joint's right down the street from the Peppermill. You went there tonight before you met with me, didn't you Billy? You were doing one of your side scams, working with a female dealer, stealing chips out of the tray."

"I don't know what you're talking about," Billy said.

"Come on, Billy, I know you too well. I got you red-handed."

Billy said, "Fuck me" under his breath.

"Maybe I'll call Slots A Fun, tell them to watch tonight's surveillance tapes of their blackjack pit. I'm betting you and your friend are on them, ripping the joint off. They'll have her arrested, and the cops will work her over real good. You don't want that, do you?"

Billy imagined Ly being grilled by the cops. She wasn't loyal to him and would roll in a heartbeat and spill her guts. The cops would arrest him, then use the information Crunchie gave them and burn his crew for the Four Queens scam. No lawyer in town could save him, or his crew, if that happened.

"No," he blurted out.

"I didn't think so. Now are you going to play ball, or do I call Slots A Fun?"

He was beaten. It was a crummy feeling, and he wanted to crawl in a hole and die.

"Yeah, I'll play ball," he said.

Crunchie glanced Doucette's way. The casino boss nodded his approval.

THIRTEEN

Billy came clean. He didn't know how the Gypsies were planning to rip off Galaxy's casino Saturday afternoon. The scam might be at blackjack, or a slot machine with a monster jackpot, or maybe they were going to take a direct run at the cage. It didn't matter; he knew enough about the operation to stop it from happening.

Crunchie didn't say very much, but his face said a lot. He knew the difference between the truth and flat-out bullshit, and he knew that Billy was leveling with him. When Billy was finished talking, he walked around the desk and spent a minute whispering in Doucette's ear.

"You sure about this?" the casino boss asked.

The old grifter grunted that he was entirely sure.

"I still don't trust him," Doucette said.

Billy's heart was pounding. He couldn't read Doucette and didn't know what the casino boss was thinking. Shaz stood behind her husband's chair and patted his shoulder while gazing at Billy with a twisted smile on her face. He hadn't figured out her deal, either.

Doucette came around the desk and stood in front of Billy's chair.

For a long moment he simply glared. His hand came out of nowhere and slapped Billy's face.

"Do you know why I did that?" Doucette asked.

"No," Billy said.

"Neither do I. Now, here's the deal. I want you to stop the Gypsies from ripping off my casino. Do that, and I won't have Crunchie turn your friends over to the law. You in?"

Billy tasted his own blood. It seemed a perfect prelude for selling his soul and ratting out another group of cheaters to save himself and his crew. "Yeah, I'm in."

"Good. If you try and double-cross me, I'll kill you."

"I get that."

"I bet you do. Now, here's the ground rules. Thomas Pico's identity is established in the casino's computer system. I want you to continue to impersonate him. That means wearing those funny-looking glasses you had on earlier and dressing like a nerd. Is that understood?"

"Your boys knocked off my glasses."

"So get another pair. You stay in disguise."

Billy nodded compliance. He was beginning to get the picture. Gaming agents regularly visited the casinos to check up on things. By having Billy wear a disguise, Doucette was making it harder for a gaming agent to recognize him. And if an agent did by chance make him, Doucette could claim that he hadn't known who Billy was. The casino boss was covering all his bases.

"Tomorrow afternoon, you'll check into the hotel using Pico's ID, and will be comped into a high-roller suite in the main tower," Doucette said. "Your suite has got hidden cameras and is wired for audio as well, so don't even think about screwing with me."

"How about the john? Are you going to film me taking a crap?"

"We just might."

He wasn't surprised to hear the high-roller suite was wired. Many casinos wired their high-roller suites to make sure their wealthy customers didn't go play at a competitor's tables.

"You'll also be comped your food and drinks, and will be given twenty grand in chips to play with," the casino boss said. "If you decide to cheat us, don't even think about cashing in your chips, because you'll be killed. Got it?"

"You think I'd cheat you now?" Billy asked incredulously.

"Damn straight I do. Cheating's in your blood." Doucette paused, then said, "You're also going to have an entourage. Ike and T-Bird will act as your bodyguards, and will accompany you wherever you go. They'll also be staying in your suite. If you stray, they'll take you down. You're going to be in our crosshairs every moment you're here. You with me?"

"Yeah, I'm with you."

"Good. If you've got any questions, ask them now."

He had questions, but he'd decided it was more important to get the hell out of here before Doucette or his crazy bride had a change of mind. They impressed him as the kind of people that could flip on a dime and turn into animals, and he didn't want to be around when that happened.

"I'm good," he said. Then he added, "You can count on me."

"Why is it every time you talk, I think you're lying to me?" Doucette said.

"Beats me."

"Get him out of here," the casino boss said, and went onto the balcony with his bride.

- - -

"Let's go, pardner," Crunchie said.

Billy rose from his chair and followed the old grifter out of the office. He had no idea how this was going to turn out, but as they rode the elevator down to the main level, he promised himself that he was going to pay Crunchie back for setting him up.

The valet stand was jamming, and they waited in line for his car. The cool desert air was bringing him around, and he could not purge the idea of revenge from his mind. Perhaps he'd throw the old grifter under the wheels of the next vehicle that came up.

"Stop looking at me like that," Crunchie said.

"Who said I was looking at you?" Billy said.

"You think I don't know? You want to kill me."

"Doesn't everybody?"

Ike and T-Bird laughed contemptuously. Billy edged closer to the old grifter. Feeling threatened by the proximity, the old grifter's watery eyes narrowed with distrust.

"You lied to me when you said you were talking to your daughter tonight," Billy said. "You were talking to that crazy bitch, weren't you?"

"How'd you know that?" Crunchie asked.

"You showed me three calls on your cell phone with a 310 area code, which is Southern California. Shaz told me she recently relocated from LA. Two plus two equals four."

"You don't miss a trick, do you?"

"Is she running things?"

"Fuck no. Doucette's running the show. She's just window dressing."

A car came up that wasn't his. There was something eating at Billy, and he decided to get it off his chest. "Why did you let her torture Ricky Boswell, and bash his head in with a baseball bat? Why couldn't you have just shot him? The poor kid didn't need to suffer."

"Who told you she tortured him?"

"She made me watch a video of it. You were in it. Why didn't you stop her?"

"I couldn't."

"I thought you said she wasn't running things."

"It's complicated. Do yourself a favor, and steer clear of her. If you don't, she'll end up snuffing you like that little bastard Ricky."

"Ricky was one of us. You don't do that to your own. You broke the code."

"Let it go," the old grifter said.

The Maserati appeared with a distinctive roar, the valet a budding NASCAR driver. Billy instinctively reached for his wallet, and came away empty.

"Give me my wallet back," he said.

"Ike's got your wallet," the old grifter said. "Come by tomorrow afternoon at three, and we'll go over things. Remember, if you mess with us, we'll destroy you and your friends."

Crunchie limped back inside. At least the story about his arthritis acting up had been true. Ike tossed Billy his wallet. Billy flipped it open to give the valet a tip, and found the billfold empty. Ike had cleaned him out. Laughing, the punishers went inside as well.

- - -

Billy burned rubber out of the valet stand. Traffic was light, the late hour thinning out the herd, and he punched the accelerator as he headed north on the neon-infused Strip, desperate to put as much distance between himself and Galaxy's casino as possible.

He felt ready to explode. He hadn't screwed up this badly since college. At the intersection of Sahara Avenue he pulled a wild-ass stunt, and with tires screaming, cut across four lanes and hung a sharp left. There wasn't a traffic cop in sight, and as he sped down Sahara, he realized it was the first lucky break he'd caught all night.

He was doing eighty when he hit the entrance ramp. With the wind blowing in his face, his fear ebbed away, and he told himself that he could beat these bastards. He didn't know how, but he could do it. They'd tipped their mitts and revealed their hands and given him enough information to mess with them real good.

Doucette was a coked-out fool, and so was his psycho bride, and neither one of them knew a damn thing about running a casino. If they had, they'd never have asked a known hustler to help them catch a gang of cheats. Only in the dumb movies did casino people do that.

Ike and T-Bird were a pair of washed-up jocks and dumber than a box of rocks. Stupid people were easily played. He was going to have fun with those two mutts.

Last was Crunchie, who'd screwed with him in so many ways that Billy had lost count. But there was a reason for it. Age had caught up to the old grifter, and Crunchie no longer had the confidence in himself to do the job that he was asking Billy to do.

Each of them had an Achilles' heel that he could stick a dagger into and twist around real good. They'd picked the wrong guy to fuck with, and he couldn't wait to pay them back.

FOURTEEN

-THE HOT SEAT: SUNDAY, MIDDAY-

At noon the gaming agents broke for lunch. Trays of food were brought up from the jail's cafeteria that weren't fit for a dog. Billy thought the session had gone well, and he sipped from a can of ginger ale while watching LaBadie, Zander, and Tricaricco chow down on baloney sandwiches on Wonder Bread and cups of greasy potato salad. Bad food was part of a cop's daily existence, and the gaming agents made sure to clean their plates.

"You haven't told us how Maggie Flynn plays into this," LaBadie asked when they were done. "That was part of our agreement."

"Mags didn't come into the picture until Thursday night," Billy explained. "I didn't want to jump ahead of myself."

LaBadie also had a briefcase, although not as pretty as Underman's. Placing it on the table, he popped it open, and removed a glossy eight-by-ten photograph of Billy and his crew taken inside Galaxy's employee parking garage a few hours before they ripped the joint off.

"Yesterday afternoon, you and eight other people were secretly photographed by one of our agents inside Galaxy's employee parking garage before the casino was robbed," LaBadie said. "We know the two black guys in the photo worked for Doucette. I want you to tell me the other six people's names."

"That photograph isn't want you think," Billy said.

"Really. Then what is it?"

"Well, I was doing a job for Marcus Doucette. Doucette thought some cheaters were staying in his hotel, and asked me to sniff them out. I asked six friends of mine to help me find them, and on Saturday afternoon we met in the employee garage to talk things over."

"You honestly don't expect me to believe that, do you?"

"Ask the woman who runs the bridal shop. Lucille Gonzalez. She knows all about it."

"This Gonzalez woman will back up your story?"

"Yes, sir."

LaBadie looked stymied. If Lucille Gonzalez backed up the story—which Billy believed she would, considering how they'd left things—the gaming board would not be able to charge him with conspiracy, which seriously weakened their case against him.

LaBadie pointed at the photo. "These six friends of yours—are they part of your crew?"

"I don't have a crew," Billy said.

"Don't get smart with us, Billy. You've been running a crew for years."

"I don't know what you're talking about."

"You had a crew when we busted you at the Hard Rock. You met with them yesterday afternoon in the employee parking lot, and conspired to rip off Galaxy's casino."

"My client was never busted at the Hard Rock," Underman said.

"He was released on a technicality."

Billy leaned forward and brought his mouth next to the tape recorder. "For the record, I've never had a crew that worked for me, and I wasn't busted at the Hard Rock, and I did not conspire to rip off Galaxy's casino with my friends."

LaBadie looked ready to pull his hair out. Billy decided to shut him down.

"Want to hear the rest of my story?" the young hustler asked.

LaBadie slammed the briefcase and dropped it on the floor. He sat down in his chair hard, making the hinges sing. The expression on his face was anything but friendly.

"Start talking," the gaming agent said.

FIFTEEN

-THURSDAY, TWO DAYS BEFORE THE HEIST-

Billy awoke the next morning sprawled across the leather couch in his living room. His body was a feverish mass of hurt from the beating Ike and T-Bird had inflicted upon him, his skin covered in bruises of every shade, from mauve to lilac to violet to plum.

In the bathroom he downed eight hundred milligrams of ibuprofen while examining his face in the mirror. He had the beginnings of a world-class shiner. How did Doucette expect him to impersonate a whale looking like this? His job had just gotten that much tougher.

He kept a collection of designer shades in his bedroom, well over a hundred pairs. He rummaged through them and settled on a pair of mirrored Ray-Bans that could have belonged to Steve McQueen. When he'd first come to Vegas, you couldn't wear shades inside a casino without drawing heat. Then the poker craze had started, and wearing shades became cool.

In the kitchen he brewed a pot of coffee and drank a cup. It had been years since he'd risen this early. Normally, he slept until noon, exercised in the building's health club or worked on his golf game, ate an early dinner at a good restaurant, and started swindling the casinos at six, his work lasting until the small hours of the morning. The next three days were going to be different. He was going to have to keep a schedule and follow other people's rules, no different than a regular job.

The coffee brought him around, and he stared at the coffee grinds swirling in the bottom. Kismet, the religion of all gamblers, was calling to him.

Three days.

There was a significance to that number, an event which occurred every three days inside a casino that had once been very important to him. Now, not as much.

Three days.

A minute slipped away. Nothing clicked.

Casinos were models of efficiency and worked on systems that were predictable and exploitable. Smart cheaters knew these systems inside out, and he was going to kick himself until he remembered what it was that happened every three days inside a casino.

The landline rang. Caller ID said it was Travis. The big man called once a day to talk shop; outside of that, they rarely communicated. Travis had recently gotten hitched and his new wife had two young sons. Karen knew about the thieving but the boys were in the dark, and Travis wanted to keep it that way.

The call went to voice mail. The enormity of Billy's fuckup suddenly hit him, and he pulled a chair out from the kitchen table and sat down. If he returned the call, Travis would want to know if the heist of Galaxy's salon was still on, and that would lead to a conversation that Billy wasn't ready to have. But if he didn't call back, Travis would get worried, wondering what had happened to him.

The phone rang again. If not now, when? Billy asked himself. He took the receiver out of the cradle and in a calm voice said, "Hey, tough guy."

"Jesus, Billy, I was starting to think you were in jail or something," Travis said. "You okay? I called your cell phone, and some asshole answered it, so I hung up."

Billy shuddered. Crunchie had answered his fucking cell phone. The damage was done, and he was going to have to tell Travis what had gone down last night.

"I had a little problem last night. What are you doing up so early?"

Travis also slept in, and rarely awoke before midafternoon.

"Karen called. Stevie got hit in the face with a soccer ball at school, and she's taking him to the hospital so they can X-ray his nose. I'm going there once I get off with you."

"Is he okay?"

"Yeah, he's a tough little fucker. Oh, shit, there's Karen calling me. Let's talk later. I want to hear how things went."

Breathing room. Billy needed some of that. It would give him time to construct the story he'd tell Travis and the rest of his crew. He started to say good-bye, then remembered that he had a question for the big man. "I need to ask you something. What procedure takes place every three days inside a casino? I know there's one, but I can't remember what it is."

Travis was the only member of the crew that had worked in a casino, and was what people in the industry called a gamer. If anyone knew the significance of three days, it was him. Travis took the call from his wife, then came back on the line.

"Is this a big casino or a little casino we're talking about?" Travis asked.

"Does it matter?" Billy said.

"In a big casino, nothing happens after three days. The smaller joints are different. Every three days they erase the surveillance tapes, and use them over. It saves a ton of money."

"How about the Four Queens? Would they erase their tapes after three days?"

"Sure. All the joints on Fremont Street do."

Billy walked into the living room with the cordless phone pressed to his ear. His crew had ripped off the Four Queens on a Wednesday. By Saturday night, the surveillance tapes of their misdeeds would be erased, and the evidence would disappear. The same was true of the gaffed-chip scam he'd pulled at Slots A Fun. By Saturday night, the tape would be blank. All he needed to do was last until Saturday night, and he and his crew would be home free.

"Did we slip up last night?" Travis asked, sounding worried.

"Last night ran perfectly," he said.

"Come on, Billy, I wasn't born yesterday. First some asshole answers your phone. Now you ask me if I thought the tapes from last night will be erased. What the hell's going on?"

Billy cursed himself. He hadn't phrased his questions right, and now Travis was suspicious, as he should have been.

"I don't want to discuss this right now. We'll talk about it later, okay?"

"Are we going down?" Travis asked, not hearing him.

"Who said anything about going down?"

"Are we?"

"No."

"Are we at risk of going down?"

"I don't want to talk about this right now."

"Fuck it, Billy, give me a straight answer, will you, man?"

There was a click on the line. Travis said, "There's Karen again," and stuck him on hold. Billy sat on the couch, feeling his world starting to implode. He hadn't come clean with Travis, and the big man knew it. If Travis didn't trust him, he'd go work for someone else. The rest of the crew would find out, and they'd leave as well. Hustling was all about trust, and right now, his was wearing thin. Travis came back on.

"Karen's fit to be tied. I've got to go. I'll call you later."

"Okay. Good luck."

"Tell me everything's cool, man. My heart's racing a hundred miles an hour."

"Everything's under control."

"You're not lying to me, are you? Because it sure sounds that way."

An invisible knife stabbed Billy in the chest. He'd discovered Travis switching dice at a sawdust joint called Palace Station, using moves he'd learned from an amateur's book on hustling he'd picked up at the Gambler's Book Club, yet still robbing the place blind. Travis was a natural, and Billy had recruited the big man on the spot. Now it was all going into the toilet because he hadn't played straight with Travis. Without truth, there was nothing.

"I screwed up," Billy said.

"Jesus Christ. You?"

"Yeah, me. Big time. I'm sorry I didn't come clean with you."

"Fucking A, what happened?"

"The scam at Galaxy I told you about was a trap, and I walked right into it. Another hustler set me up. He's working for the casino, and wants me to stop a family of cheaters from robbing them. He's got my cell phone, and knows about the Four Queens scam. He threatened to turn us over to the police if I don't play ball with him."

"Is that why you asked me about the tapes being erased in three days?"

"Yeah. If I can hold him off until Saturday night, the crew's safe."

"Jesus Christ—you're going to help him?"

"I don't have a choice."

"Do I need to lawyer up? Just in case?"

"You're not going to get arrested, and neither is anyone else in the crew. Your world is safe. Now go take care of your son."

"What about you? Are you safe?"

That was a good question. And Billy was pretty sure he knew the answer. If he didn't stop the Gypsies, his sorry ass would get dragged to an unfinished floor of Galaxy's hotel, and he'd get snuffed for his failure.

All he could hope for was that they'd get it over quickly and wouldn't make him suffer.

"I'll be fine," he said.

"There's Karen. I'll call you later."

A dial tone filled his ear. He went into the kitchen and hung up the phone. He had let Travis down, and realized that he was dreading having to break the bad news to the other members of his crew. It was going to be painful, but it had to be done.

SIXTEEN

Billy pulled into Gabe's driveway a few minutes before one. Gabe's Mercedes was missing, and he found himself getting pissed. They were supposed to be going to a Gamblers Anonymous meeting to help Gabe get the monkey off his back, so where the hell was he?

Soon Billy's hand was sore from banging on Gabe's front door. Not having his cell phone was proving to be a royal pain in the ass, and he drove out of the subdivision to a Fresh and Easy and called Gabe from a pay phone.

"Hey, Billy, what's shaking?" Gabe answered, his voice high-pitched.

"We were supposed to meet up this afternoon, remember? Where you hiding?"

"I don't want to go to Gamblers Anonymous. That shit bothers me. All those strangers pouring their guts out, talking about their problems. No thanks, man."

"You don't have to go."

"I don't?"

"Not today. But we do need to talk. Something bad went down

last night. What's that loud music in the background? You in a bar or something?"

"I'm at Misty and Pepper's place. We're having a little party to celebrate our newfound fortune. Cory and Morris are here, too. You're welcome to join us, isn't he, ladies?"

The girls' voices floated merrily in the background, inviting Billy to come over and get stoned. Billy brought his hand to his face. There was no newfound fortune, no pot of gold at the end of the rainbow. Breaking the bad news had just gotten a lot tougher.

"I'll be right over," he said.

- - -

Misty and Pepper had been sharing an efficiency apartment with their pound mutts when Billy first hooked up with them. They'd come to Vegas to be cocktail waitresses, thinking it would lead to better things. When they got tired of having their asses pinched, they'd started making porn, and discovered it was another bum deal. The actresses got paid a flat fee, with no royalties or health benefits to cover disease or injury.

They'd been at a crossroads when Billy met them. They still had their looks and could snap a man's head just by walking by. They were willing to use their charms to make a buck but didn't want to take their clothes off anymore, or go down on strangers.

Billy had come to their apartment with Chinese takeout and a DVD. While eating pork-fried rice in the cramped living room, they watched a dopey sitcom called *Sweet Nothings* that starred everyone's favorite comedic actress, Lydia Fallon. Fallon was a fixture on network TV, her giggling laugh known to millions. Misty and Pepper professed to be big fans.

When the show ended, Billy told Misty and Pepper a story. Once upon a time, Lydia Fallon had lived in Las Vegas and worked with a crew of cheaters that past-posted at roulette. Placing a wager after the little white ball had fallen was no small feat, and Fallon used her persuasive charms to distract the croupier while her partners did the dirty work.

One night Fallon was scamming a fancy Strip casino when a big-shot Hollywood producer sitting at the table spotted her and was blown away. Instead of alerting security, he whisked her away to la-la land and turned her into a household name.

There was a moral to Billy's story. Cheating wasn't the end of the road, but the beginning of a new life. With the money Misty and Pepper would make working with his crew, they could lead the kind of lives they'd always dreamed of, just like Lydia Fallon.

Misty and Pepper signed up on the spot.

It was one of the smarter things he'd ever done. When Misty and Pepper were on the casino floor strutting their stuff, the rest of his crew could operate practically unseen.

The uniformed guard at the entrance of the Las Vegas Country Club waved him through, and he drove to the three-thousand-square-foot, three-bedroom luxury house the girls now called home. Filling the circular driveway was Gabe's Mercedes, Cory and Morris's black Infiniti SUV, Misty's BMW 4 Series convertible, and Pepper's champagne-colored Lexus 350. Whoever said that crime didn't pay wasn't doing it right.

He rang the bell. A melodic chime filled the interior, followed by bare feet pounding tile floors. Misty greeted him with bloodshot eyes, her sensuous mouth parted in a loopy grin. She wore a white string bikini and a glistening diamond in her navel. She sunbathed in the nude every day and did not sport a single tan line.

"What took you so long?" she chastised him.

"I drove here as fast as I could."

"It wasn't fast enough."

Giggling, she dragged him down the hall to the living room. Gabe lay sprawled on the recliner and flipped Billy a stoner's salute. Cory and

Morris shared the couch, studying racing forms on their cell phones while taking hits off an acrylic bong with multiple rubber hoses. Bowls of junk food covered the coffee table, much of it on the floor.

"Yo, Billy. Those shades are awesome," Cory said.

"What are you guys doing?" Billy asked.

"We're working a scam with a racetrack in Santa Anita."

Misty had not let go of his arm, her nails digging hard enough to break the flesh.

"Keep moving," she commanded.

"I need to talk to everybody. Pepper needs to hear this, too."

"Well, let's go get her."

Pepper's bedroom was down the hallway. The redhead lay on the water bed in her birthday suit, watching a video playing on a flat-screen TV. In it, she and Misty were tag-teaming a very drunk Billy, whose prick resembled a bayonet.

"You trying to blackmail me?" he asked.

"No, we're trying to fuck you. Lie down." Misty tugged at his belt buckle.

"Not now. There's some serious shit going down."

They were either too stoned to hear him or too stoned to care. His pants started to fall, and he struggled to pull them back up. He was getting aroused, and that would lead to him hopping in bed with them and forgetting about life for a little while.

"He's resisting," Misty said. "Help me."

Pepper slithered sensually across the bed. Taking a big fat joint off the night table, she fired it up, then hopped to her feet and tried to shotgun him. He pushed her away.

"Stop fucking around," he said.

Pepper acted put out. She grabbed his shades and yanked them away. Seeing his banged-up face, she let out a startled cry.

"Oh my God. You get into a fight?"

"I ran into some trouble last night."

Their eyes met. In Billy's gaze she saw nothing but fear.

"Oh, fuck," Pepper said.

- - -

His crew huddled around the breakfast table in the kitchen nook, acting scared. Talking to stoned people was a waste of time, and Billy brewed an extra-strong pot of coffee and poured them each a cup. Pepper and Misty had put on grungy workout clothes and stopped being sex kittens. Cory and Morris had put away their cell phones and were looking at him, knowing that things had just gotten hairy. Gabe simply stared into space.

Billy remained standing so he could see their faces. That was important, because he needed to see if anyone was going to crack. In a calm voice, he told them the same story he'd told Travis. He'd fucked up royally and was going to spend the next three days atoning for his sins. He promised that no matter what happened, they wouldn't get arrested or go to prison.

"That's the deal. Anyone want to say anything, say it now."

At first, no one spoke. Big crocodile tears trickled down Misty's cheeks.

"Does this mean there's no giant payday?" Misty asked.

"There never was a giant payday," he replied truthfully.

"That sucks!"

Gabe blew his nose into a paper napkin. He'd been planning to use a portion of his share to pay off Tony G, and now faced the grim reality of having nothing to give the bookie.

"Billy, there's something I'm not getting," Gabe said. "Why did these assholes running Galaxy blackmail you into doing this job? Why not call the gaming board instead?"

"They didn't call the gaming board because they're afraid of the law," Billy said. "The owner of Galaxy owns a bunch of titty bars in LA. There's only so much money you can make hustling friction dances and selling drunk businessmen bottles of pink champagne. I think the place is a front, and they're laundering money."

"For who? The mob?"

"The mob, the drug cartels, who knows? They're bad dudes any way you look at it."

"Man, you sure stepped in it."

"Tell me about it."

"Should we pack a suitcase and get out of town?" Pepper asked.

Billy had never been a proponent of running when things broke bad. In the eyes of the law, a person who ran was already guilty. "Just stay here, and hang out. It will all be over by Saturday." He nearly added "One way or another" but decided he didn't want to go there.

"Will you call us Saturday night, tell us how this works out?" Pepper asked.

"You'll be the first to know," he said.

Saying good-bye had never been harder. Gabe's forlorn expression suggested that he'd dug a hole for himself that he could not climb out of. He gave Billy a bear hug and whispered, "Good luck, man," before shuffling into the living room. Pepper and Misty both kissed him on the lips as if they might never see him again.

Cory and Morris were hanging back, and Billy motioned for them to follow him out the front door so they could talk in private. They'd gotten into the rackets as teens and understood the ramifications better than the others. Billy's promise to keep them from getting busted was just that, a promise, and they might get arrested, no matter how hard Billy tried to prevent it.

Because Cory and Morris were the takeoff men, and actually stole the money during the scams, the law would seek them out first. Not the regular cops, but special enforcement agents of the Nevada Gaming Control Board, who had the power to confiscate their bank accounts, automobiles, and all their possessions. They'd go down first, and they'd go down hard.

The two young hustlers stood on the lawn, sharing a cigarette. Everything they did, they did together, from sharing a bedroom in a foster home growing up to peddling worthless coupon booklets to tourists on the Strip, which was how Billy had first met them.

"How long have you been working on this horse scam?" he asked.

"Six months. We've got a trainer at the track in our back pocket," Cory said.

"Have you tried it out?"

"A couple of times. It worked like a charm."

"You need to put it on ice. I want you to hide your computers, along with any electronic devices that might contain your communications with the guy at the track you're working with. That includes your cell phones and iPads and any devices that carry e-mails. If the gaming board pays you a visit and finds any evidence, they'll nail your balls to a wall, and try to make you turn state's evidence. That's how they operate. So don't let them find anything."

Cory flashed a brave smile. "We won't let you down, Billy."

"You can count on us," Morris added.

Billy felt confident that they wouldn't go sideways on him. To make your bones as a cheater, you had to get busted at least once and get your ass ground through the system. How you dealt with it defined the rest of your career.

"One more thing," he said. "I want you to stay away from the casinos until this is over. Work on your golf games or take in some movies. It'll be tough, but you can do it."

"Stay away from the casinos? Are you out of your flipping mind?" Cory said indignantly.

"No fucking way, Jose," Morris said.

They waited a beat before breaking into good-natured laughter. The conversation was ending on a high note. Billy appreciated that, and he beeped his horn as he drove away.

SEVENTEEN

Driving down Boulder Highway with the desert wind stinging his face, Billy remembered that Crunchie still had his Droid. Without a cell phone, he could not communicate with his crew, nor could any of them call him.

He needed to change that. There was a Verizon store located in practically every strip center in town, and his eyes searched for their distinct white and red sign. He soon found a store on the east side of the highway by Nellis Boulevard. He parked in the empty lot and went inside.

The store was a gallery, the merchandise displayed in glass cases as if precious works of art inside a museum. The manager, an alert young woman with dyed-red hair flecked with white frost and fingernails painted in a rainbow of colors, seemed eager to help him.

"I lost my cell phone last night, and need a new one," he explained.

She typed his name and address into her computer, working off the driver's license he handed her. She studied the photo on the license, then gave him a hard look.

"Something wrong?" he asked.

"Can I see you without the shades?" she asked.

He didn't like to play the sympathy card but didn't see that he had much choice if he wanted to get a new phone. Her mouth dropped open as the shades came off.

"Oh my God—were you mugged?" she asked.

"Yeah. They took everything."

"I can't fix your face, but I can get you a new phone." She stared at her computer screen. "You purchased a Droid Maxx last year and signed up for Backup Assistant. That means I can transfer your contact information from your old phone to your new phone. The Maxx you purchased also has a factory data-reset option. That will let me wipe out the information on your old phone once the new phone is up and running."

"You can really do that?"

"Sure can. What kind of phone do you want?"

"Another Droid Maxx."

He handed her a credit card. Had he gone to a Verizon store last night and gotten a new phone, the contact info on his old phone would now be wiped out. Live and learn. Soon he had a brand new phone with all of his contact info installed. The manager was sharp and knew how to think on her feet. As he signed the credit card slip, he asked if he could call her sometime. She wrote her personal number on the back of a business card and gave it to him.

"My name's Cassidy. I'm off on weekends," she said.

Cassidy had passed the first interview. If he made it out of this situation unscathed, he planned to give her a call. Over dinner and drinks he'd find out if she had moral issues with robbing casinos. If not, he could see her being a valuable addition to his crew.

Back on the highway, he decided to call Travis, and got patched into voice mail. "Hey, Travis, it's me. I had a brainstorm and bought a new cell phone. I broke the news to the others. Do me a favor, and check up on them. I'm worried about Gabe."

He bit his lip, wanting to say something that would end the message on a high note. He heard a loud beep and realized he'd hit a dead zone and the connection had ended.

He couldn't win for losing, and concentrated on the drive.

- - -

Pulling into the Galaxy's valet area, he grabbed his garment bag off the passenger seat and got out. A pair of black-and-whites were parked by the entrance, their bubble lights flashing. Cops were rarely seen inside the casinos, the belief being they were bad for business. When they did show up, it was through a back entrance or underground garage.

"Last name?" the valet asked, writing up his stub.

"Pico. Who called the five-oh?" Billy asked.

"Sorry, I'm not allowed to talk about it."

Something unpleasant had happened, and Billy was not going to venture inside without knowing why the cops were there. He slipped a twenty into the pocket of the valet's vest.

"You're not a reporter, are you?" the valet asked.

"Do reporters drive Maseratis?"

"About an hour ago a guy wearing a motorcycle helmet robbed the cage. He ran out with a bag of money, jumped on his Harley, and took off."

"How much did he get?"

"A hundred grand. Nice work if you can get it, huh?"

"You're telling me."

At the front desk, he presented the fake ID in Thomas Pico's name and learned he was staying in a luxury suite on the concierge level on the twenty-eighth floor of the first tower.

Taking the elevator up, he thought about the desperado who'd ripped the joint off. He'd known several guys who'd pulled this stunt; to a man, they were two-bit losers who'd reached the end of the line and had resorted to sticking guns in innocent people's faces to make a lousy score. He inserted the room key to his suite and entered. It was two thousand square feet of excess, the walls decorated with iconic movie stills from the days when the world was black and white. Crunchie sat on a leather couch in his cowboy attire, wearing an ugly scowl. The cage had gotten robbed on his watch, and Doucette had no doubt given him hell for it.

"Well, look who's here," the old grifter said. "Didn't I say three, asshole?"

"Traffic was a bitch," he said.

"Traffic's always a bitch. I've got something for you." Crunchie pulled Billy's cell phone from his breast pocket and tossed it to him. "I copied down the names of everyone in your address book, just to be safe. Right when I was done, the phone went blank."

"Imagine that."

"Don't pull any more shit. Now, where have you been?"

Billy wasn't about to tell him the truth. "I was getting laid," he said.

"You're a horny little fucker, aren't you?"

"It beats being sterile."

"This is getting off to a bad start. I think you need a little attitude adjustment." To the punishers he said, "Kick his ass."

Ike and T-Bird sat on the other couch, watching a mindless game show. They were sitting so close, their shoulders were touching. They rose, their hands clenched into fists.

"You guys want to flip a coin?" Billy asked.

- - -

The beating wasn't as bad this time around. They worked him mostly in the gut and around the rib cage, adding more bruises to the assortment he was already sporting. Tomorrow morning he'd piss some blood, and by tomorrow night the pain would be a memory.

A chair was produced and he sank into it. A cell phone rang. Crunchie pulled one from his pocket, said, "It's Doucette," and went onto the balcony to take the call.

The punishers stood next to the balcony's glass slider, the magnificent Vegas skyline turning them into movie stars. Billy thanked them for not messing up his face.

"Were you really getting laid?" Ike asked.

"What else would I be doing?" he lied.

They dug that. He reminded himself that Ike was the smart one. If he got on Ike's good side, T-Bird would tag along. The dumb ones always did.

"What's with the cop cars outside?" he asked.

Ike took the floor, happy to talk. "Round one o'clock, this skinny dude wearing a motorcycle helmet walks up to the cage, sticks a popgun in the cashier's face, and steals a hundred grand. Dude flies out the side door, jumps on his bike, and he's gone."

"That's a lot of money. Did he steal it in cash or chips?" he asked.

"Cash."

"Did he bring a bag with him?" he asked.

"Yeah. Flipped it to the cashier, had her fill it up. He came prepared."

Casinos got robbed every day, mostly by their own staff. Dealers stole chips off the games and hid them in secret pockets on their uniforms called subs, while technicians filched handfuls of silver dollars while emptying out slot machines. Thefts committed by outsiders were different. Usually it came in the form of the thief stealing a woman's purse, a bucket of coins, or a man's wallet. What Ike had just described was neither of these things. Or perhaps, it was a combination of both.

The door to the suite banged open, and Shaz made her entrance, dressed in a glittering hostess costume and a fake casino smile.

"Where's old smelly?" she asked.

"On the balcony talking to the boss," Ike said.

"Has he figured out how we got robbed?" she asked.

"I don't think so," Ike said.

"That son of a bitch is out there, having a laugh at our expense," she said. "If I ever get my hands on that skinny bastard, I'll kill him. You're a thief—tell me how we catch this guy."

She was looking at Billy as she spoke these words. It occurred to him that the theft would be figured out eventually, either by a smart cop or a gaming agent. It was too obvious not to be. Better for him to do it, and get something in return, he decided.

"I can catch him, if you want," he said.

"Aren't we being cute."

"I can."

"Don't fuck with me, you little shit."

"I'll figure it out in ten minutes."

She drew closer, her nose sniffing the air. "You smell like perfume. What have you been doing, banging one of your babes?"

"You want me to help you or not?"

"So sensitive. Men are stupid when they're getting pussy. Yes, I want you to help me."

"Show me the surveillance tape, and I'll tell you how to find your thief."

"You can do that?"

He nodded. He was 99 percent certain of how the theft had gone down; seeing the surveillance tape would only confirm it. Shaz produced a smartphone and punched an app. A surveillance tape of Galaxy's cage played on the small screen. A skinny motorcycle dude wearing a helmet with a black visor came up to the bars and stuck a .45 in the face of an older female cashier with a beehive hairdo. A cloth bag was pushed through the bars, and the cashier stuffed it with money and passed the bag back through. The motorcycle dude disappeared, and the cashier sounded the alarm.

He looked up into Shaz's cold blue eyes. "Cashier's involved."

"Give me a break. You can tell that by watching one time?"

"It's obvious, if you know what to look for."

"Show me."

Watching the tape again, he said, "There are three bill drawers inside the cage. The drawer directly beneath the bars contains singles, fives, tens. The next drawer contains twenties and fifties, and the last drawer contains hundreds. Watch the cashier when she's given the bag. She goes directly to the hundreds drawer. Another cashier would have dumped stacks of twenties into the bag, and only taken the hundreds if your thief had told her to. Your cashier's part of it."

Shaz lowered the phone and looked at him, still not quite there.

"The tip-off was the score. You can't steal a hundred grand without inside help," he said.

"So you knew it before I showed you the tape."

"I had a good idea. The tape confirmed what I knew."

"Why didn't that asshole Crunchie see this?"

"Maybe he needs a new pair of glasses."

She let out a mean little laugh, leaned in as if to kiss him; instead she sank her teeth into his earlobe and tugged it hard, sending him to the floor. A different kind of mating ritual, he supposed. Going to the slider, she banged on it with her fist. Crunchie came inside, red-faced from the tongue-lashing he'd just received.

"Pretty boy figured it out," she said. "We need to tell Marcus."

The look on Crunchie's face said he wanted to kill Billy. Shaz went to the door and the old grifter followed her liked a whipped pup. She turned before going out.

"Stay here," she told the punishers, "and don't take your eyes off this little bastard."

EIGHTEEN

Billy and the punishers watched *The Price Is Right* in the suite. Soon, they'd get a call telling them the guilty cashier and her partner had been arrested and the stolen loot recovered. A couple of hours at most, he guessed.

Billy felt certain about this, because he knew how the town worked. In Vegas, the only thing that mattered was the money generated by the casinos. Vegas had no industry, no port to ship out of, no mini-Silicon Valley to attract venture capital. Without the casinos' uninterrupted cash flow, the beautiful golf courses would turn brown, the hotels would go ominously dark, and ninety thousand workers would end up singing the blues in the unemployment lines.

The guilty cashier was in a world of trouble. It would start with the cops going to her house, arresting her, and tearing her place apart. If the stolen money wasn't found, they'd sit the cashier down and threaten her. If she refused to talk, handcuffs would be slapped on her wrists so tightly that the circulation would be cut off, and she'd be taken outside and shoved into the back of a cruiser, windows up, with no AC, where she'd be left to bake for a while.

The cashier would eventually break down—they always did—and roll on her accomplice. The cops would drive straight to the accomplice's house and repeat the ritual until the stolen money was recovered. Only then would the suspects be taken to jail and booked and be given an opportunity to call their lawyers.

That was how the system worked. Anyone who robbed a casino in Vegas was treated worse than a rabid dog. There were no exceptions to these rules.

The landline in the suite rang. Ike answered it, then hung up.

"Doucette wants to talk to you. You were right about the cashier," Ike said.

"Did he tell you who the accomplice was?" he asked.

"Sure did," Ike said.

"Are you going to tell me?"

"Figure it out yourself."

Ike was being a prick and not sharing information, a typical trait of lowlifes.

"It was the cashier's son," Billy said.

"How the hell did you know that?" Ike asked.

"Her age. She's in her late fifties; the dude wearing the motorcycle helmet had the body of a guy in his twenties. Not her boyfriend or her husband, must be her son."

Ike rocked back on his heels. "That's fucked," he said.

- - -

To reach the penthouse, Ike had to punch a five-digit code into the elevator's keypad, a feat that took several tries before he got the combination right.

"You took too many hits to the head," T-Bird told him.

"That's 'cause I played more than you," Ike said.

The delay gave Billy a chance to take a closer look at the two men. Both wore tailored clothes, black limited-edition Rolexes, and enough jewelry to make a pawnbroker hard. They dressed like players, and he wondered how much Doucette was paying them. Fifty grand a year? Sixty? A decent salary, but not enough to pay for the threads and the bling. The real money was coming from ripping people off, the way they'd done to him last night.

Doucette was on a call as they entered, his wife hovering behind him. The casino boss motioned toward the chair in front of his desk, which Billy took. Crunchie had been banished to the other side of the office and stood glum-faced, Stetson in hand.

"Please give my thanks to the sheriff for handling this in such a professional and timely manner," Doucette gushed into the phone, sounding like a used-car salesman. "You guys are the best, and I sincerely mean that. If there's anything I can do for the department, don't hesitate to give me a call. My door is always open for you. Thanks again. Have a great day."

Doucette ended the call. Justice had been served, and the casino boss was happy with the outcome. Billy hated to burst his bubble but did so anyway. The more information he could feed Doucette, the more level the playing field became between them.

"You're not going to get all of it back," he informed him.

Doucette's smile evaporated. "I'm not?"

"No. You might as well know now."

"The cops are going to take a cut, is that the deal?"

"Afraid so."

"Is there anything I can do about it?"

"Not really."

"Is that true?" Doucette asked Crunchie.

"Billy's telling you the truth," the old grifter said from across the room.

"How much will they take?"

"Fifteen, maybe twenty grand," Billy said.

"That's highway robbery."

"Think of it as a handling fee."

"You trying to be funny?"

"I'm just telling you how things work, that's all. You're new to town."

"What do they do, split it up among themselves?" Doucette asked, curious now.

How the Metro LVPD chopped up their ill-gotten gains was their business, and Billy said, "I have no idea. Look on the bright side. In the old days, they'd have taken half."

"You're shitting me. Did they do that to the mob?"

"Sure. Despite what people think, the mob never ran this town. The sheriff's department did, and still does."

Doucette was getting a deal; he just didn't know it. From his desk drawer he removed the gaffed Slots A Fun chip and the gaffed cigarette pack and tossed them on the desk. "I want to go over our deal again so we're clear. In return for you stopping the Gypsies from scamming me, I'll give you your toys back, and I'll have my people erase the surveillance tapes of you using your mirror at our blackjack tables. That sound right to you?"

"What about my crew?" Billy asked.

"Crunchie has their names on a slip of paper," Doucette said. "He'll tear it up, and your friends will be home free. Now, are we in agreement?"

"Sounds good to me," he said.

"You're going to be given free rein to walk around my casino," the casino boss went on. "You'll get twenty grand in chips to play with, which you'll turn in each night. We'll be watching you every minute so make sure you behave. If you try to swindle me, my wife and I are going to flip a coin to see who beats you to death with a baseball bat. I'm not kidding. I know you just saved me a lot of money, but that doesn't give you a license to rip me off. Keep your nose clean, and I won't hurt you."

Billy knew they'd do it, too, and wondered if they'd film it and watch it on the big flat screen in their bedroom while they snorted cocaine and screwed.

"I won't rip you off, and that's a promise," he said.

Doucette motioned for his guest to rise. Billy stood up.

"Lose the shades," the casino boss said.

Billy did as told. Doucette shook his head disapprovingly. "Can't have you walking around my casino looking like that. Honey, can you make him look pretty again?"

Shaz's eyes were glistening, and she seemed to be getting off on the miserable state of Billy's appearance.

"I can try," she said.

- - -

"Did you ever hustle?" he asked.

They were back in his suite, Shaz next to him in a chair, applying pancake to his bruises and his black eye, her tits in his face, her breath hot and, no doubt, filled with plans. Either she would get him in the sack or she'd bash his brains in with a baseball bat; it didn't seem to matter, just as long as she got him in the end.

"For Christ's sake, sit still," she said.

"Did you?" he asked again.

"You think I was a hooker?" she said, not sounding the least bit offended.

"I meant as a grifter."

"What do you think?"

"I think you did. You fooled me last night at the hostess stand. I never saw it coming."

She gave a sweet little laugh that didn't resemble the monster he knew. "I used to strip at a men's club called Jumbo's Clown Room in LA. I took home more money than any other girl at the club. Does that make me a hustler?"

"You got suckers to part with their money. What else did you do?"

"You talk too much. Shut up before I poke your eye out."

She dabbed his face with a small sponge and kept breathing on him. On the other side of the suite, Ike and T-Bird shared the couch, talking in a conspiratorial tone. Plotting their next rip-off, he guessed. Crunchie was outside on the balcony on his cell phone. His story about his long-lost daughter was half true. He had a drug-addicted twenty-six-year-old son in Seattle he'd recently become acquainted with, and his son had called his father to beg for money, putting the old grifter in a foul mood.

"You know how I figured it out?" he said. "It was the way you handled me. You never missed a beat, didn't give me a reason to be suspicious. You did more than just strip, didn't you?"

"How'd you like me to bite your tongue out?" she asked.

"Before or after we fuck?"

"Aren't we clever? Now shut up and let me finish."

She went back to repairing his face. Her breathing had become accelerated and her nostrils were flared. She was wound way too tight, and Billy waited for her to calm down before he spoke again.

"If you don't tell me, I'll get Ike and T-Bird liquored up tonight, and they'll tell me. I'd rather hear it from you."

She put the pancake down and rested her elbows on the arm of his chair, so close that he could have kissed her. "Why do you fucking care? What's in it for you?"

"I want to know who I'm dealing with, that's all."

"All right, here it is. I got tired of stripping and started moving blow. I dealt with people scarier than anybody you could ever dream of. Mexican cartels, guys that would cut your head off and stick it on a pole if you looked at them cross-eyed. I was good at it. Real good at it."

"How long were you in the game?"

"Five years. It taught me a lot."

"Do you miss it?"

"It wasn't that kind of work."

Before he could ask another question, she put her finger to his lips, silencing him.

"I dig you and so does Marcus, even if you are a sneaky little shit. We both think there's a place for you in the organization. Just keep your hand out of the cookie jar, and find the Gypsies before they scam us. When this is over, we'll talk again. That sound good to you?"

He mouthed the word *okay*. Ike and T-Bird weren't paying attention and Crunchie remained on the balcony getting worked over by his long-lost son. The landscape had shifted and they'd missed it. She took her finger away and planted a kiss on his lips, sealing the deal.

NINETEEN

His face repaired, he went downstairs to the main lobby and entered a coffee shop called Brando's, the walls decorated with movie stills of the famous actor before he'd gone to seed. It was the only restaurant in the hotel that served breakfast all day, and he was craving scrambled eggs. He flipped through the spiral-bound menu until he found the selections.

Ike and T-Bird sat across from him without touching their menus. They'd been quiet as mice in the elevator, and he sensed that there was something on their minds. All the thieves he'd ever known had wanted to elevate their status and make more money. House burglars longed to be bank robbers, while bank robbers imagined themselves jewelry thieves. Each rung on the criminal ladder brought new challenges and greater wealth. It was no different than any other profession, except for the penalty of getting caught.

A waitress took his order. When she left, Ike spoke in a hushed tone. "We want to talk to you later, when we can be alone."

"Do it here. There aren't any cameras spying on us," he said.

"Sure there are. They got cameras everywhere in this joint."

"Surveillance equipment is expensive, so the casinos don't put cameras in the restaurants or bars except over the cash registers. Look up at the ceiling if you don't believe me."

They lifted their heads to stare at the ceiling and both grinned. The conversation was starting out on the right note.

"How'd you get so fucking smart?" Ike asked.

"I had a good teacher."

"We want to learn the stuff you know. We're getting tired of this gig."

"You guys want to learn how to scam casinos?"

"Yeah," they said in unison.

Billy nearly busted out laughing. One of the keys to cheating was blending in. A cheater had to be just another face in the crowd, which Ike and T-Bird were incapable of, their massive size impossible to miss. If they were going to cheat, they were going to get caught.

But he wasn't going to tell them that. He did not have a problem if they got nailed. In fact, he liked the idea. They deserved a nice long jail sentence for what they'd done to him last night. But before he led them down the road to ruin, he was going to get something in return.

"I'll help you, but I want you to explain some stuff," he said.

"Name it," Ike said.

"I want to know what Shaz's deal is. And Crunchie's."

"We're not allowed to talk about Doucette's old lady," Ike said. "The topic, as they say, is off limits. But I can talk about old smelly. Doucette hired him to finger cheaters and then turn them over to us. Our job is to hurt them and send a message to other cheaters to stay away."

"Not kill them?"

"Naw. We ain't killers. Are we, T?"

"Never killed nobody in my life," T-Bird said.

"What about Ricky Boswell?"

"We didn't kill him—you saw the film," Ike said.

"But you watched."

"It was messed up. Shaz spotted Ricky casing the casino and took him upstairs and did all that sick stuff to him. She goes off the deep end sometimes."

"How did she make Ricky?"

"The hotel operators are told to listen to voice messages on guests' phones and report anything suspicious. An operator picked up a message on the phone in Ricky's room from a member of his family, and the message got relayed to Shaz. She started following Ricky around the casino, figured out his deal, and had us grab him. When Ricky refused to rat out his family, she snuffed him. It was a bad scene."

"She's a sick puppy," T-Bird added.

"Shaz got sore at Crunchie for not making Ricky," Ike went on. "She ordered Crunchie to bring another cheater in to figure out the scam. That's how you got invited to the party."

Billy played with the salt dispenser while absorbing what Ike had just said. Crunchie was skating on thin ice with his employer, so he'd blackmailed Billy to make things right.

"Is Shaz still pissed at him?" he asked.

"You bet," Ike said. "Crunchie's trying to make good by her and find the Gypsies."

"I thought that was my job."

"Not if old smelly finds them first."

Billy had planned to drag his job out until Saturday night; now, it sounded like he'd have to move quicker, or risk having the old grifter upstage him. If that happened, all bets were off.

It was T-Bird's turn to work on his vocabulary. The brooding hulk with the shoulder-length dreadlocks glanced furtively over his shoulder before locking eyes with Billy. "Me and Ike want to learn the chip scam. Can you teach us?"

"Sure. You got chips with you?" Billy asked.

T-Bird fished two chips from Galaxy's casino from his shirt pocket and slid them across the table. One was a red five-dollar chip, the other a green twenty-five-dollar chip. Billy stuck them together with a dab of saliva and launched into his explanation.

"You need a dealer working with you. You bet with the green chip showing. When you lose, the dealer turns the chip over in her rack, and you buy it back for five bucks. You can make six hundred bucks a night without drawing heat."

"That's all?" T-Bird said.

"Any more, and security will start watching you," he added.

"We ain't interested in no nickel-and-dime shit. Teach us the good stuff."

"Yeah, the good stuff," Ike chimed in.

Teaching Ike and T-Bird the good stuff would have been about as smart as giving power tools to cavemen. They were only going to hurt themselves.

"Tell us how the mirror in the cigarette pack works," T-Bird said.

"Yeah, that's a good one," Ike said.

"You're not going to get rich off that scam, either," he said. "Look, you guys can't just waltz into a casino and rip them off for a monster score without the alarms going off. It doesn't work that way. You have to build yourself in. It takes time."

"You nearly did last night," T-Bird said.

"I have experience, and I know the angles. You guys are rookies. You have to start in the farm system, and work your way up to the big leagues."

T-Bird glanced at his partner. "Pretty boy thinks we're amateurs."

"Pretty boy is going to get his face rearranged so it ain't pretty no more," Ike said.

"I want first licks."

"I'll flip you for it. Heads or tails?"

They looked ready to hurt him. The waitress served him his meal. Wanting to make peace, he slid the toasted bagel into the center of the table, speared a sausage patty with his fork, and dropped it on the bagel. "Have some grub," he said.

Reaching across the table, Ike picked up the glass of orange juice and poured it over Billy's food, the bagel as well. He slid out of the booth, as did his partner.

"Get your ass up," Ike said.

Grabbing the soggy bagel, Billy followed the punishers out of the restaurant.

TWENTY

Coming out of Brando's, Ike handed his cell phone to Billy.

"Guess who wants to bust your balls," Ike said.

"Who's this?" Billy said.

"Hey, Billy, did you have a nice meal in Brando's? What's that you've got in your hand? A wet bagel? You have strange tastes, kid," Crunchie said, laughing in his face.

Billy scanned the hotel lobby. Thursday was the beginning of the weekend in Vegas, the lobby a mob scene, with snaking lines of tourists wrestling with luggage in the check-in line. Seeing no sign of the old grifter, he said, "Where are you hiding? Under a rock?"

"I'm in the surveillance room watching you on a monitor," Crunchie said. "I just wanted you to know that I'm going to catch the Gypsies before you do."

Casino surveillance rooms were filled with the latest electronic spying equipment. Trained techs stared at a matrix of high-def video monitors, hunting for cheaters and thieves on the casino floor. The old grifter had a huge advantage and had called him to rub it in.

"Want to bet on it?" Billy asked, not willing to throw in the towel.

"You're a cocky little bastard. Ten grand says I find the Gypsies first."

"You're on. You know, Crunch, if you'd made Ricky Boswell like you were hired to do, none of this would have been necessary. You blew it, you dumb shit."

"Who told you that?"

"A little bird. Have a nice day."

He ended the call and tossed Ike the cell phone. The game was on.

- - -

He sifted through the lobby with the punishers on his heels. The hotel was big enough to hold a few thousand guests, and any one of them could have been a member of the Gypsy clan. He needed to narrow down his search if he was going to catch them.

Raised voices snapped his head. At the check-in, a comely blond reservationist was trying to calm down an irate male guest wearing a rumpled suit and a livid expression.

"I'm terribly sorry, sir, but I can't do that," the reservationist said.

"I just traveled two thousand miles," the man protested.

"Sir, the hotel is completely sold out. There are no rooms."

"Are you telling me there's not one available room? I don't believe that for a minute."

"Are you part of a group or convention?"

"No. I'm here by myself."

"Then I'm afraid I can't help you."

The man stormed off. Weekends were a hot ticket in town, with bookings made months in advance. The Gypsies would have needed to book their rooms a long time ago, unless they were part of a convention. The hotels always reserved blocks of rooms for conventions, and those rooms were held open, even when the rest of the hotel was sold out.

It made sense, when he thought about it. Being part of a group was the perfect cover to pull off a scam. Just wear the plastic registration badge around your neck inside the casino, and no one would pay the slightest attention to you. He needed to find out the names of the groups booked into the hotel and whittle down the list. That couldn't be terribly hard.

Concierges generally knew the hotel guest list inside out. The concierge on duty was tan and pretty and wore a gold uniform with a burgundy vest and a gold necktie with a crisp knot. He was talking on the phone to a guest when Billy slapped the bell on his desk.

"I need to see your welcome board."

He followed the direction of the concierge's finger. A digital welcome board the size of a movie poster hung by the elevators, with names of groups booked into the hotel crawling down the iridescent blue screen. The American Society of Podiatric Surgeons, Esurance, the CAR Group, and the Grocery Manufacturers Association, plus a slot tournament, the MacGregor family reunion, and nine weddings. Eenie meeny miney mo. Which group were the Gypsies with?

"What you looking at?" Ike said into his ear.

"Be quiet. I'm working," he said.

On the board, a calendar of Friday's events appeared, listing the conference rooms each group was meeting in. The podiatrists were in the Clark Gable lecture hall from nine until four, the car salesmen in the Humphrey Bogart room from eight until noon, followed by a golf tourney on the casino's Golden Bear course, and so on, every group on the list accounted for. Each group had their days planned out for them, morning, noon, and night. Now he was getting somewhere. Returning to the concierge's desk, he slapped the bell again, this time much louder.

"What do you want?" the concierge asked.

"Pico," Billy said, not liking the concierge's attitude.

"Excuse me?" the concierge said.

"Thomas Pico. I'm a guest in your hotel."

"You and two thousand other people."

"Are they all comped in a high-roller suite?"

Tap, tap, tap across the keyboard went the concierge's fingers. His eyes looked at the screen and grew embarrassingly wide. "Mr. Pico, my apologies. How may I help you?"

"I need to see Saturday's calendar of events."

"I'm sorry, but I'm not allowed to give out that information. House rules."

"Does the GM have that information?"

"I'm sure he does."

Billy turned from the concierge desk. "Call Doucette, and ask him to put a call into the GM," he said to Ike. "I need to see the events calendar for Saturday. The Gypsies are going to be attending a function in the hotel. If I can see the calendar, I should be able to narrow down which group they're with."

"You just figured that out staring at that stupid board?" Ike said.

Inanimate objects weren't stupid. People were stupid.

"That's right," he replied.

Ike made the call to Doucette.

- - -

A minute later, Shaz emerged from an elevator and crossed the lobby to the concierge desk, snapping heads in a black leather mini, sensuous black leggings, and a black leather jacket zippered to her neck bomber-pilot style. Her outlandish outfits seemed to change by the hour.

"Marcus said you're onto them," she said.

"I need to see Saturday's events calendar," Billy said. "The Gypsies are booked into the hotel with a group, and I want to see which groups are holding events in the hotel Saturday afternoon. The concierge said the GM has the information."

"Piece of cake," she said.

At the registration desk she got a reservationist's attention by snapping her fingers. A door beside the desk sprung open. Soon they were walking past a warren of sales cubicles to the GM's corner office. As was her custom, she entered without bothering to knock.

"Surprise," she said, as if jumping out of a cake.

The GM was on the phone putting out a fire. With the weary expression of a man who spent his day making tough decisions, he said, "I'll call you right back," and rose with a pained expression on his face, as if Shaz was the bane of his existence.

"Hello, Ms. Doucette, what can I do for you?" the GM asked.

"Hello, Jerry. We need to see Saturday's events calendar," she said.

The nameplate on the desk said his name was Jack, not Jerry. The GM tapped a command into his computer and pivoted the monitor so Saturday's events calendar faced them.

"That's the whole list. Anything else I can do, Ms. Doucette?" the GM asked.

"Disappear for a few minutes," she said.

The GM left the office with the attitude of a man who just might not come back. Billy brought his face up to the monitor to read the calendar. The foot doctors were attending a lecture from 2:00 until 4:00 p.m., as were the insurance agents. The MacGregor clan was also gathering in the hotel during that time period.

"The Gypsies are part of one of these three groups," he said.

"How can you know that looking at a screen?" she asked.

"That's what I asked him," Ike said.

"Shut the fuck up." To Billy she said, "Explain yourself."

"The timing is right. At four o'clock, a shift change will be taking place inside your casino. The day shift will be leaving, and the swing shift will be coming in. At the same time, these groups will be coming out of their conference rooms and flooding the casino floor. You can't buy a better distraction than that. You're going to get royally fucked."

"We'll post guards on the floor and catch them."

"Good luck."

"What's that supposed to mean? We know when they're coming."

"Doesn't matter. You still won't see them."

A dark cloud passed over her face. Ike and T-Bird had inched up behind Billy's chair, hanging on every word. She took her anger out on Ike and dug her elbow into the big man's gut, making him yelp.

"Out of here, both of you," she snapped.

The punishers bolted. Shaz was throwing off some seriously bad vibes, and Billy felt himself getting nervous. Lying on the desk was a sterling-silver letter opener shaped like a dagger. If she made a move for it, he was going to knock her down.

"Explain what you just said to me," she said.

"This isn't a heist. The Gypsies are cleverer than that," he said.

"If it's not a heist, then what is it?"

"It's a scam. Around four on Saturday afternoon, the Gypsies will enter your casino and rig one of your games right under your nose. Then they'll split. Later, other members of their family will play that rigged game and win a ton of money. You'll have to pay them because it will look legit. Only it won't be. Not by a long shot."

The cloud left, replaced by a look of subtle appreciation. She rested her hands on his shoulders and looked into his eyes as if trying to tear out his soul. She had to be the scariest woman he'd ever encountered.

"You ever pull a scam like that?" she asked.

"Me? Never."

"Tell me what you did."

"You get off on this stuff, don't you?"

"More than you'll ever know."

"Super Bowl, couple years back, I was part of a gang that ripped off Caesars for a million bucks, same sort of deal, rigged the craps game as the first touchdown was scored."

"Was that part of the plan?"

"Absolutely."

"Why then?"

Her breath was tickling his skin, getting him aroused. A bad idea, not that his dick ever listened to anything his brain ever said. "More money is wagered on the Super Bowl than any other sporting event in the world. A lot of the bets are proposition bets. Who will fumble first, who'll kick the first field goal, that sort of thing. The biggest prop bet is on which team will score the first touchdown. That's when we struck."

"Was that your idea?"

"Come to think of it, it was."

"I should have known. Were you the ringleader?"

"I'd rather not say."

She brought her mouth up close to his face. "Tell me, you sneaky little shit."

"Yeah, I was in charge."

She wrapped her arms around his waist, drawing closer.

"Tell me how the scam worked."

He blew out his lungs. This wasn't going to end well—he knew that going in—but boy, the ride was going to be something else. "Caesars had wheeled giant-screen TVs onto the floor of their casino for the game. The images were larger than life. Packers were playing the Steelers. Rodgers throws a twenty-one yarder to Jennings and he runs into the end zone. The casino erupts. That's when we whacked them. One of the members of my crew was a woman with a shopping bag. We used the bag to switch a bowl of dice off the craps table for a duplicate bowl filled with shaved dice. No one saw a thing. A few minutes later, a whale staying in the casino strayed over to the craps table and started playing."

"Was the whale part of your gang?" she asked, one step ahead of him now.

"Uh-huh."

"How much did he win?"

"He didn't win. He got cleaned out."

She frowned. "I thought you said he was part of your gang."

"He was."

Red flared in both her cheeks, the demon resting just below the surface.

"We set him up. He was a Brazilian playboy who wore designer sports jackets with no shirt underneath. Real asshole. We convinced him to bet a million bucks of his own money and told him he'd double it. Wrong."

"The dice were shaved for him to lose?"

"Yeah. Two other members of my crew bet against him."

"So you really stole his money."

"That's right. Caesars never felt the loss."

"That's absolutely beautiful. You enjoy fucking people, don't you?"

"Some people, yeah, I do."

"Want to fuck me?"

"Here? You can't be serious."

Her hand rose to her throat and pulled down the zipper of her bomber jacket. She was naked underneath, and her breasts spilled out with an urgency that caught the breath in his throat. Her nipples were red and hard and called to him like forbidden fruit.

"Jesus," he said under his breath.

"Impressed?"

"They're beautiful."

"Natural, too. No silicone."

"God loves you."

That got a rise out of her. Getting on her knees, she yanked down his fly and pulled his very hard cock out of his trousers. "Well, look at that. No wonder the girls adore you." She stuck his erection between her breasts while gazing up at him, very matter-of-fact about the whole thing, ready to seize the moment. "So tell me, have you ever been titty-fucked?"

"This would be the first time."

"Enjoy."

She squeezed her breasts together and moved her chest rhythmically back and forth while humming a pretty song whose name he couldn't remember. His prick got so hard and extended that it didn't resemble his anymore. Hot white stars exploded in front of his eyes and he gasped for breath. At any moment, he envisioned Doucette barging into the office and catching them in the act. Not that he cared. Every nerve ending in his body was screaming, and he tilted his head back and felt the floor start to tremble. Fifty years from now, he'd remember this orgasm while forgetting all the shit that went with it, what psychologists called euphoric recall, that wonderful mechanism that let a person forget the bad and remember only the good.

He came back to earth. She gazed up at him with a satisfied look on her face. He helped her to her feet. She swiped a Kleenex off the desk and cleaned herself off before zippering her jacket. He tried to kiss her and she shook her head. They started to leave.

"That song you were singing. Whose is it?" he asked.

"It's by Usher," she said. "It's called 'Burn.'"

TWENTY-ONE

The GM was in the hall when they emerged. Seeing something in Billy's face that tipped him off, the GM rolled his eyes.

"Thanks for the office," Shaz said in passing.

"Hope you found what you were looking for," the GM said.

"Watch your mouth," she warned him.

Billy followed her down the aisle past the sales cubicles. The heady rush of their sex was starting to fade, and he found himself wondering if he'd just dug his own grave. Illicit sex was one of those things you couldn't hide forever. If the GM had figured out the score, so would Ike and T-Bird. It was only a matter of time before the news filtered back to Doucette, and he would make Billy pay for cheating with his wife. They came to the door that led back to the hotel lobby.

"Why did you do that?" he asked.

"Because you turn me on," she said.

"What I'm asking you is, why there? You had to know how dangerous it was. Why not an empty hotel room? It would have been safer."

"Safe is for cowards."

"You could have gotten us both in trouble."

"The fuck I care."

"Let me rephrase that. You could have gotten *me* killed."

"Something tells me you would have talked your way out of it."

Laughing at him with her eyes, she entered the lobby. The punishers lurked nearby, the hotel's guests avoiding them as if they were carrying the plague.

"Call me if you get lonely tonight. My husband's a heavy sleeper," she said.

"I just might do that. Listen, I need a favor from you."

"Name it, lover boy."

"I want to get new threads for Sanford and Son, something to soften the blow. Chinos, maybe a couple of nice Tommy Bahama shirts. Where should I go?"

She cast a discerning eye at the punishers. "You want to give them a marketing makeover, turn them into a pair of dopey tourists?"

"That was the general idea."

"There's a men's clothing store next to the casino called Threads. Pick some clothes off the discount racks and charge them to your room. Are you going to call me?"

"You're an animal, you know that?"

"I know what turns me on."

"You're forgetting one little fact. Your husband is watching me twenty-four-seven. I can't just slip out of my suite without being spotted."

"For a bullshitter, you sure don't know it when you hear it. Marcus doesn't have the time to monitor your suite; he's got a casino to run. Now, will you call me or not?"

Billy had just learned something important. If Marcus wasn't watching him, he could get into all sorts of trouble and not get tagged.

"Give me your number," he said.

She gave Billy her number.

"You'd better not forget," she said, and walked away.

- - -

Every Strip casino operated high-end retail stores that sold brand-name watches, glittering jewelry, and designer clothes for prices 50 percent higher than the street. Suckers who won a few bucks at the tables entered these shops still high on their luck and got their pockets picked.

Galaxy's shops had been designed to resemble a trendy block along Rodeo Drive. Threads was the largest, its splashy windows filled with the latest men's fashions sans price tags. A sign in the window said they were closed. Movement in the rear of the store said otherwise, and Billy banged on the door. From the back appeared an animated tailor with pins stuck in his mouth. The tailor waved his visitors away before disappearing.

Billy fumed. He needed to get this done. Taking out his room key, he slid it into the vertical crack between the door and doorjamb, then bent the key in half, forcing it under the angled end of the bolt. He did this while leaning against the door. It popped open.

"Teach us that," T-Bird said.

"He just did," Ike said.

Billy entered and went straight to the rack of Bottega Veneta thousand-dollar shirts, to hell with the discounted crap, and searched for labels marked "XXL." If Doucette was too busy to watch him, he was going to take advantage of it. For Ike, he picked a canary-yellow gabardine shirt with a Parma collar, for T-Bird, an embroidered white number with mother-of-pearl buttons.

"Try these on," he said.

The punishers got undressed in the center of the aisle and tried on the new shirts. The tailor emerged from the back.

"Store's closed. You come back later," the tailor said in clipped English.

"We'll be done in a minute," he said.

"No—you leave now!"

The expression on the tailor's face bordered on sheer terror, and Billy realized he'd stepped into a bad situation. From the rear of the store came a man's booming voice.

"Didn't I tell you, no fucking customers in the store while I got fitted?"

The tailor crossed himself. The pins began falling out of his mouth.

"That sounds like Reverend Rock," Ike said.

"I thought he was in LA," T-Bird said.

"Must have decided to check the place out," Ike said.

Billy had been raised a Catholic and knew that the reverend rock was where the Virgin Mary had rested before reaching Bethlehem and giving birth to the baby Jesus. It was also a derogatory name used to describe a certain type of black sociopath who was best left alone.

He shoved the tailor. "Go take care of him."

Too late. With the magnitude of Godzilla descending upon downtown Tokyo, Reverend Rock emerged from a fitting room wearing a billowing purple shirt and cuffed dress pants. Big and round, with a shaved head and a grill of hideous gold teeth, Rock walked with the aid of a knotty stick with a polished silver handle in the shape of a human skull. It was not uncommon for casinos to fly drug dealers into town by private jet, ferry them to the hotels, and stick them in private villas hidden away from the prying eyes of the law. The only time these guests showed their faces was late night in the casinos; otherwise, they didn't exist. Flanking Rock were two slender Hispanic females wearing black leather with teardrop tattoos beneath their eyes. The tattoos were the mark of female assassins, or what the Mexicans called Las Tinkerbells.

Rock zeroed in on Billy. "Who are you?"

"Billy Cunningham."

"What's a Billy Cunningham?"

"It's whatever you want it to be."

"Don't get cute with me. See the sign in the window? Store's closed."

"We're here to get some shirts."

"You don't listen, and you don't read signs."

"How about I buy you a drink, and we'll call it a day," Billy said, wanting to diffuse the situation and get out of the store.

"I don't drink," the drug dealer said, his tone not softening.

"Can I buy a bottle of champagne for your beautiful friends?"

"They don't drink, either."

"This is Vegas, man. Everyone drinks."

"Your jokes don't amuse me, or your fucking mouth."

Rock slapped the stick against the palm of his hand. Back when Billy was hustling fake watches to suckers in Providence, he'd made the acquaintance of several drug dealers. To a man, they'd all carried a weapon, be it a knife, a handgun, or a club. Billy guessed Rock's stick was also a weapon and that the hand was hollow, filled with buckshot or small rocks.

"I'm doing a job for Marcus Doucette," he said.

"You don't say. What kind of job would that be?" Rock asked.

"Doucette hired me to sniff out some hustlers."

"I've heard said the only people that can catch hustlers are other hustlers. You a hustler?"

"Yeah, I'm a hustler."

"You motherfuckers stand aside," Rock said to the punishers.

Ike and T-Bird stepped out of harm's way. Rock lifted his stick so it became horizontal and rested the knob on Billy's shoulder. It was heavy and easily weighed two pounds. With a flick of his wrist he could crack Billy's skull open and scatter his brains across the floor.

"So you're a hustler," Rock said. "That's funny. I would have sworn you were an undercover cop."

"I tried, but I didn't pass the height requirement," Billy said.

"I'm going to give you a chance to prove you're not a cop. Fuck up, and I'll split your head open." Rock paused to let the threat take hold. "Do we understand each other?"

"Loud and clear."

"Good. Ever hear of a guy named Doc?"

"Sure, I've heard of Doc."

"Tell me about him."

"Doc is out of East LA by way of Atlanta. Maybe the best pair of hands in the world with a deck of cards when he isn't hitting the sauce, which is most of the time."

"He's got a scar on his face. Describe it."

"It's on the point of his chin. Guy in prison stuck a shiv in his face and a piece of it broke off. He doesn't have any feeling in the lower half of his jaw."

"What's Doc's specialty?"

"Depends who you're asking."

"Come again."

"Doc's a major-league bullshitter. He sits around all day practicing dealing off the bottom of the deck and hopping the cut, but he never uses that stuff in a game, too risky, even though he'll tell you otherwise. His real specialty is ringing in a cooler."

"A what?"

"Deck switching during a game."

"How's he pull that off?"

"He has a stacked deck sitting in his lap. The deck in play is shuffled and passed to Doc for the cut. Doc switches it in the act of doing the cut and passes the stacked deck to the sucker, who deals the hand. It's a perfect illusion."

"What happens to the switched deck?"

"During a break, Doc drops the switched deck into a garbage pail by the door and pours beer on it. If anyone sees the deck, they'll think it was old and got thrown away."

Rock was trying to read Billy's face. From his pocket the drug dealer removed a stack of chips and toyed with them. "Doc's done a stretch in the federal pen and has a file. Plenty of what you just told me's in that file. Tell me something that isn't, or I'll take you out right now."

Getting clubbed to death like a baby seal in an overpriced clothing store was not how Billy wanted to exit this life. Doc had visited Vegas a few years back, and a mutual friend had set up a meeting at the Ghostbar at the Palms. They'd traded stories until the sun peeked its head over the brown desert sand. Although they came from different worlds, they spoke the same language, and they'd parted knowing their paths would cross again.

"Doc's superstitious," Billy said, taking his last shot. "When he does his deck switch, he holds a fan of bills in his hand to cover the move. There's always a two-dollar bill in the fan. There's a reason for that."

The chips made a loud clacking sound in Rock's hand.

"I'm listening," Rock said.

"Doc's last name is Jefferson, and Thomas Jefferson's face is printed on the two-dollar bill. Get Doc drunk enough, and he'll tell you how his family tree starts with one of Jefferson's slaves on a plantation in Virginia."

A chip fell out of Rock's hand to the floor. "Shit. You do know him."

"I sure do. We're pals."

Rock removed his stick from Billy's shoulder. "My gut tells me I shouldn't trust you, but I'm going to let it pass. Take your pretty shirts and get the hell out of here."

The errant chip lay at Billy's feet. Bending down, he saw that it was a coveted gold chip, worth a hundred grand in Galaxy's high-roller salon. Rising, he glanced at the stack resting in Rock's palm. They were all gold. Rock was treating them as if they were pocket change, and a crazy thought went through Billy's head. If Rock wasn't listening to his gut, then he was vulnerable. Why not rip him off?

He decided to put his idea to the test. Placing the errant chip in

Rock's hand, he clicked it loudly against the other chips, then flipped his own hand over to expose a clean palm. Rock never saw the deception.

"Don't want to lose that," he said.

"Plenty more where it came from," the drug dealer replied.

It wasn't every day that Billy made a hundred large, and he walked out of the clothing store with a thin smile creasing his face.

TWENTY-TWO

Billy's head was spinning. He'd just ripped off a drug dealer and lived to tell about it. Now he had to figure out how to cash in the gold chip resting in his sleeve and not get caught. It wasn't the big score he'd dreamed about a few nights ago, but it was better than nothing.

Cashing the chip in wouldn't be easy. Many Vegas casinos embedded their high-value chips with radio-frequency-identification microchips, and he assumed Galaxy did as well. The technology could be beaten; it just took time to figure out how.

He walked through the casino with the punishers. It was hopping, the tables filled with suckers drinking free booze while slot machines rang in the background, every note in the letter *C* because it made people piss away their money faster.

He thought better with a drink, and entered a cocktail lounge. A waitress took their drink order and gave them short pencils and keno tickets before departing. Keno was a game for chumps, but that didn't stop millions of people from playing it.

He fished the gold chip out of his sleeve. The lounge was dimly lit, and he didn't think anyone watching via a surveillance camera could make out the gold color. He deliberately placed the chip on the table in front of the punishers.

"Help me cash this in, and I'll give you a cut," he said.

"You got a lot of balls, ripping Rock off," Ike said.

"Without risk, there is no reward."

The punishers talked it over. "What's our cut?" Ike asked.

"Ten percent."

"Make it twenty, and you've got yourself a deal."

"Twenty works for me."

Ike picked up the chip. "Cool. I'll get this taken care of."

"Hold on. We need to figure out how to get around the RFID chip."

"Galaxy's chips don't have those," Ike said. "Doucette was against it. He was afraid certain customers wouldn't appreciate them, if you know what I mean."

He took the gold chip from Ike and peeled back the label. There was no microchip lurking beneath. He guessed the customers Ike was referring to were criminals who didn't want to be electronically monitored during their stay.

"Better put that away. Here comes Rock," Ike said.

He sent the chip back up his sleeve just as Rock and his posse passed the cocktail lounge. Rock had slapped on funky shades and a fedora and was lugging two black leather briefcases.

"Is that what I think it is," Billy said under his breath.

"Yeah," Ike said. "One of his lieutenants usually comes."

"This is Rock's first visit to Galaxy?"

"Uh-huh. He don't leave LA much."

Rock's destination was the cage. The cage manager engaged Rock in conversation, then emerged through a side door and took possession of the briefcases. Back inside the cage, the cage manager removed stacks of money, which he placed in towering piles on the counter. Billy assumed the money had come from an army of drug pushers, the bills tainted by blood, coke, and serial numbers used by the DEA to trace them, which was why Rock had brought them to Galaxy to be laundered.

The cage manager counted the stacks. By law, casinos were required to manually count every dollar passed into the cage, the procedure filmed by the eye-in-the-sky so there was a record of the transaction. Only that wasn't happening. Instead, the cage manager was counting the stacks and writing down the total on a pad. When the cage manager was done, Rock signed a chit, and the cage manager slid a tray of chips through the bars.

It had to be one of the slickest money-laundering scams Billy had ever seen. There was no way of knowing how much money Rock had given the casino, which was exactly the idea. If a gaming agent reviewed the tapes of the transaction, the discrepancy would pass muster, unless the agent had been tipped off what to look for.

Rock dumped the chips into his pockets. They were all gold and worth millions. Rock would spend a few days enjoying the casino's lavish accommodations, then return to the cage when he was ready to leave, and exchange the chips for clean bills, with Galaxy having deducted their cut. Vegas had invented money laundering, and this was as good as it got.

Rock and his posse crossed the casino and entered the salon. Rock was a fool to be carrying around that much money, even if it was in chips. Billy had already scammed Rock once and gotten away with it. Why not again?

There were a lot of reasons not to. Doucette had warned him what would happen if he tried to pull a scam inside the casino, and he didn't think the casino boss was lying. But Doucette was a cokehead, and people who did drugs were easily duped.

Rock's bodyguards were a different story. Bodyguards in Vegas were a dime a dozen; female bodyguards were not. Billy guessed Rock's femme fatales were lethal in every way and would cut him down in a New York minute if he looked cross-eyed at their boss.

He didn't care. He was going to figure out a way to rip off Rock.

Then there was the man himself. Rock was as nasty as a heavy in a James Bond flick, not to mention the stick with the skull-crushing handle. It would be a major hurdle for *anyone* to take Reverend T. Rock down and live to tell about it.

Fuck it, he was still going to do it. He just needed to let the idea rattle around in his head for a little while, and take form. Anything was possible when he put his mind to it.

- - -

The waitress brought their drinks. Ike and T-Bird handed over their keno tickets along with their two-dollar payments. As the waitress walked away, Ike passed his phone to Billy.

"Her Highness," Ike said under his breath.

"Billy Cunningham, at your service," he said into the phone.

"I've got some bad news for you, lover boy," Shaz said. "Crunchie just made one of the Gypsies cheating at blackjack. We're going to pull her off the floor and put the screws to her, find out where the rest of her family is. I'm afraid you lose."

The Gypsies had avoided the law for decades, and Billy didn't buy that Crunchie had spotted a member of their clan so quickly, even with the help of surveillance cameras. A more likely scenario was that Crunchie had spotted another cheater doing business in the casino and had decided to rat them out, hoping it would get him back in his boss's good graces. Billy needed to plant the seed of doubt in Shaz's mind, and he needed to do it quickly.

"Crunchie's been wrong before," he said. "That's why you brought me on board."

"He's not wrong this time," she said. "This woman's marking cards with a secret substance. I watched her on the cameras and saw her digging into her pocketbook to get it. Crunchie called her a Lady Picasso."

"Maybe she was getting her lipstick."

"Admit it, you're beaten."

"The fact that she stuck her hand into her purse doesn't mean she's one of the Gypsies, or that she's cheating. Crunchie will say anything to keep his job. If you bust this woman and she's clean, she's going to sue your ass off. You don't want that, do you?"

"But she's beating us silly."

"How much are you into her for?"

"Ten grand."

"That happens sometimes. Let me take a look and tell you if she's cheating or not."

"Why do I feel you're playing me?"

"I'm not playing you. What table is she sitting at?"

"She's at the second-to-last table in the blackjack pit, sitting at third base."

"I'm going right now."

"Call me after you've had a look. I don't want to lose any more money to this bitch."

He tossed Ike the phone. Lady Picassos were skilled female cheaters who secretly marked the backs of playing cards with special substances during blackjack, allowing them to know the dealer's total before the dealer did. These substances ranged from daub to luminous paint that could be seen through special rose-tinted glasses to Vaseline jelly. Women were especially adept at this type of cheating and used their pocketbooks to hide the substance. He was acquainted with several female cheaters in Vegas who made their living this way, and he felt reasonably certain that one of them had had the misfortune of getting caught in Crunchie's crosshairs.

Rising from the table, he threw down money for the drinks.

"Let's go check this woman out," he said.

The winning keno numbers were flashing across a digital screen, and the punishers paused to stare. Keno was a carnival game, the chance of winning so poor that it was rare that anyone ever did. But Ike and T-Bird didn't know that. They didn't know the odds, and in this town, that was usually the kiss of death.

They watched long enough to find out they were losers. Throwing their receipts to the floor, they followed Billy out of the cocktail lounge.

TWENTY-THREE

Blackjack had always been a popular game, more so after the movie *21* depicted a crew of fun-loving math whizzes taking down Vegas. The movie was typical Hollywood horseshit, but that hadn't stopped scores of people from teaching themselves how to count cards and descending upon Sin City believing they could beat the house.

Billy spotted several counters in the blackjack pit. Their body language gave them away. Hunched over, never drinking anything stronger than a Coke, they stared at their cards with the intensity of accountants doing an audit. The casinos had developed measures to send them home broke, only they were usually too busy counting to notice all their chips were gone.

He came to the second-to-last table in the pit. The dealer was a woman with perfect posture who slid the cards out of the plastic dealing shoe at a rapid pace. The faster the game was dealt, the more money the house made.

He passed the table without slowing down. The woman at third base was a major speed bump. Mid-thirties, with a great face hidden behind librarian glasses and a blond wig, and a body that looked just right. He couldn't remember seeing her around before. A newbie.

He parked himself twenty feet past the table to watch her play. To determine if she was cheating, he counted the number of hands the dealer dealt, divided by the number of times she won. She was winning more than 50 percent of the time, which was what marked cards gave you. Crunchie had called it right. She was a Lady Picasso.

He kept watching, hoping to catch her go into her purse and get the substance. Every painter had a little quirk that was unique. Some only marked aces, while others marked ten-value cards. The amount of substance they applied to the card was also unique. Some painters used small marks, while others preferred the larger variety.

Lady Picasso unclasped her purse. Out came a lipstick, which she applied generously to her lips. As she returned the lipstick, her hand stayed a little too long.

Busted.

When her hand came out, her fingers were spread wide and looked frozen. She'd put the substance on all four fingers so she could mark four cards in succession without going back to her purse. It was a nice touch, something he hadn't seen before.

During the next two rounds, she marked four ten-valued cards that were dealt to her. To the eye-in-the-sky it had to look above suspicion, her fingertips lightly brushing the back of the cards she wished to mark. In reality, she was turning the deck into an open book.

"Guess who," Ike said, handing Billy the cell phone.

"Is the bitch cheating or not?" Shaz asked.

"I'm not sure. Are you filming her?" he asked.

"Of course we're filming her. The video's inconclusive."

Billy's appreciation of Lady Picasso grew. She'd honed her cheating to the degree where the surveillance camera could not discern exactly what she was doing. That kind of skill was a rarity, and he found himself wanting to get to know this woman.

"Let me watch her some more," he said.

"I've got a better idea," Shaz said. "I'm going to tell Ike and T-Bird to pull her in the back and frisk her. If she's got a substance in her purse, she's going down."

"You're going to kill her?"

"That's right. It's how we deal with people that steal from us. Put Ike back on."

He returned the phone to Ike. Lady Picasso was about to join Ricky Boswell in the closet unless he intervened. He wasn't sure how to do that without getting himself killed as well, but that didn't mean he wasn't going to try.

A slinky cocktail waitress balancing a tray walked past. Liking what she saw, she gave Billy a flirtatious wink. He stuffed a hundred-dollar bill into the tip glass on her tray, then whispered in her ear. She acted mildly disappointed, as if hoping he was in the mood for something else.

"Which seat?" the cocktail waitress asked.

"Third base, second-to-last table," Billy said.

"Will you call me sometime?"

He said yes, and she gave him her number.

"I'll take care of it," the cocktail waitress said.

- - -

The cocktail waitress walked up to the table and stood behind Lady Picasso's chair. She asked if anyone needed a drink. Several players said yes and gave her their orders. As she finished writing the orders down, she glanced Billy's way. He mouthed the words *do it.*

The cocktail waitress was right-handed. She transferred her drink tray to her left hand, then deliberately ran her right thumb down Lady Picasso's back, her thumb following the line of the spine. Gamblers called this the brush. Back in the old days, pit bosses would give players they suspected of cheating the brush as a courtesy. Move on, or else.

Lady Picasso sat up straight in her chair. Four-alarm sirens were sounding in her head, telling her to run. Standing abruptly, she left her winnings on the table and made a beeline for the lady's restroom located behind the blackjack pit. Billy was impressed. Most cheaters would have stuffed their chips into their pockets before departing and wasted valuable time.

"Hey—where'd she go?" Ike said, just off the phone.

"I have no idea," he lied.

Ike stood on his tiptoes, his height letting him look over the crowd. "I see her. Come on, T, let's nail her ass."

The punishers crossed the pit with the swagger of NFL bounty hunters preparing to cripple a quarterback. Billy followed, keeping his distance. Lady Picasso had run to the john for a reason other than her bladder being full. It was transformation time. She would lose the wig and the glasses, turn the top she was wearing inside out, and throw away her pumps for a pair of flats in her handbag, where she also kept a much smaller purse, the handbag getting stuffed in the trash. Everything about her would look different when she stepped on the casino floor again.

Only two things were capable of ruining her escape. The first was if Ike and T-Bird managed to recognize her. Perhaps she had a distinct mole on her face, or a tattoo on her neck. Those things couldn't be erased and had done in more than one cheater.

The second would be her reaction to seeing Ike and T-Bird when she came out. They were scary looking even in their new clothes. If she stopped in her tracks, brought her hand to her mouth, or displayed any of the telltale signs that guilty people showed, she'd be history. He'd done what he could; now, it was up to the gods.

He stopped by a bank of slot machines and watched the scene unfold. He put Lady Picasso's odds of making it out of the casino unscathed at fifty-fifty. There weren't many games in this town where you could get even money, and he liked her chances.

- - -

Lady Picasso left the restroom a much different person than the one who'd gone in. Her blond hair was now brunette and done up in a bun, the glasses were history, her shoes had turned into a pair of embroidered slip-ons, and her blouse had changed color. The only thing the same were her pants, a pair of stylish black capris. The punishers hardly gave her a glance.

Her escape was textbook. Not too fast, not too slow, don't run if you're not being chased, eyes straight ahead, a dead cell phone pressed to her ear as she sailed through the casino. Once outside, she'd either hit the street running or grab a cab, never to be seen again.

You rock, girl, he thought.

A scream snapped his head. A scuffle was taking place outside the lady's restroom. Ike and T-Bird had grabbed a middle-aged blond who bore a passing resemblance to Lady Picasso and were holding her down. The blond's blouse was torn, and she'd lost her shoes.

"Security! Security!" the blond shouted.

"We are security. Shut your yap," Ike said.

The blond gave Ike a swift kick in the shins. She was spitting mad, and Billy could only guess the size of the lawsuit she'd end up filing against the casino. There was no reason to let this poor woman take a beating that she didn't deserve, and he hurried over.

"She's not the one," he said.

"Say what?" Ike said.

"I'm positive. You'd better let her go."

Ike made a call on his cell phone. The blond continued to struggle. T-Bird twisted her arm and she doubled over in agony.

"Cunningham doesn't think it's her," Ike said into the phone. To Billy he said, "Crunchie says mind your own fucking business."

So Crunchie was directing the action now. That was a different story, and Billy raised his arms in mock surrender and backed off.

"Get your dirty hands off me," the blond yelled as the punishers dragged her away.

- - -

He was suddenly alone. He didn't think anyone was watching him through the eye-in-the-sky, too preoccupied with the mistaken cheater to care about him right now. He decided to try to run Lady Picasso down. He wanted to meet this woman and get to know her. She had the chops and the moxie and hadn't panicked when the ceiling was caving in. Those were admirable qualities in his line of work. Best of all, she was hot, and to the casinos that made her a dumb broad, which was the best disguise of all.

He followed her trail and headed outside to the valet stand. The cool night air was a jolt to his senses, and he shivered from the sudden drop in temperature. Stretch limos and a cluster of yellow cabs were letting passengers out, the drivers dragging luggage out of the trunks. The valet captain blew his shrill whistle while imploring the drivers to hurry up.

No sign. Had she hit the Strip and run? That was a definite possibility, only there were a lot of tourists walking the Strip tonight, which meant a lot of uniformed cops as well, a pair on every corner. Billy avoided contact with the police whenever possible, even chance meetings on the street, and he didn't think Lady Picasso was any different in this regard.

Which meant she was still here. He decided to check out the line of people waiting to take cabs out of the casino. He counted seven couples, all dressed for a night on the town, the men looking impatiently at their watches, asking themselves if it would be faster if they walked. He approached a distinguished white-haired man at the front of the line.

"Sorry to bother you, but I've lost my girlfriend. She has dark hair tied in a bun and is wearing black capris. Have you seen her?"

The key to lying was to give the lie a ring of truth. The man bought the story and consulted with his wife, who was draped on her husband's arm. The wife pointed a manicured finger at a concrete pillar behind the valet stand.

"She's over there," the wife said. "I thought she looked a little upset."

"Thanks," he said.

He cautiously approached the pillar. He could see a haze of cigarette smoke and figured Lady Picasso was on the other side, trying to calm down. He knew it would be awkward at first, but he was going to speak with her regardless. He wanted to do business with this woman.

He took out his cell phone and held it the way people did while texting, and walked around the pillar. And there she was, sucking on a menthol cigarette. The smell did a number on his head, and the euphoric recall of that first encounter came back in a flood of memories that sped up his heart. He lowered the phone and stared, just to be sure.

Mags stared right back at him. The years had been kind, and she was still as pretty as a magazine cover. She knew she'd been made, yet didn't seem to be terribly upset. It made him dig her that much more.

He'd been in love with her for as long as he could remember. Whenever he had sex, he imagined it was the magnificent Maggie Flynn that he was inside of. It was his fantasy, and so far, it hadn't gotten old.

Kismet, fate, whatever the hell you wanted to call it, they were together again. He was not going to let her go this time, at least not if he could help it.

"I guess you don't remember me," he said.

Mags ground her cigarette into the pavement. "Holy shit. You're the paperboy."

- - -

He'd been hawking the *Providence Journal* in front of DelSesto's Bakery on DePasquale Square when Mags's sputtering Toyota had kissed the curb. Irish hot and exquisitely dressed, she could have been your best friend's gorgeous sister, but in fact was a thief. The proof was the stacks of Yves Saint Laurent apparel boxes in the backseat. The easy narrative said she worked the floor at Macy's and had swiped the clothes when her boss was on break.

"Hey, cutie, want to make some money?" she asked.

"You talking to me?" he said.

"Who else would I be talking to?"

"How much?"

"Fifty bucks for a half hour's work."

He threw a plastic sheet over his papers and hopped in. She hooked him no differently than the mythical Greek sirens who lured lovesick sailors to shipwreck on the rocky coast of their island, and they floated down the uneven road as if riding upon a magic carpet.

She explained the deal. The boxes contained knockoff cashmere sweaters made out of fiberglass, cost zilch to manufacture. Folded nice and pretty, each had an impressive gold-foiled guarantee that read "Made in Ireland." Just don't light a cigarette near them, or they'll blow up. His job was to hold the boxes and keep his mouth shut while Mags gave her spiel.

They pulled into a construction site on Federal Hill, and Mags quickly gathered a crowd. It was the most amazing thing he'd ever seen. The construction workers shoved money into her hands without a second thought. Most didn't know what they were buying, just that it was hot, and they had to have one. Every line that came out of her mouth was designed to separate them from their hard-earned dough. Soon all the sweaters were sold.

They hit it off, and Mags sprang for a chocolate shake at the Mickey D's on Broad Street. They sat in her car while she sucked on a Kool. He tried to drag every piece of information about hustling out of her that he could. Finally she had enough of his questions.

"I've got to beat it. You take care of yourself," she said.

"Take me with you. We'll make lots of money."

"You're a sharp kid. Do yourself a favor, go to college."

"You sound like my old man. He wants me to go to MIT."

"Do as he says. Father knows best."

"This is better. I like you. I think you're the most beautiful woman I've ever met."

She smiled dreamily. Leaning forward, her lips brushed his, became a lingering kiss. Her breath tasted like a menthol cigarette. For the rest of his life, the smell would turn him on.

She pulled away, lit up a fresh cigarette. She was all business now. Whatever had passed between them was gone.

"You really want to fleece people?" she asked.

Billy didn't know if he wanted to fleece people or not. What he knew was that he wanted to make lots of money, wear fancy clothes, live in a beautiful house, drive an exotic sports car, date great-looking women, and he didn't want to spend thirty years getting there.

"Where do I sign up?" he said.

"Sherwood Manufacturing on 75 Eagle Street. There's no sign. Just go upstairs and bang on the door. A black guy will come out. Tell him you want to speak to Lou Profaci."

"Who's he? What do they do?"

"Lou owns the place. They make knockoffs that street hustlers sell to suckers. The big movers are the fake sweaters and counterfeit Rolex watches called one-lungers. The watches last about a week before falling apart, even though there's a lifetime guarantee on the box. Lou will pair you with a pro, and you'll learn the ropes before he turns you out. In six months, you'll be making a grand a week easy."

"Turn me out where?"

"On the street. Every street hustler in Providence rents his turf from Lou. Some guys work the malls, others the train stations; my turf is the construction sites."

"Can he teach me how to cheat at cards and dice? My old man won't."

"Sure. Lou knows all the angles. Now, let me go."

He slurped down the last of his shake. It washed away the taste of her kiss but not the euphoric rush that had gone with it. She had opened his eyes to so many things; letting go wasn't going to be easy. "Eagle Street's on the other side of town, isn't it?"

"Sure is."

"Lou Profaci."

"That's the man's name."

"You sure he'll do it?"

She reached across the seat and tousled his curly hair.

"Just tell him Maggie Flynn sent you," she said.

- - -

"That's right. I'm the paperboy. Let me buy you a drink," Billy said.

Mags knew better than to set foot back inside Galaxy. She shook her head.

"You've got nothing to worry about. They grabbed another blond," he said.

"What's that supposed to mean? I'm not a blond."

"You were back inside the casino."

"I think you've got me mixed up with someone else."

"I saw you at the table painting the cards." He held up four fingers and wiggled them playfully. "Your chops are outstanding."

"I don't know what you're talking about."

"You have a can of daub in your purse. You were sitting at third base, painting the ten-valued cards. A guy in the surveillance room made you, so the casino sent me to take a look."

Fear crept into the corners of her eyes. "You work for the casino?"

"I'm doing a job for them. Now, let me buy you a drink. I've got a business proposition to discuss with you."

"A business proposition."

"That's right. One that involves making lots of money. Does that sound appealing?"

Mags looked confused and a little scared. She hadn't figured out what Billy's deal was and didn't know if he was friend or foe.

"You're not going to bust me?" she asked.

"Hell no," he said.

She glanced furtively at the valet stand, as if weighing an all-or-nothing dash down the sidewalk to the Strip. Taking her arm, he steered her toward the entrance.

"You're safe with me," he said.

TWENTY-FOUR

He found a bar off the lobby with TVs showing mindless sporting events whose outcomes only bookies cared about, and steered Mags to a corner table where they could talk in private. She fired up another cigarette after they sat down, and he detected a slight tremble in her fingers. She was doing a good job of hiding her emotions. For all she knew, Billy was working undercover with the gaming board and could make her life miserable in so many ways.

A waitress dolled up like Marilyn Monroe took their drink order. The hotel's celebrity theme was wearing thin and in a few months would probably get scrapped, the employees forced to wear the same tired uniforms that every casino in town made their employees wear.

"Your name is Billy, isn't it," she said.

"You've got a good memory. It's Billy Cunningham."

"What's mine?"

"Maggie Flynn. Your friends call you Mags."

"You sent that cocktail waitress over to give me the brush, didn't you?"

"Guilty as charged."

"Why'd you do that?"

"I didn't want you to get busted."

Their drinks came. Mags stirred her club soda with a straw and watched the bubbles explode. He could almost hear the gears shifting in her head as she tried to figure out his deal.

"I always wondered what happened to you," she said. "Did you make your old man happy and go to MIT?"

"Sure did. I split after two semesters."

"So what do you do now? Catch hustlers for casinos? You're sure good at it."

She'd been caught red-handed, yet still was trying to control the conversation and get him to warm up to her. Lou Profaci had taught her that little trick, along with every other hustler who'd worked for him.

"You need to stop asking so many questions, and listen to what I have to say," he said.

"I'm just interested. No harm in that, is there?"

She flashed a smile. She had perfect rows of teeth, bee-stung lips, and soft emerald eyes that he could have stared into all night long without getting bored. All the feelings bottled up inside him for so long bubbled to the surface and he gazed down at his drink.

"There are two things I need to tell you," he said. "The first is, don't ever come back to this place. These aren't casino people running this joint. They're drug dealers, and they'll beat you to death with baseball bats and no one will ever see you again. Got it?"

"Shit. Who told you that?"

"It doesn't matter. Just don't come back here. Okay?"

"Sure, Billy."

Mags had been in the game a while and knew that self-preservation was the most important thing of all.

"You said there were two things," she said after a moment had passed.

"I have a business proposition for you."

"What's that?"

"I put together a crew after I moved out here. We've been raking in the dough, taking down ninety grand a week. I've been thinking of expanding and working a few new scams. I'm going to need help."

Her reaction was a slow one. She teetered ever so slightly in her seat.

"You're a cheater," she said under her breath.

"It sure took you long enough."

"Jesus H. Christ. I thought you were an undercover cop."

"Hardly. I've been scamming casinos in Vegas for ten years, and I've seen a lot of hustlers. I dug what I saw back in the casino. You've got the routine down pat. I want you to join my crew."

At first, she didn't know what to say.

"You can think about it, if you want to," he said.

"It's just . . . I've never worked with a crew before."

"It's different than running solo. You've got people covering your back all the time, so there's less chance of getting busted. The money's also stronger. You'll never have to worry about making your rent or car payment again. You'll clear three hundred grand the first year, more as we grow. We can talk about the rest of the details later, if you're interested."

"You're serious about this, aren't you?"

"Damn straight."

"I'm flattered. Yeah, I'm interested. I've never made that kind of money in my life."

He paid for the drinks. "Give me your number, and I'll touch base in a couple of days."

"Do you have something to write with?"

"I'll memorize it."

She recited her cell number and he committed it to memory. She'd been working solo when they'd first met, and he was surprised she was still going it alone. It was a tough world to survive in by yourself.

"I need to go," he said. "It's been a blast seeing you again."

"You, too. I'm looking forward to this. It'll be fun running together."

They stood up at the same time. Mags came around the table and gave him a kiss that made his toes tingle, then left the bar faster than someone trying to catch a train. He started to leave as well and spied a piece of paper lying on the floor beneath her chair. It hadn't been there when they'd sat down, and he guessed it had dropped out of her purse.

He picked the scrap of paper up and was introduced to a gorgeous teenage brunette. The apple hadn't fallen far from the tree. The pretty girl in the photo had to be Mags's daughter.

He slipped the photo into the billfold of his wallet. That day in Providence was forever etched in his memory, their conversation at the McD's in her sputtering Toyota as clear as a recording. Puffing on a cigarette, she'd claimed that she was leaving Providence for the greener pastures of New York. Had she been wishing out loud, and was she stuck in Providence with a daughter to raise? It made sense, and if the photo was any indication, it had worked out okay. He didn't want her to get home and find the photo missing, and he hurried outside.

She wasn't in the waiting line for cabs. That left the street, and he took the handy moving sidewalk to the Strip. Leaving the property was a bad idea, but he didn't care. Every guy had a dream girl that he fantasized about, and Maggie Flynn was his.

The Strip was the usual freak show of tourists and stumbling drunks. He walked up and down the block, bumping shoulders and taking sharp elbows, until he spotted her on the corner of Sahara, jabbering on a cell phone. Out came the photo while he worked on a clever line to say.

A black Jeep Cherokee with tinted windows lurched up to the curb, and she hopped in. He stuck his hand out with the photo just as the Cherokee pulled away. The passenger door wasn't closed, giving him a glimpse of the driver. It was definitely a man.

The Cherokee disappeared in a sea of headlights. Mags had a partner, and that put a different spin on things. He needed to find out what the guy's deal was and if he was cool and could be trusted. It would be a good way to start the conversation the next time they got together.

He took the moving sidewalk back to the hotel. A valet approached, holding a cordless phone. He raised the phone while gazing up at the surveillance camera over the valet stand.

"You left the property. I should have you beaten up for doing that," Shaz said.

"Friends don't hurt friends," he said.

"With you, I'd make an exception. We nailed the wrong bitch coming out of the restroom."

"I told Crunchie it wasn't her, but he wouldn't listen."

"Crunchie's a fucking moron. Marcus wants to talk to you. Get your ass inside, and go to the craps pit. Ike and T-Bird are waiting for you."

"Got it."

He tossed the phone to the valet and headed inside. He'd been on the job a few hours, and his employers were already at each other's throats. If he played his cards right, they just might end up killing each other.

TWENTY-FIVE

Ike and T-Bird were by the craps pit, their faces filled with bad intentions. Billy said, "I didn't know I needed a hall pass to leave," expecting they'd buy the line. Only Ike cuffed him in the head, making Billy see a bunch of stars that weren't on Hollywood Boulevard.

They pulled him into the employee lounge and slapped him around. A handful of dealers on break got up and left. When Billy had taken enough punishment, they took him down a hallway to a room, threw open the door, and shoved him inside.

Doucette, his crazy bride, and Crunchie stood in front of a two-way mirror, their faces showing collective despair. In the next room was the seething blond who'd been mistakenly pulled off the floor. Hell hath no fury like a woman with a torn blouse.

Doucette cast Billy a scornful gaze. He wore a pin-striped suit, a silver necktie, and had slicked his hair back, and looked every bit the casino boss.

"You seem to have a problem following instructions," Doucette said.

"I went outside for a breather. I didn't realize I was breaking the rules." The line wasn't getting him anywhere, and he decided to steer the conversation in another direction. "You grabbed the wrong woman, didn't you? I told Crunchie to back off."

"Like hell you did. Shit bird's lying," the old grifter said.

"Ask Ike," Billy said.

"Did he?" Doucette asked.

"Billy said she wasn't the one," Ike said under his breath.

"Then why did you grab her?" Doucette said.

"Because old smelly told us to," Ike said.

"What did you call me?" the old grifter exploded.

"Old smelly. It's because you stink. Take a shower," Ike said.

"Both of you, shut up. We'll deal with this later," Doucette said.

Doucette resumed looking through the two-way mirror at his new problem. Dyed-blond hair and a nice face, she sported an ugly purple bruise on her forehead along with the ruined blouse. Standing beside her chair was a smarmy casino host with blow-dried hair and sparkling white teeth. A hidden microphone in the ceiling picked up his spiel. He was offering her a free stay, free meals in the casino's four-star restaurants, free show tickets, and $10,000 of free credit to gamble with, provided she signed a form releasing the casino from liability for the beating she'd endured. When the host tried to shove a pen into her hands, she defiantly crossed her arms in front of her chest. Nothing doing.

"Any idea who she is?" Billy asked.

"Stay out of this," Crunchie warned him.

"Hey, old man, I'm just trying to help."

"You never helped anyone in your life," the old grifter said.

Doucette slapped his hand into the old grifter's chest. "Shut your yap. I want to hear what pretty boy has to say. Spit it out, kid. What's on your mind?"

"You're trying to make peace with her, and you don't know who she is?" he asked.

"Tell him," Doucette said to his bride.

"Her name's Cecilia Torch, and she lives in Sunnyvale, California."

Shaz read off a xeroxed sheet of the woman's driver's license that security had made after pulling her off the floor. "That's all we know about her. She hasn't spoken a word."

"Did she ask for a lawyer?"

"No."

"How about a husband? Did she want to call him? She's wearing a wedding band."

"I didn't hear her ask. Did you?"

"No," Doucette said. "You think she's hiding something from us?"

"It sure seems that way," he said. "Maybe she's supposed to be on a girls' weekend, but came to Vegas to shack up with her boyfriend. Or she told her hubby she was heading downstairs to shop, but blew a few grand on the tables and is too ashamed to tell him. Whatever the reason is, she doesn't want to talk about it."

Doucette saw the wisdom of what Billy was saying. He spent a long moment studying the problem on the other side of the glass. "I'm still not letting her walk out of that room until she signs that release. Fuck, she'll sue me for everything I have, and probably get it."

"You can't bargain if you don't know what her deal is," he said.

"How can I find out what her deal is if she won't talk?"

"Can I see her ID?"

"Give it to him," Doucette said.

Billy spent a moment studying the sheet. The woman's last name was familiar. He could remember every score he'd ever pulled off, right down to the date, time, and the money he'd made. So where had he seen the name Torch? Then it hit him: the name had been on the welcome board in the lobby. Bradford Allaire and Candace Torch were getting hitched in the hotel's wedding chapel on Saturday followed by a private reception.

Cecilia Torch was the mother of the bride. The punishers had humiliated her, and she was hesitant to call the cops or get her husband involved, fearful she'd ruin her daughter's upcoming nuptials. That was why she wasn't responding to the host's offers.

"I saw the name Torch on the welcome board in the lobby," he said. "This woman's daughter is getting married in your hotel Saturday, and she's afraid she's going to spoil the wedding. That's why she's not talking."

"Is that all that's bothering her?" Doucette looked relieved. "Hell, I can fix that."

Doucette straightened his necktie and went next door. He was as smooth as a snake charmer, and he apologized to Cecilia Torch for the terrible injustice that had occurred, and began to pile on the goodies. Along with all the free stuff the casino host had offered, he was going to throw in free spa treatments for the ladies in the wedding party, free golf for the men, and, best of all, the surprise appearance at the reception of Grammy Award–winning singer Tony Marx, who was appearing in the casino's theater and who would serenade the bride and groom.

Everyone had their price. For a mother, it was seeing her daughter happy on the most special day of her life. Rising from her chair, Cecilia Torch gave Doucette a motherly hug before snatching the pen from the casino host and scribbling her name across the release.

Together, Cecilia Torch and Doucette walked out of the room.

- - -

Billy stared at the empty chair long after Cecilia Torch was gone. It could just as easily have been Mags sitting in that chair, only Doucette wouldn't have been bribing her but having Ike and T-Bird beat the living daylights out of her. That would have been hard to watch, and he wondered how he would have dealt with it.

"Billy."

He turned around. While he'd been daydreaming, the punishers and Shaz had left the room, leaving him and Crunchie alone. The old grifter held his arm at chest height, fist cocked, a set of car keys protruding from his fingers, ready to plunge into Billy's face.

"Going to poke my eyes out?"

"Yup," the old grifter said.

"I got it worked out, didn't I?"

"You made me look bad."

"You already looked bad. Get over it."

"Don't play cute with me. I saw what you did in the casino. You paid that cocktail waitress to give Lady Picasso the brush, and she bolted from the table and ran. That one's working with you, isn't she? Another of your hot numbers."

"You think I'd let one of my friends work this place, after what you did to me last night? Get real. I wouldn't do that to my worst enemy."

Crunchie's face softened, if only a little. The story added up.

"Then why did you have the waitress give her the brush?" the old grifter asked.

"I wasn't sure she was marking the cards, so I had the cocktail waitress brush her to see how she'd react. When she jumped from her chair, I knew she was a cheater."

"How clever. You still let her go."

"What was I supposed to do, tackle her? That was Ike and T-Bird's job, and they blew it. When they grabbed the wrong woman coming out of the restroom, I told them to let her go, but did they listen? Did you listen? Hell, no. Stop blaming me for your fuckups."

"You're a slick son of a bitch."

"It's the truth. Believe what you want."

The old grifter lowered his fist and pocketed his keys. "Maybe it is the truth, but know this. This little stunt doesn't change a fucking thing. You still have a job to do, and that's to find the Gypsies before they scam us Saturday afternoon. If you don't come up with the goods, your crew is going down, and so are you."

"You'd really hurt my crew?"

"Damn straight I will. And don't give me that bullshit about the code saying you can't rat out another cheater. Nobody believes that anymore."

"I do."

"Like hell you do."

"We live by the code. The rules when it comes to other thieves are clear. Don't expose another thief's identity. Never rat out another thief to the law. Help another thief whenever you can. Those are the rules, man."

"Do you really believe that, Billy? With all your heart, and all your soul?"

"Damn straight I do."

"Then why'd you agree to rat out the Gypsies? Wait, I'll tell you why. Because you want to keep your crew from going to jail. They mean more to you than the fucking code, don't they?"

The real answer was right there, but Crunchie was too blind to see it.

"You're no different than me, kid. You just don't want to admit it."

Crunchie walked out of the room thinking he'd won the argument. Billy followed him into the hall knowing otherwise. The deal he'd struck with Doucette had been nothing more than a bold-faced lie, born out of necessity to save his friends. By lying, he'd bought himself time to work his way out of his jam. If he put his mind to it, he'd find a way to make sure no harm came to the Gypsies, while continuing to abide by a strict set of rules that he'd lived by for most of his life. He may have been a criminal, but he wasn't an animal. There was a difference, despite what the old grifter believed.

TWENTY-SIX

Mags awoke with a start and spent a moment collecting her thoughts. She hated screwing in hotel rooms, but that was the price you paid for sleeping with a married man.

She slipped naked out of bed. From the closet she grabbed a fluffy white bathrobe several sizes too big, then fixed herself a stiff drink at the minibar.

"You want something?"

Special Agent Frank Grimes stood on the balcony in his striped boxers, gazing down at the Strip. After picking her up outside Galaxy, they'd come to Harrah's for a good screw and a nice room-service meal. She hadn't been in the mood, but there was no arguing when Frank wanted it. His wife had cut him off years ago, and he was hornier than a pack of Cub Scouts.

She'd known a few cops in her time. Most hated their jobs and longed for different careers. Gaming agents were a different breed. The state gave them unlimited power to police casinos, and they spent their days running down cheaters and collecting tax revenue. Crooks feared them, and casinos hated them. For Frank, that was just fine.

"How about a cold beer?"

No response. Normally, Frank jumped at the sound of her voice. Her purse lay on the dresser, the contents pulled out, including the metal tin containing the daub she used to mark cards. The breath caught in her throat.

When she'd become an informant for the gaming board, she'd promised Frank she'd stop cheating, and had gone right on doing it, thinking he was too infatuated with her to figure it out.

Stupid her.

The room had matching leather chairs. Drink in hand, she parked herself in one and let her bathrobe part. She wanted Frank to see her pussy when he came inside. It was crude, but what the hell else could she do? Her body was all she had left.

Her death spiral had started four years ago. She'd been in Atlantic City painting cards at one of Trump's carpet joints when a square john at her table had alerted security, who'd looked at the surveillance tapes and arrested her. Instead of copping a plea and doing time in a country club prison, she'd skipped bail and moved to Sin City and set up shop.

It had worked for a while. She'd cheated the casinos and flown under the radar and life had been good. She'd gotten set up in a condo, had a closet filled with nice clothes, and took an occasional vacation to the warm beaches of Cancún.

Her undoing had come two years later. Her daughter was graduating high school and Mags had decided to call her. Her grandparents had raised Amber, and she hardly knew her own kid. She'd let the call drag on, never guessing Amber's phone was tapped. An hour after hanging up, two Metro LVPD cruisers had invaded her drive, and her life on the lam had ended.

Right before trial, Frank had paid her a visit in the county lockup and offered her an undercover job with the gaming board in return for dropping the charges. Frank was comic-book ugly and had no class. She couldn't see herself doing it, and said no.

If nothing else, Frank was persistent. He showed her a letter from a female inmate incarcerated in a notorious prison called Ely. In the letter, the woman stated that rotting in hell was better than her situation and that by the time her family read this, she'd be dead. Then Frank showed Mags a photograph of the woman hanging from a bedsheet. Mags caved, and a snitch was born.

Frank came inside. He glanced guiltily between her legs before sitting down.

"Ready to go another round, big boy?" she asked playfully.

"You're in real trouble," he said.

"How about a blow job?"

"Stop talking like that."

"It never bothered you before. You want it—I can see it in your face."

She crawled across the carpet on her knees, ready to go down on him. She looked into his eyes for compliance, and he pushed her away.

"You promised me you'd keep your nose clean," he said.

She returned to her chair. "I must have forgotten."

"I'm paying you five grand a month—isn't that enough?"

"I can always use a little more."

"I sent you into Galaxy's casino to find a drug dealer named Reverend Rock. You weren't supposed to scam the joint, you stupid bitch."

His voice was turning harsh. If she wasn't careful, he'd start slapping her around if the answers she gave him didn't ring true. She closed her bathrobe. "You told me Rock's game was blackjack, so I sat down at a game, thinking he might show his face. I started cheating without realizing it. I know it sounds stupid, but it's just habit. Then a cocktail waitress asks me if I want a drink. I say no, and she gives me the brush."

"A cocktail waitress made you?"

"Another hustler paid her to do it."

"You ran into another hustler?"

"That's right. Name's Billy Cunningham. I knew him when he was a kid."

"Billy Cunningham saved your ass?"

"You know him?"

"I nearly nailed that little fucker at the Hard Rock, and he turned the tables on me. If I ever catch him, I'll put him away for the rest of his life."

Mags grew quiet. She was joining Billy's crew, to hell with her deal with Frank. Billy had offered her a fresh start, something she'd been trying to do since the quarterback of the high school football team had knocked her up in his car, and she'd quit school to have Amber, and her life had become one long slippery slope of failure and brushes with the law. She hadn't thought there was a way to climb out of the hole she'd dug for herself, and then Billy had said, "You don't remember me, do you?" and it had all changed.

"Okay, finish your story," Frank said.

"The cocktail waitress gives me the brush, so I ditched my disguise in the restroom and ran. I'm outside waiting for you when Cunningham comes out. We went inside to a bar and had a drink. He told me the people running Galaxy were bad news, and that they'd kill me if they caught me. He told me never to come back."

"Think he was protecting you?"

"I guess."

"Does he have the hots for you?"

"Probably. I turned on his love light a long time ago."

"Did you fuck him?"

"For Christ's sake, he was fifteen years old."

"What was he doing in Galaxy? Running a scam?"

"He didn't say. I got the impression he was doing a job for them."

"He wouldn't be the first criminal on Doucette's payroll."

Frank stared absently into space, processing the things she'd said. In a moment of weakness after sex, he'd told her that millions in drug money was being laundered through Galaxy's casino by a dealer out of LA named Rock, and that the gaming board had gathered enough evidence to raid the place, and that they wanted Rock on the premises to make the case stick. How Billy's working for Doucette played into this was anyone's guess, although she felt certain that Frank would figure it out. Frank always did. It just took a little time.

She went to the minibar and fixed a Jack and Coke extra strong. Kneeling beside his chair, she served him, and his cop mask melted away. If she didn't ask him now, she'd never find out.

"Tell me what Cunningham did to you at the Hard Rock," she said.

- - -

Frank had been chasing Billy for a while. Whenever Billy was in a casino, money flew out the door, a sure sign that cheating was taking place.

Gaming agents were rated by the number of busts they made. To accomplish this task, agents could freeze games in casinos, enter restricted areas, and tap phone lines of employees and guests. They had unlimited authority and did not hesitate to use it.

Frank had gone around town and given Billy's head shot to several casinos and asked them to videotape Billy if the young hustler showed his face.

Eventually, Billy appeared in one of the casinos and was taped. Frank studied the tape and determined that Billy and his crew were bringing gaffed dice onto the craps table. Billy's crew was slicker than snot on a brass doorknob, and no jury would convict them based upon the fuzzy images on the tape. To make an arrest stick, Frank would have to catch them red-handed.

Frank did some more digging and learned that Billy lived in a luxury condo at Turnberry Towers, even though the condo was in someone else's name. He got a warrant from a judge to tap Billy's phone and for several weeks listened to Billy's calls.

Everyone slipped up, even the smart ones. One day while talking to a friend, Billy mentioned wanting to check out the Rehab pool, which was part of the Hard Rock. The remark made Frank believe that Billy had the Hard Rock in his sights and was planning to rip it off.

Frank decided to set a trap and camped out in the Hard Rock's surveillance room, living on sandwiches and black coffee. His intuition paid off. Two days later, Billy and his crew appeared in the Hard Rock's craps pit and started scamming. Frank alerted casino security and went downstairs. He was determined to catch Billy with the gaffed dice, and parked himself directly outside the front entrance.

A few minutes later, Billy came through the front doors, his right hand cupped by his side. Frank approached in his rumpled suit and two-day-old beard. Smelling a cop, Billy tried to run. Frank drew his sidearm and took dead aim at the young hustler.

"Don't tempt me," he said.

The Hard Rock's entrance was distinguished by a giant neon electric guitar balanced atop a rectangular concrete awning. Drawing his right hand back, Billy made a heaving motion at the awning. The bottom dropped out of Frank's stomach. He grabbed Billy's arm and shook open his hand. The gaffed dice were gone and so was Frank's case.

Frank went on tilt. He ordered Billy to drop to his knees and stick his arms behind his back. He handcuffed Billy, squeezing the cuffs so tightly that they cut off the circulation in Billy's hands. Then he smacked Billy in the face.

"You're going down once I get those dice back," Frank said.

"What dice?" Billy replied.

"The gaffed dice you just threw onto the awning. I'm onto your scam."

"I don't know what you're talking about, mister."

Deny, deny, deny—that was the hustler's refrain. A blue platoon of security burst through the front doors and circled the two men. Traffic coming into the casino ground to a halt, causing a line of yellow cabs waiting to drop off fares to back up to Paradise Road and down Harmon. Frank was in deep shit now. He wasn't supposed to get in the way of casinos making money. But at that point, Frank didn't care. He hated Billy, hated his lavish lifestyle, his sleek Italian sports car, and most of all, the harem of women Billy had at his disposal. Frank was going to nail this little candy-ass hustler if it was the last thing he did.

A metal ladder was produced, and Frank tried to climb atop the awning. It wasn't tall enough, and Frank could not get up without fear of falling. By now, the Hard Rock's general manager was begging Frank to reconsider. Couldn't Frank see the casino was losing money? Frank told the GM to get lost and summoned Las Vegas Fire and Rescue to bring a fire truck with a retractable ladder to the casino.

While Frank waited for the fire truck, a KLAS news van appeared. Local TV news crews weren't allowed inside the casinos and were forced to slum around town, looking for stabbings, shootings, and other mayhem suitable for the evening news. The front entrance to the Hard Rock was fair game, and a female reporter stuck a mike in Billy's face.

"Care to make a statement?" the reporter asked.

"They grabbed the wrong guy. I didn't do anything," Billy declared.

By now, Frank was sweating bullets. If he didn't find the gaffed dice, his long-overdue promotion would disappear, and he'd be stuck pounding the pavement. He got on the horn and asked for a team of agents to help search for the missing dice.

The fire truck was wailing as it pulled into the Hard Rock. A team of gaming agents arrived, including Frank's boss, a hard-ass named Tricaricco. Under Frank's direction, the fire truck's ladder was stretched onto the awning, and the gaming agents scampered up the ladder. Frank was the last to go. He was afraid of heights and kept gazing down at the pavement. He spotted Billy staring up at him, his boyish face curled in a shit-eating grin.

It was at that moment that Frank knew he was fucked.

"Fucked how?" Mags asked.

She continued to kneel by Frank's chair. She could not imagine how Billy had gotten out of this jam, and she gave Frank's arm a tug.

"Come on, tell me."

Frank's glass was empty. He belched into space, consumed by the memory. "We looked everywhere on that awning for those fucking dice. It was so hot, the soles of our feet got burned. We couldn't find them."

"Did they skip over the other side?"

"That's what I thought at first. We climbed down the ladder and scoured the bushes where the dice would have fallen. The branches were sharp and cut our hands and arms. The dice were nowhere—it was as if they'd vanished. My review was coming up, and I knew this was going to sink me. Ten years busting my ass down the drain."

She pretended to be sympathetic, only she wasn't sympathetic at all. She didn't give a rat's ass about Frank's promotion or how bad he'd looked in front of his boss. What she cared about was how on earth Billy had managed to weasel his way out of this.

"What happened to the dice? They didn't just disappear."

"They got flushed down a toilet inside the casino."

"What?"

He found the strength to meet her gaze. "The Hard Rock's surveillance director broke the news to me. He said the tapes showed Billy passing off the gaffed dice to one of his bimbos before coming outside. She ran to the bathroom and flushed them away."

"So what did Billy throw on the awning?"

"Nothing. His hand was empty."

"He faked you out?"

"Yeah, and I fell for it. We had to let him go."

It was as delicious a cross as Mags had ever heard, and a tiny laugh escaped her lips. Her mother had warned her never to laugh in a man's face. The difference between men and women, her mother had claimed, was that men were afraid of women laughing at them, while women were afraid of men killing them. Somehow, she'd forgotten her mother's sage advice.

Frank's hand slapped her face. The next thing Mags knew, she was lying on her back, watching the room spin like a pinwheel. Frank threw on his rumpled clothes and grabbed his wallet and keys off the bureau. Standing over her, he spoke in a dead, emotionless tone.

"Don't ever laugh at me again."

"Sorry," she whispered.

"You okay?"

"I'll live."

"That's my girl. I'll pick you up tomorrow at noon."

"Okay."

"Mad at me?"

"I'll get over it."

"Good answer."

The door slammed, and Mags listened to his footsteps tread down the hall to the elevators. Only when she was certain he was gone did she pull herself off the floor.

She sat on the edge of the bed. She was seeing double, and she tried to will it to stop. It seemed a perfect metaphor for the two worlds she was living in. She'd gotten herself into this mess, and she was the only one who could get herself out.

The room returned to normal. She went to the slider on wobbly legs and pressed her face to the glass. The Strip's neon bathed her in false colors, and she forced herself not to cry.

TWENTY-SEVEN

At midnight, Billy scratched the podiatrists off his list of groups the Gypsies might be using as cover. Wearing a waiter's uniform and balancing a tray on his palm, he'd been canvassing a banquet room where the foot doctors were having dinner. Older, bespectacled, with big marriage bellies and soft hands, they wore suits that only saw the light of day a few times a year, and sat at round tables drinking decaf and discussing such scintillating topics as foot fungus, ingrown toe nails, and plantar fasciitis. Nearly all had spouses, an equally unexciting group of half-asleep women with stiff heads of beauty-parlor hair. None appeared in any great hurry to visit the casino, or take advantage of the other pleasurable pursuits Galaxy had to offer, and he couldn't imagine any of them being a member of the Gypsy clan. Too dull, too old, and too heavy. The Gypsies had started out as shoplifters, meaning they were fleet of foot and as lean as circus acrobats. Not a single person in the banquet room fit that description.

As he took a final swing through the room, his brand new Droid hummed in his pocket. Caller ID was local but unfamiliar. He walked over to a dessert table with a melting ice sculpture and took the call.

"Billy, it's me," Ly said. "I'm in trouble."

"What's wrong? What's that noise in the background?"

"I got busted for cheating at the casino tonight. I only got one phone call, so I call you."

"You've got to be kidding me."

"Don't get mad. Not my fault."

"How can it not be your fault?"

"Because I don't do nothing wrong. Come bail me out."

She made it sound like an order. And maybe it was; if he didn't bail her out, she might get pissed and spill her guts about their little enterprise to the cops. He couldn't take that risk and decided he'd better spring her out of jail.

"I'll get there as soon as I can," he said.

"Hurry. This place scary," she said.

He put the phone away. A podiatrist at a nearby table with his wildly drunk wife was trying to get his attention. He was done playing waiter and flipped the podiatrist the bird.

- - -

He came out of the banquet hall tugging off his waiter's jacket. Ike and T-Bird hadn't strayed far, and waited in the hall. Trying to slip away was out of the question, and he said, "Interested in making a quick five grand?"

Money made the world go round. They decided they wanted to hear more and followed Billy down a hallway past the hotel lobby until they were standing outside the entrance to the casino. It was packed, the air electric. A hot zone.

"What's the deal?" Ike asked.

"I need you guys to cover for me while I bail a friend of mine out of jail."

"You want to leave the property?" Ike asked.

"Just for a couple of hours."

"Whatta ya think?" Ike asked his partner.

"We could get our asses fired," T-Bird said, the voice of reason.

"They ain't paying us shit anyway," Ike reminded him.

"I ain't risking my job for a lousy five grand. Get more."

Ike shifted his attention to Billy. "You willing to go higher? You go higher, we might agree. Marcus and his bimbo left an hour ago, and old smelly has gone home, too. Nobody will know you left but us. We'll keep quiet, but it's got to be worth our while."

Shakedown time. Billy had half a mind to ask Ike the last time someone had paid him five grand for keeping his mouth shut, but knew that line of reasoning wouldn't go very far. Ike had him by the short hairs and was going to extract every penny out of Billy that he could.

"I'll give you five grand apiece," he offered.

"You're offering us five grand each," Ike said, just to be clear.

"That's right. Cash."

"That's good, because we don't take credit cards. Try ten."

"I just offered you ten."

"Each."

He rocked back on his heels. To pay Ike that much, he'd have to visit his condo and make a withdrawal from his wall safe.

"Come on, give me a break," he said.

Ike's eyes turned cold. "That's my final offer. Take it, or leave it."

He almost said fuck you. But a little voice inside his head said no, you need to get Ly out of jail before she goes south on you.

"You've got a deal," he said instead.

Ike smiled. "Pay up."

"The money's in my condo. I'll get it while I'm out and pay you when I come back."

Ike grabbed Billy by his shirt and lifted him off the floor so he was dangling in the air. A gang of pretty young things strolled past and shot pouty looks his way. In any other city, they would have snapped a photo on an iPhone and called the cops. But Vegas had a way of desensitizing people to pain and suffering, and the girls entered the casino without breaking stride. Bringing his face close, Ike said, "We want the money now, asshole."

"The money's in a wall safe in my condo."

"Hear that, Bird? Man's got so much fucking money, he needs a safe to keep it in." Ike's eyes narrowed. "Give us the combination. We'll take care of the rest."

"You can't go into my building. The night guard won't let you onto the elevators. Trust me, I'll get the money for you."

"You've got other things to do," Ike reminded him. "Give me the combination, and we'll get our money while you're bailing out your friend. Call the night guard, and tell him we're coming. That's the deal."

Billy knew when he was beaten. "I live in Turnberry Tower, Building B, in the penthouse. The safe's in the clothes closet. Get a piece of paper, and I'll give you the combination."

"Hoowee. You got a penthouse at Turnberry? All the rich motherfuckers live there. Being a cheater must pay real good."

"It beats working. Let me down, will you?"

Ike lowered him to earth and patted down the front of his shirt. T-Bird got a piece of paper and a pen from the front desk, and Billy wrote down the combination, having to believe it was the stupidest thing he'd ever done. Fifty grand was sitting in the safe along with a Rolex gold submariner he'd ripped off from a snotty trust-fund kid during a not-so-friendly game of backgammon at the pool, and he knew damn well that the punishers were going to take it all.

"What's the night guard's name?" Ike asked.

"Joey, but everyone calls him Jo-Jo," Billy said.

"Call him, and tell him we're coming."

- - -

Billy called Jo-Jo and set the wheels in motion for the punishers to rip him off. It felt funny setting himself up to be taken down, and he supposed someday he'd have a good laugh over it, just not today. They went outside to the valet area, and Ike patted him on the shoulder.

"Be back before dawn, junior."

"Yes, Dad."

Laughing to themselves, the punishers headed down a walkway that led to the employee parking garage, the money already burning a hole in their pockets. They were the lowest form of thieves, and he could not wait to pay them back for taking advantage of him like this.

"It's going to be about ten minutes. We're jammed right now," the valet said.

He waited on a bench for his car. He'd done a bad job of ending his partnership with Ly and had probably hurt her feelings. He needed to fix that, and he went back inside.

The gift shop was just off the lobby. He pored through racks of T-shirts and knickknacks that lined the shelves. It was made-in-China crap, all of it outrageously priced. Once upon a time, Vegas had been a bargain—cheap hotel rooms, inexpensive show tickets, endless buffets. Those days had faded; now the town was a rip-off, everything overpriced. He found a sleeveless blouse that matched Ly's eyes, and took it to the counter.

"Fifty dollars," the salesgirl said.

"Can you wrap it in some nice paper?" he asked.

"Gift wrapping is an extra two dollars."

"I can handle it."

As the salesgirl wrapped the blouse, his eyes were drawn to a display case. Among the rings and bracelets was a magical gold color.

His heart skipped a beat. They couldn't be that stupid, could they?

He reminded himself that Doucette was not a gamer, and therefore susceptible to a variety of scams that seasoned casino people would never fall for.

He pointed into the case. "Let me see that."

The salesgirl slid open the back panel and grabbed a flashy cigarette lighter.

"No, not that. The key chain next to it. The one with the gold chip."

The salesgirl removed a souvenir key chain with a rubber gold chip and handed it to him. Its gold color looked just like Galaxy's hundred-thousand-dollar gold chip.

He took the gold chip he'd stolen from Rock from his pocket and compared it to the rubber chip. The colors were *exactly* the same.

Casinos guarded the formulas they used to make their chips the way Coca-Cola guarded the formula to its soft drinks. Only Doucette had slipped up and let an outside vendor use the gold color to make a souvenir key chain. He looked for the manufacturer's mark on the chip, hoping it wasn't made in China. Finding none, he said, "Where do you get these? I want to get some made for my company."

"A vendor here in town makes them for us," the salesgirl replied. "The salesman was just here filling up the case. We move a lot of them."

"Do you have his business card?"

The salesgirl rifled through a drawer and produced the salesman's card. AAA Novelty & Gift, located on Industrial Road on the north side of town.

"Keep it. I'll get another the next time he's in," she said.

He slipped the salesman's card into his billfold. His heart was pounding in his chest and he could barely contain his excitement. He'd hit the mother lode.

"That will be another twenty dollars plus tax," she said, ringing up the sale.

The key chain probably cost nothing to make. Another rip-off, but one that he was happy to swallow. Not many times in his life would he be able to say that he'd turned twenty bucks into several million, and he sensed that his run of bad luck was about to change.

TWENTY-EIGHT

He drove north on the Strip with the souvenir key chain hooked over his thumb. With the help of this fake gold chip, he was going to take Doucette down for the count.

Every casino in Vegas had gotten ripped off by counterfeit chips. The scam was so common that the state required each casino to have a set of spare chips with alternate markings in case the chips on the floor needed to be quickly changed.

He hung a left on Bonneville and was soon at the jail. The Strip did not have its own jail, and people arrested in Strip casinos were transported to the Clark County Detention Center, as depressing a place as he'd ever visited.

He'd been busted several times for scamming. Because he had a slick lawyer and was luckier than a two-peckered puppy, he'd never spent more than a single night in the CCDC. But the experience had still been hair-raising. Cheaters were not liked, and he'd spent ten hours lying freezing naked on a futon before getting to talk to his lawyer.

He parked in the visitor lot across the street and went inside. There was a line of people waiting to speak to the front-desk sergeant. Soon, it was his turn, and he learned that Ly had appeared before a judge, who'd set her bail at ten grand.

Next stop was a depressing chamber called Pre Trial Services, where a hand-printed sign announced a new forty-dollar filing fee for bond payment. Dealing with the system was no different than getting your pocket picked. He dropped a Visa card on the counter and proceeded to bail Ly out of jail.

- - -

Ly emerged from the jail still wearing her purple dealer's vest and ruffled tuxedo shirt, her hair released from its bun. Seeing Billy standing in the sidewalk, she scowled.

"What take you so long?" she asked.

"I got here as fast as I could," he said.

"How much they make you pay?"

"Ten big ones."

"Hah. That nothing to rich guy like you."

Thank you was not in her lexicon. They got into his car. Ly picked up the blouse on the passenger seat and tore away the tissue paper. She tossed the gift into the backseat.

"Not your color, huh?" he said.

"I'm hungry. Take me some place nice," she said.

He decided on the El Cortez in old downtown. It would be quiet at this time of night, and they'd be able to sit and talk things out. Ly had gotten busted for cheating a casino, and he didn't think she understood how miserable her life was about to become.

- - -

The El Cortez was a faded throwback to the days when the mob ran the casinos. Its two restaurants served terrific food in generous portions and were open all night long.

A hostess seated them in a corner booth. They read the menu, which was the length of a short novel. Ly decided on the matzo ball soup and Chicago corned beef sandwich, while Billy went for the shrimp cocktail and the signature New York pastrami sandwich served high on rye.

He studied her face while waiting for their food. The false bravado was gone, and she looked scared out of her wits. Their drinks came. Coffee for him, a sweaty Heineken for her.

"Tell me what went down," he said.

"This afternoon, my neighbor come over," she said. "He tell me he been practicing chip scam all day, that he ready to go tonight. I tell him, 'You not ready yet,' and he leave."

"You were practicing the chip scam with your neighbor."

"Yeah. His name Funky Freddie because he wear funny socks."

"Let me guess. Your neighbor came into your casino anyway."

"Yeah. Funky Freddy come in tonight, start talking to pit boss. I freak out, you know? He sit at my table, and I see the double-chip in his hand. Under my breath I say, 'Go away, you dumb shit,' but he don't hear. Very first bet, he put down double-chip. Then he realizes wrong side showing, so he flips chip over. Everyone see it not real."

"Jesus Christ. What'd you do?"

"I back away from the table. I don't want no part of this crap. Funky Freddie realize what he done and runs out of casino. Pit boss comes over, picks up the double-chip, look at me real suspicious. He says, 'This guy's a friend of yours, huh?' I say I never see him before, but pit boss busts me anyway."

If it went to trial, Ly's attorney could tell a jury that she'd refused to take Funky Freddie's bet. Every BJ game in Vegas was videotaped, and the tape would show Ly backing away from the table and not touching the gaffed chip. A good defense attorney would hang his case on that, and Ly would walk. She'd probably lose her work card and never deal blackjack again, but that was a small price to pay to beat a cheating rap.

"Tell me what you told the police," he said.

"Police ask me if I know Funky Freddie. I say I never seen this crazy guy before. Police say pit boss tell them my table not doing so good, that I may be stealing."

The pit boss had cast a shadow of doubt over Ly's integrity. He felt himself growing worried. "Did Funky Freddie leave a paper trail inside the casino that could be traced?"

"What you mean?" she asked.

"Did he buy anything with a credit card? Or use the ATM?"

"I see him at ATM machine before he sit down."

"Did the pit boss see him?"

"Pit boss see him, too."

This was bad. If the pit boss alerted the police to Funky Freddie's use of the ATM to make a withdrawal, the police would get Funky Freddie's credit card info and hunt him down. That was a problem, because Funky Freddie lived in Ly's trailer park. The police would make the connection and charge Ly and her neighbor for conspiracy to cheat a casino. There were over a hundred slick defense lawyers in town, and not a single one could beat a conspiracy rap.

Their meals came. Ly still didn't understand the gravity of what she'd done. She speared the matzo ball and tore a piece out of its side with her teeth.

"We need to move you," he said.

"What you mean?" she said.

"You're not safe at the trailer park anymore. Let's go."

- - -

Ly lived in the Rolling Ranchette Trailer Park off Boulder Highway. The roads were quiet, and he did ninety most of the way, hoping to beat the gaming board.

During the drive, she talked about growing up in Vietnam. Billy didn't know much about the country except that the United States had fought a protracted war there whose validity was still being argued by old guys with ponytails in bars.

At sixteen, she'd paid a human trafficker for passage to LA, where she'd worked folding clothes at a laundry. One day, a well-dressed Vietnamese customer named Vicky had made Ly an offer. Vicky was also a refugee, and owned a nail salon in Garden Grove in the heart of Southern California's Vietnamese community. All of the salon's manicurists were Vietnamese girls trying to make a life for themselves. Vicky had offered Ly a job painting nails, where Ly would make good money and even better tips.

There had been one hitch. The cost of entry was twenty grand.

Billy parked in front of Ly's trailer. It was dark, and he saw no sign of the gaming board.

"Explain the deal to me," he said.

"Deal simple," she said. "Vicky send me to work at Slots A Fun, where I pretend to be a Vietnamese girl named Ly. I live in Ly trailer, drive her shitty car, pretend to be her. I send Vicky money every month so I one day work in salon."

"You're not the first one Vicky's done this with, are you?"

"All girls in Vicky's salon have been Ly. No one complain."

"Does the owner of Slots A Fun know what's going on?"

"Owner knows," she explained.

"You bribed him?"

"I fuck him, same as other girls. We fuck him, and he take care of us. Back home in Vietnam, boyfriend fuck me, and when he done, tell me go make dinner. I say go make own dinner, lazy dog. Boyfriend knock me down, kick me. I tell my father, thinking he protect me. My father say, 'Chồng chúa, vợ tôi.' That mean 'Man master, woman servant.' So I run away. That's what my country like. Women get nothing in return. At least when I fuck a man here, I get something back. You have problem with that?"

She had it all figured out. Why she was here, the things she'd done to get here, the risk, the reward—nothing had escaped her.

"No, I don't have a problem with that," he said.

A few trailers down a porch light came on, and a geezer in handcuffs came out the front door. He was followed by a pair of gaming agents with badges pinned to their lapels. The geezer's wife stood in the doorway, bawling her eyes out. On the geezer's feet was a pair of hideous multistriped socks. Funky Freddie was going down.

Billy started to back away while trying not to smash into anything. One of the gaming agents spotted them.

"Stop right there, and get out of the vehicle," the gaming agent called out.

"Get your head down," Billy said.

Ly dropped in her seat. Goosing the accelerator, he flew in reverse down the street.

"Get back here!" the gaming agent shouted.

He flashed his brights, just to get the gaming agent's goat. The gaming board employed nine hundred field agents, the majority in Sin City. Rookies were relegated to the night shift; if they lasted a year, they got to work days. It was a lot harder than it sounded.

He reached the intersection, performed a backward turn, hit his brakes, and threw the car into drive. As they raced past Ly's street, the gaming agent appeared with his gun drawn. It was strictly for show. If the gaming agent fired and missed, the bullet might hit a trailer and wound someone. No agent wanted that on their resume, unless they were Dirty Harry.

Billy exited the trailer park without any more problems. A minute later, he and Ly were flying down Boulder Highway with the windows down and their hair blowing in their faces.

"You my hero," Ly cooed.

- - -

The Super 8 Motel on Koval was the best deal in town. On-site dining, a heated swimming pool, four HBO channels, all for forty bucks a night. He paid in advance and walked Ly to a room on the first floor that faced the street. Shoving money into her hands, he told her to lose the dealer's uniform first thing tomorrow.

She leaned against the doorsill. Her posture said she wanted him to come inside and screw. She was nothing but trouble, and he backed away from the door.

"I thought you like me," she said.

"I'm doing a job for some guys. I have to go or they'll get pissed."

"Make up excuse. You good at that."

"They're bad guys. They won't understand."

"Why you working for bad guys?"

"It's a long story. I'll be by in a couple of days. Stay out of trouble, okay?"

She tried to hug him. Billy knew better. Once their bodies touched, it would be all over. He gently pushed her away. Her eyes laughed at him.

"You going to take me back to LA?" she asked.

"I don't know. You have someplace to stay?"

"Vicky put me up. I still owe her money for job at nail salon. You pay her for me?"

"How much do you owe her?"

"Two thousand five hundred."

It was a small price to pay to get Ly out of his hair.

"I'll pay her the rest," he said. "Now let me go."

"You really do that for me?"

"I said I would, didn't I?"

"Remember that time we almost fuck? It was in crummy motel just like this. I never forget that night. I want you so bad inside of me. Just like now. Why don't you come inside and let me make you happy?"

Her eyes danced with the memory, and it took all his willpower to turn away and trot to his car. Not until he was speeding down Koval did he glance in his mirror. Ly remained in the doorway wearing an all-knowing look. She was the kind of woman that could get you killed, and he sped away thinking there were probably worse ways to check out of this life.

TWENTY-NINE

The hotel lobby was deserted as Billy came through the front doors, and he stuck his head into the casino before heading upstairs. The crowds had thinned, the action less frenetic than earlier. Casino games were designed to grind a player down, one dollar at a time. Over the long run you couldn't win, but that didn't stop people from sticking their heads in the buzz saw.

His ears popped on the way up in the elevator. Through the glass windows he beheld the slow-motion riot of people, cars, and blinking neon of the Strip.

His footsteps made scratching sounds on the hall's carpet. He keyed the door to his suite and entered, expecting to find Ike and T-Bird counting the money they'd taken from his condo. To his surprise, they weren't there, and he called the front desk at Turnberry.

"Good evening. Can I help you?" answered Jo-Jo, the lethargic night manager.

"This is Billy Cunningham in 28D. I'm looking for a couple friends of mine. Have you seen them around?"

"Hey, Mr. C. If your friends are a couple of mean-looking black dudes, then yeah, I saw them. They came in earlier and introduced themselves. I saw those big Super Bowl rings, and we got to talking. I remember those guys when they played for the Steelers."

"Were they any good?"

"Naw, they sucked. The tall one nearly cost them the title."

"Any idea where they are now?"

"They're still upstairs in your condo."

"They haven't left yet?"

"Nope. I would have seen them, and I've been at my desk all night."

An alarm went off in Billy's head. Emptying his safe shouldn't have taken Ike and T-Bird very long. What had they done, called some high-priced call girls and thrown a party? He had to assume that they were up to no good. That was a mistake, because he had the capability to screw them in a bad way, right from where he was.

"What's the name of the security company that installed the hidden camera system in the building last year?" he asked.

"A1 Security and Alarm," Jo-Jo said.

"Do you have their website?"

"Yeah, it's taped to my computer: a1security.com, all lowercase. Is something wrong? Are those guys ripping you off?"

"That's between me and them. Later, Jo-Jo."

"Have a good night, Mr. C."

He got on the Internet with his Droid and soon was on the A1 site. A year back, a cleaning woman had gotten caught trying to pawn valuable jewelry she'd stolen from a resident at Turnberry. To prevent further theft, the building's management had hired A1 to install hidden CCTV cameras in each unit's ceiling smoke detectors. These cameras were wired to the firm's main location and could be accessed with a few simple commands.

He'd been happy to have cameras installed in his unit. He wasn't worried about theft as much as what the gaming board would take if they ever raided his place. Chances were, they'd rip him off, and wouldn't it be fun to have a tape of it? He went to the log-in page and typed in his password: *cheater*.

The interior of his condo appeared on the Droid's screen. The CCTV cameras filmed in four-color, and his condo looked as sharp as the set for a late-night infomercial. He flipped between rooms and stopped at the master bedroom. As he'd expected, the wall safe was open and had been cleaned out, the stacks of money piled on the floor.

But there was more. His clothes had been removed from the closet and laid out across the bedroom. Dozens of silk shirts, designer slacks, cashmere sports jackets, and Italian shoes. Some articles had never been worn and still had price tags. His collection of men's watches was also on display, along with the fancy cigarette lighters that he used to light beautiful ladies' cigarettes when he went clubbing. They had decided to take inventory of his stuff.

Ike stood in the center of the bedroom lecturing T-Bird, who sat on the bed, staring at the floor. T-Bird's posture was peculiar: sagging shoulders, head down, like a boxer collapsed on his stool between rounds of a fight, getting ready to call it quits.

Ike kept talking to his partner, and T-Bird kept staring at the floor. Not a lecture, Billy decided, but a pep talk. Ike was trying to cheer up T-Bird, who was clearly depressed.

He tried to put himself in T's shoes. The bird man was past his prime, maybe nursing a bad knee or suffering memory loss from too many hits to the head, all the while holding on to some thin dream of wealth. Then he'd seen Billy's mind-blowing collection of threads and jewelry, and the crushing weight of his own crummy reality had hit him, and all he wanted to do was go to a bar and get loaded, because that's what dumb guys did when they got depressed.

And Ike was saying no, we got a job to do, come on, man.

He had caught them at a vulnerable moment, and a Roman candle went off in his head with the most glorious of colors. They were his for the taking. He just had to handle them right.

He picked up the room's phone and dialed 9 for an outside line and called his condo. On the Droid, he saw the punishers' heads snap as the phone in the condo rang. He repeated this three more times. On the fourth try, Ike snatched the phone off the bedside table.

"Who's this?" Ike said.

"It's me, Cunningham. I'm watching you and your partner."

"You're watching us? How the fuck can you be doing that?"

"Through my cell phone."

"Don't fuck with me, asshole."

On the Droid, Billy saw T-Bird get off the bed and stand next to his partner with a pensive look on his face. T-Bird wasn't sure what was going on, and he started to gather the stacks of money they'd pulled out of Billy's safe and cradle them in his arms the way a nervous parent might hold a newborn baby. T-Bird was going to bolt—Billy was sure of it—and he said, "I'm not fucking with you. T-Bird just got off the bed and is now grabbing the money you took from my safe. Tell him he needs to hear what I have to say."

"How can you be spying on us?" Ike said. "There ain't no surveillance camera in here."

"The smoke detector on the ceiling has a closed-circuit TV camera with a fish-eye lens hidden in it. There's one in every room."

"You're shitting me."

"I shit you not. Take the cover off one if you don't believe me."

Ike found the smoke detector on the ceiling and yanked off the cover. His arm was so long that he didn't need a chair to stand on.

"Fuck, look at this," Ike said.

T-Bird stared into the tiny camera, his face so close that Billy saw forests of nose hair.

"It's Cunningham," Ike explained. "He's watching us."

"That's fucked up," T-Bird said.

"So what do you want to talk about," Ike said to the camera.

"I have a job for you. I'll pay you life-altering money."

"What kind of money?"

"Life altering. As in lots."

"How much?"

"Enough to retire on. You interested?"

Ike turned to stone, thinking hard.

"Ain't no harm in talking to him," T-Bird said into his partner's ear.

"When?" Ike said into the phone.

"Right now," he replied.

"Where?"

"In my suite at the hotel. I'll order room service. You guys hungry?"

"We're always hungry. Get me a filet, well done, french fries, hollandaise sauce on the side. Same for T, only make his medium rare with a baked potato and sour cream."

"Got it. See you soon."

"Listen, Cunningham, you'd better not be fucking with us."

"I'm not fucking with you."

Ike ended the call. He slapped his partner on the shoulder at their sudden good fortune, then remembered the CCTV camera in the ceiling. He flipped Billy the bird before ripping it out.

THIRTY

Billy ordered the punishers' steaks from room service along with a large shrimp cocktail for himself. The room service attendant explained that the kitchen was backed up and that it would take forty-five minutes for the meals to be delivered. Billy wanted the food on the table when Ike and T-Bird arrived, and he said, "Make it twenty, and I'll be happy."

"I'm sorry, sir, but that's impossible," the attendant replied.

Nothing was impossible inside a Vegas casino. "What's your name?"

"It's Hinton, sir."

The incoming caller ID on Hinton's phone said that Billy was calling from a high-roller suite. "If you don't get those meals up to my suite right now, I'll check out of this crummy dump and tell the rodeo clown at the front desk you were rude to me. Got it?"

"Please don't do that, sir," Hinton said.

"I didn't hear you. What did you say?"

"You'll have your food in twenty minutes. I'll deliver it myself."

"I'm counting on you, Hinton."

While waiting for the food to arrive, Billy went to work on the suite. He was about to sell a bill of goods to Ike and T-Bird, and to do that, he needed the suite to look just right. He started by positioning the chairs at the dining room table so that Ike and T-Bird sat together and would face him while they ate. He wanted to gauge their expressions while he made his pitch and know how each man was leaning. More importantly, he didn't want them communicating with each other, even if it was with their eyeballs.

The suite's bar was filled with top-shelf brands. He set a bottle of Hennessy XO on the marble bar top along with three snifters to toast their newfound partnership. By setting the bottle out ahead of time, he was signaling his desire to work with them.

Hinton arrived with a few minutes to spare and set the covered plates at the appropriate spots on the table under Billy's instruction. When he was done, Billy shoved a hundred-dollar tip into Hinton's breast pocket and made a new friend.

Ike and T-Bird arrived a short while later. T-Bird carried the money from the safe in a Nike duffel bag he'd taken from Billy's closet.

The bag was popping at the seams, and Billy wondered how many other items they'd filched from his condo.

"What's your fancy?" he asked from the bar.

"Whatever's cold," Ike said. "You having a party?"

He pulled three bottles of beer from the fridge, popped their tops, and brought them across the room. "Call it a celebration. Here's to getting rich together.'

"Sounds good to me," Ike said.

"Same here," T-Bird said.

They took their spots at the table and started to eat. Ike and T-Bird were vacuum cleaners, weapons of mass consumption. Billy took his time and savored his shrimp cocktail. More shrimp got eaten in Las Vegas than anywhere on the planet, and the shrimp were always succulent and delicious. When he was done, he sprayed lemon on his fingers and washed away the remaining taste with beer. The punishers had already crossed the finish line and were watching him.

"Taste good?" he asked.

Ike grunted that his steak was decent, nothing great. T-Bird said the same. They did not act nearly as fierce with their bellies filled with red meat and potatoes.

"Want some dessert? The kitchen's open all night," he said.

"What we want is for you to talk to us about life-altering money," Ike said.

"That's right, tell us about the money," T-Bird chimed in.

They wanted to hear about the payoff before they knew the risk. It was an amateur mistake, born out of desperation and greed. He took another swig of beer, just to make them wait. "Let me ask you a question. If I said there was a rich guy that could be ripped off, and that you'd walk away with enough money to retire on, would you do it?"

"Someone we know?" Ike asked.

"The right Reverend Rock."

"What you smoking? It's making you talk crazy."

"Hear me out. Rock's a drug dealer, and he's using the casino to launder drug money. If Rock gets scammed while he's here, he can't call the police and file a report. Rock's money is ours—he's just holding it for us. It's a perfect job."

"Maybe for you it is," Ike said. "If me and T get involved, we'd have to go into hiding, get new identities, the whole shebang. Rock has a long memory."

"So what if you go into hiding? The way I see it, you guys have a problem. You're too big to be thieves. Wherever you go, you stand out. That's hard when you're a thief. Look at me—I'm five eight and weigh a hundred sixty pounds. Stick a baseball cap on my head, and I look like your average schmuck."

"You don't look average," Ike said.

T-Bird had pulled his chair closer to his partner. In the reflection in the mirror on the other side of the suite, Billy saw the bird man foot-tapping Ike on the leg the way cheating couples did at bridge, as if to say, *Listen to the man.*

"There's another problem—you're also famous," he said. "You played football for the Steelers, won a Super Bowl, your faces televised to a billion people during the game. How many times do you get recognized? I bet it's a lot."

"Guy recognized us tonight," T-Bird said.

"There you go. You're not cut out to be thieves. You need to make one big score and vanish into the wind." He paused to let the idea set in. "So what do you say? Do you want in?"

T-Bird gave his partner another foot-tap. Ike scratched his chin, thinking.

"All depends on what our take is," Ike said.

"Twenty-five percent."

"Twenty-five percent of what?"

"Twenty-five percent of whatever was in the bag Rock passed through the cage last night. It looked like six million. Twenty-five percent would be one point five million. That's your take."

"Try eight million," Ike said. "That's what gets laundered each week."

"All right, then your take would be two million. That's enough to spend the rest of your life eating cheeseburgers in paradise, don't you think?"

"That's a nice number," Ike said. "We could live off that. Couldn't we, T?"

"Fat and happy," T-Bird said.

The vibes coming off the punishers were of the feel-good quality. Billy had planted the seed; now he needed to make it grow.

"On Saturday afternoon, the Gypsies are going to scam Galaxy's casino, and Doucette is counting on me to stop them. If I tell Doucette that the scam's going to happen in front of the craps pit, he'll send every security guard to the craps pit. You couldn't ask for better shade to make a run at the cage."

"Shade?" Ike asked.

"Distraction. Every hustler uses it. By the time Doucette realizes Rock's eight million is missing, you two gentlemen will be gone."

"Are you talking about a heist with guns?"

"Hardly. I'm talking a scam. The cashier will hand T-Bird eight million in laundered money, and T-Bird will waltz out the front door. Does that sound like fun to you?"

"I dig the way you describe things," Ike said. "But it won't be cash. It will be eight million in money orders. Doucette uses a chain of check-cashing stores in town to launder the money."

"Can the money orders be traced?" Billy asked.

"Nope. Each money order is for ten grand. Rock comes to the casino with two big leather briefcases, and he leaves with a small one."

"That will make your job even easier. This is going to be a piece of cake."

"Keep talking," Ike said.

- - -

It was time for the reveal. From his pocket, Billy removed the souvenir key chain with the rubber casino chip he'd purchased at Galaxy's gift shop, and let it dangle on his finger.

"See this hundred-thousand-dollar gold chip? I bought it in the hotel gift shop. It's the key to the kingdom. We're going to get rich off this."

T-Bird jumped out of his chair. "Are you fucking kidding? That thing's rubber. No one's gonna be fooled by that."

"Sit down, and let him talk," Ike said, knowing there was more.

T-Bird dumped his body back in his chair and folded his massive arms.

"You're right, it is made of rubber," Billy said. "Now, look at the color. It's the same color as the hundred-thousand-dollar gold chip in the casino. The *exact* same color."

T-Bird started to protest. Ike silenced him with an elbow to the ribs.

"What's the one thing the casinos are most afraid of?" Billy went on. "Counterfeit chips. A talented forger can wipe a casino out. To stop this from happening, the casinos employ different measures to stop forgers. The two measures that have worked best are RFID microchips and using special colors that can't be duplicated. You with me so far?"

"Yeah," the bird man grunted.

"Galaxy doesn't use RFID microchips, so that just leaves the special colors. And Doucette let a promotional company have the formula to make this rubber chip. I'll get the paint from them, give it to a forger that works for me, and he'll counterfeit gold chips. Get it?"

Ike nodded approvingly; he was on board. T-Bird still needed convincing.

"Passing counterfeit chips inside a casino has a name," Billy said. "It's called making a run at the cage. It's a difficult scam to pull off. You've got to fool the cashier, the cage manager, and the eye-in-the-sky. If any of those folks think you're trying to pass bogus chips, they'll hit an alarm, and you'll get busted."

"This sounds hard," T-Bird said.

"It won't be when we do it. In fact, it's going to be a piece of cake."

"Why's that?"

He'd already told them the answer, only T-Bird was brain dead and had forgotten. Ike's brain was still working, and he slapped the table with his enormous palm.

"We're going to make a run at the cage while the Gypsies are pulling their scam," Ike said. "You understand what the man is saying? We're going to pull a scam while another scam is going down. Security will be dealing with the Gypsies, while we're ripping the joint off. Douche bag won't know what hit him."

T-Bird had a funny look on his face. Rising from the table, he pointed at the door to the master bedroom. "In there," he said, and walked into the other room.

Ike rose as well. "Be right back."

The bedroom door closed, and they started to argue like a married couple having a spat. For a couple of ex-jocks about to run out of road, it was the deal of a lifetime, and he wondered what the problem was. At the end of the day, it really didn't matter. Ike was the brains of the duo, and T-Bird would eventually agree to what Ike wanted, because that was how it worked.

The Nike duffel bag sat on the floor. It had been eating him to know what they'd stolen from his condo. The zipper made a harsh sound as he tugged it open. The bag was filled with the money from his wall safe—no surprise there. In the side pockets they'd stuffed watches, jewelry, and fancy cigarette lighters.

He took everything back. The pieces that didn't fit in his pockets went into drawers at the bar. He also helped himself to the money, and left twenty grand. That was the amount they'd agreed to, and he was not going back on his word.

Harsh words floated out of the bedroom. He went to the couch, flipped on the TV, and stared at images that made no sense. Sleep was calling to him. It had been a long fucking day, and he needed to recharge his batteries for tomorrow, which promised to be an equally long fucking day. He still had to find the Gypsies, and that was no small order.

The punishers came out of the bedroom and stood in front of the couch, blocking the TV.

"We got a question," Ike said. "How do we know you won't rob us and take all the money come Saturday? What's to stop that from happening?"

"You have first touch," he said.

When neither man responded to this most incredible of offers, he explained.

"You're going to rob the cage while I'm catching the Gypsies. The cashier will hand you the money orders, and you'll walk outside and jump into a car with my crew. I'll meet up with you later and split the money. Sound fair?"

It was more than fair, and erased any doubts that Billy wasn't being on the level with them. Both men stuck out their hands.

"You've got yourself a deal," Ike said.

THIRTY-ONE

-THE HOT SEAT: SUNDAY, LATE AFTERNOON-

The sunlight was starting to fade when the gaming agents decided to take a break and walked out of the interrogation room. Billy had been talking nonstop, and his vocal cords were turning hoarse. He uncapped the last water bottle on the table and chugged it down.

"Let me have your pen," he said.

His attorney handed over his gold pen. Billy scribbled on the pad. His attorney gave the question some thought.

"I'd put your odds at less than even money," the attorney said truthfully.

It was better than having no odds at all. The gaming agents returned and took their places at the table. LaBadie replaced the cassette in the tape recorder on the table.

"Let's continue," LaBadie said.

"Ready when you are," Billy said.

"We want to hear more about the rubber chip you found in Galaxy's gift shop. You said the gold color matched the casino's hundred-thousand-dollar chip, and this led you to believe that your crew could counterfeit these chips and use them to rob Galaxy's casino."

He'd told them a faithful rendition about the first two days, except for the details about his crew. Those things he'd glossed over, referring to his crew simply as a group of friends that he occasionally got together with.

"I already told you, I don't have a crew," he said.

"Stop playing games, Billy. You and your crew made a run at the cage and ripped the place off Saturday afternoon."

"Never happened."

"Did Maggie Flynn know your plans?"

He glanced sideways at his attorney. "Tell them."

"For the record, my client does not have a crew," Underman said. "If you continue to put words in my client's mouth, I'll have to ask you to stop this interrogation immediately."

"We're not putting words in his mouth," LaBadie said defensively.

"I beg to differ."

LaBadie had been around the carnival a few times and knew that Underman was establishing a line of defense to use at trial.

"Have it your way. Carl, go get the bag," LaBadie said.

Zander left the room. When he returned, he was holding a paper bag. LaBadie took the bag and poured its contents onto the center of the table. Gold chips from Galaxy's casino rained onto the table, their color so rich they sparkled in the light.

"Recognize these?" LaBadie asked.

Billy shook his head, playing dumb.

"They're counterfeits. Your crew used them to steal eight million bucks."

"I don't have—"

"We have this on videotape, Billy. Now are you going to come clean with us or not?"

Billy picked up one of the chips and gave it a cursory glance. If they had it on tape, then he was fucked, no two ways about it. So why hadn't they shown him the tape and gotten it over with? Why go to the trouble of making him tell his story? Either LaBadie was lying or something else was going on. All he could do was keep talking and hope for the best.

"You want to hear the rest of my story?" he asked.

"You're not going to confess?" LaBadie asked.

"To what?"

"To all the crimes you committed."

"I didn't commit any crimes. I'm innocent."

"You're making this tough on yourself, Billy."

"Why don't you just listen to the rest of my story? I mean, isn't that why we're here?"

LaBadie parked himself in a chair. The three gaming agents put their elbows on the table, their eyes boring a hole into their suspect's face.

"Spit it out," LaBadie said.

THIRTY-TWO

-FRIDAY, ONE DAY BEFORE THE HEIST-

Billy awoke to being kicked in the shins. It wasn't ideal, but it was better than being bonked in the head with a lead pipe, shot in the face at point-blank range, or strangled with a rope, which occasionally happened to people who cheated for a living. He'd fallen asleep on the couch in the living room of his suite, an empty snifter in his hand. Painful sunlight streamed through the picture window as bright as a police interrogation.

"Get up, you sneaky little bastard."

A plumber's dream of Cleopatra stood before him. Baby doll red dress, five-inch spiked heels, her lips a tight red scar, and enough cleavage to open a Hooters. He still hadn't figured out what her deal was, and decided to make it a priority over the next two days.

"I resemble that remark," he said.

She kicked him again. He saw it coming and shifted, letting the couch absorb most of the blow. She was on tilt, and in no mood for jokes.

"Hey—what did I do?"

Her hand made a sweeping gesture of the plates from last night's feast. "Marcus doesn't appreciate people running up bills in his name, and neither do I. Do it again, and I'll cut your balls off. Now, get up. We have a lead on the Gypsies to check out."

The words gave him pause. His plan to rip off Galaxy was contingent upon the Gypsies not getting caught before Saturday afternoon.

"Who got the lead on them?" he asked.

"I did."

Crunchie stood at the bar wearing black cowboy attire. He'd scraped a razor over his face and cleaned himself up, yet still looked like death warmed over. The hustler's life got bumpier the longer you stayed in the game; if you didn't quit the business, the business quit you.

Their eyes met. Billy mouthed the words *up yours*.

"Same to you," the old grifter said. "I set a trap for the Gypsies and just caught one of them. Appears I won our little contest."

"You couldn't catch the clap in a whorehouse."

"Watch it, you little punk."

"Just remember: you wouldn't have had to blackmail me if you hadn't screwed up."

Angry spittle formed at the corners of Crunchie's mouth, and the old grifter took off his cowboy hat and punched the crease. "I've had enough of your crap, Billy. I want to be treated with respect. Stop talking to me that way, or I'll take you out myself."

Billy laughed derisively. The old grifter charged across the suite. Shaz clapped her hands, stopping him in his tracks.

"Enough of your macho bullshit," she said. "Go out in the hallway, and cool your jets. And don't dare do that again."

"He's trying to divide us—can't you see that?" Crunchie said.

"He's just playing with you. Now get lost."

Crunchie shot a parting dagger before retreating to the hallway. Divide and conquer was the only way to fight when you were outnumbered. Billy went to the bar, pulled a carton of OJ out of the fridge, filled two glasses, and brought one to her.

"You enjoy riding his ass, don't you?" she said.

"Whatever gave you that idea? So tell me about this trap."

"Ricky Boswell is registered in the hotel. Crunchie thought one of Ricky's family might try to contact him before Saturday, so we kept his room open. Our operators have been monitoring phone calls to the room, hoping one of his family would call him."

"Did they?"

"No. But this morning someone visited the room, and the door clicker went off. A security guard was sent. By the time the guard got there, the visitor was gone. Crunchie wants to search the room, see if this person left anything."

Security in Vegas was more elaborate than most guests realized, not just in the casinos but in the hotel rooms as well, the fear being that guests might stage private card games, which were illegal. To prevent this from happening, electronic door clickers counted the number of times guests visited their rooms each day. If the number of visits exceeded a certain level, the hotel would send security guards to the room to make sure nothing improper was going on. Since Ricky Boswell was dead, *anyone* visiting his room would set off an alarm.

"What time did this happen?" he asked.

"Around eight thirty this morning."

"That was hours ago. Why wait so long before doing anything?"

"Crunchie thought the person might come back, so we had a pair of security guards camp out in the hallway inside the emergency exit and wait for him."

"But the person didn't come back."

"No. How'd you know that?"

"Because Ricky was a scout. His job was to check out your casino before his family took it down. From what you told me last night, Ricky had already given his family the green light before you killed him. That meant Ricky's job was done. He wouldn't have any contact with his family until Saturday afternoon. No phones calls, no e-mails, no texting, and certainly not any visits."

"So who visited his room this morning, Santa Claus?"

"Probably a cleaning lady. Crunchie's wrong to think a family member would make contact with Ricky prematurely. They're too smart for that. If you want my advice, you need to stop listening to what old smelly says. He's poison."

"Really. And what does that make you?"

"I know what I'm talking about, and he doesn't. It's as simple as that."

His shirt was halfway unbuttoned, and she placed her finger on his hairless chest and drew an imaginary line down the center as if preparing to do open-heart surgery.

"But what if you're wrong? What if one of their family screwed up and went to Ricky's room? Can you deal with that, Billy?"

"I'm not wrong."

She pulled his shirt open and touched his nipple, making circles around the dimpled flesh with her white-painted fingernail. "You're a cocky little son of a bitch. Let's bet on it."

"What do you want to bet?"

"Let's bet to see who gets to be on top. Sound good to you?"

She pinched his nipple and gave it a twist. It was easy to imagine having sex with her—no foreplay or soft romantic music to get them in the mood, just hitting the box springs with the force of two overheated Greco-Roman wrestlers. He supposed he'd have a better chance of surviving if he started on top.

"I'm game," he said.

"Let's check out Ricky's room and see who's right. Where are those two clowns that are guarding you?" She went to the punishers' bedroom and banged on the door. "Hey, you dumb slobs, get moving." No answer, so she opened the door. "Oh, my. Isn't that cute."

Billy glanced over her shoulder into the room. A naked Ike and T-Bird were spooning on the bed. No wonder they argued so much. They were married.

"Get up," she said.

T-Bird appeared in the doorway holding a sheet around his waist. In celebration of their deal, they'd polished off the bottle of Hennessy, and T-Bird looked wildly hungover.

"Wass up?" the bird man asked.

"Brush your teeth and throw some clothes on, and tell your lazy partner to do the same."

"Which lazy partner is that?" he said, screwing with her.

"Don't get smart with me, or I'll have Marcus fire you."

"I thought we were buds."

She poked him in the gut. "Get moving, before I get mad."

"Don't do that. Nobody likes you mad."

"Stop talking back to me, asshole."

T-Bird laughed to himself. He was going to be a rich man soon, and it had filled his head with grand plans. He went back into the bedroom without another word.

- - -

To reach Ricky Boswell's room, they rode an elevator downstairs, crossed the hotel lobby, and boarded a second elevator, which ascended to the nineteenth floor of Tower B, home to the hotel's lesser-priced accommodations, its rooms facing a hideous unpainted garage. Billy stood in the corner so that he faced Crunchie. In the fashion of old-time gunslingers, they'd put each other on notice; now it was simply a matter of time before one called the other out.

He was not looking forward to their showdown. Fighting was for people not clever enough to anticipate the future. That was how he saw it, anyway. Still, there were times when the person standing before you was going to destroy your life, and you had no choice but to act out of self-preservation. The doors opened and they marched down a hallway littered with room service trays. Shaz was reading door numbers. She stopped and held out her hand.

"Give me the key."

Crunchie produced a plastic room key. She shoved the key into the lock and waited for the green light to come on. Billy glanced at the hallway's end where the emergency exit was located. The door was ajar, and he counted to himself. One potato, two potato, three potato. A pair of security guards emerged with guns drawn and came hustling toward them.

"Put your guns away," Shaz said.

The guards obeyed and holstered their weapons.

"Sorry, Miss Shazam. No one said you were coming up," one of the guards said.

"Don't let it happen again," she said.

The guards returned to their post, and Shaz led the others into Ricky's room. Billy came in last, his eyes doing a sweep. The room had as much personality as a pod, which was what a hundred and fifty bucks a night scored you on the Strip. Square-shaped, with a double bed, a desk that would never be used attached to the wall, a cheap dresser, and the prerequisite wall TV showing the house station, the modern equivalent of Chinese water torture.

"All right, so what are we looking for?" she asked.

"I'll know it when I find it," Crunchie replied.

"So find it."

The old grifter began pulling open the dresser drawers. Finding nothing, he searched the closet, which contained two dress shirts and two pairs of slacks hanging on the bar, along with a dark suit in a plastic dry-cleaning bag.

"There's nothing here," she said.

"Somebody came into this room. The door clicker wouldn't lie. Let me look around some more. I'm sure I can figure it out."

"Spend all fucking day. It's not like I have anything to do."

Crunchie was desperate now. Entering the bathroom, he tore apart Ricky's toilet kit, as if within the razors and lotions was hidden the secret to the Gypsy's scam. He emerged with his eyes downcast, mumbling to himself like a dispirited old geezer at the mall.

"Are you done?" she asked.

"There's a reason someone came into this room this morning. I just can't find it."

"Marcus is going to love it when I tell him what a fuckup you are," she said. "You had him convinced the Gypsies were about to get caught. Nice going."

She left in a huff, brushing Billy's sleeve the way strippers in clubs did to get your attention.

"You win, lover boy," she said under her breath.

Crunchie followed, his shoulders sagging. Billy waited until he heard the door click shut before addressing the punishers.

"Who came into the room this morning?" he asked.

The dull look of their hangovers had blunted their faces.

"Wasn't me," Ike said.

"Me, neither," T-Bird chorused.

"It was a hotel employee. The evidence was right in front of Crunchie's face, and he missed it. Did either of you see it?"

Both men shook their heads.

From the closet he removed the dry-cleaned suit in the plastic bag that the hotel concierge had delivered to the room, and shoved it in their faces. "It was the concierge. You want to run with me, you need to be on your toes. Got it?"

"Yeah, boss," Ike said.

"No more getting smashed or trash-talking."

"Got it," Ike said.

"Right," T-Bird chorused.

"Your life is going to become one big party after Saturday. Until then, you need to act like soldiers and walk the straight and narrow line. You with me?"

"Right," they both said.

Billy was glad to have that out of the way. He hung the suit back up in the closet and realized the garment was bothering him. It was the only piece of formal clothing that Ricky had brought with him. For Ricky to have it cleaned by the hotel meant he planned to wear it while he was in Vegas; otherwise, he would have had it dry-cleaned when he returned home.

Billy tore away the plastic for a closer look. Single breasted with a notch lapel, dual vents, and handpick stitch on the borders. The label said "Extrema by Zanetti," a decent line. The suit was too stiff looking for the casino, and not something you'd wear to a club. Outside of the casinos and clubs, there weren't any other things to do that required getting dressed up.

Three pairs of shoes lay on the closet floor: Nike running shoes, casual loafers, and black patent-leather shoes that looked new. He picked up the patent-leather pair and held them next to the suit. They went together.

He took another look at the shirts hanging in the closet and found a light blue dress shirt with herringbone stripes and French cuffs tucked away in the back. He pulled it out and placed it next to the suit. They also went together.

He laid the suit and shirt on the bed, placed the shoes beside them, and rifled the dresser drawers that Crunchie had searched. He discovered a pair of gold cuff links in a box, and a silk navy necktie. Innocent items, unless you knew what they were for. The cuff link box also contained a ticket to a mixed-martial-arts contest taking place at the Mandalay Bay on Saturday afternoon, the first contest starting at 1:00 p.m.

It all added up. He knew how Ricky had planned to spend Saturday afternoon, and he also knew the Gypsies' cover for scamming Galaxy's casino, all because he'd spotted a dry-cleaning bag in the closet. He turned around holding the objects in his hands.

"What you got?" Ike asked.

Billy handed him the cuff links and tie, while keeping the ticket. Ike examined the items, then studied the clothes lying on the bed.

"Looks like somebody's going to a wedding," Ike said.

"You're a star," Billy said.

THIRTY-THREE

"Ricky Boswell's family is staying in the hotel as part of a wedding party," Billy said. "That's their cover."

"Was Ricky supposed to be part of the wedding?" Ike asked. "If he was, they're gonna notice he's not here, being that he's dead and all."

"No, they won't. Ricky's job was to scope out the casino. Right before you grabbed him, Ricky sent a message to his family, telling them everything was George. After that, he wouldn't connect with his family until the scam was finished. That's how crews operate. Each member only shows up when necessary, and contact is limited."

Ike nodded, getting most of it. "Sorta like that movie *Reservoir Dogs*, the gang members having aliases and all, not talking to each other before the heist."

"You got it."

"Who's George?" T-Bird asked.

"George is an expression that means everything's cool. If I say everything's George, it means the scam's good to go. If I tell you everything's Tom, it means the scam is off."

"Who's Tom?" T-Bird said, now really confused.

"There ain't no Tom," Ike said. "It's a made-up expression that means the shit is gonna hit the fan. Even I know that."

T-Bird was getting pissed. Rather than face off with Ike, he took his frustration out on Billy. "Just speak English, okay? I'm in no mood to learn a second language."

"Sure. So where was I? Oh yeah, Saturday afternoon. So here's how it's going to happen. The Boswells are part of a wedding party. They go to the wedding in the afternoon, and then at four o'clock as the shift change is taking place, they hit the casino. They use the commotion inside the casino as their shade, and pull their scam."

"But why won't they miss Ricky?" Ike said. "If he don't show, they're gonna know."

"No, they won't."

"Why not?"

"Ricky was planning to see mixed martial arts at the Mandalay Bay Saturday afternoon. When the fights were over, he was going to come back here, throw on his duds, and go downstairs to meet up with his family as they hit the casino."

"Why would he wait?" Ike interrupted. "Why wouldn't Ricky go to the wedding in the afternoon along with the rest of his family?"

"A casino employee might remember seeing Ricky snooping around the casino earlier in the week and get suspicious. That would bring heat. Better for Ricky to appear as the family hits the casino. He'll blend in easier."

"You still haven't answered my question," Ike said. "Ricky ain't showing up Saturday afternoon. His family's gonna notice."

"Of course they'll notice, but that won't stop them. Ripping off casinos is the family business. There are bills to pay and mouths to feed. They won't shut the operation down because Ricky pulls a no-show at the last minute. Trust me, I know."

"Man, that's cold," Ike said.

A cheater's first job was not to get caught. Ricky had slipped up and had paid for his mistake with his young life. The family would eventually realize what had happened to him, and they would mourn his passing, but that wouldn't stop them from scamming casinos. If anything, losing a member would only strengthen their resolve.

"How you going to know which wedding these people are a part of?" Ike asked. "Aren't there a bunch in the hotel?"

"According to the welcome board in the lobby, there are nine weddings in the hotel on Saturday. It shouldn't be hard to figure out which one they're a part of."

"Why's that?"

"The Boswells are Gypsies, and Gypsies have strange habits. They're nuts about cleanliness, always washing their hands, clothes are always spotless. They're obsessive-compulsive—it's in their genes. I'll figure out who they are, no problem."

Billy was sick of talking. He'd only allowed Ike and T-Bird to question him because he didn't want them getting cold feet Saturday. So he put up with their bullshit. But it was tiring.

Ike said, "So how do we fit into all this?"

Billy had told Ike last night what their role was, and he guessed the booze had erased the memory. "While the Boswells are pulling their scam, I'll blow the whistle, and security will bust them. While security is hauling them away, you guys will rip off the cage with the counterfeit chips. By the time Doucette realizes he's been robbed, you'll be wasting away in Margaritaville."

"That don't sound so hard," Ike said.

"It isn't. The hard part comes now," Billy said.

"What you mean?"

"This stuff isn't going to happen by magic. I have to go see my guy so he can counterfeit the chips. I also need to figure out who the Boswells are. And, I need to keep Doucette and his crazy wife in the dark so they don't get a wild hair and decide to kill me."

"How you gonna do all that and not get caught?"

"Simple. You two are going to cover for me."

"We are?"

"That's right. You don't work for Doucette anymore, you work for me, and that means you're going to cover my ass so I can set this thing up. Dig it?"

"But what if Shaz calls us on the cell phone, and wants to speak to you, and we say you ain't here, and she goes psycho on us? What do we do then?"

"Make up a story. Tell her that I discovered the Boswells are part of a wedding party, and that I'm running around the hotel trying to figure out which wedding it is. That will get her excited. Then call me. I'll call her back and string her along some more."

"You think she'll fall for that bullshit?"

"She will if you say it right. It's all about the delivery, and the conviction in your voice."

"Sounds risky, you ask me."

Every job he'd ever pulled was risky; without the risk, there was no reward. He poked the larger man in the chest so hard that it made Ike's eyes bulge. Ike wasn't used to someone half his size pushing him around, and it showed.

"It's called the big time. The question is, are you guys ready to play?"

"I'm ready," Ike said.

"Me, too," T-Bird said.

"Good. I need two things from you. First go downstairs, and buy a few thousand in chips from the cage, and put them in my gym bag. My guy is going to need them so he can set the molds correctly. Then get your car, and bring it around so I can get out of here."

"You want to use our car?" Ike asked.

"If I drive my own car out of here, I might get spotted. Better to take yours."

"Well, all right. Our ride's a refurbished '68 Camaro. Just go easy on the gas. There's a tiger under the hood."

"I'll remember that. Use the money you took from my safe to buy the chips from the cage. My guy will want to see lots of them. He claims that it makes counterfeiting easier."

"I thought that was our money," T-Bird objected.

"It's *our* money, and we need it to pull this thing off. By the way, I took my jewelry out of the gym bag and hid it. That wasn't part of our deal."

"That Rolex with the diamonds was *mine*," T-Bird said, clearly upset. "It went perfect with my Super Bowl ring."

"You can buy yourself a watch with your share of the haul. Now give me your cell phone numbers so I can get a hold of you."

The punishers gave him their cell numbers, which he entered into his Droid's memory bank. Two nights ago, as he was getting the crap beat out of him, he'd promised himself he'd pay Ike and T-Bird back. Revenge was sweet, especially when the other guys didn't see it coming.

"Our car's parked in the employee garage," Ike said. "We'll bring it around to the rear exit. It's usually pretty quiet this time of day."

"I'll be waiting," Billy said.

THIRTY-FOUR

He drove to Gabe's place in the punishers' vintage '68 Camaro. Vegas was the pits during the day, and he kept his eyes on the road. Without a million watts of neon to light the place up, it was just another tourist town, the sandblasted hotels showing every dimple and crack.

The Nike gym bag sat on the passenger seat. As instructed, T-Bird had visited the cage and purchased several thousand dollars of chips, from lowly five-dollar red chips to coveted five-hundred-dollar purple chips. Gabe would need these to make his knock-offs. Not just to duplicate the look and color, but also the feel and weight, which varied from casino to casino.

The Strip ended and the highway turned straight and uninteresting. Gabe's subdivision was dead ahead, with its manicured lawns and indistinguishable track houses, where nothing exciting ever went on. He couldn't imagine living in these surroundings. Not in a thousand years.

A parade of cars was parked in front of Gabe's house: Misty's Mercedes, Pepper's Beamer, Cory and Morris's Infiniti, and Travis's Windstar. His crew was having a meeting, and he hadn't been invited. He didn't have a problem if his crew got together socially, but the fact that Travis was present—Travis who never left home except for work—told Billy this wasn't a book club meeting. They were talking business without the boss.

He parked and cut the engine. He needed to handle this in steps. Step one: find out who the ringleader was and toss his sorry ass on the street. Step two: sit down with the others and read the riot act to them. He didn't need them, but they sure as hell needed him.

He stared at the house while working up the courage to confront them. The sheers in the front window fluttered, and a man's face materialized behind the glass. Suntanned, big jawed.

Travis.

He punched the steering wheel. Travis had been challenging him lately, and he'd passed it off to the fact that Travis had gotten married and now answered to a higher authority. *Wrong*. Travis was trying to take over and had called everyone to Gabe's house while Billy was dealing with the mess at Galaxy. The big man had betrayed him.

He shouldn't have been as upset as he was. Part of running a crew was dealing with problems: members got sick, divorced, thrown in jail, all the usual fun stuff. There wasn't anything he couldn't handle except having a knife stuck in his back.

The face in the window disappeared. He could remember recruiting Travis as if it were yesterday. Travis had been drowning in debt, with a house in foreclosure and a car about to be repossessed. Within six months of joining his crew, Travis had been back on his feet, the wolves no longer at his door. *And this is how the bastard repays me.*

He got out and unlocked the Camaro's trunk. Pulling up a piece of carpet that covered the spare, he grabbed a tire iron. It felt nice and firm in his hand.

His heart was pounding as he banged on Gabe's front door. To his surprise, no one answered. "Come on, you chickenshits, open up."

Nothing. In a rage, he called Gabe's number on his cell phone and got voice mail. "It's me. I'm standing outside your front door. Let me in, goddamn it."

When Gabe didn't call him back, he hopped off the stoop and pressed his face to the front window, straining to see inside the furniture-less house. His view went straight to the family room in the rear. A group of people was moving through a slider onto the lanai, trying to escape. Bad thoughts raced through his head. Had his crew taken a vote and decided to dump him? *Fuckers.*

He marched around the side of the house, clutching the tire iron. A little voice was telling him to turn around, nothing would be accomplished by violence. A bigger voice was saying go ahead, break some bones, you stuck your neck out for these people, made them lots of money, and this is how they thank you, the dirty rat bastards.

Coming around the house, he hit the brakes. His crew was on the lawn, trying to scale the picket fence in the back of Gabe's property. Misty and Pepper had on the skintight exercise outfits that they wore for Pilates, while Cory and Morris appeared to have just rolled out of bed, their boyish faces unshaven, hair uncombed. Gabe was a different story: beat up, face bloodied, his right leg hurting. Travis had a gun and was saying, "Hurry, we've got to get out of here."

A hard object dropped in the pit of his stomach. He'd read the whole situation wrong. Something else was going on here; his crew hadn't finked on him. Ashamed at his miscalculation, he tossed the tire iron into the bushes.

"Hey, guys, what's up?" he called out.

Travis spun around and took aim. Billy's bowels loosened, and he raised his arms into the air.

"Don't shoot."

"Billy—Jesus Christ, is that you?" Travis asked.

"No, it's his evil twin brother. Stop aiming that gun at me, will you?"

The others had assembled behind Travis. The big man lowered his weapon and pointed it at the ground. "Was that you in the pimp mobile out front?"

"Yeah, that was me."

"You scared the shit out of us. Some guys are after Gabe. We thought it was them."

"Tony G's boys?"

"Yeah. He's into them real deep."

He saw it clearly now, most of it, anyway. Tony G had sent his enforcers to put the heavy on Gabe. Hurt and bleeding, Gabe had called the crew, being they were the only friends he had, and the crew had dropped what they were doing and come to Gabe's rescue, because that was what friends did. Billy had been left out because his crew knew he was at Galaxy, dealing with his own problems. No one had betrayed him. It was all good.

"I can fix that," he said.

- - -

They went inside to the living room to talk things out. Except for an old-fashioned La-Z-Boy recliner that populated the room's center, the space was bare. Folding chairs and stools were brought from the kitchen so that everyone could get comfortable.

Gabe dropped his pummeled body into the La-Z-Boy and gazed at the ceiling, horrified that it had come to this. Billy was late to the party and started by asking Gabe a question that the rest of them already knew the answer to.

"How much are you into Tony G for?" he asked.

"Does it matter?" Gabe said, the shame bunching up his face.

"I can fix this, but you've got to be straight with me."

"You can't fix this, Billy. I fucked up, and now I've got to blow out of here. I'll go to another state, and get a job in a mall fixing watches. I'll get by."

"No, you won't. Tony G has got a flag in every state," Billy said.

"A what?"

"Tony G's got mob enforcers he can call in every state. They'll hunt you down, and pump a bullet into your head, and send Tony G photos of your corpse. You can run, but you can't hide. Now, how much do you owe this guy?"

"Three hundred big ones."

"You've got to be kidding me."

"It's the truth. That's why I've got to run. I don't have another choice."

"You're not going anywhere."

"I'm not?"

"No, I need you for a job. Now shut up, and let me think about this."

The living room went quiet. Billy kept a stash of cash buried in the desert for emergencies, but it wasn't enough to cover Gabe's debt to Tony G. Had the amount been smaller, Tony G might have been willing to take a down payment, with the rest coming later. But the amount was huge, and Tony G's reputation was at stake. If the bookie didn't collect, every gambler in town who owed him money would renege on their obligations.

The seconds dragged on. Misty got behind Billy's chair and began to massage the knotted muscles in his shoulders.

"You're all tense. Relax," she said.

He tried. The tightrope he was walking was getting harder by the step. The safety net was gone, and the pole he used for balance had fallen out of his hands. If Gabe left town, Billy couldn't scam Galaxy, and the biggest payday of his career would go down the toilet.

Cory and Morris were checking e-mails on their cell phones. It had to be the worst habit in the world next to picking your nose. Billy remembered they had a scam going at a racetrack in Santa Anita, and he guessed this was how the agent at the track was communicating with them.

"Is that horse-racing scam still alive?" he asked.

"We were about to shut it down, like you told us," Cory said.

"What would you say if we used it to clean the slate with Tony G?"

Cory glanced at Morris. The horse race scam was their baby, and Billy did not own the rights to it. Cory and Morris could say no, except they were in this for the long haul, and Billy was their ticket to the big time.

"I'm okay with that," Cory said.

"Me, too," Morris said.

"Cool. Lay it on me," he said.

"A horse trainer named Sal Lopez is fixing races at Santa Anita," Cory said. "Sal's a smart operator. He only fixes one race a day, and sends us the name of the horse a few minutes before post time. That way, we can get our bets down right before the race starts, and the other gamblers following the race can't react when they see the odds change."

"What's Sal's cut?"

"Half."

"What kind of odds are you getting?"

"It varies. Yesterday, the ringer ran at twenty-to-one."

"How does it work?"

"Sal's got a stable of Brazilian horses he keeps nearby that are ringers. He dyes the ringers so they're identical to the horses at the track's stables, and switches them at night. The only problem is if it rains. Then the dye runs off, and the ringer changes color during the race."

"I'd like to see that," Misty said, still massaging Billy's back.

"It must be the dry season in Southern California," he said.

"Sal just sent us an e-mail saying the scam was on for today. It's going to happen during the twelfth race at four twenty-five," Cory said. "It's yours if you want it, Billy."

Billy played with it. He'd once scammed a bookie in Providence with a fixed boxing match, but that was Providence. Vegas bookies were smarter than that. They knew the angles and took precautions to protect themselves. That didn't mean Tony G couldn't be fleeced; it just meant that it was going to take a certain level of sophistication to make it work. But before Billy set the wheels in motion, he wanted to be sure that Cory and Morris would not harbor any hard feelings.

"Are you guys sure about this?" he asked. "I'm planning to take Tony G for the full amount Gabe owes him. Tony G might realize the race was fixed, and make some phone calls. Sal could get some heat down the road."

"That's Sal's problem," Cory said. "We work for you, Billy."

"Yeah, we work for you," Morris said.

Billy turned his attention to Gabe. "How do I get in front of this guy?"

"Tony G plays golf every day on the Bali Hai course. That's where he does most of his business," Gabe said. "I know the pro at Bali Hai. I'll call him, and set it up."

"You're saying Tony G take bets while he plays."

"His cell phone never stops ringing. It's annoying as hell."

"Do it." Billy rose from his folding chair. He needed to get back to Galaxy and put in some face time. Gabe was looking at him, as were the others, all put out.

"Something the matter?" he asked.

"You said you needed me for a job," Gabe said. "You going to tell me what it is?"

In all the excitement, Billy had forgotten why he'd come to Gabe's home in the first place.

"Hold that thought," he said.

Going outside, he retrieved the Nike bag from the Camaro, came back in, and dropped it on Gabe's lap. Gabe unzippered the bag and had a look.

"You want me to counterfeit these, is that the deal?" the jeweler asked.

"No, I want you to counterfeit this." He took the souvenir key chain from his pocket and showed Gabe the rubber gold chip. "Use the chips in the bag to get the weight and texture, and this for the color. I need eighty of them. They're worth a hundred grand apiece."

"How am I going to match the color? There are a thousand different shades of gold."

From his wallet Billy extracted the AAA Novelty & Gift business card he'd gotten from the cashier in the hotel gift shop. "The company that makes them is local. Go see them, and tell them you need a paint match for a job you're doing for the hotel."

Gabe stared at the card. "Shit, I know these guys. Getting the paint won't be a problem. When did you say you need these by?"

"Tomorrow afternoon."

"Well, that's a problem. This isn't something you can rush."

"I know that. But if anyone can make it happen, it's you."

Gabe was a perfectionist; every job he tackled was handled with the utmost thoughtfulness and care. From the open Nike bag he removed a stack of colored chips and let them fall into his other hand, nice and flat and downward. They fell with a uniform correctness, landing on top of each other with a cushion of air that broke their fall due to their perfect construction. Under his breath Gabe said, "Eleven grams, blended plastic, silver inserts." He climbed out of the recliner still hurting from the beating he'd taken, and stood next to Billy.

"Eighty gold chips it is," the jeweler said.

"You're the man. Later, everyone."

Billy headed for the front door. Travis was right behind him, and in a breathless voice said, "Are we stealing eight million bucks from Galaxy tomorrow?"

"That's right. I'll call you later with the details."

"Billy, wait!" Misty called after him.

His crew had come out of their chairs, their faces filled with hopeful expressions.

"What about us?" Misty asked. "Are we part of this deal?"

"Of course you're part of it. All for one, and one for all, and everyone gets their usual cut. I'll fill you in later, and explain what your roles are. Now let me go. I've got work to do."

He jogged across the lawn and climbed into the oven-hot Camaro, the flesh on his back burning up as it touched the driver seat. His Droid lay on the passenger seat, and he picked it up to stare at its face. He hadn't gotten any distress phone calls from Ike or T-Bird. No news was good news, and he fired up the ignition and made the engine roar.

This was going to work. The pieces were falling into place, the stars aligning in his favor. By tomorrow night, he and his crew would be rolling in dough, while Marcus Doucette and his murderous wife would be scratching their asses, wondering where the hell their money was.

He pulled onto the street. His crew had come outside to stand on the front lawn. They began waving to him. They looked so damn happy that he welled up with emotion. He hadn't had much of a family life growing up—his mother in prison for stabbing a man to death with a pair of scissors, his father having to cheat at cards to make ends meet—and he'd always wondered what it would have been like to have a gang of brothers and sisters to hang out with. He guessed this was the next best thing, and he waved as he burned past.

"We love you, Billy!" Misty shouted.

THIRTY-FIVE

Mags stood outside her town house, cooling her jets. Frank had said noon, and it was now twelve fifteen. He could have called, but that would have been the polite thing to do.

The desert air was heating up, the air scorching hot. Sometimes, she toyed with the idea of skipping town and starting her life over in another city, but deep down, she knew that wasn't going to happen. Her contract with the gaming board was ironclad. In it, she'd admitted to her crimes and had agreed to work off her punishment by becoming a paid informant. If she ran away, she'd become a wanted felon, and the police would run her down at warp speed. Hanging on her kitchen wall was a calendar that she used to count off the days. In eleven months and twenty-six days she'd become a free woman. If she only lasted that long.

Twelve twenty came and went. Murphy's Law said light up a cigarette when you want something to happen, so she fired up a Kool and took a few puffs. Sure enough, Frank pulled into her drive and his window came down.

"Get in, and get rid of that butt," he said.

She ground out her cigarette and hopped in. Frank had cleaned up. His unruly hair had gel in it, and he was wearing a pretty blue necktie. A box of candy appeared on her lap.

"I'm sorry about last night," he said.

She undid the bow and popped the lid. Chocolate-covered strawberries. Considering he'd smacked her in the face, she'd been expecting a piece of jewelry. The candy made her feel cheap, and she placed it on the floor between her feet.

They drove in silence. The relationship was starting to feel like a bad marriage. Sleeping with Frank had been a good idea at the beginning of their arrangement. It had let her exert control over him and had given her the upper hand. Now that control was gone, and she felt apprehensive when they were together, never knowing what he might do.

Soon they were driving past a wasteland of strip malls on South Decatur. Frank pulled up in front of a breakfast joint called Mr. Mamas and parked.

"Sit in the back. I'll be in after I make this call," he said.

"You want something?" she asked, trying to act nice, when all she wanted to do was hurt him.

"Get me some coffee and a breakfast burrito," he said. Any mention of food always perked him up. "Order yourself something as well; just don't go overboard."

She went in. The restaurant had black linoleum tables, a counter with stools, and tables filled with Mexican workers eating chicken-fried steak smothered in gravy. She took a table in back where a printed menu sat on the table. She decided on a Greek omelet and ordered from a waitress who gave her a sympathetic look. She glanced in the mirror behind the table and saw the puffiness around her jaw. It made her want to hurt Frank that much more.

Coffee came, and she sucked it down. How was she going to pay Frank back for last night without fucking up her already fucked-up situation? She didn't know. All she knew was that when the opportunity presented itself, she was going to stick the knife in.

Outside, a black sedan pulled up. A thickset man wearing a dark suit climbed out, said good morning, but didn't shake Frank's hand. The man's face was a blunt instrument. His eyebrows were connected, his forehead sloped. This had to be Frank's ill-tempered boss Trixie, who'd denied Frank a promotion after Billy had pulled the wool over the gaming board's eyes at the Hard Rock. They spoke for a minute before coming inside and sitting down.

"This is my boss, Special Agent Bill Tricaricco," Frank said. "Bill, this is Maggie Flynn, the paid informant I've been working with for the past year."

"I've heard a lot about you," Trixie said.

"I'm sure it was all lies," she said.

Their food came. It smelled delicious, and she blew on a mouthful of omelet before taking a bite. Frank's breakfast burrito also looked good, although Frank didn't touch it. The waitress asked Trixie if he cared to see a menu. He grunted no and told the waitress they wanted some privacy. He placed his wallet on the table so his gold badge was showing. The waitress shot Mags another sympathetic look before walking away.

"Sure you don't want a bone to gnaw on?" Mags asked.

"Don't get cute on me, little lady," Trixie said. "I can make your life miserable in more ways than you can imagine."

"More miserable than Frank has? That would take a lot."

Frank leaned in. "Bill has a deal for you. Listen to what he has to say."

"A deal? As in, *Let's Make a Deal*? Oh boy, I can't wait."

"Just shut up, and hear Bill out."

She liberally sprinkled salt on her eggs and resumed eating. A broomstick was about to get rammed straight up her ass, and there wasn't a damn thing she could do about it. The knuckle-scraper sitting across from her cleared his throat.

"You have eleven months left on your contract with the gaming board," Trixie said. "What would you say if we tore your contract up?"

"Who do I have to sleep with?" she asked.

"No one. Frank tells me that you ran into Billy Cunningham at Galaxy's casino last night, and that Billy is doing a job for Marcus Doucette. Is that true?"

"Yeah, that's right."

"Frank also said that you two know each other from the old neighborhood."

She rested her fork on her plate. With cold eyes she gazed at Frank, then at his boss. "If you're asking me to do something that will hurt Billy, the answer is no."

"Billy's a menace," Trixie said. "He and his crew have ripped off every casino in town, many of them multiple times, and we've never been able to put him away. Now we can, and you're going to help us."

"Take the potatoes out of your ears. I said no."

"No is not an option. If you don't play along, I'm going to take you downtown and throw your pretty ass in jail, and no smart-talking lawyer in town will be able to get you out. I've got the goods on you, Maggie. Take a look if you don't believe me."

Trixie parted his suit jacket and removed a folded sheet of paper. He smoothed out the creases before placing it on the table in front of her. On the page were five cancelled checks captured on a color Xerox machine. Each check was from a wealthy widow who'd made the mistake of playing a friendly game of gin rummy with Mags poolside at one of the Strip's fancy hotels, fifty cents a point. The amounts on the widows' checks ranged between $2,500 and $4,000, payable to Maggie Flynn.

Fuck, fuck, fuck, she thought.

"These checks are from five wealthy dowagers who recently visited Las Vegas," Trixie said. "You cheated these women at gin rummy, and stole their money. That's shameful."

"Those checks don't prove a thing," she said, unwilling to go down without a fight. "You're drinking your own bathwater, Trixie."

"Who told you my name was Trixie?"

"A little bird."

"I'm afraid you're wrong. One of your victims, Mrs. Goldie Hill of Pembroke Pines, Florida, filed a complaint with the Vegas police, who passed the case to the gaming board. I handled the investigation because I knew you were on our payroll. I called Mrs. Hill, and she told me how she'd written you a personal check to cover her losses, and that you got all teary eyed and said you didn't want her money. You tore up the check and burned it in an ashtray. End of story, or so Mrs. Hill thought. When she returned home, a bank statement was waiting for her, saying the money was gone from her account. Admit it, you ripped Mrs. Hill off."

The walls of the restaurant were starting to close in, the air difficult to breathe. Mags shifted uncomfortably in her chair, feeling trapped.

"I contacted your bank to see if there were more victims," Trixie said. "They provided me with four more cancelled checks. I called the women whose names were on the checks, and got the same story. A pretty Irish lass cleaned them out at gin rummy by the pool, took a personal check, then had a fit of conscience and tore it up. When they got home, the money was withdrawn from their bank accounts."

"That still doesn't prove I cheated them," she said.

"You're not going to play ball with me, are you?"

"Not if it means hurting Billy."

"Have it your way. Give me your purse."

"No."

"Give it to me, before this gets ugly."

"Do it," Frank said.

Mag's satchel purse hung off the back of her chair. She tossed it to the gaming agent and the bag struck him in the face. Trixie reached for his belt as if to grab his handcuffs, then thought better of it. He poured her purse's contents onto the table and sifted through the lipsticks, birth control pills, and other personal items as if prospecting for gold. The waitress hovered by the counter, watching with the same morbid fascination that drew motorists to car wrecks.

Trixie hummed to himself while picking through her things. Stripping Mags of her dignity was the kind of dehumanizing activity that made his day. Frank, on the other hand, was not having any fun at all and sadly shook his head.

I'll get both of you back, Mags promised herself, if it's the last thing I do.

Trixie checked her wallet last. It was made of faux leather and matched her purse. He pulled it apart, tossing her money and credit cards onto the pile. Inside a hidden compartment he found a stash of folded checks, which he held triumphantly in the air.

"These blank checks are my proof," Trixie said. "When your victim is writing you a check, you dive into your wallet, find a check that matches the color, and hide it in your hand. The victim gives you the check, and you go into your act and pretend to tear up the check. But you don't—you rip up the blank and burn it, destroying the evidence. That's the scam, isn't it?"

Mags was beaten. The scam was called the Tear Up and had been devised by card cheats to be used on long railroad trips, the idea being that the sucker would forget about the loss once the check was destroyed. It was one of the first scams that Lou Profaci had taught her.

"Now, are you going to play ball, or do I run you in?" he asked.

The moment of truth had arrived. Long ago, she'd decided that she was willing to do just about anything to stay out of prison. She took a deep breath before replying.

"What do you want me to do?" she asked.

"Tell her," Trixie said.

"We want you to make sure that Cunningham is inside Galaxy's casino on Saturday afternoon," Frank said. "We're going to take Cunningham down along with Doucette."

Her skin for Billy's. Another deep breath.

"All right," she said.

"You're going to have to connect with Billy before the raid," Frank said. "Find out where he's staying inside the casino and tell us. He's a slippery little shit, so we'll need to know."

"If I do that, will you tear up my contract?"

The two gaming agents nodded solemnly, as if those gestures meant anything.

"And this shit with the checks will go away?"

They both nodded again.

"I want it in writing," she said.

"You'll get it." Trixie consulted his watch and rose from the table. "I'm glad we came to this understanding, Mags. I'll let Frank fill you in on the details."

"There's one thing I'm not getting," she said. "How are you going to take Billy down? You don't know what he's doing in there."

"Doesn't matter," Trixie said. "Billy's scum. We'll trump up a charge if we have to. Just make sure he's inside the joint when the raid happens. If you do that, you're home free."

She drew back in her chair. "You're going to frame him? What kind of assholes are you? Just because you can't catch him doesn't give you the right to trump up a charge."

"Keep your voice down," he cautioned her.

"You're pathetic excuses for human beings. Both of you."

"Watch your damn mouth."

"Fuck you."

"We're out of here." Frank threw down money for the food. "Let's go."

Standing, she began tossing her things into her purse, the words spilling out in a mad rush. "Billy comes into your casinos and beats your games in front of your cameras and your so-called security experts, and you're not clever enough to figure out how to stop him. People do that at the racetrack or the stock market, and they call them geniuses and give them their own fucking TV shows. Not you guys. When someone's smarter than you, you frame him. And you wonder why people in this town think gaming agents are shit heads."

"Don't play self-righteous with me, you little cunt," Trixie said. "Cunningham is a plague, and I'm going to do whatever I have to do to put him away. Did you know that he went to MIT on a full scholarship? Kid's a mathematical wizard, could have been the next Steve Jobs or Bill Gates, but no, he decides to quit after a year, and come out here, and start stealing. He could have made a difference in the world, but he chose not to. That makes him a world-class scumbag in my book. And so are you for thinking he's some kind of prince."

She tossed her purse over her shoulder. The difference between cops and criminals was that criminals knew when they were breaking the law, while cops rarely did. Trixie had stepped over to the dark side, just as Frank had stepped over, and there was nothing she could say to either one of them that was going to convince them how wrong it was.

"Whatever you say," she said, and headed for the front door.

THIRTY-SIX

Billy parked the Camaro in the employee garage. It was easy to tell it was the employee garage; half the cars were falling apart. He knew a cheat named Ace who frequented bars where casino employees hung out. Ace would scour the lot to see whose car was in the worst shape, find the owner, and begin the recruitment process.

The elevator was on the blink so he took the stairwell. He had a lot on his plate, all of which needed to get done in the next thirty-six hours. He had to make the Gypsies, get Tony G off Gabe's back, and prepare his crew for an eight-million-dollar takedown. A few hours ago, he might have said forget it, but not now. Being around his crew did that to him. By himself, there was only so much stealing he could do. With his crew, the possibilities were endless.

A blast of cold air greeted him upon entering the casino. Urban legend had it that the casinos pumped oxygen to get customers to gamble more, but it wasn't true. They just kept the joints bone-chilling cold, and the lure of easy money did the rest.

He found Ike and T-Bird inside the sports book, an area reserved for gamblers wanting to bet on sporting events. Both wore new designer threads that signaled a step up in the world. As the scores faded away on the digital screen, their betting stubs were tossed to the floor.

"Know how to make a small fortune inside a casino? Start with a large one."

"Shit, man, we got to gamble," Ike said. "What else is there to do in this town?"

"No gambling while you're doing a job with me. People will get suspicious if you start losing money they don't think you have. Got it?"

They reluctantly nodded agreement.

"Good. Now what's going on?"

"We got everything under control," Ike said, his tone indicating a willingness to impress. "Crunchie had to go see the doctor because his ulcer's bleeding. He called me from the doctor's office, and I told him we were watching you like a hawk. Then we got a call from psycho bitch. She was at the airport picking up a rich oilman flying in from Houston. She says, 'Put that sneaky little bastard on, I want an update,' and I messed with her real good."

"What did you tell her?"

"I said, 'Billy thinks the Gypsies are part of a wedding party. He's inside the chapel, checking out a rehearsal. You want him to call you?' and psycho bitch says, 'Just keep an eye on him,' and hangs up."

"She wasn't suspicious?"

"Nope. Everything's good."

"What time did she call?"

"About a half hour ago."

"I want to know the exact time."

"I told you—about a half hour ago."

"Take out your cell phone and check."

"You think I can't keep track of the fucking time?"

"I'm sure you can keep track of the time. I just think you're wrong."

Ike took out his cell phone and found the incoming call in the memory bank. Casinos were designed to make people lose track of the time—no clocks, no windows, the outside world shut out—and Billy would have bet Ike was wrong, only he didn't want to make an enemy.

"Holy shit, she called an hour ago," Ike said.

An hour was a lot different than a half hour. In an hour, Shaz could meet the oilman at the airport, bring him back to the hotel, and check up on Billy. And if she didn't find Billy at the chapel, she'd know that Ike had lied to her and that his allegiances had shifted.

"Let's get over to the wedding chapel before this thing blows up in our faces," Billy said.

- - -

Just off the hotel lobby, the wedding chapel was far enough away from the casino to make it feel real, a pretty room painted in champagne hues and delicate shades of brown, with cut-glass chandeliers and amethyst glass windows traced in gold leaf. Billy sat down in a pew with the punishers. Up at the altar, a white-haired minister was conducting a rehearsal with two nervous kids who kept peeking at the door, as if expecting an irate parent to appear and call the whole thing off. He guessed that the bride-to-be was underage and that she and her boyfriend had eloped. It was easy to get hitched in Vegas. No waiting period, no blood test, just buy a fifty-dollar certificate, and find a man with a turned collar to read from the black book.

The rehearsal dragged on, with the kids comically stepping on each other's vows. The groom tried slipping a wedding ring on his bride's finger and dropped it on the floor, where it rolled beneath a pew and disappeared. The girl looked ready to brain him.

The rehearsal ended, and the kids walked down the aisle squeezing hands. The minister wiped his brow with a hanky. A door beside the chapel opened, and a new couple appeared for their rehearsal. It was an assembly line. Billy rose from the pew.

"I need to take a look at something. I'll be right back."

He walked around the chapel to the door the couples were coming through and twisted the knob. Crammed into the adjacent room were ten more couples, waiting their turn. Returning to the pew, he asked Ike to call Shaz. As the call went through, he left the chapel with Ike's cell phone pressed to his ear and parked himself on an overstuffed couch in the lobby.

"What do you want?" Shaz said by way of greeting.

"It's me, Billy. I hear you've been looking for me."

"That's right. Did you make the Gypsies yet?"

"I've hit a little snag. According to the welcome board in the lobby, there are nine weddings taking place on Saturday. I'm at the chapel, and I've already seen twelve couples rehearsing. What's the deal?"

"Price points. You have to pay to get your name put on the welcome board."

"So how busy is Saturday?"

"We start at ten a.m. and run them until five. Three weddings an hour, no overlap."

"I believe you just said twenty-one."

"Don't be a wiseass. It isn't healthy."

If he knew one thing for certain, it was that Ike and T-Bird weren't going to lay another hand on him, and he could not help but smile into the phone. "One more question. Do small wedding parties stay in the hotel, or can they just rent the chapel?"

"Anyone who gets married has to stay in the hotel. That's the deal."

He ran his free hand through his hair. The joint was a wedding mill. No doubt the Gypsies had taken this into account when they'd decided to scam the casino. It made it that much easier for them to blend in. The mountain he was climbing had just gotten steeper.

"Who deals with all of these couples?" he asked.

"We have a full-time wedding director, Lucille Gonzalez."

"Can I talk to her?"

"Be my guest. Lucille's office is in the bridal shop; she deals with all of the parties. I'll call her and let her know you're coming. But be careful. Lucille will take one look at you and start spinning her web. You know the kind I'm talking about."

"I'll let you know what I turn up."

"Don't hang up. Why do I think you're fucking with me every time I have a conversation with you? You're scheming away, I just know it."

Billy's cheeks burned. "I'm not fucking with you. Ask Ike if you don't believe me."

"Like that moron would know? I used to strip, remember? I can hear it in a man's voice when he lies. You're lying. If I find out what you're planning, I'm going to take you down. That's a promise, Billy, so help me fucking God."

She was onto him. But would she pull the trigger when the time came? If the snuff film of Ricky Boswell was any indication, she would, and he'd become another notch on her belt.

"Why don't you trust me? I haven't hurt you," he said.

"Give it time," she said.

THIRTY-SEVEN

The bridal shop was a factory. Weddings were big business for the hotel, and a staff of dress fitters and wedding planners scurried about the spacious room, altering the gowns of the frantic brides-to-be and their doting mothers. The brides were bitchy and tearful and tossed verbal bombs at their mothers or anyone else in range.

The girl at the front desk was on happy pills, immune to the carnage around her. She called into the back for Lucille. Hanging up, she pointed at a door that led to the fitting rooms. "Last door on the left. Don't bother to knock—Lucille's expecting you."

Billy checked out the fitting rooms while walking to Lucille's office. They were equally tense, the brides frowning at their reflections, the beautiful gowns they were wearing somehow just not right. Maybe that was the key to finding the Gypsies. Find the bride that wasn't a nervous wreck, and she'd probably be part of the Boswell clan.

The door to Lucille's office was ajar. A sunny Hispanic woman showing head-snapping cleavage sat at a desk, talking on a landline. Her sensuous brown eyes locked on him, then dropped to his hand to see if he wore a wedding ring.

"I'll call you back." She nestled the receiver into its cradle. Rising from her swivel chair, she slowly grew as she stepped into her heels. "You must be Billy."

"I hope I'm not disturbing you."

"Never." She came around the desk with a little swing to her hips. High cheekbones, small mouth glossed pink, azure-shadowed blue eyes. A nice package.

"Shaz said you were a consultant the casino had hired to sniff out a crook, and that I might be able to help you," she said. "Wait—I've seen you on TV. The Discovery Channel, right? They did a show about casino scams, and you were on it, being interviewed."

"Wrong," he said. "It was actually A&E."

"Hah! Shaz said you were the devil. Have a seat, make yourself comfortable."

He took a chair. Lucille sat on the edge of the desk and let her feet dangle playfully in the air. She was a live wire, that was for sure. She offered him a cigarette, which he declined. She lit up and inhaled pleasurably. Multiple lines on the desk phone were blinking frantically, and she paid no attention to them. He dug that. She had focus.

"I'm looking for a family of crooks that are staying in your hotel posing as a wedding party," he explained. "I'm guessing you might be able to help me figure out who they are."

She brought her hand dramatically to her chest. "You want me to help you catch these people? How exciting. What do you want me to do?"

"I need you to think back over the past week. Have you seen any brides that weren't crying or picking fights with their mothers? That seems to be the norm, from what I've seen."

Lucille went into thought mode, her face a study in concentration. "Sorry," she said.

"Have they all had meltdowns?"

"Good expression," she said, the cigarette's ash glowing. "Yes, they all have. It's part of the marriage process. The anticipation is too much, and they blow their stacks."

"And you rescue them."

"I most certainly do. That's why they pay me the big bucks." Her laugh sent a stream of blue smoke over Billy's head. "I'm not helping, am I?"

"You're doing great. Do you dance?"

"All the time. How'd you know?"

"Lucky guess. Which clubs?"

"I used to go to the Bank, but it got tired after a while, same DJs every week. Now I hang out at the Tryst. The DJs change every night and it's much fresher. Fridays are the best, but not until after midnight. I bet you're fun on the dance floor."

"I've got some moves. Let's get back to business. Have any of the brides acted strangely, or done something to give you a funny feeling about them?"

"You mean in my gut? Not that I can remember."

"How about their mothers?"

Lucille's eyes sparked as she ground her cigarette into an ashtray on the desk. He had hit a nerve, and he waited expectantly for her to continue.

"The mothers are a pain in the bitch, if you'll pardon my language," she said. "A few days ago, a bride was getting her gown altered, and I'm there with her mother, making sure it looks right. The mother says she paid twenty grand for the gown from a bridal shop. I took one look and knew the gown was a knockoff. Bridal shops sell fake wedding gowns made of synthetic fiber. The shops mark up the price ten times, pocket the difference. It's a big scam."

It sounded like the fake-sweater scam, only on steroids. He didn't have a problem selling knockoffs—bridal gowns got worn once and got stuck in mothballs—and he wondered if Lucille might be amenable to starting up a business on the side, with him fronting her.

"How many gowns do you sell from your shop?" he asked.

"Don't go getting any ideas," she said.

She was a square. He smiled pleasantly, as if making a joke.

"Tell me about the mother," he said.

"I had to tell the woman the truth. Her poor daughter's about to go down the aisle in a dress that was probably made in China, for Christ's sake. So I took her aside and said, 'I hate to tell you this, but your daughter's gown is a knockoff. When you get home, go to the bridal shop where you bought it and tell the owner you know the RN number printed on the label isn't real, and that you'll report him if he doesn't refund your money. That should do the trick.'"

"How did the mother react?"

"That was the strange part. Momma got real quiet. In a whisper she tells me to mind my own business, then turns around and walks away."

"You don't think she'll go to the shop when she gets home?"

Lucille shook her head. The story had riled her up, and she lit a fresh cigarette and filled her lungs before responding. "I'll tell you what I think. I think Momma knows her baby's gown is a fake. It was written all over her face. Maybe she bought it through the mail to save money, or maybe there's some other reason. But she knew."

He had to think about that. He motioned with his hand, and Lucille passed him the cigarette. He took a taste, the smoke tickling his tongue, then gave it back.

"Have you ever had that happen before?"

"Never, and I've been in the business a while. Families skimp on things, sure, but never on the gown. The gown represents the family as much as it does the bride."

She had nailed the discrepancy on the head. A family marrying off their daughter could be excused for buying a supermarket wedding cake, serving cheap New York State champagne, or having a drunk uncle sing "Just the Way You Are" for the first dance, but they couldn't get away with buying a fake gown. There was something else in play here.

"How can I find this woman?"

"She and her daughter are here right now. Shall I make an introduction?"

"If you don't mind."

From a desk drawer Lucille found a name tag that said "Director of Special Memories" and clipped it to Billy's shirt. Her hands lingered on his chest. She was sexy and smart and knew the angles. It was too bad she was a square.

She backed away, expecting him to say something, embarrassed when he didn't. She'd helped him, and he didn't want to bruise her feelings. He took a business card from a box on the desk and slipped it into his breast pocket. Her eyes danced with possibilities.

"Can I call you sometime?"

"I don't see why not," she said. "Walk with me."

- - -

Lucille led him to a dressing room. He'd been hearing tales about the Gypsies for as long as he could remember, and he was excited at the prospect of finally meeting a member of the clan, even if under strained circumstances. Lucille stopped at a door marked with a gold star and tapped lyrically, the sound like raindrops dancing on a roof.

"Hi, it's Lucille, just checking to see if everything's going okay."

The mother of the bride opened the door. Late forties with dyed-blond hair and circles under her eyes, she gave Billy the once-over before focusing her gaze on Lucille. She didn't look any different than the other mothers he'd seen, and was either doing an Oscar-caliber acting job or wasn't part of the Boswell clan.

Behind her, the bride-to-be stood before a three-way mirror as a tailor applied the final touches to her strapless gown. She bore a striking resemblance to her mother: same face, same figure, only no dye job. The gown was a disaster and made her look thick around the middle.

"Hello, Mrs. Torch," Lucille said. "This is my associate, Mr. Cunningham. I just wanted to check in and make sure you and Candace were doing all right."

"My daughter's driving me nuts," the mother of the bride said, dropping her voice. "Otherwise, I guess everything's fine."

Billy did a double take. It was the same woman that Ike and T-Bird had roughed up coming out of the restrooms. Cecilia Torch, the one who'd played it cool as the casino had tried to bribe her with gifts so she wouldn't sue. He'd pegged her for a distraught mother, desperate to save her daughter's wedding from disaster. Had she pulled the wool over everyone's eyes and actually been hiding the fact that she was part of a family of cheaters?

The two women discussed tomorrow's wedding. Listening to them talk, he couldn't tell if Cecilia was faking it. He had an idea. You could learn a lot by listening to a person talk with your eyes closed. The mouth spoke the lie, but the face sold it. But without the face, the lie was just a lie and could be picked up.

He pretended to take a call. What he actually did was shut his eyes and listen to Cecilia talk. He quickly picked up the hint of three-card monte below the surface, the bullshit smooth and expertly delivered. Whatever rancor Cecilia had shown to Lucille when confronted with the accusation of her daughter's fake gown was history; now Cecilia was respectful and polite, and he knew it was all an act.

He said good-bye into his cell phone and put it away. Then he took a closer look at the daughter's wedding gown. It made the girl look pregnant. Somehow, the gown played into this.

The conversation between Cecilia and Lucille ended. Lucille said the usual pleasantries and shut the fitting room door. She walked Billy out to the reception area, where his journey had started, her face a question mark.

"Are they the ones?" she asked.

"Afraid not," he said.

“Damn, I would have sworn it was them.”

Clasping her hands, he gave her a gentlemanly kiss on the cheek.

“You’ve been a huge help,” he said.

“I’m sorry I couldn’t do more.” As he headed for the door, she called out to him. “Don’t forget to check out Tryst. The place gets really hot after midnight.”

“I’ll do that,” he said.

Ike and T-Bird stood outside the bridal shop with their cell phones, surfing websites with splashy layouts of Italian sports cars soon to be in their futures. Bye-bye, Camaro, hello, Lamborghini Roadster and Ferrari Spider. His cautionary talk about lying low after the heist had gone in one ear and out the other. Living large was all they cared about.

Their gazes lifted in unison.

“Any luck?” Ike asked.

“Home run,” he said.

THIRTY-EIGHT

Billy talked to Cory from the balcony of his high-roller suite. Standing by the rail, he sipped on a bottled mineral water while letting the desert sun bake his face.

"Did Gabe have any problems getting the paint?" he asked.

"Nope," Cory said. "Gabe's in the garage now, starting to make the fake chips. He gave me and Morris a lecture on negativity. You should have heard it."

"You be nice to Gabe. Agree with whatever he says, and don't you dare piss him off. That goes for Morris, too. Gabe's our ticket to paradise."

"I know, I know. He's a downer sometimes."

"Deal with it. How's the horse-race scam looking?"

"We're all set. You're playing with Tony G at the Bali Hai at three thirty. Morris and I will be playing in front of you. The scam is for the twelfth race at Santa Anita. Once we know which horse is the ringer, we'll pass the information to you, and you'll place a bet with Tony G and fleece him. The ringers are always long shots. Once we had one at fifty-to-one odds, if you can believe it."

Vegas bookies were tough to fleece. Billy couldn't see Tony G accepting a large bet on a long shot from a stranger, couldn't see it at all. Cory was leaving something out.

"You're telling me you've been fleecing bookies with this scam, and none of them wised up? What are you doing, hitting them over the head with a lead pipe?"

"We're not fleecing bookies, we're hitting sports books," Cory explained. "Sal, the guy who's fixing the races, has a web. Morris and I are part of the web. I probably should have told you sooner how this worked. Sorry."

Billy's blood began to boil, and he sipped his water to calm down. Webs were used by fixers to place bets on rigged sporting events. Most webs were spread across the country and employed a dozen or more bettors in different cities whose job was to place medium-sized wagers on rigged events with different bookies. The beauty of a web was that it spread the pain around, and no one bookie got beaten for too much money. The drawback was that it required a large group of people to pull off, as well as a large pool of victims. For Cory to think that the horse race scam at Santa Anita could be used against a single bookie—i.e., Tony G—was insane.

"If I didn't care about you, I'd throw your ass on the street," Billy said. "Morris, too."

"I'm sorry, Billy. I didn't think it through," Cory said.

"We'll talk about this later. In the meantime, I want you and Morris to stop smoking weed. It's killing your brain cells."

"Will do. You want me to ice the round of golf?"

"Fuck no. I need to get Tony G off Gabe's back. Meet me in the Bali Hai parking lot at three fifteen sharp. I'll think of something between now and then."

"I'm really sorry, Billy. I'll make it up to you, I promise."

"Yes, you will."

The sound of scratching glass snapped Billy's head. Inside the suite,

Ike stood with his back to the slider, using the diamonds on his Super Bowl ring to let Billy know that they had company. Marcus Doucette, his crazy bride, and Crunchie had appeared in the living room wearing angry faces. Making his cell phone disappear, he went inside to face the music.

- - -

"Hit the little bastard," Doucette said.

"What did I do—at least tell me that," Billy said.

"Fuck you, you little rat shit. Ike, do as I say."

Ike was unusually fast for a big man. He grabbed Billy by the front of the shirt, lifted the young hustler clean off the carpeted floor, and smacked him in the mouth with a loose fist. It was a pussy punch, real loud, but without mean intentions. Their eyes met. Ike winked.

Billy knew that he had to sell the idea that Ike was beating him up. Otherwise, he and Ike were both in a world of trouble. He flopped his head to one side as if his neck were broken. Ike threw another pussy punch and he flopped his head to the other side. To sell the notion that he was being hurt, he bit down hard on his lower lip, causing it to bleed. Opening his mouth, he pushed the blood out with his tongue.

"Want me to smack him again?" Ike asked.

"No, that's enough. Sit him down," Doucette said.

Ike grabbed a chair and threw Billy into it.

"You know why I had Ike do that?" Doucette asked.

Billy continued to play hurt and shook his head.

"Because you're waltzing around my casino grilling my employees, and not bothering to tell me what you've found. From now on, you're going to communicate with me. No more bullshit games. Are we clear on this?"

"Yes, sir," Billy said softly.

Doucette turned to his bride. "Tell him we're ready."

Shaz's eyes were glistening, the sight of blood turning her on. Going to the hallway door, she unchained it and stuck her head out.

"We're ready for you," she called into the hallway.

Rock and his two leathered-up bodyguards entered the suite and stood directly in front of Billy's chair. Rock wore pretty, fat-man clothes—black pants with billowing legs, a tent-sized purple shirt hanging out of his pants, and a snappy fur hat—and clutched his walking stick as if he planned to use it very soon. His bodyguards flanked him like a pair of backup singers.

"I want you to tell me what's going on in the casino Saturday afternoon," Rock said. "If you leave anything out—anything at all—I'll crack your skull open. Now, start talking."

Billy didn't understand what was going on. Why should he be telling Rock about the scam? His eyes found Doucette's face. The casino owner dipped his chin. *Tell him.*

He looked back at Rock. The man acted as if he owned the joint. And the other people in the suite acted as if Rock owned the joint as well. Which could only mean one thing: Rock *did* own the joint; Doucette was fronting for him and was on Rock's payroll.

It made sense, when he thought about it. Bugsy Siegel had built the Flamingo Hotel with mob money, the Cleveland Outfit had built the Stardust, Fremont, Marina, and Hacienda Hotels with mob money, and Rock had built the Galaxy Hotel and Casino with drug money. The more things changed, the more they remained the same.

The realization made him look at Rock differently. Beneath the clownish clothes and swagger was a man of superior intellect and street smarts who'd built an empire in a business where a single mistake or slipup meant loss of life or a lengthy stretch in the pen. To Billy's way of thinking, it made Rock smarter than Donald Trump or Warren Buffett, because those men had all fucked up at one time or another in their illustrious careers, while Rock had never fucked up. Not once. Because if Rock had fucked up, he wouldn't have been standing there.

It also made him look at Rock's bodyguards differently. The women were not physically imposing, nor did they appear to be carrying weapons of mass destruction strapped to their bodies. But they were lethal. They had to be, because their boss was a constant target.

Knowing these things made him choose his words carefully. If he tried to bullshit Rock the way he'd bullshitted Doucette and his bride, it would end quickly, in bloodshed.

"On Saturday afternoon around four, a wedding party staying in the hotel is going to rip the casino off for a major score," he said. "The party is named Torch-Allaire, although they're really part of a Gypsy clan that specializes in taking casinos down for huge scores."

"Define *huge*," Rock said.

"Millions."

"How long have you known it was these people?"

"Since I spoke with the mother of the bride in the hotel's bridal shop. Her name's Cecilia Torch, and she's as phony as a three-dollar bill."

"You didn't answer my fucking question. How *long* have you known?"

"Not long. Maybe a half hour."

"Why didn't you call Doucette and tell him?"

Rock's fingers tensed on the grip of his stick. If Billy's answer didn't ring true, he was going to split Billy's head open, causing Billy's lovely brains to ooze out of his nostrils. He took a deep breath, hoping it wasn't his last.

"I didn't call Doucette because I didn't have any proof," he explained. "Shit, I don't even know what their scam is. Without knowing that, the information's worthless."

"Why's it worthless?" Rock demanded.

"Say I tell Doucette I think the Torch-Allaire party is the Gypsies. If he tosses them out of the hotel, they'll just come back under different names and rip the place off. If Doucette has security rough them up, they're going to fight back, and that could get messy. The best way to deal with them is to figure out their scam and catch them in the act, with videotape evidence as backup. By doing that, you own them."

The suite fell silent as Rock considered what Billy was telling him.

"That might be true, but it doesn't explain why you didn't tell nobody," Rock said. "You were holding out. I get mad when people hold out on me."

Billy sat up straight in his chair. "I did tell someone. I told Ike and T-Bird. Ask them if you don't believe me."

Rock directed his attention to the punishers. "Is this candy-ass nigga telling the truth?"

T-Bird knew better than to open his yap and get caught in a lie. Instead of responding, he simply nodded, his dreadlocks bouncing on his broad shoulders. Ike took up the slack.

"Yeah, he's telling the truth," Ike said. "Cunningham came out of the bridal shop, and I asked him how it went. Cunningham said he'd made the cheaters, now he just needed to figure out what their scam was so he could tell Marcus. Those were his exact words."

"You think he was trying to pull a fast one?" Rock asked.

"No, suh."

"Could he have been stalling or plotting something?"

"Cunningham knows what we'll do to him if he double-crosses us. Marcus told us to keep him in line, and we're keeping him in line."

"Is that so. How many times have you smacked him around?"

Ike counted on his fingers. "Four."

"Did you make him bleed?"

"Yes, suh. Every time."

The answer seemed to satisfy Rock, and he shifted his attention back to Billy. "I'm buying your story this time. But from now on, no holding back. Next time you learn something of significance, call Doucette right away. Am I making myself clear, pretty boy?"

"He'll be the first to know," Billy said.

"How come every time you open your mouth, I think you're lying to me?"

"I must remind you of someone."

"You're right—you do remind me of someone."

Rock flicked his wrist as if executing a trick Ping-Pong shot. The walking stick became horizontal and sliced the air with a sharp hissing sound. An invisible hand grabbed Billy by the nuts and gave them a squeeze.

The inquisition was over. Rock's bodyguards sprang to life and went to the door. They both instinctively touched the sleeves of their leather jackets, and Billy guessed each was packing a knife sharp enough to slit a man's throat. They unchained the door, stepped into the hallway, and cautiously looked both ways. Rock's enemies were everywhere, their actions seemed to imply, even in a hotel he'd built with his own money.

"We're good," one of the guards called into the suite.

The drug kingpin shuffled out of the suite, followed by Doucette, his bride, and Crunchie, who hung back long enough to flash Billy the evil eye. It occurred to Billy that what had just happened was the old hustler's doing in an effort to take him out of the picture.

"Pistols at ten paces," he said.

"I can't wait," the old grifter replied.

The door clicked shut. Ike was grinning from ear to ear.

"So how'd we do?" Ike asked.

Billy got three cold ones from the fridge and popped the tops. If he'd had any doubt about the punishers' desire to rip off their boss, it had been erased, and they clinked bottles in a toast.

"I'd say you both have a real future in this business," he said.

THIRTY-NINE

The afternoon was slipping away, and Billy decided to head out to the Bali Hai golf club for his three-thirty game with Tony G. But first, he needed to transform himself into a sucker and get decked out in an overpriced polo shirt and obnoxiously loud pants in the casino's men's shop.

"Do me a favor and call Shaz," he said to Ike. "I need to leave the property for a few hours and want to get her permission."

"You think she'll let you?" Ike said.

"Sure. She's got a thing for me."

"What are you going to tell her?"

"I don't know—I'll think of something."

Ike put his half-finished beer on the bar and made the call on his cell phone.

"What do you want now?" came Shaz's greeting through the phone.

"Cunningham needs to speak with you," Ike said.

"Is that so? Put him on."

He took the cell phone and raised it to his face. "I need your permission to go play a round of golf with three members of the Torch-Allaire wedding party. Your concierge pulled some strings and got me invited to their group at the Bali Hai course at the Mandalay Bay this afternoon. I want to schmooze them, see what I can pick up. You cool with that?"

The lie was filled with enough information to make it sound right. Her tone softened.

"Little Billy plays golf. How cute. You any good?"

"Good enough to hustle."

"Go ahead. Just be sure to pass any information to Marcus."

"I'll do that. I need to get some clothes from your men's shop so I look the part. I promise not to spend too much."

"Aren't we being polite. Crunchie told my husband that he thinks you already know what the Boswell's scam is, and that you're holding out until Saturday afternoon so you can keep us to our word." She paused. "Is that true?"

"I know part of the scam. It's tied into the wedding."

"Tell me, and I'll go down on you."

Normally, that kind of invitation got him all hot and bothered. Not this time around. Their last sexual encounter was still fresh in his mind, and he wasn't about to take that kind of risk again. "Here's what I figured out," he said. "On Saturday afternoon, all of the men will be wearing tuxedos, while the bridesmaids will be wearing matching dresses. That's important, because it's going to let them trick your security guards while they rip you off."

"Trick them how?"

"It's called the Dazzle. The wedding party will converge around a designated area of the casino. The ringleader will give a signal, and everyone will start moving around and talking loudly. The movement will cause their outfits to blend together, and trick your security guards into losing count of how many people are in the party. A member of the party will duck out of sight, rig one of your games, and rejoin the group, with no one being the wiser."

"You're saying we won't see a thing."

"That's right. Totally invisible."

"Which game are they going to rig? You must have some idea."

He'd given that aspect of the scam a lot of thought. The Gypsies would rig a game with the capability of a monster payout, like craps or blackjack, and would avoid games like keno, which rarely paid out. Telling her this was not in his best interest, and he stalled.

"That's what I'm trying to find out," he said.

"You're bullshitting me. I can hear it in your voice."

"No, I'm not. I'll call you if I learn anything."

"Liar."

"Would I lie to you?"

"Every chance you can."

The connection ended, and he tossed Ike the phone.

- - -

Downstairs in the casual men's shop he grabbed a few pairs of loud slacks off the racks along with several crayon-colored polo shirts. A peppy salesgirl followed him into the back and unlocked a dressing room stall with a brass key attached to the belt of her dress. She counted the slacks and shirts before letting him enter the stall.

"Sorry, but I got burned the other day," the salesgirl said.

"Get a lot of shoplifters?" he asked.

"It only takes one. Anything stolen gets deducted from my pay."

"Don't they have a security camera in the store to stop that?"

"I wish. Let me know if you need anything. I'll be out front."

"What about the other stores in the casino? Same deal?"

"Yup. The employees are responsible for the merchandise. It sucks, if you ask me."

He went into the stall to try on the clothes. Every Strip casino had security cameras inside their retail stores to protect the merchandise. Galaxy didn't, and he guessed there was a reason for that. By entering through a back way, Rock and his bodyguards could visit the casino's different stores and not be filmed, letting the drug kingpin come and go as he pleased.

He had learned something important. He could use the retail stores inside Galaxy to move around the property and not be detected by the eye-in-the-sky.

He settled on a pair of hideous red slacks and a clashing navy polo shirt with wide green stripes. The clothes scored high on the ugly meter, and he spent a moment appraising his reflection in the full-length mirror inside the stall to make sure he hadn't gone overboard.

A knock on the door. The salesgirl, checking up on him.

"I'm almost done," he announced.

"Let me in," a female voice said.

Not the salesgirl, too sultry. He unlatched the door, and a woman wearing oversized shades and a floppy straw hat meant for the pool stood outside. The face was too hidden to ring any bells, but her body's tight curves left no doubt who it was.

"For the love of Christ, what are you doing here?"

"Oh my God, what are you doing in those clothes?" Mags asked.

"I'm going to hustle a guy on a golf course."

"It figures you'd be up to something. I came here because I wanted to see you. I couldn't stop thinking about you, or your offer to join your crew. I want in, Billy."

He'd told Mags he'd call in a few days, and that should have been enough to keep her happy. Before he could voice his displeasure, she tore away the shades and pulled off the hat, letting her dark locks fall on her shoulders and frame her gorgeous Irish face. That day in Providence came back in a thrilling rush, and his unhappiness melted away.

"God, you look beautiful," he said.

She smiled and just stood there, torturing him.

"How'd you track me down?"

"I came to the casino earlier and was playing the slots. You came out of the elevator and entered the store, and I followed you."

"I told you not to come back here. These people are animals."

"I wore a disguise. I had to see you."

Mags had been hustling nearly twenty years. She hadn't lasted this long as a grifter by intentionally walking into bad situations. Her story wasn't ringing true. He wanted to ignore it, but that was a mistake. He needed to find out why she was here.

"Let me pay for these clothes. Then we can talk," he said.

- - -

He paid with his own money. It was quicker than charging the clothes to Doucette and having the salesgirl make a phone call to the casino boss to verify the charge. The salesgirl put his old clothes into a plastic bag and passed them over the counter.

"Have a nice afternoon," the salesgirl said.

When he turned around, Mags was gone. A quick search of the store found her on a couch by the pants section. Knowing the store had no surveillance cameras made him feel comfortable enough to sit down beside her.

"I can't believe we hooked up after all these years," he said.

"Or that we're going to be working together. When can I start?" she asked.

"I need to get this job finished up. Then I'll introduce you to my crew."

"When will you be done here?"

"Saturday afternoon. Let's hook up on Sunday, grab some lunch."

The answer seemed to satisfy her. She wasn't prodding him for information or asking bad questions, and his earlier suspicions that she was up to something faded away, replaced by the delicious idea of them ripping off Vegas casinos together. What a wild ride that would be.

"I just remembered something. You dropped a photograph of your daughter on the floor in the cocktail lounge the other night." He took out his wallet and rifled through the billfold. "Damn. It's not here. I must have lost it."

"Don't worry, I've got plenty more. How'd you know Amber was my kid?"

"Come on—she could be your clone."

"Acts like me, too, got a mouth on her you wouldn't believe. She's in community college, going to graduate in the spring. I've already got my ticket booked."

"You must be real proud of her. What's she majoring in?"

"I'm embarrassed to tell you."

"Why?"

"She's studying CSI. My baby wants to be a cop."

They shared a laugh. Mags had a deep, throaty laugh, and he imagined hearing it in bed and how pleasing it would be. Hooking up hadn't been right fifteen years ago, but now it felt okay. The age difference between them no longer mattered. He had caught up to her, and the long-awaited prize was about to be his. He decided to test the waters and dropped his hand on her knee and gave it a gentle squeeze. She didn't seem to mind.

"How did you manage to go to MIT? I hear the tuition's crazy," she said.

"I got a full ride," he said.

"You must be some kind of brainiac."

"School always came easy to me. During my first semester, they gave me the Bucsela Prize for outstanding achievement in mathematics. The funny part was, I hardly ever studied."

"Your old man must have been proud."

"Not for very long."

"What do you mean?"

"I only lasted two semesters."

"Why'd you quit?"

The words hit him hard. Mags hadn't asked him if he'd flunked out or been thrown out. She'd asked him why he'd quit, as if it was a statement of fact. Every time he'd been busted by the gaming board, a nosy gaming agent had dug into his past, seen he'd gone to MIT, and wanted to know why he'd only lasted a year. Rather than tell the truth, he'd made up a lie, and now Mags had repeated that lie. It could only mean one thing: she was an informant working for the enforcement division of the gaming board.

He jumped off the couch, startling her.

"I'm going to be late. I'll call you Sunday," he blurted out.

She rose as well. "What's wrong? Your face is all red."

"Talking about college isn't my favorite subject."

"Did something bad happen? Come on, you can tell me."

What had happened was that a woman he'd been carrying a torch for had stuck a dagger straight into his heart, and it hurt so bad that he needed to get away from her as fast as he could.

"It's a long story. I'll tell you another time," he said.

"I'm going to hold you to that."

She pressed her body against him. Their lips touched. It was all he could do not to put his hands around her throat and choke the life out of her.

FORTY

The Bali Hai golf course was part of the shimmering-gold Mandalay Bay Resort. Billy parked his Maserati in the gravel lot and sat very still. It didn't seem real. Mags had gone over to the dark side. And to think that he'd asked her to work with him ripping off casinos.

A tap on his window got him out of the car. Cory had a bag of golf clubs slung over his shoulder, Morris a racing form. Cory passed Billy the golf bag.

"Tony G's waiting for you by the first tee in his cart," Cory said. "He's got his enforcers with him, Guido and Snap. Guido won the Las Vegas bodybuilder championship last year; Snap fights mixed martial arts. Guys who don't pay get their arms snapped."

Morris handed him the racing form. It was for today's races at Santa Anita. It was in the twelfth race that Sal the fixer would switch in the Brazilian ringer. Sal was purposely not letting his web of bettors know which horse was the ringer until right before post time. That way, his web couldn't share the information and bring down the ringer's odds.

"How are we going to work this?" Billy asked.

"Sal will text me a few minutes before the race starts with the ringer's name," Cory said. "I'll text the information to you, and you'll scam Tony G."

"If Tony G sees me reading a text and then betting on a long shot, he'll feel a breeze. Try again," Billy said.

"We can send the information to you by code on your Droid," Morris suggested. "You'll put your cell phone on vibrate and stick it in your pocket."

"Vibrating cell phones make noise. If Tony G hears the vibration, he'll get suspicious. Try again."

"Here's an idea," Cory said. "The club has a drink service. Cute girl drives out in a cart, brings you an ice-cold beer. I'll bribe her into passing you the information on a cocktail napkin."

"What if she gives the napkin to Tony G by mistake? Is that when Snap breaks my arm?"

Beaten, Cory and Morris gazed shamefully at the ground. They were the little brothers that he'd never had, yet there were times when he wanted to throw them both down a flight of stairs. Still holding the racing form, he slapped it against Cory's chest.

"Find a pencil, and draw circles around the horses that should win the other races, but don't draw anything on the twelfth," he said.

Cory went inside the clubhouse to get a pencil. An idea was brewing in Billy's head, and he popped the Maserati's trunk. He carried a variety of stuff in the trunk, including a box of magic props. He frequented the local magic shops, always on the lookout for a new gimmick that could be used to beat the casinos. His favorite shop was Houdini's inside the MGM Grand, where every purchase came with a free lesson from one of the demonstrators.

He removed a swami gimmick from his collection and shut the trunk. It was made of brass and prefitted with a tiny piece of lead that fit comfortably under his right thumbnail. With it, he could secretly write on a piece of paper—or a racing form—without being detected.

Cory came back outside. He'd done as told and circled the favorites on the racing form while leaving the twelfth race blank. Billy stuck the form in his back pocket.

"Do either of you know semaphore?" he asked.

"I learned in the Boy Scouts," Morris said.

"Good. Here's what I want you to do. When Sal texts you the ringer, drop your beer on the ground and curse. Then grab two clubs from your bag and start loosening up. Use the clubs to signal the first three letters of the ringer's name. That's all I need to find it on the form."

"Got it," Morris said.

It was 3:20 p.m. Billy still needed to buy golf shoes from the pro shop before heading out to the first tee. He put his arms on their shoulders and drew them close.

"Tell me you're ready," he said.

They swore to Billy that they were ready.

"I want to ask you a question. If you found out that someone you knew was a snitch and was working with the gaming board, what would you do to them? Be honest with me."

"I'd kill them," Cory said without hesitation.

"So would I," Morris said.

Billy felt the same way. It didn't matter that he'd carried a torch for Mags all these years. The betrayal was too great.

- - -

The first pair of shoes he tried on fit perfectly. He paid up and left the shop with his bag of clubs slung over his shoulder. Painted signs directed him down a crunchy gravel path to the first tee. Tony G used the Bali Hai course as his office and was probably a strong player and would hustle Billy once he'd sized up Billy's game. That was how it usually went.

Golf was not a friendly game in Vegas. Every club had hustlers who paid golf pros to arrange matches for them. Some hustlers were scratch players who practiced in shaded areas and had pale white skin that matched the tourists they fleeced. Others resorted to cheating, and spread Vaseline jelly on their clubs' faces to better control their shots, or wore golf shoes with the soles removed, allowing them to move their balls out of unfavorable lies with their toes.

Billy guessed that Tony G also had tricks that he used. That was fine. While Tony G was hustling him on the greens, he'd be hustling the bookie at the racetrack.

He came to the first tee. Tony G sat in a cart with an iPhone, making book. Late fifties, fat as a tick, with a thick matte of white chest hair creeping out of his V neck.

Behind the bookie was a second cart with the enforcers. Guido was at the wheel and wore a sleeveless black muscle shirt that showed off his massive arms. He was jotting down the bets his boss was making on a legal pad and paid Billy no attention. Snap sat next to him and had a wiry body without an ounce of fat. Snap's nose had been honked a few times and was as thick as a blood sausage. His weak spot, Billy guessed.

"You must be Billy," Tony G said, covering the mouth of the cell phone. "Toss your bag in the cart and grab a drink. There's beer and spritzers in the cooler. We're up next."

"Appreciate it," Billy said.

Cory and Morris had strolled onto the first tee and were hitting their drives. They were both out of practice and needed to work on their games if they planned to pull off any more golf scams. Done, they got into a cart and drove down a dirt path.

Billy pulled a driver out of his bag and walked onto the tee, where he took several practice swings. Tony G approached holding a sleeve of new golf balls.

"Let's use these," the bookie said. "You can have the number-one ball."

They hadn't even started, and Tony G was already hustling him. During their match, Tony G would make Billy's ball vanish and would drop a ball with identical markings in a sand trap, costing him several valuable strokes.

"How long you in town?" the bookie asked, making small talk.

"I'm here for the weekend. Weather sure is great."

"You're telling me."

Tony G got a call from a client. The bookie stepped off the tee and passed the information to Guido. Knowing Tony G wasn't looking, Billy removed the racing form from his pocket, refolded it lengthwise, and returned it to his pocket so it was partially exposed.

"Let's play some golf," Tony G said. "You like to gamble?"

"Doesn't everyone? What's your handicap?" Billy asked.

"I'm an eight. How about you?"

"I'm an eight, too. How about we bet five hundred a hole?"

"I'm game. You do the honors."

Billy teed up and hit his drive. Every golf course in Vegas followed a basic premise. If a player drove his ball straight and stayed out of the rough, he was rewarded with a decent score.

Tony G went next and hit a powerful ball that sailed forty yards past Billy's. Like hell you're an eight, he thought.

They drove down the path. Halfway down the fairway, they got out and found their balls. Up on the green, Cory and Morris were putting out. Tony G waited until they had left before taking his next shot, which landed five feet from the flag. Billy's shot sailed over the green into the rough. They returned to the cart.

"You into the ponies?" Tony G asked.

Like a shark smelling blood in the water, Tony G had spied the racing form in his pocket.

"Love 'em," he said.

"What's your favorite track?"

"Santa Anita. My father used to take me there when I was a kid, taught me how to handicap. He died a few years ago, left me his company. He was the best."

He turned his head and pretended to wipe away a tear.

"I'm happy to take your action," Tony G said. "You can bet on the races while we play."

"I think I'll take you up on that."

He pulled the racing form from his pocket. It was 3:50 p.m. Each race had a post time, and he flipped the pages and stopped on the eighth race of the day, which was listed to start at 3:55 p.m. Cory's pick for the eighth race was a horse named Solid Gold.

"Five grand on Solid Gold to win," he said.

"Five grand? That's some serious money, kid."

"I can handle it."

Tony G pulled out his iPhone. Most bookies relied on apps to check the results of sporting events in real time to prevent being swindled on events that had already occurred. Using an app named Today's Racing, he checked the eighth race at Santa Anita.

"There's a lot of money riding on Solid Gold. The odds have dropped to even money. You still want it?" Tony G asked.

Billy said yes. He needed to stick to the script and not improvise. Tony G drove to the green, and they finished the hole, which the bookie won by two strokes.

When they returned to the cart, the eighth race was over. Tony G pulled up a replay on his phone using the Today's Racing app, and they watched Solid Gold stumble out of the gate and finish sixth. Billy had lost the hole and the race, and was down fifty-five hundred bucks.

"Too bad," Tony G said without a hint of sympathy.

Billy hid a smile. The fish had taken the bait. All he needed to do now was reel him in.

FORTY-ONE

Billy proceeded to lose the next three races at Santa Anita. A half inch of rain had fallen at the track earlier in the day, and the conditions were sloppy. It seemed to be affecting many of the favorites, all of whom were falling out of the money.

His golf match wasn't faring any better. On the front nine, he lost six holes and tied the other three. On the holes that he tied, Tony G purposely missed a couple of makeable putts, just to keep Billy in the game.

His losses were adding up. He was going to win it all back, but that didn't matter. He hated losing, even if only for a short while.

Tony G parked the cart in a shaded spot by the teeing ground of the tenth hole. It was 4:53 p.m. The twelfth race was listed to start at 4:58 p.m. Cory and Morris were on the tee, preparing to take their drives. They had purposely slowed down and were holding up play. Tony G bit off the end of a cigar and said, "Who invited these jerks?"

"They sure are slow," Billy said.

"You're telling me. I've never seen them before."

Clutched in Cory's hand was a sixteen-ounce can of Budweiser. The can appeared to slip out of Cory's grasp, and hit the ground.

"Shit," Cory said.

The scam was on. Cory grabbed a towel from his bag and dried off his shirt. Morris picked up his partner's driver and, along with his own club, pretended to loosen up. As Billy watched, the clubs formed letters in the air using the semaphore code.

Morris held the club in his left hand by his side, the club in his right hand at twelve o'clock. The first letter was *D*. The club in his left hand stayed by his side, while the other club went to eight o'clock. The second letter was *A*. The club in his left hand went to four o'clock, while the club in his right remained at eight o'clock. The third letter was *N*.

That was all Billy needed to know. He stuck his left hand into his pants pocket, located the swami gimmick, and jammed it under his thumbnail. He brought his hand out of his pocket and held it in his lap. With his right hand, he grabbed the racing form off the dashboard. Turning sideways in his seat, he opened the form to the twelfth race so the page was hidden from Tony G.

"I'm on a losing streak," he said.

"Happens to the best of us," the bookie said.

He scanned the horses entered into the twelfth race. The ringer was named Dana's Boy, listed at seventy-to-one odds. He circled the name with the swami gimmick.

"Here she is. I think my luck's about to change."

He passed the racing form to Tony G and pointed at the ringer that he'd just circled.

"Five grand on Dana's Boy."

Tony G studied the form. As he'd done with each of Billy's bets, he pulled up the twelfth race on the app on his cell phone and studied the true odds, which fluctuated before the start.

"This horse is dog food, kid. Why'd you pick it?" the bookie asked.

"My mother's name was Dana, and I'm her boy," he said.

Tony G relayed the bet to Guido. By now, Cory and Morris had hit their drives and left. Billy got his driver and went to the teeing ground. Tony G joined him moments later.

"Youth before beauty," the bookie said.

Billy teed up and hit his drive. He was laughing inside, and his ball flew straight and true. For his next shot, he chipped to the green, then sank a twenty-foot putt for his first birdie of the day. Tony G couldn't touch him and lost the hole.

As they left the green, Tony G pulled up a replay of the twelfth race on his iPhone, and they watched Dana's Boy tear up the wet track at Santa Anita and beat the field by five lengths.

"Dog food my ass!" he shouted into the bookie's ear.

- - -

Dazed, Tony G stumbled to the cart as if he had two left feet. Billy grabbed a bottled water out of the cooler and handed it to the bookie. The enforcers hopped out of their cart.

"What's the matter, boss? You look pale," Guido said.

"We just got taken for three hundred and fifty thousand big ones," Tony G said.

"What? By who?"

Tony G smirked, as if to say, *Who do you think?* He leaned against the hood of the cart and gulped down the bottled water. His eyes were blinking, his brain playing back the events of the past hour and analyzing them, frame by frame, word by word, looking for a clue that might lead him to understand how Billy had scammed him. Long shots did not win horse races, and Tony G knew that the race had been fixed. But knowing something and proving it were two entirely different things, and if Tony G didn't pay Billy off, his reputation would be ruined.

"Was it this little twerp?" Guido poked Billy in the arm.

"Leave him alone," Tony G said.

"Wait a minute—I know this guy. I've seen him in the clubs around town, picking up all the hot chicks. He's nothing but a two-bit hustler."

"That's great. Now, leave him alone," Tony G said.

"Fucking piece of shit—you think you can scam us?" Snap jumped in, his chest puffing up like a rooster's. "Maybe I should teach him a lesson and break his arm."

"I said leave him alone," Tony G said, growing irritated with them.

Snap backed off, only he didn't back off. His eyes held the promise of future mayhem down the road. One day, Guido and Snap were going to hurt Billy. They'd do it in a parking lot or a lavatory or some place where no one was watching, and they'd mess him up real good.

Or not. Billy still held his putter. By extending his arm, he brought the putter's head into Snap's face and struck the bridge of his damaged nose. Snap groaned and took a knee with blood pouring out of both nostrils. Guido's turn. Billy feinted and Guido shielded his head with his arms. The putter found the magic spot between Guido's legs, and muscles went down in a heap. Billy tossed the putter into the cart and dusted his hands.

"You didn't need to do that," Tony G said.

"Yes, I did. You and I need to talk."

"About what?"

"Stuff."

- - -

Billy drove the cart while Tony G rode shotgun and listened.

"Let's start out by talking damages," he said, his eyes glued to the narrow path. "I lost twenty-three thousand five hundred bucks between my first four bets at Santa Anita and the golf, and you lost three hundred and fifty thousand on my last bet at the track, which puts me ahead three hundred and twenty-six thousand, five hundred bucks. Does that sound right to you?"

"Yeah, that sounds about right." Tony G grabbed the roof as they took a curve. "Look, kid, I know you scammed me. Your reputation will be shot when I'm done with you."

He jammed on the brakes, nearly throwing his passenger out of the cart.

"Don't threaten me," Billy said.

Tony G started to reply, but didn't, knowing that a display of anger would solve nothing at this stage in the game. He looked at Billy the way a parent looks at a misbehaving kid.

"You're a tough little fucker," the bookie said.

He took off down the path. "I have a business proposition for you. You and I have a mutual acquaintance named Gabe Weiss. Gabe is currently into you for three hundred large. I want to wipe away Gabe's debt with the money I just won. Interested?"

"How do you know Gabe?"

"That's none of your fucking business."

"But I owe you more than that."

"Keep it."

The path ended. Billy parked by the pro shop and killed the cart's engine. Las Vegas was the land of the unforgiving; there were no gimmes, freebies, or torn-up IOUs. Tony G waited to hear what the catch was.

"I don't want any hard feelings down the road," he said. "No threats or bad-mouthing. What's done is done."

"Trying to buy me off, huh," the bookie said. "What the hell. I'll take your deal."

They shook hands on it. Billy got out and grabbed his clubs from the back. He started to walk away but not before giving Tony G a parting look to make sure things were good.

"Those two kids playing in front of us were part of it, weren't they?" the bookie said. "They must have lost twenty balls, but they still kept playing. I should have known."

"Have a nice day," Billy said.

- - -

Cory and Morris were horsing around when he exited the clubhouse into the parking lot. They did that a lot, and he'd decided that they were too cocky for their own good and needed to be knocked down a peg. He tossed Cory the golf bag.

"Tony G made you," he said.

Their faces crashed. The apprenticeship to become a grifter was filled with tests, and they'd failed this one miserably.

"How bad did we fuck up?" Cory asked.

"Bad enough. Your horse racing scam is weak. Those goons could have messed me up, put me in the hospital. The good news is, it still worked. Gabe's a free man."

"Sorry," they both said.

"Fuck sorry. You need to do better, start thinking things through. Got it?"

They both promised that they'd do better next time. Talk was cheap, and he found himself wondering if they had what it took to make it in a town as tough as this one.

He drove back into town, the fading sunlight creating a blinding sheen on his windshield. At Russell Road he stopped at the light and checked his Droid for messages. He'd gotten five calls from Ike and sensed something was amiss.

"What's up?" he asked when Ike picked up.

"Doucette's looking for you. There's some bad shit going down."

"Am I in trouble?"

"That would be an understatement," Ike said solemnly.

FORTY-TWO

Hanging up, Billy wondered if his time had run out.

Doucette had ordered Ike and T-Bird to grab Billy when he came into the hotel and bring him up to room 1444 in the main tower. Room 1444 was where Ricky Boswell had been tortured and killed, the designated torture chamber.

Doucette had decided to snuff him. Billy had spun so many lies in the past two days that it was hard to know which one had finally caught up to him. Or maybe it was an accumulation of lies that had tipped the scales. It really didn't matter. Doucette wanted him gone.

He considered running. But that meant leaving his crew behind to face the music. Crunchie had promised to turn their names over to the police if he didn't play ball. His crew would go down, and eventually the gaming board would find him, and he'd go down as well.

He could run, but he couldn't hide.

Traffic was brutal. As the sunny afternoon turned to dusk, tourists poured out of the hotels and filled the Strip's sidewalks and traffic crossings, eager for the party to start. By the time he pulled into Galaxy, it was dark. He threw his keys to the valet and went inside. It had been a great ride, and he had no regrets. If he was lucky, they wouldn't make him suffer.

Ike and T-Bird were in the lobby. They'd ditched the new threads and gone back to basic black. No words were exchanged, just nods of the head. They both looked sad. Their million-dollar paydays had just gotten flushed down the toilet.

They boarded a service elevator. Ike punched a code into the keypad and appeared frustrated when the doors wouldn't close. He tried the numbers again. This time the code worked, and Ike pressed the call button for the fourteenth floor. The elevator began its ascent.

Billy imagined himself making a run for it before they tried to kill him, and knew that he'd need the service elevator to facilitate his escape. Having watched Ike punch in the code, he said it three times to himself and stored it away in his memory for future use.

The doors parted on the fourteenth floor. He cleared his throat and said, "It's been a gas, gents," and heard them grunt in the affirmative. They got out and started their long walk. A lack of progress on finishing the floor was evident—electrical wires popping out of walls, unpainted drywall, piles of dust. Reaching number 1444, Ike paused.

"You scared?" Ike asked.

He shook his head. His old man had set the bar on dying and had demonstrated to his only child how a man was supposed to check out of this world. Three days off life support with no food or water, gasping for breath on rotted lungs, his body finally succumbing when his heart couldn't take it anymore, fading away in his son's arms with a satisfied expression on his face, as if to say, *See, kid, this is what tough is.*

"Bring it on," he said.

They entered the suite. It had not changed since two nights ago—the prerequisite movie stills of iconic dead celebrities on the walls, the flat-screen TV showing the house channel.

"Anybody home?" Ike called out.

"We're in the bedroom," came Shaz's voice from another room.

Billy started down the hall, prepared to face the music. It was how his old man would have handled the situation, and he was his old man's son. Ike and T-Bird scrambled to catch up. The bedroom door was cracked. Kicking it open, he went in.

"I hear you're looking for me," he said.

Doucette, his bride, and Crunchie were having a party and sat in chairs, gorging on BBQ ribs, chicken wings, and other finger food they'd ordered from room service. A low-budget slasher film was playing on the TV, the sound muted. Other things stood out. Lines of coke on the coffee table. Duct tape on the night table. And a body wearing a black hood lying beneath the bedspread, struggling to free itself from crisscrossing ropes holding it down. The first thought that went through Billy's mind was that he wasn't going to die. The second thought was that the poor schmuck lying on the bed *was* going to die.

"What took you so long?" Doucette asked, licking BBQ sauce off his fingers.

"I got stuck in traffic. Who's this?" he asked.

"Crunchie caught another cheater in the casino this afternoon."

"Did he trip over him?"

"Fuck you, you little turd," the old grifter said.

Billy edged up to the bed to get a better look at their prisoner. He was on a first-name basis with most cheaters in town and wondered if the poor bastard was someone he knew.

"Is this necessary?" he asked.

"Rock's rules," Doucette said. "Any cheaters we catch, Rock wants snuffed. Except you, of course. You're special."

The body on the bed let out a muffled cry. There was nothing Billy could do, and he watched Doucette snort up a line of coke that could have gotten an army on its toes.

"Let's hear about your golf game. Are these people the Gypsies?"

"It's them," he said.

"How can you be sure?"

"I got them apart on the golf course, caught them in a few lies. Stupid stuff, like the name of the high school they went to. It's definitely them."

"Good. Now tell me how they're planning to rip off my casino."

Billy had been planning to hold on to this piece of information for as long as possible but didn't think that was prudent anymore. "The scam involves the wedding gown," he said.

Doucette's handsome face went blank, not understanding.

"The bride's gown is part of the scam. She's wearing a Chinese knockoff made of a synthetic material. I saw her wearing it in the bridal shop, and it occurred to me that a gown made of synthetic material would not tear as easily as one made of silk. That was the tip-off."

"Do you know what he's talking about?" Doucette asked Crunchie.

The old grifter nodded. "Billy's onto something. Keep talking, kid."

"The gown will be used to bring gaffed equipment into the casino. The bride wears a leather harness around her waist with a strap that hangs down the front, another strap down the back. The gaffed equipment hangs between her legs. She might walk stiffly, but that's not uncommon with women in gowns. My guess is, she'll be carrying a gaffed shoe to rip you off."

"You think there's a dealer involved," the old grifter said.

"Yeah, and a pit boss. I noticed a number of high-stakes blackjack tables in the pit. They'll target one of those."

"How's the shoe going to be gaffed?"

"Stacked and marked. Bleed the joint all night long."

The old grifter flashed a crooked smile. "Like we did at the Mirage, only we used a floppy lady's handbag to switch the shoe in. How much did we steal that night?"

"Two hundred large."

"What the hell are you two talking about?" Doucette said, wiping his runny nose with a cocktail napkin. "Back this conversation up, and give it to me in plain English."

Billy had never heard a casino owner admit he didn't understand. Doucette's days were numbered if he kept broadcasting how stupid he was.

"The bride will be carrying a dealing shoe beneath her gown," he explained. "The shoe contains eight decks removed from your casino by a pit boss. These decks are stacked and also marked. The Gypsy wedding party will enter your casino and stand in front of a particular table. This table will be locked up: the dealer, pit boss, and players will be involved. The wedding party will create a distraction, and the shoe will be switched with the one on the table. The normal shoe will be stashed in the gown, and the wedding party will leave.

"The players at the table will win every hand because the cards are stacked. When the shoe is exhausted, the dealer will shuffle up, and a new round will be dealt. The players will read the backs of the cards and keep ripping you off. You'll lose a fortune."

"But the shoes are chained down," Doucette said. "They can't be switched, can they?"

Every time Doucette opened his mouth, he weakened the nation. Billy glanced at Crunchie, giving the old grifter the floor.

"The chain will be cut with a battery-powered saw hidden in the pit boss's jacket," Crunchie explained, "and the gaffed shoe will be secured to the table with a duplicate chain."

"You've done this before," Doucette said.

"In my previous life, yeah," the old grifter said.

"So this is how we're going to get ripped off? Pretty boy isn't lying to me?"

"Billy's telling the truth. This is the real work."

The body on the bed begged for mercy. It was pitiful to hear, and the room's occupants pretended not to. The last gasp of a dying man, Billy thought.

His education complete, Doucette crossed the bedroom and jabbed Billy in the chest. "You still rub me the wrong way. That's a problem, because I'm depending on you to catch these fuckers. If this breaks bad,

Rock will go off the reservation. You understand what I'm saying? The man takes no prisoners."

"You can trust me. I won't let you down," Billy said.

"That's the point, kid—I don't trust you, and never will. In my world, trust has to be earned. So I'm going to make you earn my trust."

Billy almost said "How?" but bit his tongue. He knew what was coming; it was as clear as the nose on his face. Doucette moved to the side of the bed and grabbed the black hood covering the prisoner's head.

"I want you to put a bullet in our friend here," Doucette said. "Do that, and you'll earn my trust. Think you're up to it?"

Billy weighed his options. The poor son of a bitch on the bed was a goner, and there wasn't a damn thing he could do about it. But he could save himself. Viewed in that light, he really didn't have any other choice.

"Sure," he said, swallowing the lump in his throat.

"Say it, you slimy little snake," Doucette said.

"I'll shoot him."

"Very good."

The body torqued beneath the covers. Maybe the poor bastard will suffocate and save me the trouble, he thought.

Doucette jerked away the hood. A large piece of duct tape covered the prisoner's mouth. Recognition was like a splinter in the chest, and Billy thought he might get sick.

It was Mags, crying her heart out.

FORTY-THREE

"Crunchie tells me this little lady is a friend of yours," Doucette said.

The words hung in the air. The old grifter had been waiting for a chance to get back at him, and Billy hoped there was more than one bullet in the gun they gave him to shoot Mags.

"She's no friend," he lied.

"But you know her," the casino boss said.

"I caught her painting cards at blackjack in your casino and had a cocktail waitress give her the brush. She left her chips on the table and ran. End of story."

"Why help her out? What was in it for you?"

"I felt bad for her. I knew what you were going to do to her."

"That's it? You felt bad for her? Give me a fucking break."

"She also has a great ass."

"That's more like it. Were you going to hook up with her, and get it on?"

"That was the plan. Wouldn't you?"

Doucette's eyes did a little dance. Every guy in Vegas was a pussy hound; Doucette had checked Mags out while she was being tied up, and liked the merchandise. Talking about her ass was crude—especially after having agreed to kill her—but sometimes crude worked, and Billy wasn't surprised when the casino boss slapped him on the shoulder.

"I could learn to like you," Doucette said.

- - -

They waited another hour before moving her. Now tied to a wheelchair with the duct tape still in place, Mags was taken by service elevator to the basement garage, where Ike and T-Bird placed her struggling body into the cramped trunk of a limited-edition Mercedes-Benz AMG Black Series, a racecar capable of devouring any track in the world. She wasn't the first cheater to take her last ride in the trunk of a car, and probably wouldn't be the last.

"Be careful," Doucette said. "The last time, you scratched the paint."

"Can she breathe?" Billy asked.

The casino owner shrugged indifference and slammed the trunk. To Ike he said, "Meet us in the usual place. Thirty minutes. Don't be late."

"Got it, boss," Ike said.

With Doucette at the wheel, Shaz riding shotgun, Crunchie in back, the Mercedes hurtled up the exit ramp, the roar of its engine echoing in the garage long after it was gone. Ike and T-Bird trotted toward a stairwell with Billy on their heels. He had agreed to kill someone to save his own skin. There was no doubt in his mind that he was capable of pulling the trigger. What he didn't know was if he was capable of living with himself in the days and weeks that followed. His conscience would eat at him, and he was afraid it might eat him alive.

They took the stairwell to ground level. Went outside to the employee garage, climbed three levels, and got into the Camaro's front bench seat, sitting three across. It was tight, but Billy wanted to talk to Ike and T-Bird during the drive and gauge their facial expressions.

Ike made his tires scream going down the spiral exit ramp, and hit the street doing sixty.

"Think you can make it to Lake Mead in thirty minutes?" Billy asked.

"Who said we were going to Lake Mead?" Ike said.

"That's where all the cheaters get buried."

"Is there anything you don't know, man?"

The deserts of Las Vegas were pockmarked with shallow graves that had no tombstones or markers. The nameless dead surrounded the city and often became unearthed during new home construction and road projects. In the past two decades, 150 had been discovered; it was believed there were many more. The police told the media that these deaths were the work of hit men and roaming serial killers, but Billy knew otherwise. The dead, in fact, were cheaters who'd gotten caught one too many times plying their trade. Not all cheaters met this gruesome fate, just those damn fools who didn't know when to quit. The casinos got tired of busting them, so they whacked them instead.

Where the bodies popped up often indicated where the cheater was caught. The Apex area near Nellis Air Force Base was used by casinos on the north side of town, the roads leading to Mount Charleston were favored by old downtown's casinos, and State Route 160 from Blue Diamond to Pahrump was popular with casinos on the Strip's south end. But in terms of sheer numbers, the recreation area around Lake Mead won the prize, with half the city's nameless graves having been found there, usually near campsites or hiking trails.

Ike took the 215 east into Henderson, got off on Lake Mead Parkway, and followed the signs toward Boulder Basin, a brightly lit Albertsons and Walmart the only stores for miles. It was a different world out here, the vast space easy to get swallowed up in. Billy realized he had broken into a cold sweat, and glanced at his car mates. Ike and T-Bird were sweating as well.

"Tell me how this is going to work," he said.

"There's a campsite up the road where we buried Ricky," Ike said. "We'll pull in there, and me and T will dig a grave. You'll shoot the bitch, and we'll plop her into the ground. That's about it."

"What's Doucette's role?"

"Doucette sits in his car with his sick wife and watches. They get off on this shit, especially her. She enjoys seeing people suffer."

"Has she always been like that?"

"Once upon a time, she was cool. Wasn't she, T?"

"Way cool," T-Bird said.

"So what happened?"

"Doucette happened," Ike said. "Shaz went to work stripping for him, and he started sending her down to Tijuana to get naked in a club he owns. Each time she came back, she was loaded with blow. The stuff is ninety percent pure, worth forty grand an ounce. All the strippers in Doucette's clubs move blow for him. Rock fronts the operation, sells the stuff on the streets."

"How did she get so messed up?"

"I'm getting to that part," Ike said. "The girls carry the blow inside of them. Doucette's rule—he thinks it's safer that way. Some girls swallow the bags; others shove them up their assholes. Shaz used her pussy. One day she's driving back from Tijuana and the bag broke. She passed out, crashed the car. Two days later, she woke up half-dead in a hospital bed with a diamond ring on her finger. Doucette married her while she was out."

"So if she got arrested, she wouldn't testify against him."

"You got it."

"Was she okay with that?"

"Yes and no. She got off on the ring. What made her crazy was that she couldn't have no babies. The doctors had to take out her sex organs to save her life."

"They gave her a hysterectomy."

"Yeah. It screwed up her head. Shaz got out of the hospital and was arraigned. Judge felt sorry for her, gave her probation. That night, she was in the club, drinking champagne at the bar with Doucette. Another stripper comes over, kisses him on the mouth. Shaz grabs the bottle off the bar and crushes her skull. Poor kid bled to death. Shaz laughed over her dying body."

"She got off on it?"

"Uh-huh. It was scary."

"She's a liability. Why doesn't Doucette get rid of her?"

"She's his wife. If she disappears, people will start asking questions. He's stuck with her. Here's our turn. So what are we going to do? You going to kill this bitch?"

"I don't know what I'm going to do," Billy said truthfully.

"Well, you'd better decide, because if you don't, they're gonna kill you."

- - -

Ike drove down a bumpy gravel road to a deserted campsite. Lake Mead offered cheap lodging to campers and RVs, which included electrical hookups along with water and sewer, and the campsites were often full. This particular campsite was deserted, without a single tent or recreational vehicle. A sign tacked to a pine tree explained the situation.

CAMPSITE CLOSED FOR REPAIRS
USE BOULDER BEACH, CALLVILLE BAY,
OR ECHO BAY UNTIL FURTHER NOTICE

A pair of headlights blinked from the other side of the campsite.

"You make up your mind yet?" Ike asked.

"I need to play this situation as it lays. I won't put either of you in jeopardy."

"I hope you know what you're doing."

Ike parked and they climbed out of the Camaro. Billy's skin was tingling and butterflies filled his stomach. Ike grabbed two shovels from the trunk and tossed one to this partner, striking him in the chest. T-Bird cursed him.

"Chill out," Ike said.

They crossed the campsite to where the Mercedes was parked beneath the pine trees. The driver window came down and Doucette stuck his head out. He was holding a cell phone and appeared to be taking a call. "What took you so long? You forget how to get here?"

"My car don't go as fast as yours," Ike said.

"Here, take this." Doucette passed Ike a handgun enclosed in plastic wrap. "It's only got one bullet in the chamber, in case he tries to do something stupid."

Ike lifted the front of his shirt and slipped the gun behind his belt. Then he and T-Bird walked into a clearing and started to dig, their bodies silhouetted by the moon's glare.

Billy lingered behind, staring at the Mercedes's trunk.

"Is she still alive?" he asked.

"She cried all the way here," Doucette said.

He told himself not to think about it and walked into the clearing. Near where Ike and T-Bird were digging was a fresh mound of earth. Ricky Boswell's final resting place, he guessed. A flashlight's beam hit him in the face. Shaz, watching from the car.

"Are they going to join us?" he asked under his breath.

"They don't want to leave fingerprints, so they stay in the car," Ike said.

Shaz ran the flashlight's beam over their faces. She eventually grew bored with the procedure and shut the flashlight off.

"You make up your mind yet?" Ike asked.

"Still working on it," Billy said.

Soon the grave was ready. Coffin shaped, three feet across, six feet long. Ike tossed his shovel to the ground and went to the Mercedes to tell Doucette it was time. The Mercedes's trunk popped open. Ike returned to the campsite dragging Mags by the collar of her blouse. She looked bad, hair in her face, sobbing through the duct tape, losing it.

Ike brought her to the edge of the grave, then retreated. Mags found the courage to stop crying and gazed at Billy with the same bewitching eyes that had frozen him on the street corner in Providence so long ago. If he hadn't jumped into her car that day, he would have gone on to become an engineer or a college professor the way his old man had wanted him to, his life filled with endless repetition and boredom. Mags had changed his universe, and if she died here tonight, a part of him would die as well.

He made Mags face the grave. His lips brushed her ear. Four words came out of his mouth, barely a whisper. Then he stepped back.

The campsite was quiet. No one around for miles. He had never shot anyone before. There was a first time for everything, he supposed.

"Give me the gun," he said.

Ike drew the gun and tore away the plastic before handing it to him. "You ever shoot a Glock before? There's nothing to it—just aim and squeeze the trigger."

"Got it."

The gun felt heavy in his hand. It was black, boxy, with a dull polycarbonate sheen. He spent a moment finding the sweet spot on the back of Mags's head that was his target. He took a deep breath. Raising his arm, he aimed, then stole a sideways glance at Ike and T-Bird to gauge their reactions. They had turned into statues, their mouths wide open as if catching flies. He squeezed the trigger. The bang reminded him of a firecracker going off. A tuft of hair flew into the air, and Mags tumbled into the grave. One second she was there, the next, gone. The shot echoed across the distant lake before finally coming to rest.

"Fucking A. I didn't think he was gonna do it," T-Bird said.

"Me, neither," Ike said.

He lowered his arm, unsure what came next. Shaz rushed into the clearing clutching a Maglite. Grabbing his wrist, she pulled him to the edge of the grave. Her flashlight found the back of Mags's bloodied head and she squealed with perverse delight.

"You did it," she gushed.

"You sound surprised."

"I didn't think you had it in you. You whispered in her ear. What did you say?"

"Have a nice eternity. I saw it in a movie once."

"That's cool. I'll remember that."

"Are we done?"

"We're more than done. Good job."

"You want the gun?"

"Bury it with her."

He tossed the gun into the grave. She had not let go of his arm, and he walked her back to the Mercedes. The sparkle in her eyes said he'd won her over, but what about the others? As she got into the passenger seat, the car's interior light came on. Doucette was still on his call and shot Billy a thumbs-up. Crunchie was retrieving e-mails on a handheld device and ignored him. Whatever reservations they'd had were gone. He'd passed the test.

The Mercedes's taillights grew faint as it rumbled out of the campsite. Billy waited until he was certain they were gone before returning to the clearing. Ike and T-Bird had remained by the grave, prepared to finish the job. P. T. Barnum once said that you couldn't fool all the people, all the time. Barnum was wrong. You could fool all the people, if you played your cards right.

He got down onto the ground, lying flat on his stomach. Reaching into the grave, he tapped Mags on the shoulder.

"Get up. It's safe now," he said.

FORTY-FOUR

They entered the urgent-care clinic on the corner of Eastern and Flamingo at just past ten. Mags had a bloody towel pressed to her ear, and fit right in with the rest of the clinic's walking wounded. The clinic was run by a drunk named Dr. Gregorio Ibarra. Ibarra specialized in treating the city's criminal element, the reception area's cheap plastic seats filled with drug dealers and tattooed gang members. Ibarra treated their gunshot and knife wounds without bothering to report their injuries to the police, as the law required. That was his racket, and he made a good living from it.

A female receptionist reading a celebrity magazine sat behind a plate of bulletproof plastic. Billy sweet-talked her, his breath fogging the plastic. Soon Mags was being ushered into an examining room ahead of the other patients.

The examining room was without decoration. Mags sat on a steel table bolted to the wall and kept shaking her head, pissed off that she hadn't been taken to a regular hospital. Billy stood against the wall with his arms crossed, refusing to wilt under her hostile gaze.

"This place is a dump. The floors aren't even clean."

"I can't take you to a regular hospital without the cops getting involved. You'll be fine here. Your wound isn't that bad."

"You could have blown my head off with that crazy stunt."

He had shot Mags on the side of her head directly above her left ear. He hadn't meant to take a sliver of her ear off, but shit happened. To everyone in the campsite it had appeared that the bullet had entered her skull, when in fact the bullet had only grazed it. The timing of her fall into the grave had sold the play, and he didn't think it could have gone better.

"You're alive, aren't you? Show some gratitude," he said.

"A piece of my ear is gone. I'll be scarred for life."

"So wear your hair long."

"My hearing's fucked up as well."

"Learn sign language."

She angrily threw the towel at him. "I thought you cared about me."

He started to steam. He'd risked everything to save her. It had seemed the right thing to do; now he wasn't so sure. But he was stuck with the decision, and he decided to let the situation play itself out. If he played her right, maybe she'd tell him what her deal with the gaming board was.

"I do care about you," he said.

"Then why didn't you use the gun to shoot those bastards instead of me?"

"The gun had only one bullet." He retrieved the towel from the floor and placed it on the examining table. "Let's not talk about this right now, okay?"

"You're not making any sense."

A noise in the hallway ended the conversation. Ibarra entered, his eyes watery from too many liquid meals. In his hand was a clipboard containing Mags's personal information, all of it lies. Ibarra gave her wounded ear a cursory examination before addressing Billy.

"Gunshot?" the doctor asked.

Billy acknowledged that Mags had indeed been shot.

"You look familiar."

Billy acknowledged that he'd visited Ibarra's clinic in the past.

"I'm assuming you know the drill."

Billy said that he did.

"Six hundred, cash, and I'll make your friend as good as new."

Ibarra's rates had gone up. Billy was in no position to argue, and he extracted six crisp hundred-dollar bills from his wallet. Ibarra held the bills up to the overhead light to ensure they were not counterfeit before stuffing them into his lab coat. Then he got busy stitching Mags up.

- - -

The closest Walgreens was on the corner of Flamingo and Maryland Parkway. The aisles were empty as they walked to the back of the store to where the twenty-four-hour pharmacy was located. The pharmacist on duty was a pleasant guy with a goatee and a silver ponytail and said it would take fifteen minutes to fill Mags's prescription for painkillers.

They waited on a short bench outside the pharmacy window. Mags's ear was covered by a flesh-covered bandage that didn't look so bad, until you saw her face and knew that she'd just stepped one foot in hell. He felt bad for her, even if she was a snitch, and held her hand.

"You going to be okay?" he asked.

"I'll survive. I want to finish our conversation. What was going to happen to you if you didn't shoot me? Were the people in the car going to kill you?" she asked.

"Probably."

"Who are they?"

"The good-looking guy is named Marcus Doucette. He runs Galaxy. The wacky blond's his wife. The old guy is a grifter I once ran with who switched sides."

"What's your deal with them?"

"They caught me cheating their casino and blackmailed me into doing a job for them. I'll be done tomorrow afternoon, and then they'll let me go."

"What happens tomorrow afternoon?"

"I can't tell you that. What's wrong?"

"My ear's starting to throb."

He coaxed the pharmacist into giving him a single pain pill. Mags swallowed it dry and thanked him with a thin smile. He decided it was time to level with her. "I followed you out of the casino the other night. You got into a Jeep Cherokee on the corner of Sahara. There was a guy behind the wheel. You want to tell me about him?"

She hesitated, the gears shifting, thinking hard.

"He was my partner," she said.

"Was, as in past tense?"

"We're splitting up. I'm done with him."

"He treat you bad?"

"The fucking worst."

"Explain why you came back to Galaxy."

"I wanted to see you again. I want to run with your crew. It's what I wanted my whole life. When you made me the offer the other night, I thought, shit, it's finally come true."

He didn't believe that was her motivation for coming back to Galaxy. The gaming board had made her do it, then left her hanging in the wind. They were bastards that way. But maybe she was being truthful about being done with them. After what had happened tonight, he didn't think she was very useful to the gaming board anymore.

"Your prescription's ready," the pharmacist announced.

He paid for the drugs. The pain pill had taken hold and Mags was acting spacey. Taking her by the arm, he guided her to the front of the store.

"I'm dying for a smoke," she said.

"You still smoke Kools?"

"You remembered. How sweet."

He bought a pack and they went outside. The Camaro was parked by the entrance, windows down, the blaring rap music loud enough to stir the dead. Ike and T-Bird occupied the front seat, playing chauffeur because he'd asked them to.

He helped Mags into the backseat. She lived on the east side of town in a town house development. The drive was short. As Ike pulled into the driveway, Billy glanced up and down the street, just to make sure no gaming agents were hanging around.

He walked Mags to the front door. She was fighting to stay awake and struggled to get the key into the front door. She invited him inside, and he heard an urgency in her voice that caught him by surprise. They entered the foyer. The door slammed behind him.

"I want you to stay," she said.

"I can't do that."

"Not even for a little while?"

"No. You need to rest up. You took a real beating tonight."

"I really want to run with you, Billy. We'll make a good team."

He'd been sincere when he'd asked Mags to join his crew. It seemed out of the question now, considering what he knew. Her days as a grifter were over. She needed to find another line of work, go back to school, get a degree in a profession that paid the bills. Anything but this.

"Let's talk about this in a couple of days," he said.

"You're not backing out, are you?"

"Of course not."

She wrapped her arms around his waist, and kissed him on the mouth with everything she had. She had smoked a cigarette in the car, and the menthol taste did a wicked number on his head. When their lips parted, he could hardly breathe.

"Why won't you stay?" she asked. "Don't I turn you on?"

"I just can't," he said, the words unconvincing.

"You never forgot that day in Providence, or me."

"I've got to beat it."

"Admit it. You want me so bad your pants are about to burst."

"Not tonight."

"You'd better not stand me up on Sunday, or I'm going to hunt you down."

Her eyelids had turned heavy and she could barely stand up. He guided her through the town house to the master bedroom and made her lie down on a bed covered with a collection of teddy bears. She was asleep within moments of her head landing on the pillows.

He found a blanket on the top shelf of the closet and covered her, then stood beside the bed and drank in the sight of her for the very last time. She was the definition of everything he found beautiful in a woman. Never seeing her again was the right thing to do, even if it was going to tear him apart.

"You take care of yourself," he whispered.

He walked out of the town house and locked the front door behind him. He needed to wash away the memories with a few stiff drinks. Ike and T-Bird were chilling in the driveway, and he offered to buy them dinner. They climbed into the Camaro with Billy riding shotgun. Ike fired up the engine and backed out of the drive.

"What are you gents in the mood for?" he asked.

"You've got some explaining to do first," Ike said.

"About what?"

"That shit at the campsite. Me and T think you're trying to pull a fast one on us."

Before Billy could explain, Ike cuffed him in the mouth, and the car took off.

FORTY-FIVE

Ike and T-Bird took turns smacking him around inside the car. A slap in the face, a poke in the back of the head, all the usual fun stuff. The beatings were getting old, and he raised his arms protectively to shield his face from a cheap shot.

Finally the beating ended. Being of diminutive stature, he'd taught himself to fight with whatever objects happened to be handy, and the car's cigarette lighter was just itching to get shoved into Ike's eye. But he didn't do it. One day, he'd pay them back in spades, but not today. Today, he needed them to help him rip off Galaxy's casino, and he repeated his offer to buy them dinner, thinking a few slabs of bleeding red meat might settle them down. He suggested a fancy Brazilian restaurant tucked away on East Flamingo called Fogo de Chão.

"What kinda food do they serve?" Ike asked.

"Bleeding red meat. It's one of the best steakhouses in town," he said.

"I can always eat a steak. What do you say, T?"

"If he's buying, I'm flying," the bird man said.

Fogo was one of the town's better meateries, bolstered by a waitstaff willing to do backflips to get your order right. Billy bribed the host into seating them at a table away from the other parties, and a waiter dressed in a gaucho outfit went over the specials before taking their orders. Ike chose the beef ancho, T-Bird the *costela de porco*, which were fancy names for rib eye and pork ribs, while he ordered a traditional filet mignon. Soon their drinks came.

"You guys must really enjoy beating me up," he said.

"We don't appreciate being messed with," Ike said.

There was real menace in Ike's voice. Billy proceeded cautiously.

"Messing with you how?"

"What happened at the campsite, where you faked shooting that bitch. You've got some kind of side deal going with her, don't you?"

"Her name's Mags. She's a grifter I met back in Providence when I was a kid. I ran into her the other night in the casino and told her to stay away. She came back anyway, and Crunchie busted her. You know the rest. To answer your question, no, I don't have a side deal going with her. We're just old acquaintances."

Ike put his elbows on the table. He had an enormous wingspan, and it was easy to imagine him scooping up defenseless quarterbacks and throwing them savagely to the ground.

"Do I look like I was born last night? Me and T saw what happened. She jumped into the grave when you faked pumping a bullet in her head. It was staged. You guys are a team."

"We're not a team. It was spur of the moment," he said emphatically. "Look, I'm not trying to double-cross you, if that's what you guys are thinking."

"Then how'd the bitch know to jump in the grave? Answer me that."

"I cued her."

"Say what?"

"I gave her a verbal cue. When you led Mags across the campsite, I turned her around and whispered in her ear. That's when I told her to jump in the grave."

"Your mouth touched her ear for a half a fucking second. You're trying to tell me that's when it happened? There was no prior conversation?"

"That's right. I said, 'Jump in the grave,' and she played along."

"That's the biggest pile of bullshit I've ever heard."

"Man's messing with us," T-Bird said under his breath.

The conversation had taken a brutal turn and Billy knew that he'd lost their trust. Without trust, there could be no partnership, and the scam would die before it ever got off the ground. He decided to start the conversation over, from the beginning, and bring them back into the fold.

"You guys want to hustle, right?" he asked.

"What kind of question is that? You know we do," Ike said.

"All right, then hear me out. To hustle you have to be able to gain a person's trust and get them to play along with you. It isn't easy, yet hustlers do it all the time. It's what separates the men from the boys. Want to know what the secret is?"

"Lay it on us."

"You have to know what a person's thinking. That's not as hard as it sounds. I'll give you an example. I'm standing under the clock tower outside the Providence railroad station hustling fake watches for fifty bucks a pop. The watches resemble expensive Swiss timepieces, only the inner workings are as sophisticated as a rubber band. Suddenly, a sucker comes toward me, holding the fake watch I just sold him. Stupid bastard dropped it on the ground and the back's popped off and he's seen it's junk. So what's he thinking?"

"He's mad, and he's going to call the cops," Ike said.

"You're half-right. He's mad, but he isn't calling the cops. If he were going to call the cops, he'd stay a safe distance away from me. Try again."

"He wants his money back."

"That's right. He's mad, and he wants his money back. You just figured out the two things that were on his mind. That wasn't so hard, was it?"

"Easy as pie," Ike said.

"So what do I do?"

"Give him a refund."

"In front of the other suckers and risk exposing myself? No way. I stick my hand into my pocket where I keep my wad, peel two fifties off the roll, and palm them in my hand. I bring my hand out of my pocket and stick the money into the sucker's palm as I shake his hand. The other suckers think we're friends. I whisper in his ear. I say, 'Play along.'"

"Did he keep his mouth shut?"

"Damn straight he did. He paid fifty for the watch, got a hundred back. He just made a one hundred percent return on investment. He goes home happy. End of story."

A trio of waiters brought their meals to the table with the precision of a military exercise. The meats were cooked to perfection, the smells mouthwatering. Ike and T-Bird picked up their cutlery and dug in. He had hooked them with a story from his youth. Now came the hard part, which would be to reel them in. He ignored his meal and watched them eat.

Ike finished his rib eye in record time and wiped his mouth with a cloth napkin. The look on his face was skeptical. "You ever try this in a casino? You know, during a scam."

"I use it all the time," he said.

"How's that work?"

He glanced furtively over his shoulder. None of the waitstaff were near the table, but he did it anyway, just for the effect. "It's Friday night, and I'm scamming Planet Hollywood at roulette. The ball falls, and one of the ladies in my crew deliberately places a late bet. The croupier sees her and says, 'Lady, you can't do that!' The croupier slides her late bet back to her. He does this real deliberately, so everyone can see he's got things under control.

"At the same time, the other lady in my crew makes a second late bet. She's sitting next to the red-black boxes on the layout, and she drops five hundred on the red, which happens to be the color that just won. No one sees a thing because they're preoccupied watching the croupier. His movements block out her movements. The scam's totally invisible.

"Suddenly, a little old lady standing next to me says 'Holy crap' under her breath. She's seen the whole thing. So what's she thinking?"

Ike rubbed his chin in thought. "She's thinking, shit, I wish that was me."

"You nailed it. What tipped you off?"

"'Cause she didn't broadcast it."

"There you go. If she'd wanted to expose us, she'd have said it out loud. So I slipped a few hundred in chips into her hands, and I whispered, 'Be nice.' When you whisper to a stranger, you're making them an accomplice. She walked away with a big smile on her puss."

"Very cool," Ike said.

"Think about what happened at the campsite. I knew what Mags was thinking as you brought her toward me. She's praying I wouldn't shoot her. When I whispered 'Jump in the grave,' her prayers came true, and she played along."

"But what if she hadn't played along?" T-Bird said. "What then?"

"They always do. You just need to play it cool, and they'll come around."

He was done talking and ate his now cold filet while watching the punishers converse with their eyes. Eyebrows arched up, eyebrows down, a few short snorts, each man speaking his mind. Ike was sold, the jury still out for the bird man. They both needed to be on board if he was going to rob Galaxy's casino, and he raised his arm and clicked his fingers.

Their waiter hustled over. "Is everything to your satisfaction?"

He waved the waiter closer and whispered to him. The waiter nodded and left. To T-Bird he said, "I just told our waiter it's your birthday. Just watch. He's going to bring out a piece of cake with a candle and get the entire staff to sing 'Happy Birthday' to you."

"Did you ask him to do that?" the bird man asked.

"I didn't have to."

"Then how you know he's going to?"

"Because our waiter thinks we're high rollers. I could tell by the way he served us and how overly polite he's been. Our waiter thinks that if he takes extra special care of us, we're going to take care of him, so he's going to pull out all the stops."

"A cake with a candle and everybody in the fucking kitchen singing 'Happy Birthday' to little ole me, and you didn't tell him to," T-Bird said skeptically.

"That's right."

"You're messing with us again."

"Bet you I'm right. Loser picks up the tab."

"You're on."

Sixty seconds later, their waiter returned to their table holding a dessert plate containing a slice of molten chocolate cake with a lit white sparkler on top, which he placed in front of a slack-jawed T-Bird. The rest of the waitstaff appeared and gathered round the table, along with the female bartender, both the cooks, and a gang of grinning busboys. On the count of three, they broke into a rousing rendition of 'Happy Birthday' sung in Portuguese while enthusiastically clapping their hands. By the time they were done, every diner in the restaurant was applauding, and Ike was laughing his fool head off.

FORTY-SIX

While T-Bird settled the tab, Billy waited outside. It was a faultless night, and he watched a jet pass beneath the stars. He couldn't remember ever gazing up and not seeing a plane. With the same ferocious determination of lemmings, suckers flocked to Vegas to gamble their money away. One day, they were going to collectively wake up and realize the town was a big scam. Until that happened, he'd ride the wave along with everyone else.

His Droid vibrated. Ly calling. The late hour spelled trouble. If she hadn't been his friend's girlfriend, he wouldn't have taken the call.

"What's up?" he asked.

"Gaming agents come to motel looking for me," she said. "They bang on everyone's door, tell people open up. I climb out bathroom window, hide by pool. Finally they leave."

"Tell the manager to move you to another room."

"You tell him. I scared."

"Come on, work with me."

"You want gaming board to arrest me? Maybe I tell them how we cheat Slots A Fun. I bet they like to hear about that."

Blackmail. As if he didn't have enough problems right now. He told her to hold tight and ended the call. Ike and T-Bird came outside. He sensed a subtle change in them. They'd accepted the fact that they were clueless and needed to do what he said.

"I need you to cover for me for a few hours," he said.

"No problem," Ike said.

Ike took Flamingo to Koval and pulled into the motel parking lot where Ly was holed up. Billy checked for unmarked vehicles and saw none. As he started to get out, Ike stopped him.

"Me and T want to hear details about tomorrow's scam," Ike said.

"Yeah, like what are we supposed to do?" T-Bird asked.

He'd purposely avoided talking about details, knowing they'd wake up tomorrow having forgotten. It was the problem when you worked with morons.

"I'll go over the details tomorrow over breakfast," he said. "Just make sure you get a good night's sleep. You need to be on your toes."

"Sleeping's never been a problem." Ike shot T-Bird a disgusted look.

"That's not funny," T-Bird said.

Billy didn't want to hear anymore, and jumped out. The Camaro roared away. He took another look around the parking lot before approaching Ly's room and tapping on the door.

"It's me, open up," he said.

She let him in. She'd lost the dealer's uniform and wore tight-fitting designer jeans, a sleeveless pink top, and a gold necklace with a crouching-tiger ornament.

"Any sign of the gaming agents?" he asked.

"There were no gaming agents," she replied.

"Then why'd you call me?"

She gave him a kick in the nuts. Pools of black opened before his eyes, and it took all his willpower not to go down. The lost snapshot of Mags's daughter lay on the dresser, and he guessed it had gotten stuck in the money he'd given her.

"I hate you! You ruin my life!" she exclaimed.

"You're the one who wanted to cheat casinos," he gasped.

"Yeah, but I didn't know you were piece of shit."

"I saved your ass, didn't I?"

"Yeah, then you leave me in this dump, go play around with other girl. Fuck you!"

The snapshot had set her off. He picked it up and waved it in Ly's face.

"She's the daughter of a woman I know. There's nothing between us."

"You lie. Billy Bullshit should be your name."

"I'm not lying. And by the way, I'm not your boyfriend."

She snatched the snapshot from his hand and tore it in half.

"I hate you," she said again.

- - -

Women were complicated. There was nothing between them, yet Ly had gotten her feelings hurt. He needed to set her straight, so he took her outside to the pool, where they sat in lounge chairs by the water's edge. Next to the diving board was a metal sign explaining all the reasons hotel guests weren't allowed to swim at night. Ly still had the pieces of Amber's graduation photo clutched in her hand.

"Her mother's a grifter named Maggie Flynn," he explained. "Mags got me started in the rackets. I ran into her the other night, and we had a drink and talked about her joining my crew. After she left, I found her daughter's photo on the floor. I stuck it in my wallet and mistakenly gave it to you. That's the story—okay?"

"This woman going to work with you?"

"No. I found out she's a snitch for the gaming board."

"How you know *that*?"

"She tripped up. When we first met, I told her how my old man wanted me to go to college. I left after a year, and Mags asked why I quit.

I never told anyone that I quit, except the gaming board. When Mags repeated the lie, I knew she was working with them."

"This woman no good."

"Tell me about it."

"Why you quit college? Something bad happen?"

He stared at the pool's still surface. He'd traveled three thousand miles to escape the utter shame of his failure, yet there were times when the distance wasn't nearly far enough. Ly put her hand on his arm.

"What you do? Sleep with all the girls and make them cry?"

"I wish it was that simple."

"You not going to tell me?"

"No."

"I tell you my secrets. Why won't you tell me yours?"

She was prying, and he gave her a hard look.

"Why do you care? There's nothing in it for you."

"I just trying to be your friend."

"Do you really mean that?"

She took her hand away and nodded solemnly.

"All right. Here's why I left," he said.

- - -

The beginning of the end of his days at MIT had begun early one Saturday morning with a visit from two big-gutted Boston cops. Rubbing the sleep from his eyes, he'd stepped into the hallway outside his dorm room to discover the boys in blue banging on doors, looking for him. When he'd asked what the problem was, the one in charge had wagged a finger in his face.

"You're the problem. Get dressed. We're going for a walk."

As they crossed the campus and walked down bitterly cold Mass Avenue, Billy wondered what he'd done. He'd tried to keep his nose clean since entering college, but it had been tough. There were too many stuck-up rich kids that needed to be knocked down a peg, and he'd cheated them at weekly poker games for extra spending money. The scores had been chump change, and he couldn't imagine that it had led to anything serious.

His attitude changed as they'd entered the office of the dean of undergraduate education. The dean was at his desk, a squirrely fellow wearing a dated striped suit and tie, his face a study in odd tics and twitches. The dean had presented Billy with his award a few weeks ago, and they were on a first-name basis. With him was a lanky detective with a badge pinned to his suit coat. Parked in chairs by the window were two juniors named Brett Wolf and Dan Fleshman. Wolf and Fleshman were his buddies, although judging by their refusal to make eye contact, he sensed they'd just thrown him under the bus.

"Hello, Billy," the dean said solemnly.

"Good morning, Dean," he replied. "How have you been?"

"To be honest, I've been better. Do you have any idea why you're here?"

"Because my friends are assholes," he nearly said. Instead he said, "No, sir, I don't."

"Brett and Dan have implicated you in a plot to scam the Mohegan Sun Casino in Connecticut. They claim you masterminded the operation, and attempted to steal a quarter of a million dollars from the casino."

Billy swallowed hard. What had these two clowns done?

"I don't know what you're talking about," he said.

"We have proof, Billy. Why don't you fess up and save us the trouble?"

"Because there's nothing to fess up to."

"You're making this hard on yourself, son."

"I'm Detective Peret with the Boston Police Department," interrupted the man with the badge. He had the ruddy complexion that came from too many pints, what the locals called a saloon tan. "As you probably know, the Mohegan Sun is run by the Pequot Indian nation.

I've been asked by the head of Pequot's tribal police department to speak with you. The Pequots are very disturbed by what your friends have done. Do you mind if I call you Billy?"

He wanted to kill Wolf and Fleshman. Instead of ripping off the Pequots for a few grand a week as they'd agreed to, they'd gotten greedy and gone for the big enchilada.

"Not at all," he said.

"Good. Perhaps this will refresh your memory." From the dean's desk Peret picked up a kid's video poker game made by Bally Gaming. The game had been a big seller last Christmas and in all the department stores. "Last night, your friends got caught stealing a two-hundred-and-fifty-thousand-dollar jackpot from a video poker machine at the casino. The video poker machine that got scammed was made by Bally Gaming. According to what your friends have told us, you figured out a way to use this kid's game, also made by Bally, to scam the casino version. Is this ringing any bells, Billy?"

"They're lying," he said.

"Really? You created the software program they used to scam the game. We found the original on a computer in your statistics class. Your name was on it."

Whoops. So much for covering his tracks.

"I want to speak to a lawyer," he said.

"No, you don't," Peret said.

"Yes, I do."

"No, you don't. I'm here to cut a deal with you. The Pequots want to know how your friends knew the cards that were going to come up on their video poker machine. If you explain how you did that, they won't press charges, and I won't arrest you."

Rule number one of cheating was never to explain, because an explanation was an admission of guilt, and once you admitted your guilt, your goose was cooked. But the other option was no fun, either. Arrest, plea bargain, or maybe a trial, and jail time.

"Detective, you have yourself a deal," he said.

Peret's disposition grew more hospitable. The detective crossed the office and handed Billy the video poker game. "Explain how you did it, and don't leave anything out."

"You got it." He hit the play button on the machine and the game came to life. "I saw this game in a store last Christmas, and it got me to thinking. I knew Bally made casino video poker machines, and I wondered if they'd programmed the game's internal clock using the same software that they'd used for their casino games. It would save time, and lots of money."

"Did they?" Peret asked.

"Yes, although it took me a while to figure it out. First, I analyzed the game on a computer, and discovered it used a random function to shuffle its internal deck of cards. The random function generates starting values, called seeds, which are randomly changed each time you play. It's a simple formula. When a player hits the game's start button, the random function looks at the number of milliseconds which have elapsed since twelve a.m. and uses that number to create the seed. With me so far?"

"Keep talking, smart-ass," Peret said.

"Since there are eighty-six million milliseconds each day, the seeds should be totally random, ensuring a fair game. Because I knew the starting point was twelve a.m., I was able to work my way backward, calculate the seed, and then calculate which cards would come out. I was able to cheat the store game within a few hours.

"Cheating the casino version of the game came next. Brett, Dan, and I visited the Mohegan Sun, and Brett played a game of video poker while Dan read the cards off the screen to me with his cell phone. I was in our hotel room on my laptop, and I ran the cards through my software program using the twelve a.m. starting point. Sure enough, the internal clock on the casino game was identical to the store game. We started beating the casino game right away."

"How much did you win?" Peret asked.

"Two grand. I told them not to win too much. You know they say hogs get fed, pigs get slaughtered. I guess they didn't listen."

"That would be an understatement," the detective said.

- - -

Tired of talking, Billy bought a bottled water from a vending machine, which he split with Ly when he returned to their poolside chairs.

"You get thrown out?" she asked.

"Yup. Packed my bags and left that morning. The dean took the award back, gave me a real dressing down. It was humiliating. Then I went home. That was worse."

"What happen?"

"My old man was in the kitchen reading the Saturday paper. I came in through the back door and dropped my suitcases on the floor and told him flat out what had happened. I didn't even take my coat off. When I was finished, my old man didn't say a thing. He just took off his reading glasses and wiped the tears from his eyes. I never saw him cry before. Not even when my grandparents died or my mom got thrown in jail. You understand what I'm saying? The man didn't cry. I broke my father's fucking heart."

"What you do then?"

"I took a Greyhound bus to Vegas."

"You no make up?"

"It was too late for that."

He'd called his old man every week until he'd passed, but it had never been the same between them. Every man worth his salt dreamed of a better life, if not for himself, then for his children, and he'd shattered his father's dream with the reckless disregard of a drunk shattering an empty beer bottle on the curb. It was a hurt that he could not fix, and he hadn't even bothered to try.

"That sad," she said.

"Tell me about it," he said.

She rose from her chair and held out her hand.

"Let's go back to room. I make you feel better."

He looked up into her pretty face. It was tempting, but he wasn't going there.

"You go," he said.

"But . . ."

"Just go."

"Don't you want to feel better?"

"It's too late for that."

She left without a word. She'd gotten to hear his story, and that was all she was getting.

He stared at the pool's flat surface for what felt like an eternity. If he had to do it over again, would he have done things differently? For his old man's sake, he liked to think so. He could have enrolled in a community college and gotten a degree in math or engineering and still made his old man proud. That wouldn't have been so hard.

But he hadn't done that. Instead, he'd headed to Vegas and never looked back. It was the life he'd chosen and he had no regrets, except when his old man's birthday came around.

Then he cried like hell.

FORTY-SEVEN

-THE HOT SEAT: SUNDAY, LATE-

"Tell us about Saturday," LaBadie said. "We want to hear what happened in Galaxy's casino. Don't leave anything out."

LaBadie, Zander, and Tricaricco were not happy campers. Their all-day deodorants were starting to fade, their chins sprouting five o'clock shadows. Dinnertime had come and gone, along with any hope of spending Sunday night with their families. Billy wasn't going anywhere, and he took his time drinking a warm can of soda before answering the question.

"A strange thing happened on Saturday," he said. "I discovered that another crime was being hatched, right under Doucette's nose, and he didn't know a damn thing about it."

"Another crime besides the Gypsies?" LaBadie asked.

"That's right."

"Tell us about it."

"Doucette had a pair of gay football players on his payroll named Ike and T-Bird. I got to know these guys pretty well. They told me that Doucette's strip clubs were a front for a drug dealer named Rock, and that Rock had bankrolled Galaxy. Needless to say, I got upset."

"You got upset."

"That's right. I know how hard the gaming board tries to keep drug money out of the casinos. I mean, it's what you guys get paid for, isn't it? And here I'm being told that a drug dealer pulled the wool over your eyes and actually got a casino built with drug money."

"You're not funny, Billy."

"I'm not trying to be funny."

"Keep talking."

"Where was I? Oh yeah, Ike and T-Bird told me that Doucette was using check-cashing stores in town to launder the profits from Rock's drug operation and turn the cash into money orders. They said Doucette was laundering eight million a pop, which I couldn't believe. Doesn't the gaming board monitor those stores to make sure stuff like that doesn't happen?"

"Make another remark like that, and you'll pay for it."

"I'm just trying to be helpful."

"I'm sure you are. Tell us about this crime Ike and T-Bird were planning."

"Ike and T-Bird were planning to steal the eight million in money orders from the cage and wanted my help. Of course, I said no."

"Those money orders were stolen yesterday afternoon," LaBadie said, barely able to contain his anger. "Are you saying that you and your crew had nothing to do with the theft?"

"I already told you, I don't have a crew."

"You're lying."

"My client did not rob Galaxy Casino and does not have a crew," the attorney said, having not spoken a word for several hours. "Please stop repeating these false allegations."

LaBadie retrieved his briefcase from the floor and placed it on the center of the table. From it, he removed a stack of eight-by-ten glossy photographs taken from a casino surveillance camera. Each photo had the date and time stamped in the corner.

The gaming agent placed the top photo on the table so it faced Billy. It showed Ike standing at the cage, cashing in the fake gold chips. T-Bird was also in the shot, accompanied by Misty and Pepper in their disguises.

"Admit, it, these two women work for you," LaBadie said.

"Never seen them before," he said.

"They're not part of your crew?"

"Stop saying that."

"Then explain this."

Three more surveillance photos were produced and placed on the table. The cameras had caught his crew doing the pigeon drop and stealing the eight million in money orders from Ike and T-Bird.

Shit, he thought.

LaBadie had a smug look on his face, having backed his suspect into a corner.

"Ready to confess?" the gaming agent asked.

"To what?" he asked innocently.

"We're willing to cut you a deal, provided you give us the names of the people in your crew. And, we want the eight million in money orders returned. Give us those two things, and we'll go light on you. Think about it, Billy."

Even the best cops made mistakes, and LaBadie had just made a major one. The gaming board didn't know the names of Billy's crew.

"I'm not interested in cutting any deals because I didn't do anything," Billy said. "Do you want to hear the rest of my story or not?"

LaBadie left the incriminating photos on the table and returned to his chair.

"Go ahead with your story," he said. Then he added, "It's your funeral."

FORTY-EIGHT

-THE HEIST-

Saturday morning, 6:00 a.m., the dingy motel room filled with harsh sunlight. It was a rude way to wake up, and Billy crawled off the couch to pull the blinds.

His eyes adjusted to the darkness. Ly murmured in her sleep, and he looked at her lying in the big bed by herself. He'd stayed up late, come into her room to watch a little TV, and had crashed. He checked his Droid to see if he'd been missed, and saw no messages.

He took a short walk to the 7-Eleven at the end of the block. The pastries had just come out of the oven, and he bought doughnuts and chocolate cookies. He held the mouth of the bag beneath her nose upon returning to the room.

"Here's some yum for your tum," he said.

She rolled over and started to snore. He turned on the TV, and checked the weather while munching on a doughnut. It rained less than five inches a year in Vegas. The rest of the time, it was hot and dry. Today would be no different.

He thought about his old pals Wolf and Fleshman. He'd done a search not long ago and discovered that Fleshman was a personal injury attorney, while Wolf had gone to work for one of the financial institutions that had bankrupted the country. Their gutless betrayal had ruined his life, yet he didn't think they particularly cared. It had been a good lesson. He chose his partners carefully now and did not tolerate betrayal.

Time to go. He took half the money from his wallet and left it on the night table.

He made sure to hang the "DO NOT DISTURB" sign before walking out.

- - -

A cab dropped him off at Galaxy's entrance. The joint was a tomb, and he heard a lone slot machine being played as he walked through the lobby. He would have bet that the player had blue hair and a Popeye-sized forearm, only there was no one to take his action.

He went upstairs to his suite. An empty bottle of Jack sat on the bar, the TV showing the porn channel, a pair of hot blonds doing each other while a tattooed dude masturbated. According to Pepper and Misty, the porn shown on hotel channels was shot in an industrial warehouse. It took the fun out of watching it, and he killed the picture.

The door to the punishers' bedroom was ajar. He stole a look inside and saw them passed out in each other's arms. He'd told them to dial back the partying, and they'd gone and gotten shit-faced anyway. He couldn't wait to lose these two guys.

He got a bottled water from the fridge. A message pad lay on the bar. The top sheet had been written on, then scribbled over. People only scribbled over things they wanted to hide. He tore away the top sheet and studied the indentations on the sheet below. It was a woman's name—Amanda Fernandez. And a long phone number that suggested another country.

It didn't feel right, and he decided to call the number. A Mexican woman answered in Spanish. Should he pretend to be Ike or T-Bird? He covered the mouthpiece of the phone.

"This is Ike Spears. Did you call me?"

"Mr. Spears? I didn't recognize your voice," the woman said, switching to English.

"I've got a cold. What's up?"

"I sent you an e-mail last night. Did you get it?"

"Afraid not. My cell phone's been acting up."

"I'll resend it. Take a look, see what you think. It's a wonderful property—perfect for you and your partner. I will tell you up front that the price is firm. It's a hot market these days."

"I'll look for your e-mail."

"Talk to you soon. Feel better!"

He ended the call. So Ike was talking to a Mexican real estate agent about buying a house. Not a bad idea, only he didn't understand why Ike had gone to the trouble of scribbling out the woman's name. Was Ike trying to hide something?

He searched the suite for Ike's cell phone. Not finding it, he decided to chance it and slipped into the punishers' bedroom, where he discovered Ike's cell phone lying on the dresser. It was a newer-model Droid. He left the bedroom and silently shut the door.

He locked himself into the bathroom. The Droid needed a password. He guessed it was something easy, and typed Ike's name in, no spaces. The phone unlocked itself. The screen was covered with apps. He pressed the e-mail app and went to Ike's inbox. In it were two e-mails from Amanda Fernandez, one sent moments ago. Its subject matter: "Your house—SMDA."

He read the e-mail. SMDA stood for San Miguel de Allende, a small colonial town tucked away in the heart of central Mexico. The property Fernandez was trying to sell Ike was called Ranchos de los

Olivos. Fernandez claimed it was "perfect for two gentlemen" and that it offered "all the amenities." Included was a link, which he clicked on. Soon he was taking a virtual tour of the ranch of the olives.

It was opulent by anyone's standards. Twelve acres of lush landscaping with a kidney-shaped swimming pool, four-stall horse barn, and a magnificent eight-thousand-square-foot ranch house with high-ceilinged rooms, polished wood floors, working fireplaces, and plenty of old-world charm. The asking price was $2,550,000, which Fernandez had said was firm.

The price raised a red flag. Ike and T-Bird's take from the scam was two million. Not enough to pay for this joint. So where was the rest of the money coming from? It certainly wasn't going to fall out of the sky.

He hadn't been born yesterday. Ike and T-Bird were planning to double-cross him and take it all.

- - -

He returned Ike's cell phone to the bedroom without waking them. Soon he was descending in an elevator to the main floor, where he got out and boarded a service elevator. He punched in the code that Ike had used the day before and hit the button for the fourteenth floor.

He started to rise and realized he was trembling. The fourteenth floor was his personal house of horrors, a place that he'd never wanted to return to. But it was also an area of the hotel that only a limited number of people had access to, and that made it valuable to him.

The doors parted and he stepped out. The floor was humming with activity—electricians installing light fixtures in the ceilings, carpenters firing nails, dusty men laying Sheetrock. The last unfinished rooms were coming together. Soon they'd be filled with guests, and the ghost of Ricky Boswell would have someone to keep him company.

He spent a moment checking the ceiling light fixtures in the hall. The covers had not been installed and the security cameras used to monitor guest activity were in plain view. The tiny red light that flashed when the cameras were operating was dark, and he guessed these cameras would not be operational until the floor was finished.

He entered an unfinished suite. The layout was identical to the suite where Ricky had died, and he walked down a hallway to the master bedroom. An electrician wearing dirty blue jeans and sneakers wrestled with ductwork for the room's AC handler inside the closet. The closet's back wall had been removed and was propped against the bed. The space behind the wall looked perfect for what he needed.

The electrician stepped out of the closet. "Who are you?"

"I'm in charge of decoration," he said.

"Where's your badge?"

"I don't have one. Is that a problem?"

"Everyone working on the floor is supposed to have a badge. Union rules. I'm going to have to report you, pal."

The guy had a chip on his shoulder the size of Mount Rushmore. It was the same with most people that worked for the casinos. The casinos made billions while their employees made jack. The imbalance created resentment that carried over into every phase of the employees' lives.

"I really wish you wouldn't do that. I don't need the union harassing me," he said.

The electrician said nothing, unmoved.

"Look, I've got a surplus of movie stills that aren't going to be used. I'll give them to you if you don't report me."

"Movie stills, huh. How many?" the electrician asked.

"Two dozen."

"What do they run?"

"A couple hundred apiece."

"No kidding. Anyone I've heard of?"

"Clint Eastwood, Marilyn Monroe, Jack Nicholson. Want them?"

"You bet I want them." The electrician wiped his hand on his pants leg and stuck it out. "My name's Buzzy. Nice doing business with you."

"Same here. I'll bring them by tomorrow."

"I'll be here. We're working all weekend."

He left the bedroom convinced the electrician would not call the union and report him. In the hallway he stopped to read the number on the brass door plaque. Room 1412.

By the elevators was a utility room. He went in and flipped on the overhead light. The room was a catchall and filled with garbage pails overflowing with debris. One man's garbage was another man's treasure, and in one pail he found a pair of painter's coveralls that reeked of turpentine. More digging revealed a painter's hat and a used surgical mask. He stuck everything on a shelf behind some equipment where the clothes would not be seen.

He came out of the utility room thinking he'd covered all his bases. If Ike and T-Bird thought they were going to rip him off, he'd let them continue to believe that, right until the bitter end. He was going to pay them back for every punch and every slap, so help him God.

Riding down to the main floor, he started to hum. The day was starting out right, and he had a sneaking feeling it was only going to get better.

FORTY-NINE

Gabe liked a good challenge. That was what separated the men from the boys, the rich from the poor. It was why he enjoyed working for Billy; a week didn't go by when the young hustler didn't present him with a new way to rob a casino, and challenge Gabe to manufacture the apparatus necessary to make the scam work.

So far, Gabe was batting a thousand. Not once had he let Billy down. But there was always a first time, and the challenge of counterfeiting fake hundred-thousand-dollar gold chips in his garage had proven harder than he'd anticipated.

Once upon a time, Vegas casinos got counterfeited on a regular basis. Clever thieves took advantage of inexperienced cashiers and lax security and passed off handfuls of bogus chips before sprinting to the exits with their loot.

Casinos hated to get robbed, even for a measly dollar. Over time, they'd devised a series of elaborate tests to stop fake chips from appearing in their cashiers' trays. These tests had proven highly effective, and today, it was rare to hear of a casino being counterfeited.

It was this hurdle that Gabe was attempting to overcome. He had to beat a series of tests that the industry considered foolproof. If he succeeded, endless days of wine and roses. If he failed, a life of banging out license plates in a prison machine shop.

Eight a.m. Saturday morning, after no sleep, he shuffled from his garage into the kitchen of his house carrying a tin can containing the forged chips that he'd spent the night slaving over. He yawned without covering his mouth.

The rest of the crew huddled around the kitchen table, eating scrambled eggs on paper plates. They'd spent the night bringing him coffee and keeping him company. Gabe had liked that. He missed his wife and kids, and it had been nice to have people in his house again.

"Ladies and gentlemen, may I have your attention, please. The show is about to begin," the jeweler announced. "Please remove your plates."

The kitchen table was cleared. Pouring the gold chips from the can, Gabe spread them out so each chip was exposed. Eighty chips in all, they covered a large portion of the table.

"Our first act is called pick the winner. One of these little beauties is the real hundred-thousand-dollar gold chip that Billy gave me to work with. The rest are counterfeits. I defy you to pick the winner. No touching, please. You have to do it by sight alone."

"How many chances do we get?" Misty asked.

"Three," Gabe said.

"What do we win if we pick it out?"

"You get to watch a grown man cry. On your marks. Ready, set . . . go!"

While the crew studied the chips, Gabe fixed himself a cup of coffee with the Keurig coffee machine and laced it with enough artificial sweetener to kill a lab rat. His ex-wife hadn't left much in the way of household furnishings, but the items she had left, like the Keurig, he used every single day. It made him think she still cared about him, if only a little bit.

"Time's up. Make your selections, please. Ladies first."

Misty picked three chips from the middle of the pile. Gabe explained that the real chip had been x-ed with a Sharpie on its opposite side. He flipped over Misty's selections.

"Sorry, you lose," he said.

"Fuck," she said.

Pepper went next, followed by Morris, Cory, and Travis. Each failed to find the real chip. Gabe smiled to himself. The color on the fake chips was a match. If it hadn't been, the real chip would have jumped out like a sore thumb.

"Which chip is real?" Travis asked.

"Beats me."

Gabe flipped the remaining chips over until he found the ringer. Each member of the crew took it and compared it to the others on the table.

"You're a genius," Travis declared.

"You're only saying that because it's true. Save your applause until we're done."

Billy had given Gabe a gym bag filled with chips from Galaxy's casino to work with. Gabe removed ten of these chips from his pocket and stacked them. He then made a second stack using ten fake gold chips and placed the two stacks side-by-side.

"New game," he said. "Who wants to play?"

"I do," Misty said.

"How good is your vision?"

"Twenty-twenty."

"Perfect. The chips in Galaxy's casino weigh eleven point five grams, are thirty-nine millimeters in diameter, and are exactly four millimeters wide. The fake chips I counterfeited should be exactly the same size. If

I erred, it will show up in these two stacks. I want you to visually compare the stacks and see if they're identical."

Misty placed her chin on the table and eyed the two stacks of chips. Gabe held his breath and waited. If he'd made even the slightest miscalculation in the width, it would be exposed when multiplied by the number of chips in the stack.

"They're exactly the same. What do I win?" Misty said.

"My never-ending gratitude."

"I've heard that one before."

Gabe had the others check as well. They all agreed that the stacks' heights were exactly the same. Every race had a finish line; his was now in sight.

Time for the third and last test. He asked Pepper to assist him. He arranged the chips into three stacks of five chips. Two of the stacks were real Galaxy chips, while the third contained five fake gold chips.

"Are you right-handed or left-handed?" he asked.

"I'm a rightie," Pepper replied.

"I want you to pick up one of the stacks of real chips and let them fall to the table. Do it slowly, and let each chip brush past your fingertips."

"What for?"

"I want you to get a feel for them. Casino chips are made from sand, chalk, and the same clay they use in kitty litter. It's what gives them that special feel."

"Cat litter? Come on, be serious."

"I am being serious. Now try it."

Pepper picked up a stack of real Galaxy chips and let them fall from her fingertips to the table. She repeated this several times.

"You're right. They do have a special feel," she said.

"Okay. Now close your eyes," Gabe said.

"Ohhh, this sounds like it's going to be fun."

Pepper shut her eyes. Gabe moved the stacks around the table as if playing the three-shell game. Then he guided Pepper's hand toward the stacks and had her repeat the process with each stack. All of the human senses could be tricked, except for human touch. If the stack of fake chips felt different than the others, her fingers would sense it.

"Which stack is the fakes?" Gabe asked.

"I'm not sure. Can I feel the stacks again?"

"Be my guest."

The process was repeated. Pepper seemed intent on picking out the phonies, and Gabe felt himself getting nervous. A female bank teller in Hong Kong had broken up a major counterfeiting ring while counting a stack of fake hundreds at work. The fake hundreds had beaten all the bank's detection devices but not the teller's acute sense of touch.

"Time's up. Please make your selection," he said.

"They all feel the same. I can't tell the difference," Pepper said.

"Pick one anyway."

Pepper picked up the center stack and opened her eyes. "Whoops, you got me."

She'd chosen a stack of real chips. Gabe walked around the kitchen collecting high fives from the rest of the crew. His work was done; now it was their turn to shine.

He took a place at the kitchen table and let them serve him breakfast. As the food was being prepared, Travis pulled up a chair. Picking up one of the fake gold chips, Travis rolled it across his hairy knuckles in dexterous fashion.

"What happens if we get caught with these babies?" Travis asked.

"You don't want to know," Gabe said.

"Got to. I've got a family now."

For the crime of dropping a slug in a slot machine, the state would put a person away for three years. For more sophisticated counterfeiting crimes, the penalties were more severe.

"You'll do five to seven for trying to pass the fake chips, and I'll do life for manufacturing them. I'm sure Billy's taken all of that into consideration."

"How so?"

"He'll get a sucker to cash in the fake chips. That's how major counterfeiting scams work. A sucker takes the risk, while the cheater gets the lion's share of the reward."

"What's the risk to us?"

"Inside the casino? None."

"How about outside the casino?"

"Just the equipment in my garage. If that gets found, we're screwed."

"Have you thought about dumping it?"

"I've already reserved a moving truck. On Sunday morning, I'll load up the equipment and make a trip to the landfill in Boulder City. You're welcome to come along."

"Boulder City's a haul. Why not dump it in a landfill nearby?"

"Vegas landfills use transfer stations, so the employees see what you're dumping. Boulder City doesn't have a transfer station. Once we dump the equipment, it's gone."

"You've thought this all out, haven't you?"

Gabe nodded and sipped his coffee. He was a stickler for cleaning up after a job. The more you cleaned, the less chance of getting caught. It had become so ingrained in Gabe's head that he thought about how he was going to clean up before every job he did.

"I've got a wife and kids, too, you know," Gabe added.

FIFTY

Mags awoke in the middle of the night with her ear on fire and chugged down a pain pill along with a glass of scotch to make the burning sensation go away. It had done a number on her, and at ten o'clock the next morning, she could not get out of bed. That would have been okay, only some jackass was pounding on her front door.

"Go away," she said.

The pounding grew frantic, the sound busting up the protective coating around her poor brain. It wasn't going to stop until she made it stop. Still wearing last night's clothes, she cleaned her teeth, brushed down her Bride of Frankenstein hair, and when she'd taken possession of herself, went into the living room and parted the curtains to the window that faced the street.

Frank was on the stoop, banging on the door. His SUV idled in the driveway, the black exhaust belching warning signals into the air. He was the last person she wanted to talk to, and she went into the kitchen and poured herself a glass of juice.

The pounding continued. If need be, Frank would break the door down. She got her courage up and ventured into the front of the house.

"Leave me alone," she said through the door. "I had a bad night. Go away."

"Open the door, Mags. You know what I want," he said.

"What if I say no?"

"You can't say no."

She opened the door and sunshine flooded the foyer. Frank brushed past her on his way to the living room. His hair was neatly parted and he'd trimmed the bushes from his ears. He only groomed himself when he was going to make a bust and thought he might get his picture taken. She didn't like it when he came to her place unannounced.

"You left your car on. Someone might steal it," she said.

"My boss is with me," he said.

"You mean Trixie? What a piece of shit that guy is. How do you put up with him?"

"I'm not going to be putting up with him for much longer. How about a cup of coffee?"

"Forget it."

"Thanks a lot. What's with the bandage on your ear?"

"It's a long story. I don't want you here. Say your piece, and get out."

"You're in some mood."

He ducked into the kitchen and poured himself a glass of water. Glass in hand, he returned to the living room and took the couch. He pointed at the lone chair in the room. "Sit down. In case you forgot, the gaming board is planning to bust Cunningham this afternoon, and you're going to help us. Give me any crap, and my boss will throw you in jail. Am I making myself clear?"

So much for Custer's Last Stand. She positioned her chair so she faced him. Frank drank his water and put the glass down on the coffee table. He smiled with the sincerity of a phony TV preacher. She was tempted to throw a lamp at him, just to wipe that smile off his ugly mug.

"This afternoon, the gaming board is going to raid Galaxy," he said. "The joint was built with drug money, and now it's being used to launder more drug money. We plan to bust the kingpin of the operation, Reverend T. Rock."

He took out his iPhone and keyed in a command. He turned the screen so Mags could see a live feed of a humongous black guy sitting poolside in a cabana. With him were two tattoo-covered Hispanic babes wearing leather bikinis.

"The women are named Margarita Jimenez and Damaris Olivio," he said. "They used to work for a Mexican drug cartel before Rock lured them away. Rumor is, they're absolutely lethal."

"What does this have to do with me?"

"Shut up, and let me finish. Two days ago, Rock brought eight million dollars in drug money to Galaxy's casino and passed it through the cage. The money was laundered through a chain of check-cashing stores in town and turned into money orders. Eight hundred of them, to be exact. Later today, Rock will go to the cage and get a leather briefcase with the money orders. We're going to bust Rock once the transfer is made."

Her wounded ear throbbed. She needed to take another pain pill and climb into bed. But first, she needed to get Frank out of her house.

"We plan to nail Cunningham as well and make it seem as if he's working for Rock," Frank said. "Kill two birds with one stone, if you will. To do that, we need to bust Cunningham inside the casino. That's where you come in."

"You don't say."

"Don't get smart with me. You struck a deal with us, and I'm going to hold you to it."

Whatever promises she'd made to Frank and his boss had gotten flushed down the toilet. Billy had saved her life last night, and she was not going to double-cross him, even if it meant lying through her teeth to Frank.

"You still haven't told me what you want me to do."

"We want you to establish contact with Cunningham before the raid, to verify where he is inside Galaxy."

"I'm not going back inside that place."

"Don't worry. There will be more gaming agents inside that joint than you can shake a stick at. You'll be totally safe."

"I'm not going back inside. The people running that place are crazy."

"You can't say no."

"Try me."

"Don't do this, Mags. You'll regret it."

"I'm not your slave. No."

"All right, have it your way. You can draw Cunningham out to the valet area. Then you don't have to go in."

"Is that your idea of a compromise?"

"Yes. I've got a lot riding on this. My career's at stake."

Frank's last promotion had gone up in flames because Billy had outsmarted him, and she guessed another promotion was now on the line and would be granted if Frank went where no gaming agent had gone before, and put Billy's cute little ass in the slammer. It was the opening she'd been looking for, and she said, "I'll do it, but I want something in return."

"You're not in a position to bargain with me."

"Really."

"Don't even think about it, Mags. You're wasting your breath."

Frank had tipped his mitt and told Mags that he needed her. It was leverage, and she went to the front door and flung it open. "Get out of my fucking house."

"You can't throw me out."

"Yes, I can. This is my place, and I didn't ask you in. If you don't leave, I'll call 911."

"Don't be stupid."

She took out her cell phone and started punching numbers. Frank jumped off the couch and rushed her. His movements suggested he might do something irrational.

"Don't. Please, Mags. I can't let this one get away."

She stopped dialing. "This is all about your fucking job, isn't it, Frank?"

His eyes fell shamefully to the floor, and he did not reply.

"Answer me," she said tersely.

"Yeah," he mumbled.

"I thought so. I want this arrangement to be over. I'll draw Billy out this afternoon, but from that moment on, my agreement with the gaming board is over. I also never want to see you again. Do you understand?"

Still looking at the floor, he nodded.

"Good. Now, go talk it over with your boss. Don't come back until he says yes."

Frank walked out of the town house. She watched him climb into the idling vehicle in the driveway before slamming the door.

- - -

She gulped down a pain pill before going to her study. Got on her desktop and drew up a letter of termination between her and the gaming board, to take effect at 5:00 p.m. tonight. She cleaned up the typos before making two copies on the laser-jet printer she'd bought at Staples. From the front of the house came a pounding on the front door. Return of the caveman.

She opened the door and Frank just stood there, scared of her now.

"Trixie's not happy about this," he said.

"Shocking. Tell him to get in here."

"Don't order me around."

"I have something you want, Frank, remember? Go get him."

"You're being really stupid, Mags."

She laughed in his face. She had a job waiting with Billy's crew when this was over. That, and a brand new life. Frank could go to hell, for all she cared.

Frank got his boss from the car and they came inside. Mags slapped the termination letter on the dining room table for them to read. When they were done, she asked them if they had any questions. None were forthcoming, so she signed each letter next to where she'd printed her name, then stuck the pen in Frank's hand. Frank signed each document next to where his own name was printed. The pen was passed to Trixie, who initialed both signatures and dated them. Mags walked them outside to the car, feeling elated.

"I'll be by at twelve thirty to pick you up," Frank said. "And don't try to cross me. I'll throw your ass in jail if you do."

"And deny you your promotion? I wouldn't dream of it," she said.

Frank got into the SUV and disappeared behind the tinted glass. Trixie remained in the driveway.

"I'd suggest you pack your belongings and get out of Vegas when this is done," Trixie said. "The other hustlers in town won't be very accommodating when they hear you're a snitch."

"Do you plan on telling them?" she asked.

"Word will get out. It always does."

"Hold that thought. I'll be right back."

Mags got her cell phone from the bedroom. Coming outside, she opened the Gallery app and stuck the phone in Trixie's face. With her thumb, she scrolled through the shots she'd secretly taken of Frank and her doing the nasty in various hotel rooms during the past year. There were over sixty. Each had a date. Frank was big on cunnilingus, and the dreamy look in his eyes as he was going down on her made his boss turn crimson.

"That's extortion," Trixie said.

"You hurt me, I hurt you," she said.

"Are you threatening me?"

"Why yes, yes, I am."

"The gaming board will destroy you. Or did you forget that?"

"My girlfriend has a memory stick with these photos on it. If anything ever happens to me . . . Well, you know the rest."

Trixie's face was a blank, but behind his eyes a bad movie was playing where everybody died in the end. Mags touched his sleeve.

"Call it a truce. You can't win all the time, you know," she said.

"We'll see about that."

They left and she went inside. She was going to call Billy and tell him about the raid. She didn't know how to break the news without telling him she was a snitch, but she'd figure it out. But first, she was going to lie down before the side of her head exploded.

FIFTY-ONE

In Billy's opinion, Vegas hotels served the best food around. Take the late-morning room-service breakfast he was eating in his suite. A mouth-watering frittata made from organic cage-free eggs, grilled chicken, roasted tomatoes, and a slice of sourdough toast on the side. Growing up, he'd never dreamed a meal could taste this good.

His Droid beeped. Travis had sent him a text. The counterfeit gold chips were done and had passed muster. The last cheat to take down Vegas with fake chips had been another Providence native, Lou "The Coin" Colavecchio, and that was over twenty years ago. Billy sent Travis a reply and told him to bring the crew to the hotel for a meeting, then resumed eating his breakfast.

Ike and T-Bird sat across from him, battling their hangovers with coffee.

"What are you smiling about?" Ike asked.

"That was my guy. The fake chips are ready," he said.

"You still haven't told us how this scam's going to work," Ike said, holding his mug with both hands. "It would be nice to know, considering we're a part of it."

"Yeah, let's hear the details," T-Bird chimed in.

The time for secrecy was over. Clearing the table, he took a pair of salt and pepper shakers and placed them on the table's edge. On the left side of the table, he placed a sugar bowl; on the right side, the purple zinnia in a small vase that had come with his meal.

"This table represents the casino, and these salt and pepper shakers are you guys," he said. "The sugar bowl is the blackjack pit. The flower is the cage. With me so far?"

"Which one of us is the salt?" T-Bird wanted to know.

"Shut the fuck up," Ike said.

"Here's what's going to happen. At three forty-five, the Gypsy wedding will take place inside the chapel. The ceremony will last fifteen minutes. When it's over, the Gypsies will walk down the hall through the lobby and enter the casino." He walked two fingers across the table, stopping at the sugar bowl. "Upon reaching the blackjack pit, they'll stop to have their picture taken. This distraction will allow them to perform a little act called the Dazzle. The Dazzle is designed to fool security into not seeing that a member of the wedding party is gone."

"One of them's going to disappear?" Ike asked.

"It will seem that way. The invisible member will remove a dealing shoe hidden inside the bride's gown and switch it for a shoe on a high-limit table. At that moment, I'll alert security, and they'll pounce and expose the scam. That's when you rob the cage."

"How we going to do that?" T-Bird asked.

He pushed the salt and pepper shakers toward the single flower. "At four o'clock, Ike will call the cage and tell the cage manager that Rock is ready to cash out. A few minutes later, you guys will appear. T-Bird will have two lovely ladies with him who work for me. He'll pass the fake chips to the cage manager and get the money orders in return. You'll leave through the hotel's back exit with my crew. We'll chop up the money later."

"But I don't look nothing like Rock," T-Bird protested. "The cage manager's gonna notice and sound the alarm."

"No, he won't. According to a blackjack dealer named Jazzy I spoke with, the Saturday employees are starting their workweek. Since this is Rock's first visit to the hotel, it's a lock the Saturday employees have never seen him. They don't know who Rock is."

"So how's the cage manager going to know?" T-Bird asked.

"He'll have to take Ike's word for it," Billy said.

"So I gotta be convincing when I call the cage," Ike said.

"That's right. You have to sell the cage manager that T-Bird is Rock."

"I can do that," Ike said.

T-Bird didn't look comfortable with the explanation.

"If it makes you feel better, I'll have my girls put you in disguise," he said. "They can shave your head and tie a pillow around your belly. By the time they're done with you, you'll pass as Rock's twin brother."

The bird man mulled it over. "Well, all right. Sure hate losing my dreads."

"So grow them back. One more thing. Two members of my crew will be stationed by the cage. If an employee happens by, they'll turn him. Any questions?"

"I'm good," T-Bird said.

"What about the Gypsies?" Ike said.

"What about them?"

"You know how Doucette is about cheaters. You gonna let him kill them?"

"Why do you care what happens to the Gypsies?"

"I don't care. I just wondered if you were gonna let him."

He'd been avoiding the question for days, believing that when the time came, he'd come up with a clever way to save the Gypsies from getting their brains bashed in. The time was now, and he balled up his napkin and tossed it onto his plate.

"Let me think about it," he said, and went outside to the balcony.

- - -

He hung on the railing, racking his brains. How was he going to stop the Gypsies from getting hurt without getting himself hurt in the process? No good solution came to mind.

The Strip was jumping: tourists, peddlers, hookers, and plenty of nut jobs. He was looking at one right now, standing in the crosswalk of Sahara wearing bright blue underwear and a Superman cape with a screaming gold *S* stitched crookedly on the back. Nutso flapped his arms, as if preparing for liftoff. Traffic ground to a halt. Horns blared.

A swarm of uniformed cops appeared in the crosswalk. The cops pinned the would-be Man of Steel's skinny arms behind his back, slapped on the cuffs, did a thorough frisk, and led their man to a cruiser parked by the curb, where they shoved him into the back. The cruiser sped away with ruby-sapphire lights flashing, the crown jewels of trouble.

As busts went, it was as pretty as a ballet. Vegas had one of the largest forces of street cops in the world, over two thousand strong. The largest concentration was deployed around the convention center and the Strip, where the tourists were. Using bike patrols, motorcycle units, and cruisers, they did a good job of keeping things safe. Dozens of cops were right outside Galaxy's front doors every day. Just a simple call to 911 and they'd appear.

That was it. He'd call the cops and tell the operator a psycho was inside Galaxy's casino, shooting up the place. The cops would appear and save the Gypsies from getting hurt. If the Gypsies handled themselves right, they might even be able to sue Galaxy for damages.

It was all good, but it wasn't good enough. By ratting out the Gypsies, he was breaking the code never to hurt another cheat. That required making things right with them. Perhaps he'd hear about a casino with a flawed security system and pass the information to them. Or, he'd let them know where Ricky was buried so they could retrieve the body and give the kid a proper send-off. Whatever he did, it needed to be significant enough to erase the harm he'd caused. He went back inside. Ike and T-Bird were still sucking down coffee.

"That was fast," Ike said.

"Compared to you, anything's fast," T-Bird said.

"Shut up," Ike said.

The sound of the door being unlocked snapped their heads. Even to a casual observer, the unusual layout on the table would arouse suspicion and lead to questions Billy did not wish to answer. With a sweep of his arm, he sent the salt and pepper shakers, sugar bowl, and flower vase to the floor, where he swept them under the couch with his foot. Evidence gone.

Shaz entered wearing a white pantsuit and a string of white pearls. To keep the color theme correct, her eyes were dilating, and she appeared to be riding the white pony.

"Reverend Rock requests the presence of your company," she said, making it sound like a death sentence. "Get moving."

FIFTY-TWO

As Billy followed Shaz to the pool area, a group of bikini-clad young things strolled past. Weekends were his favorite time in Vegas. On Friday nights, cars with California plates pulled into the hotels, and throngs of girls climbed out clutching overnight bags and pillows. These girls often stayed five to a room, sleeping on floors and sharing food they brought from home. The casinos were cool with it because they drew men the way honey draws bears.

Shaz pulled out her cell phone and stopped by the pool. It was a replica of the magnificent pool at the Beverly Hills Hotel, with pink cabanas and striped lounge chairs.

"I've got Cunningham with me—where are you?" she said into her phone. "You're having lunch? We'll be right in." She turned to him. "Rock has some business to discuss with you."

"What kind of business?" he asked.

"Our business."

The café had a checkerboard tile floor and metal tables and catered to the pool crowd. A hostess escorted them to a doorway with a velvet rope stretched across it. The rope came down, and the hostess led them into a second dining room, where Rock sat at a corner table, eating lunch. The drug kingpin wore ridiculously small bathing trunks and could have passed as a chocolate Buddha. His bodyguards wore bikini bottoms and T-shirts with long sleeves to hide the knives they kept strapped to their forearms.

"Leave," Rock said to the hostess. To Ike and T-Bird he said, "Stand in the corner."

The punishers moved away from the table, and the hostess disappeared.

"You two pull up a chair," Rock said.

Billy and Shaz made themselves comfortable. Rock resumed eating an artery-clogging double-bacon cheeseburger. When it was gone, he picked at a mountain of french fries covered in ketchup. The conversation would not begin until he was ready for it to begin. Back home, Billy had known drug dealers who'd drag a subject into a bathroom stall and make him watch while they crapped. It was a form of intimidation, designed to remind you who was boss.

"I hear you killed a woman last night," the drug kingpin said. "That your first time?"

Billy realized he was being tested and grew rigid in his chair.

"Yeah," he said.

"How did it make you feel?"

He shrugged, not sure what to say.

"Answer me."

"I was numb, but then it wore off," he said.

"What did you do after you buried her?"

"Had dinner."

"You were hungry?"

"Yeah."

"You're not bullshitting me, are you?"

"No. We were hungry, so we went out for a late dinner."

Rock gave him a cold stare. "Which restaurant?"

“We went to a Brazilian steakhouse called Fogo de Chão on East Flamingo. You should try it sometime. The steaks are great.”

“You don’t say.” Rock addressed the punishers. “Is pretty boy telling the truth?”

“Uh-huh. Best steaks in town,” Ike said.

“Don’t fuck with me, asshole. Did you eat there last night?”

“Yes, suh,” Ike said.

Rock crossed his hands over his enormous belly and belched. “I once had a guy working for me went by the name Freeway. Freeway’s deal was that he sold bags of coke at exits off the freeway. Freeway wanted to move up and become a lieutenant in my organization, so I decided to test him. I needed a rival killed, so I ordered Freeway to take the guy out. I drove Freeway there so I could watch. He walks up to the guy on the corner, caps him, and jumps into my car. As we’re leaving, he pukes on the upholstery. The blood upset him.”

Rock shook his head at the memory. His Mexican bodyguards laughed to themselves.

“Freeway was a weakling, so I got rid of him,” the drug kingpin said. “You, on the other hand, have the right stuff to join my organization. You interested?”

It was a job interview. Billy tried to keep a straight face.

“You want me to push drugs for you?” he asked.

“I got a hundred guys selling drugs for me,” Rock said. “I want you to police my casino, keep hustlers from stealing my money. I’ll pay you real good, give you a car, penthouse, all the blow you want, pussy, too. You won’t regret coming to work for me. Will he?”

“Rock’s the best,” Shaz said.

“What do you say?” Rock asked. “You in?”

Billy believed in seizing opportunities whenever they presented themselves to him. Only one person stood in the way of him ripping off Galaxy’s casino this afternoon, and that was his old pal Crunchie. If

Crunchie's grift sense kicked in, he'd blow the whistle on Billy and his crew and bring everything crashing down on Billy's head.

"The last time I checked, Crunchie was policing your casino," Billy said. "Is he staying? If he is, then my answer is no. I won't work alongside that prick."

Rock was not a man to be challenged. He picked up his walking stick from the floor and dropped the handle on Billy's shoulder, causing the young hustler to wince in pain.

"You got a lot of balls, little fellow. I'll answer your question, but only this one time. Crunchie's history."

"Then I'm in," he said.

"Good. We're meeting in Doucette's office at two to discuss how we plan to deal with these Gypsies trying to rip me off. Don't be late."

"I'll be there," he said.

"Don't make me regret this decision."

"You won't."

"Get out of here, and let me finish my lunch." To Shaz he said, "Hang around for a few minutes. We have some things to discuss."

"Sure, Rock," she said.

Billy tried not to laugh as he walked out of the café with the punishers. He'd pulled some major snow jobs in his time, but this one ranked at the very top.

His Droid was talking to him. Another text from Travis. His crew was camped out in the employee parking lot, waiting for Billy to show his face.

"It's time for you to meet my crew," he said to the punishers.

FIFTY-THREE

Billy had used casino employee parking garages to stage meetings in the past. The casinos were too cheap to install surveillance cameras or pay guards to police them, making the garages safe havens for thieves and scammers plotting their next big score.

The elevator was still out, and he trotted up the stairs to the garage's fourth floor. The stairwell was as hot as a furnace, and Ike and T-Bird were gasping when they reached the top landing. He'd assumed that they were in good physical shape but was having second thoughts. Cheaters had to be fast on their feet for all the obvious reasons.

"You sure this is a safe place to meet?" Ike asked.

"You didn't see any cameras in the ceiling, did you?" he pointed out.

"What if we run across some security or surveillance people? Those guys are suspicious of everybody. They see you having a meeting, they'll know something is going on."

"Security and surveillance people are required to park in a different garage and use a different entrance to the casino. The casinos don't want them fraternizing with other employees, for fear if they catch them stealing, they won't report it. So they separate them."

"Man knows all the angles," T-Bird said.

They exited the stairwell. Every parking space was filled except for two handicap spaces by the door. Cory and Morris's Infiniti SUV was squeezed into the narrowest of spaces. Billy's crew stood outside the vehicle engaged in small talk. To a casual observer, they appeared to be a group of friends out for the day. Nothing about their appearance said crook.

"Good afternoon. How's everyone doing?" Billy said.

"We're the only ones up here. I checked," Travis said.

"Good. I want to introduce my friends, Ike and T-Bird. They're going to be a part of our operation this afternoon. If you're nice, they'll show you their Super Bowl rings."

The punishers mumbled hello. His crew responded in kind. Each side spent a few moments sizing the other up.

"Let's see the goods," Billy said.

Gabe removed the Nike gym bag from the SUV and passed it to Billy, who took a look inside. Eight million in glittering gold casino chips stared back at him.

"You tested them?" he asked.

"Every which way but Sunday. They're perfect," Gabe said.

"Good job."

He stopped talking. A blinking light had caught his eye. It didn't look natural, and he walked between two cars until he was standing at the wall that faced the rear of the casino, where there was a pool area and a pair of bright blue tennis courts. He tried to pinpoint the light's origin but could not. Travis edged up behind him.

"Something wrong?" the big man asked.

"I thought I saw a reflection," he said.

"Binoculars?"

"Maybe. Or a high-powered camera."

"Think someone's spying on us?"

"There's always someone spying on us in this fucking town."

"What do you want to do?"

"I don't see it now. Maybe it was nothing."

Travis dropped his voice. "So where'd you find these jokers?"

"It's a long story," he whispered back.

"I don't trust them."

"Nor should you."

"Got it."

Billy turned from the wall and went back to his crew. Ike was showing off his Super Bowl ring to Cory and Morris, while T-Bird was chatting with Pepper and Misty. Gabe stood off to the side, clutching the bag of counterfeit chips protectively against his chest.

"Everyone, listen up," he said. "In a few hours, we're going to pull off the biggest heist this town has seen in a while. I need your undivided attention for a few minutes."

The conversations stopped, and they huddled around him.

"Here's the deal. At a few minutes past four o'clock, Ike and T-Bird are going to make a run at the cage and hand over the counterfeit chips to a cashier in return for a briefcase containing eight million in untraceable money orders. That in a nutshell is how we're going to rip the joint off. T-Bird will be impersonating a drug dealer and will need to have appropriate threads. You're also going to have to shave off his dreads.

"I've been thinking about where this transformation should happen, and decided my suite at the hotel would be best. Misty and Pepper, come to my suite at two thirty with clothes for T-Bird to wear. Sound good, ladies?"

Misty and Pepper both said sure, no big deal.

"Each of you has a role in today's heist," he went on. "T-Bird needs two Mexican female bodyguards to accompany him. Misty and Pepper, that's you. Dark wigs and lots of makeup should do the trick. You'll also need some dangerous attire."

"Who has female bodyguards?" Pepper asked skeptically.

"Prince had female bodyguards when he was doing the *Purple Rain* tour," Misty reminded her. "They came with him to one of the awards shows."

"I remember them. They were wicked looking," Pepper said.

"Think you can handle it?" Billy asked.

They both said yes.

"Gabe and Travis are going to play dumb tourists, and need to be hanging around the cage when the chips are cashed in," he continued. "Their job will be to intercept any employees that walk by, and turn their attention away from the cage."

"I can do that," Gabe said.

"Same here," Travis said.

"Cory and Morris, you drive the escape car. Go to the airport, and use fake ID to rent a red Chevy Malibu from a rental company. Bring the car to the rear exit of the casino at ten minutes before four. Park by the exit, and have the trunk unlocked. Got it?"

"Why a red Chevy Malibu?" Cory asked.

"It's the number-one rental car in Vegas. Harder for the police to locate in case you're chased."

"Got it," Cory said.

"At a few minutes past four, there's going to be a major commotion by the blackjack pit that will draw security. That's when Ike and T-Bird will cash in the fake chips. Once they have the money orders, they'll leave through the back exit, where Cory and Morris will be waiting for them. The four of them will head back to Gabe's house, where they'll hole up.

"Gabe and Travis will hang around the cage for a few minutes to make sure everything's cool. Then they'll hook up with Misty and Pepper and leave the casino. I'll meet up with everyone later tonight. We'll chop up the score and go out for a victory meal."

He paused to gauge their expressions. It was a lot of information to absorb, and he wanted to be sure that each person understood what his or her role in the operation was.

"If you have any questions, ask them now," he said.

"What kind of commotion?" Cory asked.

"I'm going to sic security on a family of cheaters scamming the casino."

"You're ratting out another group of cheaters?" Cory sounded incredulous.

"Not in the way the casino wants. They won't go to jail, and they'll come out on the winning end of things in the end."

"How you going to pull that off?" Cory asked.

Billy had taught Cory the cheater's code, along with every other cheater that had run with him. The code spelled out how the game was played and what the rules were that they lived by. He tousled Cory's hair until the younger man loosened up.

"Trust me on this," he said. "It will all work out."

"Okay," Cory said.

They were done, and he said good-bye to his crew. If things broke bad, he might not see them again for a while, and he took the time to speak to them individually. Done, he walked toward the stairwell with the punishers. At the entrance he stopped as if he had forgotten something.

"I didn't give the girls the key to my suite. I'll meet you downstairs."

The punishers headed down the stairs. He turned around and walked back to where the SUV was parked. His crew had gotten in, ready to leave. The passenger window came down, and Misty stuck her head out.

"Hey, stranger, what's shaking?" she said.

He took the room key from his pocket and handed it to her. "You're going to need this. I'm staying in Tower A, suite 1841. What do you think of my friends?"

"They're a couple of two-bit hustlers," Misty said.

"I'll second that," Pepper said, wedged in beside her. "They're scum buckets."

"I wouldn't trust them with my kid's lunch money," Gabe added from the backseat.

"We don't like them, either," Cory said.

He rested his elbows on the open windowsill. "Your instincts are good. These boys are planning to rip us off. Forget everything I said about leaving with them in the rental. Once the exchange is made at the cage, I want you to do the pigeon drop, then get out of the casino as fast as you can. Does everyone remember the pigeon drop?"

The pigeon drop was the first street scam that Billy had learned when he was apprenticing, and he'd taught the scam to everyone who'd run with him. It was a surefire way to separate a sucker from his money. Everyone inside the vehicle said they remembered the scam.

"Good. Travis, you'll be the steerer. Gabe will do the switch while Misty and Pepper keep the boys distracted. You'll need to get a leather briefcase for the switch. Cory and Morris, that's your job. Everyone clear on what they have to do?"

Another group yes. They were all on board.

"Here's to getting rich together."

With that, he rapped his knuckles on the roof and walked away.

FIFTY-FOUR

Mags punched the horn of her rental. A hard rain was falling that had turned the streets treacherous, and traffic wasn't moving. She jumped out to see what the problem was. Up ahead, two vehicles had collided, the drivers standing in the road inspecting the damage.

She decided to hoof it. Leaving the keys in the ignition, she hustled down the sidewalk with the university's majestic spires in view. No member of the Flynn dynasty had ever made it to college, her family tree filled with losers and two-bit thieves, a tradition she'd faithfully carried on. Amber was about to break the mold, and Mags was determined not to miss the seismic moment.

It was her first visit to the college, and the manicured grounds and stately buildings made her choke up. Tuition had to be expensive. Had Amber gotten a scholarship? Mags didn't know. Some mother she was.

The gymnasium's shimmering glass walls captured her quiet desperation as she hurried inside. For all these years she'd carried around the belief that she and Amber would one day form a bond beyond the infrequent phone call. It happened on the Hallmark Channel all the time.

The lobby was deserted. She went to the nearest set of doors and tugged at the handles. The doors opened, and a black maintenance man gave her a scornful look.

"It's over, lady. You're too late," the maintenance man said.

She rushed past him onto the polished parquet floors. The gym was a sea of bleachers covered in discarded programs, while up on stage, two workers dismantled the podium.

She choked back her tears. She imagined Amber receiving her diploma to no applause. How many other grads had suffered that ignominy? She wanted to blame someone for being late, but in reality, she had no one to blame but herself.

"Wake up."

Her head came off her pillow. Frank stood beside the bed, holding a steaming mug. He put it under her nose, the fumes snapping her awake.

"How . . . did you get in?" she stammered.

"When you didn't answer your phone, I picked the lock," Frank said.

"You said you were coming at twelve thirty."

"It is twelve thirty. We need to get moving. I told my boss we'd be there at one."

The coffee brought her around. She hadn't contacted Billy to warn him, and she slipped out of bed and took her iPhone off the night table. Frank intercepted her at the bathroom door and yanked the cell phone out of her hand.

"Give me that," she said.

"You don't need your cell phone in there," he said.

"I want to send my daughter a text. I haven't been in touch with her in a while."

"Do it later, on your own time."

– – –

The Strip was a madhouse. Thousands of tourists oozed along the sidewalks clutching plastic cups of draft beer and yard-glass containers filled with potent rum concoctions. Every day was Mardi Gras in Las Vegas, every night a Super Bowl party.

"Where are you taking me?" Mags asked.

"See those NV Energy vehicles parked the next block over? There," Frank said.

Parked in front of Galaxy was a convoy of Nevada Energy vehicles. This included a truck with a cherry picker, two white vans, and a camper-sized vehicle with a satellite dish on the roof. A crew of utility workers was fixing the spaghetti power lines running to the hotel. It looked legit, until Mags noticed that the man in charge was Frank's piece-of-shit boss Trixie.

"There's something you're not telling me," she said.

Frank's hands clutched the wheel as if clinging to a life jacket.

"We have a deal," she said. "If you're changing the deal, I want to know."

Frank took out his cell phone and punched in a command.

"The changes are about this," Frank said.

She squinted at the screen. Eight people gathered inside a covered parking garage. Billy, two big black dudes, a fat guy holding a gym bag, two kids with curly mops of hair, a big man with his back to the camera, and two babes pretty enough for porno.

"That was taken inside Galaxy's employee parking garage earlier," Frank explained. "We think Cunningham's planning to rip off Galaxy today, and that's his crew."

"You're going to catch him in the act."

"Damn straight. He'll do serious time."

"What do you mean serious time?"

"Twenty-five to life, no parole."

"You think you can nail all of them?" she asked, swallowing hard.

"That's the plan. We've doubled the number of agents for the bust."

It wasn't adding up. The gaming board was raiding Galaxy to bust a drug dealer and shut down a money-laundering operation. Billy was just icing on the cake, or so she'd been led to believe.

"Why all this attention on Billy?" she asked. "This other guy's a drug dealer. He's more important, isn't he?"

"Rock's goose is already cooked. The gaming board just wanted to arrest him inside the casino because it was good publicity. Busting Cunningham is a different story. That little motherfucker humiliated us. We've got a score to settle with him."

"So this is personal."

"You got it, baby."

"You still haven't told me how my deal's changed."

"You're going to help us catch the whole crew."

"But that wasn't our agreement."

"It is now."

Harrah's was across the street from Galaxy. Frank pulled in and gave the valet his keys. Then he came around to Mags's side of the vehicle and told her to get out.

"I'm warning you, don't try anything stupid," he said.

They walked down the Strip to an elevated walkway, took the escalator up, and crossed over. The walkway was crowded and Frank pushed his way through. Another escalator took them down to the opposite side of the street, and they headed toward the convoy of NV trucks.

Mags decided it was time to end her relationship with the gaming board. She started to make a run for it, but Frank forced her up the stairs of the camper-sized vehicle. He opened the back door and brusquely shoved her inside.

The door shut behind her. Three gaming agents sat before a matrix of video monitors. Gaming agents were voyeurs; they eavesdropped on phone conversations, opened other people's mail, and stuck their noses where they didn't belong. A gruff female agent with steel-gray hair appeared in charge.

"You must be the snitch," the female agent said. "What's your name?"

"Maggie."

"Okay, Maggie, I want you to sit over there in the corner. Don't open your mouth unless I speak to you. Am I making myself clear?"

"Yes, ma'am."

Whatever chance she'd had to warn Billy had been lost. She sank down in the chair under the female agent's wilting gaze.

"And don't get any bright ideas," the female agent added.

FIFTY-FIVE

At two o'clock, Billy entered Doucette's office. A makeshift home theater had been erected in the room's center. Four seventy-inch flat-screen TVs on rolling flat-panel stands, each set turned on, showing a live surveillance feed from the casino floor. The cameras were in four-color *and* HD, and the images literally popped off the screens.

On the first screen was a feed from the wedding chapel. Next to it, a feed from the bustling hotel lobby. The third feed was the entrance to Galaxy's casino, the fourth from the casino floor. Now dressed in pretty clothes, Rock sat on the couch, accompanied by his female bodyguards. Doucette and his bride stood behind the couch, sipping bottles of mineral water. His old pal Crunchie was not on the premises, and he guessed the old grifter had been relieved of his duties.

"Like it?" Rock asked.

"I'm impressed," Billy said.

Rock picked up a walkie-talkie and spoke into it. "Show your faces." On the second screen, hotel security came out of the woodwork and filled the lobby. They were big men wearing ill-fitting suits and ultra-mean faces, just spoiling for a fight.

"Go back to your stations," Rock said to them.

The security goons faded away.

"I'd say you're ready for the Gypsies," Billy said.

"We're more than ready, my little friend." Rock exchanged the walkie-talkie for a remote. "I'm going to show you the meaning of Big Brother."

Rock tapped the remote. On the first screen appeared a Hispanic couple at the chapel altar. The bride had a small tattoo on her forearm. Another tap, and the tattoo grew in size to show a brown-skinned Virgin Mary standing on a crescent-shaped moon held up by an angel.

"I want one of those," the bodyguard to Rock's left said.

"I'll get you one when we get back," Rock promised.

"You can operate the camera's PTZ from your remote?" Billy asked.

"That's right. Ain't nothing down there I can't see," Rock said.

Pan-tilt-zoom cameras had ruined more than one cheater's career. PTZs could read the date off a dime and, when enabled with auto tracking, would follow a cheater around the casino while recording his every movement. It was going to make his crew's job this afternoon a lot harder, but not impossible. Nothing was impossible when eight million bucks were at stake.

The ceremony ended, and the Hispanic couple left the chapel and entered the lobby. As the groom patted his brow, Rock fingered the remote. Beads of sweat filled the screen.

"Look at that poor bastard," Rock laughed. "He's cooked, isn't he, Marcus?"

"I'll say," Doucette replied.

Shaz shot her husband a murderous look.

The Hispanic couple entered the casino and celebrated by shooting craps together. The bride blew on the dice for luck before sending them down the table. Rock hit a button and the dice filled the screen. A seven, a winner.

"You've got that down pretty good," Billy said.

"Yes, I have," Rock said. "When the Gypsies are getting married this afternoon, you're going to be down on the floor, following them, and I'm going to be watching you."

Good, Billy thought. *Watch me, but don't watch my friends.*

"What exactly do you want me to do?" he asked.

"Expose the Gypsies' scam so we can get it on video," Rock said. "Once you do that, security will haul them into the back and teach them a lesson."

"You going to rough them up?"

"That's none of your fucking business," Rock snapped, "but since you asked, I'll tell you. We're going to take the leader of the gang and his wife and crush their fucking skulls in. We'll tell the police they put up a fight and had to be subdued. I'd kill the whole fucking party, but I don't want the publicity." He studied Billy's face. "You have a problem with that?"

Billy shook his head.

"Come again," Rock said.

"No, I don't have a problem with that."

"I might even ask you to help us. Got a problem with *that*?"

"Nope."

"Glad to hear it. Now get outta here. I hate looking at guys prettier than me."

Rock glanced over his shoulder at Shaz. "Show our friend out."

Shaz came up beside Billy and locked arms. Instead of escorting him to the door, she marched the young hustler across the office to the paneled wall. With a press of her palm, a hidden door sprung open, followed by a gentle push that said he was to go first.

He entered the ultimate man cave. Full bar, the latest pinball machines, the biggest flat screen he'd ever seen, and a collection of lewd paintings of delicious black chicks. This had to be Rock's secret hangout. Shaz went to the bar and pulled a bottle off the shelf.

"How do you like your scotch?" she asked.

"Straight up."

"In case you haven't realized it, Rock digs you."

"But he doesn't trust me."

"Don't sweat it. Rock doesn't trust anybody."

"I'm not appreciating the difference."

"Rock likes your style. He didn't like Crunchie at all. He thought the old hustler was looking down his nose at him because he was black."

"I didn't see Crunchie hanging around. Did you lose him?"

"In a manner of speaking, yes." She came around the bar with the drinks and handed him one. They clinked glasses.

"Here's to joining our team."

"I'll drink to that."

The scotch burned going down. Shaz drank hers like it was water and rattled the ice cubes in her empty glass.

"Come here. I want to show you something."

She led him to a private elevator in the corner of the room and hit the call button. The doors parted, and the breath caught in his throat. Crunchie was inside, tied to a chair, his mouth frozen in agony. Cause of death was two knife wounds. The first a lateral slash across the forehead. An old street-fighting trick, designed to blind an opponent with a sheet of blood. The second a stab to the heart, the knife left in to prevent excessive bleeding. The knife's handle was carved to resemble a Mexican sugar skull.

One of Rock's bodyguards had done this. Or maybe both had.

"It's time you and I got to know each other a little better," she said.

"In there?" he asked incredulously.

"Yeah, in there."

They got in, and she hit a button. As they descended, she covered his face in kisses while undoing the front of his shirt. Billy put his arms around her waist and drew her close. She shut her eyes and moaned pleasurably. She was lost in the moment, and his hands went through Crunchie's pockets and found a wallet. He extracted the slip of paper with the information about his crew that Crunchie had taken off his cell phone. He did all of these things while trying not to look into Crunchie's face out of fear he might never forget.

The elevator bounced to a stop, and the doors parted.

"You ready?" she asked.

"You serious?"

"I'm always serious when it comes to sex. I can use the key and lock us in. We can fuck standing in the corner, or on top of him. Ménage à trois with a dead man is the ultimate turn-on."

"You've done this before?"

"You bet. Why are you looking at me that way?"

The dead were not meant to be messed with. Had he killed the old grifter himself, it would have been with a bullet to the back of the head. He would not have made him suffer.

He stepped out of the elevator and spent a moment getting his bearings. He was in a private parking garage beneath the hotel, and he started walking toward an exit.

Shaz called his name, begging him to come back.

Even bad people had souls. They were hidden most of the time, but they were still there. His soul had been scorched, and he wondered if it would ever be the same.

He found the stairwell and hurried up it.

FIFTY-SIX

Mags sat in the NV Energy van, waiting for the trap to be sprung. Billy's crew was going to get busted, and it was all her fault because she'd overslept.

It was the story of her life. She couldn't blame fate or bad luck for the dumb mistakes she'd made. The choices had all been hers, and she'd screwed up every single time.

Thinking about it wasn't going to do her any good, and she stared at the video monitors trained on Galaxy's hotel and casino. The gaming agents were using a facial-recognition software program to locate Billy's crew as they entered the casino. The agents had scanned the photo of Billy's crew taken inside the employee parking garage into a computer, and now the computer's software program was comparing those faces against the tourists going inside.

Poor Billy was a goner. The gaming board had the joint surrounded, determined to get their man. Their reputations, and Frank's promotion, were riding on it.

At two forty-five, the gruff female agent said, "I've got two on monitor number five."

Mags located monitor number five on the wall. The sex kittens from Billy's crew were entering the hotel with garment bags slung over their shoulders, while one also carried a Nike gym bag. The female agent relayed the news with a walkie-talkie.

Frank charged into the van. "Show me," he said.

The tape of the sex kittens was replayed. Frank brought his ugly face up to the screen.

"What about the other members of the crew?" he asked.

"They haven't arrived yet," the female agent said.

"You sure?"

"Of course I'm sure. The facial-recognition program would have made them."

"What do you think's in the clothing bags?"

"Disguises. They'll change in a stall in the ladies' room, or have a room in the hotel. They won't look the same when they're robbing the place."

"Play the tape again, and do a close-up of their faces," he said.

"What for?"

"Just do it."

She shot him a simmering look while fingering the toggle on her keyboard. It gave Mags small comfort knowing that she wasn't the only female that Frank treated like dirt. The tape ran again and was frozen. The sex kittens' faces expanded and came into sharp focus on the monitor.

"Send that shot to everyone on the team," he said.

"Anything else?"

"That's it for now."

Frank made for the door, then pretended to notice Mags. He knew all the ways to cut her down, and said, "Billy likes them pretty. I hear he gets more ass than a toilet seat."

"I bet he does," Mags said under her breath.

- - -

Misty and Pepper had been mistaken for call girls enough times to know how to fool hotel security. Dressed in casual clothes and wearing a smattering of makeup, they chattered about a dumb Channing Tatum flick as they strolled past the guards posted inside the front doors.

Soon they were riding an elevator to Billy's suite. Misty carried the Nike bag with the fake chips, which she tried to avoid peeking into. In a few hours, she was going to be rich, and the thought made her giddy with excitement. She unlocked the door with the spare room key.

It was said that the best things in Vegas were free, only no one could afford them. Billy's comped high-roller suite was a perfect example, the furniture and decorations to die for.

"I could live here," Misty said.

"Me, too," Pepper said.

"Anybody home?"

"I'm on the balcony," came Billy's voice through the open slider.

They dropped their things on a couch and stepped outside. Billy stood by the railing, watching the action down below with a pair of binoculars with the sales sticker still on them.

"We didn't expect to find you here," Misty said. "What are you doing?"

"I came upstairs to get a better look at those NV Energy trucks parked in front," he said.

"What's the matter with them?"

"They've been there for a few hours. When was the last time you called the power company on a weekend, and they came out?"

"You think it's the heat?"

He lowered the binoculars. First the flash of light in the covered parking garage, now the trucks parked out front as if preparing to raid the joint. It could have been nothing more than his imagination taking a trip down paranoid lane, but he wasn't ready to dismiss his feelings just yet. With his hand, he motioned for Pepper to close the slider.

"No, I don't think it's the heat, but I've been wrong before," he said. "If you smell an undercover cop when you're in the casino, dump the chips and run."

"But what about our big payday?" Misty pouted.

"There will be more of those down the road. You with me on this?"

"I guess," she said sadly.

An awkward silence followed. He had instilled the fear of doubt into them. It was the worst possible way to start a job. Putting his hands on their shoulders, he drew them close.

"It's just a precaution. You never can be too careful in this game. Especially with the people you care about."

"Awww," they both said.

They shared a group hug, and things were good again.

- - -

Back inside, Billy rapped on the punishers' bedroom door. Ike and T-Bird emerged a few moments later. T-Bird's dreadlocks were history, his skull a shiny brown dome.

"Look what the cat dragged in," Billy said.

"Shut up," T-Bird said, clearly disgusted. "Took me two years to grow my dreads. They're part of me, know what I mean?"

"You can grow them back while you're enjoying your money."

"We brought some clothes for you to try on." Pepper unzipped a garment bag and pulled out a pair of billowing slacks, a black silk shirt with mother-of-pearl buttons, and an alligator belt with a gold-plated barbwire accent. "See how these look."

T-Bird went into the bedroom with the clothes hanging over his arm and returned wearing them. The belt was a nice touch, the type of outlandish accessory that a drug peddler might wear.

"Pants too long," the bird man grumbled.

"We'll pin them up," Pepper reassured him. "Otherwise, what do you think?"

"I guess they're okay."

"You look like a player," Billy said. "Sit down so the girls can give you a makeover."

T-Bird lowered his body into a chair. Pepper removed a makeup kit from the garment bag, and she and Misty went to work on transforming him into a menacing drug dealer. They trimmed his eyebrows, attached a diamond magnetic earring to his left earlobe, gave him a grill of fake gold teeth to stick into his mouth, and fitted a pair of rose-tinted Ray-Bans on his nose. Finished, they both took a step back and nodded approvingly.

"I'd say he's done," Pepper said.

"I'd buy an eight ball from him," Misty said.

T-Bird went to the mirror hanging over the bar to appraise his new look. Ike came up from behind him, offering encouragement.

"You really think this is going to fly?" T-Bird asked.

"Yeah," Ike said. "You having second thoughts?"

"I don't know, man. I just don't know."

- - -

The girls still needed to put on their disguises. They went into one of the bedrooms with the garment bags and shut the door. Billy turned to Ike. "Call Shaz on your cell phone and tell her T-Bird's sick. Make it convincing."

Ike made the call. "Hey, it's me. I'm up in the suite with T-Bird. He's sick as a dog, can't get out of bed. Cunningham's here, too. Sure, I'll put him on."

Billy took the cell phone. "Hey."

"You shouldn't have run away from me like that," Shaz said. "I didn't like it."

"I guess I'm just the bashful type."

"What's wrong with T-Bird?"

"I think he got food poisoning. It's not pretty."

"He'll live. Meet me outside the wedding chapel wearing a sports jacket. We're going to mike you up. Rock wants to be able to talk with you while you're on the casino floor."

Wearing a mike would be the same as having an electronic dog collar around his neck, and Billy told himself he'd just have to work around it.

"I'll be right down," he said.

The call ended. He entered the bedroom and shut the door behind him. Misty and Pepper stood at the dresser, turning themselves into Mexican hit women. Misty wore a leather mini, leggings, fake eyelashes, and was applying dark pancake to her face. Pepper had chosen a leather jumpsuit that hid her freckled arms and legs, a black wig that spiraled to her shoulders, and the same dark pancake, liberally applied to her pale skin. They could both pass as Hispanic, and he smiled to himself, seeing the pieces falling together.

"What do you think?" Misty asked.

"I think this is going to work."

He grabbed the sports jacket he'd brought with him from the closet and slipped it on. "I've got to blow. Remember, the pigeon drop is still on."

"What are we going to do with the extra two million we steal from these guys?"

"Split it up, same as always," he said.

"Goody."

He walked out of the bedroom to find Ike waiting for him.

"Let's go downstairs and rob this joint," Billy said.

FIFTY-SEVEN

The elevator dumped them in the lobby. Instead of going to the wedding chapel as Shaz had instructed, Billy visited the casino instead. The joint was jumping, the players yelling with each turn of a card or roll of the dice, the sound of a ringing slot machine cutting through the air.

"People acting crazy in there," Ike said.

It was called a hot zone, and it occurred when a player got on a lucky streak. The euphoria quickly spread to other players and caused them to behave like drunken sailors on a navy payday. He could not have asked for a better distraction for making a run at the cage with the fake chips.

They headed to the wedding chapel. Shaz stood outside the chapel's double doors, not happy at being made to wait. Billy said, "Sorry, but the elevators were slow."

"Why do I think you're lying every time we talk?" she said.

She approached an unmarked door across from the chapel and punched a combination into the door handle. It led to a storage room. Along with the fake flowers and wall decorations was a small army of muscle-bound, plainclothes security guards. Shaz introduced Billy by saying that he was a consultant the casino had hired to catch a gang of cheaters who were planning to rip them off this afternoon. Each guard gave Billy a cursory nod.

"Chase, mike him up," Shaz said.

Chase was as big as a sumo wrestler and he gave Billy a funny look.

"You look familiar," Chase said. "Ever work for the Trop? I used to run security there."

Billy had ripped off the Tropicana many times, right under this idiot's nose.

"Can't say I've had the pleasure," he said.

"That's funny. I'd swear I've seen you before."

Chase clipped a receiver onto Billy's belt from which ran two transparent plastic wires. The first wire contained a receiver embedded in a flesh-colored earplug, the second a miniature black microphone with a clip. Billy stuck the earplug into his left ear and clipped the mike to his right lapel. He flipped the power button on the receiver and static filled his ear.

"You're set," Chase said. "What's your name again?"

"Billy Cunningham."

"I'll figure out where I know you from eventually."

Shaz pulled him out of the storage room. In the lobby outside the chapel was another couple ready to take the plunge. The bride was chewing gum while her husband didn't appear old enough to have pubic hair. The doors to the chapel opened and they filed in with the rest of their party. Billy checked the time. Three thirty on the nose. At three forty-five, it was the Gypsies' turn.

"Walk with me," Shaz said.

He followed her into the hotel lobby, where she stopped at a large potted plant positioned by the wall. "This is where we want you and Ike to stand. Don't move until Rock tells you. Remember, we can see everything you're doing. No funny stuff."

He thought back to the four large-screen TVs in Doucette's office. A large potted plant had been on TV number two, at the very periphery of the surveillance camera trained on the lobby. They had framed the play without knowing it.

"Got it," he said.

She grabbed his chin and squeezed it. "I'm heading upstairs to my husband's office. Don't you dare try and fuck us. I'll kill you myself if you do."

"I won't fuck you," he said.

"That's only because we're watching you."

Ike laughed under his breath as she hurried away.

- - -

When Shaz was gone, Billy took a step backward. If memory served him correctly, he was now at the very edge of the surveillance camera's range. Framing the play was a powerful weapon when taking down a casino. By knowing where a surveillance camera was pointed, a cheater could position himself at the edge of the frame and be hidden enough to go about his business and not get caught.

He checked the receiver clipped to his belt. The green light was on. He found the power switch and flipped it off. The green light faded away.

"You ready?" he asked.

"I don't know—what am I supposed to do?" Ike said.

"You're going to walk away, and no one's going to see you. Rock and Marcus can see us on the surveillance camera, but only barely. If you take a giant step backward, you'll disappear from their view. When the Gypsy wedding party comes marching down the lobby, all eyes will be on them. That's when you split."

"You sure they won't see me leave?" Ike asked.

"Positive."

"Man, I sure hope you know what you're doing."

"No more talking. I'm turning the receiver back on."

He flipped the switch and the green light came on. He shifted his attention toward the elevator bank at the end of the lobby and waited for the Gypsies to show their faces.

- - -

Cory and Morris were sweating through their underwear, and it had nothing to do with the dry desert heat. Following Billy's instructions, they'd used a fake driver's license to rent a red Chevy Malibu from Hertz's airport location, then driven the vehicle back to Galaxy. They'd allocated an hour for their task, which was plenty of time on a weekday but never enough for a Saturday. Stuck in a bottleneck on the Strip, the two fledgling hustlers stared at Galaxy's flashing neon sign a mere stone's throw away.

"Billy's going to kill us," Cory swore, clutching the wheel. "He's already pissed about the golf scam. If we don't show on time, he'll fire us for sure."

"You really think he'd do that?" Morris said.

"Damn straight. He doesn't put up with any crap."

"Maybe we should stop smoking dope before jobs."

"There's a thought."

The idea of no longer being a member of Billy's crew terrified Morris. He'd never held down a real job, and he had no intention of starting now. He threw open his door and stuck one foot onto the pavement.

"What the hell are you doing?" Cory asked.

"The resourceful professional failing to improve the method changes the moment," Morris said. "Billy told me that once, said it came from a famous book on cheating. Don't ask me what it means, because I don't know."

Leaving the rental, Morris walked calmly into the next lane, causing the already sluggish traffic to grind to a halt. Horns blared in disapproval and drivers shook their fists. Morris waved to Cory to cut in. The rental jumped to the front of the line, and Morris got back in.

"You're a superstar," Cory said.

They reached Galaxy's back entrance with minutes to spare. There were a handful of available parking spaces by the back entrance. Cory backed into one and they both got out. Except for an NV Energy company crew working on a pole, everything looked George.

Cory popped the rental's trunk. He reached in, hoisted a Kenneth Cole leather briefcase off the spare tire, and placed it inside a flat-handle, brown-paper shopping bag so that the briefcase would be hidden when he entered the casino.

"This feels heavy. Are you sure it's the right weight?" he asked.

"I did the math," Morris said. "Eight hundred money orders weigh ten point six pounds. That's how much weight I put in the briefcase."

"It feels heavier," Cory said.

"It's not. Get moving, will you? Gabe and Travis will be wondering where you are."

"You going to wish me luck?"

"Luck is for amateurs. Get moving."

"Why are you so pissy?"

"Who the fuck knows? Go."

Cory entered the rear of the casino carrying the shopping bag. Twenty feet from the door, he spotted Gabe tapping the screen of a Jacks or Better video poker machine. Gabe was playing geezer and wore a floppy white fishing hat and wraparound shades that covered half his face. Cory came up beside the older man and dropped the shopping bag on the floor by his chair.

"Where you been?" Gabe said under his breath.

"Traffic was a bitch. You know how it is. Where's Travis?"

"He's scouting the cage area. You know why you show up to jobs early? Because then you're not late."

"I got here, didn't I? Stop yanking my chain."

Gabe peeled his eyes away from the video poker machine long enough to give Cory a blistering stare. His frown turned into a snarl. "You're not wearing your disguise."

"Shit, I forgot to put it on," Cory stammered.

"How can you forget something like that?"

"I don't know, man."

"Where is it?"

"It's still in the car."

"A lot of fucking good it's going to do there. Now the casino knows what you look like. If this thing blows up in our faces, it will be because of you."

"I didn't do it on purpose."

"You're pathetic. Get out of here, before I smack you in the mouth. I mean it."

"Stop talking to me like that."

"Leave."

Cory kicked the shopping bag. Hadn't he and Morris helped this big sack of fertilizer settle his huge gambling debt? But it was the wrong time and the wrong place to be having this discussion, and he left the casino without another word.

FIFTY-EIGHT

The sky was falling, and Mags didn't know what to do.

All of Billy's crew were now inside Galaxy. Just a few minutes ago, the last two members had parked a red Chevy Malibu in a spot next to the casino's back entrance. Both had curly hair and boyish faces and reminded her of Billy, long ago. One had gone inside the casino with a brown shopping bag. When he'd come out, no shopping bag.

Frank and Trixie had joined the three gaming agents inside the truck. The tape of the Chevy was replayed, and watched again. Frank's boss shook his head.

"That car is a problem," Trixie said. "They can use it to run over our agents. Call the guys working the back of the casino, and tell them to set up roadblocks on the street."

"Roadblocks?" Frank said. "How long is that going to take?"

"I don't care how long it takes," Trixie said. "Just do it."

Frank went outside the truck to make the call. Mags leaned back in her chair. It was now or never to alert Billy. Not having Frank in the truck emboldened her, and she rose from her chair.

The three gaming agents sat in front of a large console onto which they'd tossed their car keys and cell phones. Mags backed up to the console, looking at Trixie as she did. As their eyes met, one of the agents' cell phones found a home in her back pocket.

"Go sit down," Trixie said.

"I need to take a piss," she said.

"You've got some mouth on you, you know that?"

"Want to wash it out?"

Trixie led her to the lavatory and jerked the door open. It was smaller than the johns on airplanes, and she had to wedge herself inside.

"Make it fast," Trixie said, shutting the door.

The overhead light flickered on. She pulled out the stolen cell phone and sat on the toilet. She was in luck; it did not require a password, and she unlocked the screen and located the phone icon. She got an outside line and got the main number for Galaxy's casino from information. The call went through. Through the door came the unmistakable sound of Frank's voice.

"Where's Mags? She didn't slip out, did she?" Frank asked.

An operator answered her call. Mags covered the phone's mouthpiece.

"Hi. Can you please page someone in your casino for me? It's an emergency."

"Let me check. What's their name?" the operator asked.

"Billy Cunningham."

"Please hold on."

Recorded music filled her ear. Frank pounded his fist on the door. "You dirty little shit! Who the hell are you talking to in there? Open the fucking door, goddamn it, or I'll break it down."

"I'll be right out," Mags said, trying to buy more time.

"Right now!"

"I'm taking a leak. You can watch. I won't charge you."

Frank hit the door with his shoulder, causing the hinges to give way. He was going to kill her, only Mags didn't care. Billy's crew meant more to her than any promise she'd ever made to the gaming board. She was going to join them one day, even if it meant first going to jail.

- - -

Billy was glued to the potted plant in the lobby. The three-thirty wedding had wrapped up, and the chapel was ready for the next couple to tie the knot.

An announcement over the PA snapped his head. He glanced at Ike. "Did you hear that?"

"I think you're being paged. Want me to check?" Ike asked.

"Yeah, do it."

Ike crossed the lobby and picked up a white house phone that hung on the wall. He had a short conversation before returning to Billy's side. "Operator said some woman urgently wanted to speak to you, only she hung up," he said.

"Did the operator get a name?"

"Nope."

Only a handful of people knew that Billy was here; those that did would never have him paged. Was someone trying to warn him? It sure felt that way. Crackling static filled the earpiece he was wearing, and Rock's voice invaded his head.

"Here come the Gypsies," the drug kingpin said.

"I'm not seeing them," Billy said into the mike pinned to his lapel.

"They just got off the elevators. They'll be down your way in a second."

It was time to rip off Galaxy, and Billy put the page out of his mind. Slipping his hand into his jacket, he flipped off the power on the receiver clipped to his belt.

"Get ready to bolt," he told Ike.

"I got butterflies in my stomach," Ike confessed.

"Just do as I told you, and you'll be fine."

He flipped the receiver back on. Rock was talking to him.

"You see them now?" the drug kingpin asked.

"I sure do," he said into the mike.

The Gypsies were booking down the lobby. At the front of the pack were the bride and groom. They were holding hands, and he realized that the groom was helping the bride keep her balance as she hustled along with the plastic dealing shoe strapped between her legs. Behind them was the bride's mother, Cecilia Torch, wearing a subdued burgundy dress. Her husband strode beside her, fifteen years her senior, well tanned and fit. The husband had the air of being in charge, and Billy pegged him as the ringleader. Behind them was another older couple, posing as the groom's parents. Bringing up the rear was a drop-dead-gorgeous bridesmaid, a smiling best man, and three twentyish couples posing as guests. The shared bloodline was easy to spot. Each member of the party had a full head of wavy hair and a swarthy complexion. They moved with springs in their steps and reminded him of an acrobat troupe about to enter the big top.

"I count fourteen. How about you?" Rock asked.

"Fourteen it is," he said into the mike.

"The tan guy is running the show, isn't he?" Rock said.

"Yeah."

"I'm looking forward to killing that motherfucker."

"You going to do him yourself?"

"I sure am."

The Gypsies entered the chapel and the doors closed behind them. Billy felt certain that Rock was watching the ceremony unfold inside the chapel on the TV screens and was not paying the slightest attention to him, or Ike. It was time for Ike to make himself scarce. He gently kicked the big man in the shin with his heel. Ike stepped backward, out of the frame.

Billy waited for Rock to say something.

Rock didn't say a thing.

Billy reached into his jacket and turned off the receiver.

"Go," he said without moving his lips.

Ike hurried away.

Billy flipped the receiver back on. Standing as stiff as a statue, he focused on the wedding-chapel doors, waiting for the Gypsies to emerge.

- - -

Ike had touched greatness in his life before, and come up short. In college during a nationally televised bowl game, he'd allowed the opposing team's running back to slip past him, the play repeated endlessly on ESPN during their end-of-year bloopers festival. In the Super Bowl, he'd tripped over another team member during a crucial play and also made the ESPN idiot reel. And so it had gone—remembered for the times he'd messed up, not for his achievements.

That was about to change, and a new chapter would be written. Walking to the elevators, Ike called upstairs to the suite and, when T-Bird picked up, said, "Everything's set. Come on down."

"See you by the elevators," his partner said.

Ike hung up, called the cage, and spoke to the cage manager, a guy named Don Winter. Don was part of the casino's inner circle and knew about the money laundering. Ike said, "Hey, Don, this is Ike Spears. Reverend Rock's ready to cash out."

Don said, "Bring him down. We've got the goods ready for him."

Ike said, "See you in a few," and ended the call.

Ike tried to stay calm as he waited by the elevators. Soon, he and T-Bird were going to be living the good life in Mexico, lounging by the pool and doing all the fine things that rich people did. He was sorry to be taking Billy's share—the little guy had grown on him—but the way he saw it, Billy had plenty of big paydays down the road, while he and T-Bird were at the end of their playing days. The elevator doors parted, and T-Bird and the two sexy ladies from Billy's crew waltzed out. T-Bird had the drug dealer persona down flat and walked with the swagger of fast cash. The girls wore trashy clothes and makeup so dark they looked like hot Mexican bitches. The one named Misty carried the Nike bag with the fake chips swinging by her side.

"You guys look sharp," Ike said.

"I feel sharp," T-Bird said. "Lead the way, my man."

Ike led them through the packed casino. The shift change was taking place, and he saw blackjack dealers leaving their tables to be replaced by fresh dealers. It was a perfect time to be pulling off a heist, the room in a state of flux.

By the time they reached the cage, the sweat was pouring off him, the memory of those fuckers blowing past him in college and the pros still haunting him. No more blooper reels, he told himself. If anything, he might get profiled on *The Ones That Got Away*.

There were long lines at the cashiers' windows. Ike looked over the people's heads and spotted Don. The cage manager held up a finger as if to say, *Give me a minute*.

They stood off to the side to wait. There were surveillance cameras in the ceiling, but Ike wasn't worried. Rock, Marcus, and Shaz were watching the Gypsy wedding and paying zero attention to the cage. Billy had suckered them good.

"What are we waiting for," T-Bird said impatiently. "Don't they know who I am?"

"Cool your jets," Ike said. "Our ship's about to come in."

FIFTY-NINE

At four, Frank got the word that the roadblocks were in place.

"Okay, folks, we're ready to roll," he announced.

The three gaming agents watching the monitors rose in unison and filed out through the side door of the truck. Frank looked at Mags, who sat handcuffed in her chair.

"You, too," he said.

Mags stood up and held out her wrists. He shook his head.

"Why are you treating me this way?" she asked, fighting back tears.

"Because you can't be trusted. You're a cheater and always will be," he said.

"You sure enjoyed sleeping with me."

He shrugged as if to say, *What did you expect?*

"You still haven't said what I'm supposed to do," she said.

"My team is responsible for busting Billy and his crew," he said. "When you see Billy in the casino, I want you to call out his name and start walking toward him. Be real friendly."

"You want me to bring his guard down."

"That's right. Billy's no dope. He'll see you cuffed and realize he's done. Let's go."

"Can I have my cell phone back?"

"You're funny."

They went outside to where a small army of gaming agents dressed in NV Energy uniforms were gathered on the sidewalk. Each agent had a firearm strapped to his side and a seven-pointed gold star pinned to his uniform. Trixie was giving them their final instructions before going in. "Remember, we have the exits to the hotel and casino covered, and that includes the underground garage," Trixie told his troops. "If either Cunningham or Reverend Rock tries to make a run for it, let them go. Our men outside will chase them down. Got it?"

There were murmurs of yes and a collective nodding of heads.

"I got a phone call from the mayor earlier. I promised the mayor that we would not discharge our weapons inside Galaxy's hotel or the casino unless there was a life-threatening situation, and I expect you to uphold that promise," Trixie said. "Am I making myself clear?"

More agreement. Vegas was strange when it came to firearms; the police and gaming agents regularly gunned down bad guys in the street, yet rarely fired their weapons inside the casinos, fearful of the effect it would have on the town's tourism business.

Mags breathed a sigh of relief, knowing that Billy wasn't going to get shot.

"Any questions, ask them now," Trixie said.

There were none.

"Let's roll," Trixie said.

- - -

"The Gypsies are coming out," came Rock's voice in Billy's earpiece.

It was four o'clock, and Billy stood frozen by the potted plant. Ike had been gone for several minutes, and Rock hadn't said boo. Across the lobby, the chapel's double doors sprang open and the Gypsies spilled out, all grins and good-natured laughter. They made a beeline down the lobby toward the casino, the bride still holding the groom's hand, the weight of the hidden dealing shoe making each step a treacherous one. The rest of the party was yucking it up and having a swell time, enough of a distraction that no one would notice the bride wasn't walking right.

"Ready to nail 'em?" Rock asked.

"Ready," Billy said.

"Wait for Chase and his group. They're coming out now."

The storage room was directly across from the wedding chapel. The door opened, and Chase and the mob of muscle-bound security guards poured into the lobby as if being released from cages. Chase came over to Billy and pointed a finger in his face.

"I finally remembered you," Chase said. "You and your friends ripped off the Tropicana at craps. Took us for a whole bunch of money."

"Live and learn," Billy said.

"I lost my job because of you, asshole."

"Get moving," Rock said into his earpiece.

Billy headed down the lobby with the posse of security guards breathing down his neck. The Gypsies had a good head start and had already passed the hotel check-in. Taking a hard right, they made their way into the casino and briefly disappeared from view.

Billy picked up his pace. If there was anything he loved as much as cheating a casino, it was watching someone else do it, and he didn't plan on missing one beat of the Gypsies' scam.

"Where's Ike? I don't see him," Rock said into his earpiece.

He feigned looking over his shoulder and shrugged.

"You don't know?" Rock said.

"He was here a second ago," he said into the lapel mike. "Want me to go find him?"

"Fuck no. Keep doing what you're doing."

He passed the check-in, turned right, and entered the casino. The Gypsy wedding party was dead ahead. They had stopped to form a line so the best man could take a photo on his cell phone. Not liking the arrangement, the best man asked several members of the party to shift places.

Billy halted, and so did the security guards. Before his eyes, there was a swirl of bodies and a rustling of fabric as members of the party brushed past each other, the effect as dizzying as watching a square dance. Only the bride stayed still, as if glued to her spot.

Was this the Dazzle? It sure seemed to be, only the wedding party was nowhere near the blackjack pit, and that was where they needed to be standing if they were going to pull the stacked dealing shoe out of the bride's gown and make the switch. Something else was going on.

Chase edged up beside him. "What are they doing?"

"I don't know," Billy said.

He edged closer for a better look. The dance now over, the wedding party formed a new line, and the best man took several shots. Billy had no idea what they were doing.

"Hey, buddy, would you mind taking our picture?"

The best man motioned to him. Billy hesitated. This was cutting it too close.

"Go take their picture," Rock said into his earpiece.

Billy relieved the best man of his cell phone. The best man slipped into the line and slung his arm around the groom's waist. Everyone in the party broke into a smile.

Billy took his time. By staring at the cell phone's screen, he counted heads without being obvious about it. Fourteen members of the wedding party had entered the casino; now there were only thirteen. One of them had disappeared right in front of his nose.

He scanned the faces. Dear old Papa was gone.

"Let me get a few more of the beautiful bride. What's your name?" Billy asked.

"Candace," the bride replied.

"Say cheese, Candace."

The bride said cheese, and Billy took several shots of her. She was standing in front of a Money Vault progressive slot machine with her gown spread wide. Progressive slot machines let players from around the state compete for a gigantic jackpot. Not long ago, a nurse from Reno had won five million bucks playing a Money Vault machine, and it had made all the papers.

There was a paddle for everybody's ass, and his ass had just been spanked. The Gypsies weren't here to pull a blackjack scam. They were rigging the jackpot on a slot machine, and they were doing it right in front of his nose.

He didn't need X-ray vision to know where dear old Papa had gone. Hiding behind the bride's gown, Papa had opened the Money Vault machine with a skeleton key, the machine's internal security alarm put on standby mode by a powerful earth magnet the bride had been carrying in her gown. Using a small handheld computer loaded with a DEPROM software program, Papa was now overwriting the machine's jackpot code that resided on its random-number-generator chip and replacing it with a code of his own. It was so damn beautiful that Billy nearly cried.

Instead, he handed the best man back his cell phone.

"Thanks a lot," the best man said.

"My pleasure," he said.

"Hey, cutie, want to make some money?"

He spun around. A small army of gaming agents dressed in NV Energy uniforms had appeared behind Chase and the security goons. At the front of the pack was his old nemesis Frank Grimes; beside him, Mags. She flashed a sad smile and held up her shackled wrists as if to say, *Look at me!* He thought back to the page and realized it was Mags who'd tried to warn him. And for that little indiscretion Grimes had slapped the cuffs on her.

He glanced over his shoulder at the Gypsies.

"Last one out's a rotten egg," he said.

The Gypsies broke ranks and bolted into the casino. The bride was moving awkwardly, the earth magnet back beneath her gown. The door on the Money Vault machine was closed, and the machine looked no different than before. They were going to get out of this with their skins.

He shifted his attention back to the casino entrance. The gaming agents were bumping into the security goons, telling them to get out of the way. Not liking the treatment, the security goons were mouthing off to them. Testosterone was flying high and tempers were flaring. There was a real opportunity here, only he couldn't see himself starting a ruckus. He was too damn small and would end up getting crushed.

But Mags was not so shy. She didn't give a flying fuck on a rolling doughnut about her own situation, and she threw herself into Grimes while sticking her leg out. The gaming agent toppled to the floor along with several security goons in a massive scrum.

Fists started to fly. Within moments, bedlam broke out, and the goons and gaming agents began mixing it up in a good old-fashioned brawl. Seeing his chance, Billy ran forward, prepared to grab Mags and make a run for it. The girl of his dreams pulled back.

"No," she said.

"No?" he said.

"I can't run away anymore."

"You sure?"

"Positive. You go."

All the bad feelings he'd had toward her vanished, and it tore him apart leaving her behind. Grimes was pulling himself off the floor, and she sent a knee into his face.

Billy started walking backward into the casino. Not too fast, not too slow, his steps measured—don't run if you're not being chased. Rock shouted in his ear.

"Who are those fucking guys beating up my men?"

Someone was going to pay for this, and Billy wished he could be there to see it happen. He ripped the receiver off his belt and threw it onto the floor along with the earpiece.

SIXTY

The brawl could be heard on the other side of the casino. Ike, T-Bird, and the pretty girls from Billy's crew exchanged nervous glances, knowing something was not right.

"What the hell's that noise?" T-Bird asked.

"Ignore it," Ike said.

Ike heard his name being called. Don the cage manager had opened up a new window, and motioned for Ike to step forward. Ike hurried over with the gym bag and began passing the gold beauties through the cage into Don's waiting hands. Don removed a stack of real gold chips from the cashier's drawer and compared them to the fakes, checking for both color and height. Satisfied, he held the fakes in his hand and let them cascade to the marble countertop to see if they had the same consistency as the chips he handled every day. Convinced that everything was on the square, he counted the fakes, then looked at Ike through the bars.

"We're good. I'll be right out," Don said.

Ike tried not to grin. It was going just as Billy had said it would. A door beside the cage swung open, and the cage manager emerged carrying a leather briefcase with the money orders. Ike stuck his hand out for the briefcase, and Don scowled at him.

"This isn't yours," Don scolded.

Ike grinned foolishly and lowered his arm. "Sorry, I wasn't thinking."

"Why are you sweating so much?"

"I'm not feeling so hot."

"If you're sick, you should stay home. Everyone knows that."

"You're right, I should have stayed home."

Don gave him a look that said he didn't like Ike's behavior. The cage manager shifted his attention to T-Bird. The disguise put Don at ease, and he handed T-Bird the briefcase.

"I hope you had an enjoyable stay," Don said.

"We had a great time. Didn't we, girls?" T-Bird said.

The girls knew better than to say anything. It was starting to get awkward, and Ike said, "We need to beat it. Rock's got a plane to catch back to LA."

"I need his signature for our records." Don reached into his suit jacket and produced a pen and a chit for T-Bird to sign for the money orders. "Just sign on the bottom and we're done."

T-Bird passed the briefcase to Misty and took the pen and chit out of Don's hands. He made a flourish out of signing his name before handing Don the pen and the chit.

"Thanks for the good time," T-Bird said.

Don stared at the signature on the chit. "Who's Terrell Bird?"

"Me," T-Bird said without thinking.

"I thought your name was Rock."

"Well, yeah. It's actually my nickname. You see . . ."

Don whipped out his cell phone. "Stay where you are. I'm calling security."

This was bad. Real bad. Ike couldn't see them talking their way out of it, so he sucker punched Don in the side of the face. Don's eyes rolled up and he sank to the floor.

"I've got a sick man here. Somebody call a doctor," Ike called out.

A big man playing video poker jumped out of his chair. Ike recognized him as having been in the garage earlier, a member of Billy's crew. Travis was his name.

"Let's go," Travis said. "The getaway car's parked in back."

"I thought Billy said there'd be two of you," Ike said.

"No, just me," Travis said.

They moved in tandem toward the casino's back entrance. Travis walked backward, never taking his eyes off Ike or T-Bird. Ike sensed motion behind him and looked over his shoulder. Misty had gone AWOL. Pepper was still there, holding the briefcase with the money orders. Ike drew a gun from his pocket and pointed it at her.

"Eeek," Pepper said.

Ike relieved her of the money orders. "Don't follow us, or I'll clip you."

"Wouldn't dream of it," Pepper said.

Ike and T-Bird bolted out of the casino. The baby-faced guys who were part of Billy's crew had parked a red Chevy Malibu in a spot by the back entrance and were standing beside it, in anticipation of making their escape. Seeing Ike's gun, they both turned pale.

"Go stand in the grass," Ike said.

The baby-faced ones did as told. Ike got behind the wheel of the rental, while T-Bird rode shotgun. The keys were stuck in the ignition. Ike turned over the engine and hit the gas, making the engine roar. He circled the massive parking lot searching for the exit.

"We did it, man. We're rich," Ike said.

"Sunny Mexico, here we come," T-Bird said.

"Did you see their faces? Wish I had a camera."

Ike found the exit and took the turn on two wheels. He'd mapped out their escape plan that morning; they'd take the back roads to Spring Mountain Road, drive west to the freeway, and head due south to the California state line. From there it would be a leisurely drive to San Diego and across the border to the promised land, where they'd spend the rest of their days hanging out in their big hacienda, living in the lap of luxury.

T-Bird held the briefcase with the loot in his lap. “Holy shit.”

“What’s wrong?”

“It changed color.”

“What the hell are you talking about?”

“The briefcase changed color. It was black inside the casino; now it’s dark brown.”

“You’ve got to be kidding me.”

“I ain’t kidding you, man. It changed.”

It was at that moment that Ike knew they’d been double-crossed. Misty disappearing, only one guy inside the casino to help when there were supposed to be two. Billy had figured out they were going to rip him off, so the little guy had beaten them to the punch.

“Open it,” Ike said.

T-Bird popped the clasps and lifted the lid. “Fucking shit! It’s filled with rocks!”

“Surprise, surprise.”

“Turn around. Come on, do it!”

Ike wasn’t paying attention, his eyes focused on the roadblock at the end of the street. A line of men wearing bulletproof vests were pointing high-powered rifles and shotguns at the rental’s windshield, ready to mow them down. Ike’s foot touched the brake but didn’t press down. What was the point? They’d just end up rotting to death in some crummy federal pen with a thousand other losers. That was not the way he wanted to check out. Better to do it in style.

Seconds later, the first bullet penetrated the windshield. T-Bird jumped in his seat and then slumped forward with his chin resting on his chest, never knowing what hit him.

“I’m right behind you,” Ike said.

- - -

Rock stood at rigid attention in front of the flat-screen TVs, watching the mayhem unfold. Punches thrown, bodies flying, the lavish hotel lobby and its beautiful furnishings trashed by the army of determined gaming agents that had raided his casino. His security staff was putting up a decent fight but was outgunned and would ultimately lose to a superior foe. That was the law of the jungle, and it was only a matter of time before the gaming agents came upstairs to arrest him. Clutched in his hand was his walking stick, whose ornate handle he smacked viciously into his open palm. His bodyguards flanked him, unsure what to do.

The landline on the desk rang.

"Answer it," the drug kingpin barked.

Doucette and his wife had taken up positions behind the couch, afraid of Rock's wrath. Doucette sprinted to the desk and hit a button on the phone.

"Hello?"

"This is Don Winter, the cage manager. We've been robbed. The money orders are gone," came the man's weakened voice out of the speaker.

"*What?*"

"It was Ike. He and his partner stole the money orders."

"Ask him where he is," Rock said.

"Where are you?" Doucette asked.

"By the cage. I'm hurt," the cage manager replied.

"Give me the remote," Rock said.

One of the bodyguards found the remote. Rock punched in a command, and the images on the TVs changed to show Don standing outside the cage with a cell phone. Don was having trouble keeping his balance and listed from side to side.

Rock crossed the office and brought his mouth next to the speaker.

"How much did Ike steal from us?" Rock said to the speaker.

"Who's this?" the cage manager asked.

"The person you were supposed to give the money orders to."

On the screen, Don started coughing. A reflexive action, born from fear.

"Answer the question," Rock barked.

"He got all eight million," the cage manager said.

"How the fuck am I gonna pay my dealers back in LA!"

"I don't know," the cage manager said.

Rock brought his fist down on the speaker, disconnecting the call. Then Rock played back the events of the past twenty minutes and realized that while he'd been watching the Gypsies scam him, another scam had been taking place. There was no doubt in his mind that Cunningham had orchestrated this; Ike and T-Bird were too brain-dead to scam a casino and get away with it.

Rock shifted his gaze to Doucette. "Your guy ripped me off."

"You're not blaming me, are you?" Doucette said.

"Yes. I trusted you, and you failed me."

"Wait a minute—I've got an idea," Doucette said.

Doucette removed an abstract painting from the wall and spun the dial of a combination safe. It sprang open, and he pulled out stacks of crisp hundred-dollar bills, which he tried to give to Rock's bodyguards. The bodyguards refused to take the money, and Doucette tentatively approached Rock. The drug kingpin shook his head and scowled.

"Give the money to your dealers, tell them the rest is coming," Doucette said.

"Coming from where?" Rock said.

"I don't know. I'll think of something."

"You've never had a smart idea in your life."

"Come on, Rock, I've always been loyal."

In Rock's experience, those who proclaimed their loyalty were usually the first to roll on him. He clutched his walking stick with both hands and took a practice swing. The stacks of bills spilled from Doucette's hands to the floor, and the casino boss started backing up.

"No, please," Doucette begged.

"I'll make it painless, if that makes you feel better," Rock said.

Doucette tripped over his own feet and fell backward onto the couch. His arms shot out and he begged for mercy. Rock didn't know the meaning of the word and came forward.

A shot rang out. One of the TV screens imploded, the image of Don the cage manager cascading to the floor in a thousand pieces. The bullet had sailed by Rock's head, yet the drug kingpin hadn't flinched. It wasn't the first time he'd been shot at.

Shaz stood behind her husband's desk, holding a silver-plated handgun she'd pulled from the center drawer, her arms trembling in fear.

"Leave him alone," she declared.

"And if I don't?" Rock said.

"I'll shoot you, and those dumb Mexican bitches as well."

"Is that a fact?"

"I'm not kidding, Rock."

"Why you doing this? I thought Marcus was just a meal ticket."

"Maybe so, but he's the only one I've got. Stay away from him."

Rock had already decided how he was going to handle the situation. He dipped his chin, and his bodyguards drew knives from their sleeves, the polished blades sparkling in the bright daylight. Before joining his organization, they'd murdered scores of rival members of the drug cartel they'd worked for. Killing was in their blood, and their faces took on feral expressions.

"Take her out."

With feline quickness they crossed the office and attacked from opposite sides. Shaz fired at them amateurishly, the bullets spraying the walls. One of the bodyguards caught a ricochet and brought her hand up to her chest in surprise.

The second bodyguard let out a cry for her wounded comrade. She knocked the gun away and began poking Shaz in the abdomen with the point of her knife, determined to make her suffer. Shaz was a dead woman; she just didn't know it yet.

Rock shifted his attention to Doucette, who was crawling on his knees toward the door in a sorry attempt to escape. Rock despised weakness and realized what a terrible mistake he'd made trusting Doucette to run his casino. He got on top of the casino boss and raised his walking stick.

"Say your prayers."

SIXTY-ONE

Cory and Morris watched the rental peel out of the casino parking lot. Ike and T-Bird were going to be in for a rude surprise when they discovered the briefcase was filled with rocks.

Their job done, they began the long walk around the property to the Strip. The escape plan called for them to grab a cab and head back to Gabe's. Vegas cabs were not allowed to pick up rides in the street, and they had already scoped out a taxi stand a block from Galaxy.

Cory was sick with worry. He'd forgotten to wear his disguise inside the casino, which was the worst mistake a cheater could make. He decided to confess to Billy before Gabe told Billy what he'd done. That way, he'd have a chance to apologize and beg for mercy. But before he did that, he needed to tell Morris. It was only fair that Morris knew first.

"Listen, man, I've got a confession to make," Cory said.

"This sounds bad," Morris said.

"It is."

"Worse than the time we were sharing a bed and you had the runs?"

"Much worse."

"Lay it on me."

A sickening barrage of gunfire ripped a hole in the afternoon air, the sound coming from the street where the two ex-gridiron stars had just gone. Across the parking lot, a door to an NV Energy truck banged open, and gaming agents wearing NV uniforms piled out, brandishing guns.

"It's a raid. Get inside," Cory said.

Inside they found another bad scene. Cory grabbed a cocktail waitress and learned that a brawl in the lobby had spread and people were panicking.

They decided to try the front entrance and hustled across the casino floor. Mobs of players huddled around the felt-covered tables, while dealers and pit bosses stood statue-like at their posts, guarding the trays of precious chips in their possession.

The hotel lobby was no better. A crowd had gathered and was trying to leave. Blocking their way was a line of stern-faced gaming agents checking ID.

"Maybe there's another exit we can use," Cory said.

They retreated into the casino. The gaming agents disguised as NV workers were now blocking the rear exit, setting the trap, and Cory knew what that meant: arrest, bail, lawyers, and if the crew got lucky, a plea deal that would let them get out of the slammer before they were wrinkled and gray. Or maybe there was a solution right in front of his face that he wasn't seeing. He walked over to a Wheel of Fortune slot machine and fed a crisp twenty into the bill feeder.

"Are you crazy? What are you doing?" Morris asked.

"Thinking," Cory said.

"Hurry up, man."

The slots in the Strip casinos were tight, and his money was gone in the blink of an eye. As he donated another twenty to the machine, Travis and Gabe took a pair of seats beside him.

"What happened to the assholes?" Travis asked.

"I think the cops took them out," Cory said.

Pepper and Misty took the chairs next to Gabe and Travis, still wearing their Mexican hit-women disguises. Misty dropped the briefcase with the money orders to the floor.

"That sucker's heavy. Anyone seen Billy?" Misty asked.

"Billy just texted me," Travis said. "He wants to meet up in the men's room."

"Why there?" Misty asked.

"No surveillance cameras in the john," Travis explained.

- - -

Billy sat on the elevated chair in the shoe-shine stand and studied his crew as they came in. No one was freaking out or crying. That was good, because they needed to stay calm if the plan he'd hatched to get them out of the casino was going to work.

A plastic bag lay at his feet. He picked it up and passed out the ball caps, T-shirts, and cheap pairs of sunglasses he'd lifted from one of the casino's clothing stores.

"Put these on. We got made earlier in the parking lot," he explained.

As his crew donned their new disguises, he continued to study them. "I think I can get you out of here without anyone getting busted. But you need to listen closely."

That got their attention. They huddled up, and he explained how he wanted them to go to the lobby and split up. He was going to create a diversion that would allow them to get outside, and their chances of escaping increased dramatically if they ran away individually. It was an old trick dating back to the Wild West, when cheaters would escape from town by riding in opposite directions on their horses, making it harder for the sheriff to chase them down.

"What about you? How are you getting out?" Travis asked.

"Don't worry about me," Billy said.

His crew filed out of the john. He touched Misty's sleeve and told her to stay.

"How do you like carrying eight million bucks around?" he asked.

"It's scary. I keep thinking I'm going to get busted," she said.

"I've got a plan for that, too."

"You've got a plan for everything."

He'd taught every member of his crew how to count cards at blackjack. He used the basic Hi-Low system, in which point values were assigned to each card dealt that allowed the player to keep a running count of the deck's composition. He did this so his crew would have an alternate means of income, and also to test their memories. Misty had easily picked up the skill and proven to have a memory as good as his own. He explained what he wanted done with the money orders, then gave her the code to the service elevator that he'd seen Ike use the day before to reach the unfinished fourteenth floor of the hotel. She repeated the instructions and code back to him.

"Text me when you're done," he said.

"How are you getting out?" she asked, repeating Travis's concern.

"I'll think of something. Onc more thing." He placed the suitcase on the sink and transferred the money orders into the plastic shopping bag the gifts had come in.

"You think of everything," she said.

Misty left, and he doused his face with cold water in the sink. He'd forgotten to steal a disguise for himself, which was going to make it harder for him to get out of the casino, but not impossible.

The minutes slipped by. One by one, his crew texted they were ready. Misty's text came last. He'd given her a tricky job, and he wondered how she was dealing with the responsibility of hiding the score. Would she rise to the challenge, or fall flat on her face?

Reading her text, he knew he'd made the right decision. The money orders were safe.

He returned to the casino and sat down with a group of slot queens who didn't seem fazed that the joint was being raided. Slot queens came from all walks of life and all social strata. What joined them at the hip was the fact that they'd all won a jackpot the very first time they'd played a slot machine, and believed that Lady Luck smiled down upon them.

He tapped one of the ladies on the shoulder. She had dyed-red hair and wore a crushed-velvet jumpsuit, and refused to make eye contact, her eyes glued to her machine.

"Do you smell that?" he asked.

"Smell what?" the slot queen replied.

"Smoke. I think it's coming out of the air vents."

The slot queen faced him. "Do you think there's a fire in the hotel?"

"Could be. I just wanted to warn you."

"Oh my God, I do smell it. Girls, the hotel is burning down!"

The slot queens abandoned their machines and made a mass exodus to the lobby. Decades before, a flash fire at the MGM had taken so many lives that the city's leaders had been shamed into changing the town's fire code. Now there were fire alarms inside every casino. One such alarm was in the hallway leading to the lobby. One of the slot queens beat him to the punch and pulled away the steel mesh and jerked the handle. A piercing alarm went off.

The lobby was a zoo, with patrons being screened by gaming agents before being allowed to leave. Grimes was running the show and he checked faces against a piece of paper clutched in his hand. Mags was nowhere to be seen, and Billy guessed that she'd been carted off to jail.

There was a lot of noise, and it drowned out the alarm. The MacGregor family reunion took up the end of the line, recognizable by their matching lime-green polo shirts and Irish mugs. He got the attention of an elderly woman that appeared to be the family matriarch.

"Did you hear that?" he shouted.

"Excuse me? Are you talking to me?" the elderly woman shouted back.

"That sound. I think it's a fire alarm."

"I do hear it! Oh my God! *Fire!*"

The elderly woman had a voice like a longshoreman and it carried across the lobby. With all the force of a tidal wave, the patrons rushed the doors and pushed Grimes and the gaming agents aside. The doors popped open, and the patrons flooded outside.

Billy became one with the surge and was soon in the valet area. He calculated the length of hotel sidewalk to the Strip at one hundred yards. If he could reach the Strip, he'd blend in with the crowds and be home free. A hand gripped his sleeve. A man wearing a rumpled tux with the collar undone had latched onto him. It took a moment for the face to register. It was dear old Papa, the head of the Gypsy clan. He had gotten separated from his clan, and looked lost.

"Let's go for a walk," Billy said.

"I'm with you," Papa said.

"Stay right next to me, and don't slow down."

"You got it, kid."

With Papa glued to his side, Billy sifted his way through the swirling crowd toward the sidewalk that would take them to freedom.

"*Freeze, Cunningham!*"

He shot a glance over his shoulder but did not stop. Grimes was framed in the hotel entrance, his suit jacket ripped, aiming his sidearm. Couldn't the dumb bastard have come up with an original line? Billy started to trot, as did his partner.

"*I said freeze, you little shit!*"

Grimes went into a marksman's crouch. Only a damn fool would shoot into a crowd.

"Who's that dickhead?" Papa asked.

"Gaming agent."

"Figures."

They kept moving. Suddenly, a shot rang out, scattering the crowd. A geyser of bright red blood gushed out of a bullet hole in Papa's tuxedo pants, the bullet hitting an artery. Papa groaned and melted to the pavement. Billy's instincts told him to run. It was the only chance he had. He gazed down at the older man, saw the helplessness in his eyes. He'd seen that same helplessness in his father's eyes right before he'd checked out, but it had been too late to do anything about it. Now things were different. Now he could do something and give the reaper a kick in the shins. He went to his knees and pressed the palms of his hands onto the wound to halt the blood.

The world turned quiet. The patrons had run away, and the fire alarm inside the hotel was no longer ringing. The noise from the Strip was muted, almost inconsequential. He could not remember it ever being this way—not even on a Sunday.

He heard the sounds of a struggle by the entrance. Grimes was being wrestled to the ground by two gaming agents wearing NV Energy uniforms. They were trying to take away his gun, which appeared glued to his hand. And they were trying to reason with him.

"Goddamn it, Frank, get a hold of yourself," one agent said.

Grimes was having none of it and continued to struggle. He wanted to take Billy out and erase the humiliation from their encounter at the Hard Rock, the wound having never healed. Having no choice, the gaming agents cuffed Grimes's hands behind his back. Billy wondered how this was going to play out. There was no doubt in his mind that he was heading to prison for a long stretch, but with that thought came the knowledge that Grimes's career was over.

Papa groaned, his eyelids fluttering. Billy wanted to shake him so that he'd stay conscious, but was fearful of taking his hands away from the wound. Bending forward at the waist, he spoke quietly to the older man.

"Don't go to sleep on me."

Papa struggled to respond. His face had turned ashen and he started to slip away. Billy knew he had to jolt the old guy back to life. But how? Then he had an idea.

"What did your daughter do with the earth magnet?" he asked.

Papa's eyes snapped open and stayed that way until the ambulance arrived.

SIXTY-TWO

-THE HOT SEAT: SUNDAY, PAST MIDNIGHT-

It was late when Billy ended his tale. Except for the short lunch break, he'd talked for nearly fourteen hours straight and his voice had turned brittle. It had to be some kind of Guinness World Record, even for a bullshit artist like him. LaBadie, Zander, and Tricaricco sat across the table, their out-of-shape bodies having morphed with their chairs. Except for a few details better not shared, the tale he'd told them was 98 percent true. The 2 percent he'd omitted would hopefully spare him from going to prison, but that was just a guess on his part.

"I'm not clear about something," LaBadie said. "You said that Doucette hired you and your crew to sniff out a family of Gypsy scammers. What exactly happened there?"

"Come on, man. I already told you, I don't have a crew," he said.

"My mistake. You and your *friends* were hired by Doucette. So what went down?"

"We never found the Gypsies. It was a dead end."

LaBadie took out a pack of gum and offered him a stick. It was an old cop trick to offer a suspect gum or a cigarette before going for the kill, and he declined with a shake of the head. The gaming agent jammed a stick into his mouth and chewed vigorously.

"What about this wedding party you mentioned? What was their names?"

"Torch-Allaire."

"Right. Could they have been the ones?"

"No."

"But you suspected them."

"I was wrong. Check the surveillance tapes if you don't believe me."

"We did."

"And?"

LaBadie did not reply. It was at that moment that Billy knew the Gypsies' rigging of the Money Vault machine had gone undetected by the casino's surveillance cameras. If the scam had been spotted, LaBadie would have puffed up his chest and said so and taken credit for the collar.

"Excuse us for a minute," LaBadie said.

LaBadie left the room. Zander and Tricaricco unglued themselves from their chairs to join him. As the door closed, Underman kicked Billy under the table. In his attorney's hand was an iPhone tuned into CNN's flashy mobile site. The lead story was the killings in Galaxy's casino and the negative impact on tourism the crimes were already starting to have on the city. Conventions, long the town's lifeblood, were cancelling left and right. Would Vegas survive?

Information was power, and his attorney had just given him a strong hand to play with. Moments later, the gaming agents returned to the room but did not sit down. In LaBadie's hand was a large manila envelope from which he removed a stack of surveillance photos. The gaming agent placed the top photo on the table so it faced Billy. It showed Ike at the cage, cashing in the fake gold chips. T-Bird was also in the photo, accompanied by Misty and Pepper in disguise.

"Recognize these two women?" LaBadie asked.

"Never seen them before," he replied.

"You just told us that your guy counterfeited the gold chips to scam Galaxy's casino. These two women were part of the scam, and they work for you."

"I never said that I had my guy counterfeit gold chips."

"No? Then what did you just tell us?"

"I said that I asked a friend of mine to *try*. I gave him the rubber chip I bought at Galaxy's gift shop, and my friend said he would see what he could do."

"What happened?"

"He couldn't duplicate it."

"You've got to be kidding me."

"I'm not. Counterfeiting is hard. My friend couldn't hack it."

The fake gold chips sat on the table in a pile. LaBadie picked up a handful and held them in front of Billy's face. "Then where the hell did these come from? The sky?"

"Ask Ike and T-Bird. They cashed them in."

"Ike and T-Bird are dead. When we pulled them from their car, T-Bird had a briefcase filled with rocks. The women in your crew switched briefcases on them."

"I don't have a crew."

"I'm getting sick of this routine, Billy."

"That makes two of us."

"You're not going to confess?"

"Only in church."

Three more surveillance photos were produced. The cameras had caught his crew doing the pigeon drop. The first photo showed Pepper standing behind Ike and T-Bird, holding the briefcase with the money orders. The second showed Pepper handing off the briefcase to Misty, while Gabe passed the rock-filled briefcase to Pepper. In the third, Misty fled into the casino with the loot.

"Admit it, this fat guy works for you," LaBadie said, pointing at Gabe.

Gabe's disguise hid most of his face. It could have been anyone.

"Never seen him before," Billy said.

"He's not the same fat guy we photographed in the employee garage earlier?"

"Nope."

"Really? Then see if you can weasel your way out of this."

The manila envelope was filled with surprises, and another surveillance photo hit the table. In it, Cory and Morris stood by the rented Chevy Malibu they'd parked by the casino's rear entrance. Cory had forgotten to put on his disguise, his boyish face clearly visible to the lenses.

"This kid was also in the employee garage, and is part of your crew," LaBadie said.

A second photo of Cory was produced, worse than the first. In it, Cory was entering the casino holding a shopping bag containing the rock-filled briefcase whose outline could be clearly seen on the side of the bag.

"Cat got your tongue?" LaBadie asked.

The trap had been sprung, and he couldn't get out.

Smiling, LaBadie stuck his hand into the envelope, ready to produce a third photo showing Cory passing the shopping bag to Gabe. A smart prosecutor would use this photo to convince a jury that Billy's crew had set up Ike and T-Bird. The money shot.

"Confess now, and we'll cut you a deal," LaBadie said.

"We'll go easy on you," Zander said.

"And your crew," Tricaricco added.

It didn't smell right. They had all the evidence they needed. Why cut a deal with him now? Several seconds passed, the room having grown as quiet as a tomb.

"Let me guess. The kid walked into a choke point, and you lost him," Billy said.

LaBadie's face turned red. So did Zander's and Tricaricco's. Ninety-eight percent of a casino floor was policed by surveillance cameras; 2

percent was not. The areas that fell within the 2 percent were called choke points and were black holes inside every casino. Cory had passed the shopping bag to Gabe in a choke point and had not been filmed.

"We have a photograph of you with this kid in the employee garage," LaBadie said.

"So what?" Billy said.

"This kid parked a rental car behind the casino that Ike and T-Bird used for their getaway. That ties him to the heist, and we can tie you to him."

"Did this kid drive the rental away?" Billy asked, knowing damn well Cory hadn't. "Because if not, you can't tie him to the heist."

LaBadie was losing his cool and shredded the envelope. He looked defeated, as did Zander. Tricaricco's eyes grew panicked as he realized their suspect might walk.

"We have witnesses who will swear you coerced them into pulling a fire alarm, which caused a stampede," Trixie said. "Or do you have an explanation for that as well?"

Of all the charges against him, pulling a fire alarm inside the casino was the least serious. They were grasping at straws, trying desperately to make something stick. It was time to play the hand that his attorney had given him just a few minutes before.

"Come to think of it, I do," he said. "Want to hear it?"

"Spit it out," Trixie said.

"As I'm sure you're aware, Reverend Rock had three assassins working for him. Two Mexican hit women and a black guy named Lamont Paris. Lamont had a zipper scar running down the side of his face, liked to wear his pants down by his ankles."

"There's no one fitting that description on the surveillance tapes," Trixie said.

"Lamont's a little guy. Probably got lost in the crowd."

"What does this have to do with the fire alarm being pulled?"

"I was getting to that. While your agents were raiding the joint, I spotted Lamont in the casino. Lamont told me he'd had a dispute with Rock and that it had gotten ugly and he'd killed some people. Lamont was afraid your men were going to arrest him, so he'd decided to shoot his way out. I panicked and asked those women to pull a fire alarm. I mean, can you imagine how many innocent people would have died if Lamont had started shooting?"

The gaming agents knew bullshit when they heard it. He didn't care and kept talking.

"The fire alarm goes off, and people start booking out of the casino. I ran into the lobby and found Special Agent Grimes by the front doors. I told Grimes what Lamont was up to. Right then, Lamont came into view. Lamont had a gun in his hand and a crazed look in his eyes. Grimes stepped right in front of him. I mean, it was the bravest thing I've ever seen. Lamont knocked Grimes down and took off. Grimes jumped up and pulled his gun and tried to stop Lamont but wounded a bystander instead." He paused. "That's why I pulled the fire alarm."

"That's the biggest bunch of crap I've ever heard," Trixie exploded. "There was no hit man named Lamont Paris. You're making this whole thing up."

Billy folded his hands on the table. There were times when the truth didn't matter. What mattered right now was that his story painted the victims into bad guys, the gaming agents into good guys, and Grimes into a hero for saving innocent lives. It was a story with a happy ending that if properly fed to the media might erase the sewer-like stench that had engulfed the city.

"Let me make sure I've got this straight," LaBadie said. "You're saying Grimes wasn't shooting at you but was trying to take down a hit man. Is that what you want us to believe?"

"Yes, sir."

"And that this hit man killed several people in Doucette's office."

"That's what Lamont told me."

"And that this character was a threat to the well-being of every person inside the casino."

"A serious threat."

"Would you swear to this?"

"On a stack of Bibles."

LaBadie worked his gum, thinking hard. Either they ran with his bullshit story and used it to fix the mess they'd created for themselves, or they didn't.

"Excuse us," LaBadie said.

The gaming agents left to talk things over.

"This should be interesting," the attorney said.

SIXTY-THREE

Billy and his attorney talked meaningless crap while waiting for the gaming agents to return. First they discussed the weather, which was a joke, since Vegas was sunny nearly every day of the year. Then they discussed the rumor that the NBA might let a team come to town, another joke, since the league was afraid the town's gamblers would fix every game. They didn't talk about anything of significance, knowing a hidden camera in the ceiling fire alarm was recording them. The tape recorder was just a ploy, put there to lull them into complacency.

The gaming agents returned wearing their poker faces. They stood in front of Billy and his lawyer with LaBadie in the center. With the gaming board, it was never a good cop / bad cop scenario. They were nobody's friend and never would be.

"We want to strike a deal with you," LaBadie said.

"A very good deal," Zander added.

"One that you should take," Tricaricco said.

"I'm all ears," Billy said.

"We'll write up the story you just told us, word for word, and have you sign your name to it," LaBadie said. "Your story will become the official version of what happened at Galaxy's casino yesterday afternoon. You will stick to that story come hell or high water, and will not waver from it, especially if you speak to the media. Does that sound good to you?"

"I can do that," he said.

"We also want you to tell us where the eight million dollars in money orders went," LaBadie said. "Do that, and we'll let you walk out of here."

"The woman in the photo with the briefcase has your money orders," Billy said.

"We know that. We want to know her name."

"I don't know her name."

"Come on, Billy. That woman works for you."

"No, she doesn't."

"You and I both know that woman's face got captured in a surveillance photo," LaBadie said, talking straight with him. "We're going to scan every surveillance tape we can find using OCR, and we'll figure out who she is, and run her down. You've heard of OCR, haven't you?"

"Optical character recognition. Yeah, I've heard of it."

"Then you know it's not just for text anymore. Its facial-recognition capability is infallible. So do us both a favor and give us her name. We'll go light on her. You have my word."

Though originally used for scanning print, OCR was now the latest tool in law enforcement. A computer created an algorithm based upon a suspect's physical characteristics and scanned it against a surveillance tape. Each time a match came up, the computer would flag the frame. By using OCR, the gaming board would be able to find Misty on other casino surveillance tapes without her disguise and run her down.

But those things took time. Days, even weeks before a match was made. Enough time for him to save Misty's ass. Leaning forward, he said, "That woman has never worked for me, and I don't know who she is. Now, do you want me to sign your piece of paper, or what?"

"You're being a fool," LaBadie said.

"You're the one with his balls in a vise."

The lawyer's gold pen lay on the table. Billy picked it up.

"Ready when you are," he said.

- - -

Billy walked out of the detention center a free man. Underman offered to give him a lift, and they walked down Lewis Avenue to the county parking facility where he'd parked.

"Where to?" his attorney asked, driving away.

"I need to get my car from Galaxy's valet," he said.

"I would advise you not to go back there."

"I need my car."

"Can't one of your friends get it for you?"

Billy wouldn't ask a member of his crew to do something that he wouldn't do himself. Underman dropped the subject and turned on the local public radio station that played classical music when it wasn't begging for donations. They listened to one of Beethoven's symphonies while driving south on the Strip, the beautiful music colliding with the jarring sight of late-night drunks trolling the sidewalks with drink cups dangling in their hands.

"What happened to Doucette's wife?" Billy asked, figuring his lawyer would know.

"I've heard several versions," his attorney said. "The most reliable is that she shot one of Rock's bodyguards, killed the second by smashing an ashtray over her head, and bit Rock in the neck and severed his jugular. She did all of this with a knife sticking out of her chest. By the time the gaming board found her, she'd bled out. Did you know her?"

"A little."

"What was she like?"

"She had a lot of anger in her."

"I've got a question for you. Is there really a hit man named Lamont Paris?"

"Sure is. I saw his wanted poster when I went to the post office to pick up a package. His name had a nice ring to it."

Galaxy's casino was a block away, their trip almost over.

"I need you to do a couple of things for me," Billy said. "A friend of mine named Maggie Flynn needs to get sprung out of jail. That's where you come in."

"Is she a cheater?"

"No, she's a nun."

"I'll see what I can do."

Billy turned sideways in his seat. "I don't care if you have to bribe a judge—just get her out."

"Be sensible, Billy. I don't even know what the charges against her are."

"That's not the answer I want to hear."

"What do you want me to say?"

"I want you to get her out of jail. You once told me half the politicians in this town were in your back pocket. Pull some strings—I don't care how much it costs."

"I'm not going to promise something I can't deliver."

Billy grabbed Underman's arm and gave it a vicious squeeze. The pain was unexpected, and the car swerved dangerously into the next lane before the attorney righted the wheel.

"You're hurting me," Underman said.

"Get Maggie Flynn out of jail."

"All right, all right. I'll figure out a way to get your friend sprung. Now let go of me."

Billy released his lawyer's arm and resumed looking at the road. "I also want you to find out where the guy that got shot is hospitalized, and text me the information."

"Why do you want to know that?"

"I want to send him flowers. Stop asking so many fucking questions."

They had reached Galaxy's main entrance. It was open for business, an interim management team running the joint. In any other town, it would have been shuttered until the investigation was complete, but that wasn't how things worked in Vegas.

Underman pulled into the valet area and hit his brakes. With the restrained fury of a father lecturing his son, he wagged his finger in Billy's face. "I want you to listen to me. You're a sharp kid, and you've got more lives than a cat. But your luck is going to run out. It happens to every criminal that thinks they can beat this town. They eventually crap out, and it's one long downhill slide from that point on. When your luck does run out, the gaming board's going to crucify you and your crew. This woman in the surveillance photo with the money orders is especially vulnerable. She's a goner, if you didn't know it."

Misty wasn't a goner. Billy had figured out a way to save her. It was going to cost him, but that was true for most things that kept a person out of jail.

"You done?" Billy asked.

"For now," his attorney said.

"Don't forget to get me that info," Billy said, and hopped out of the car.

SIXTY-FOUR

Billy pulled in front of Gabe's place at 3:00 a.m. and killed the engine.

Human beings were creatures of habit. Upon discovering comfortable routines, they repeated them endlessly without thinking. Even criminals, who should have known better.

His crew was no different. They'd gone to Gabe's place to hole up, their cars lining the driveway. Seeing no gaming agents snooping around, Billy got the strongbox from the trunk and held it against his chest as he lugged it up the front path.

He banged the front door with his knee. Bare feet pounded the foyer, Misty and Pepper the first to greet him. They planted kisses on his unshaven face and hugged his stinking body. He followed them down the hallway to the kitchen.

"Look who's here," Misty said.

The others were at the kitchen table eating cold pizza. They came out of their chairs and slapped him on the back. He cleared a spot on the table and put down the strongbox.

"Did you post bail?" Travis asked.

"Believe it or not, I talked my way out of it," he said.

"You must have done a real snow job on them."

"We're not out of the woods yet."

The strongbox still had sand on it. He cleaned it off, popped the lid, and handed out stacks of bills to his crew. The money inside the strongbox had been his first big score. He'd scammed a blackjack game at Caesars using a perfect-strategy computer built into his shoes, the vibrating solenoids telling him how to play each hand. Instead of blowing the money on wine, women, and song, he'd bought a strongbox and buried the money beneath a large conifer tree in the desert.

"The gaming board is pissed," he said. "You need to lay low for a while, let the dust settle. Use this money to pay your bills and stuff. And whatever you do, don't go into the casinos." He turned to Misty. "You're the one they really want. They're going to try to track you down. They've got brand new technology that will be hard to beat."

"Am I toast?" Misty asked.

"You are if we don't do something."

He pulled two more stacks out of the strongbox and gave them to her. "Would you consider going to a plastic surgeon and getting a face-lift? The woman on that tape needs to disappear."

"And I thought you just liked me more," Misty said, fingering the stacks. "Shit, Billy, I'll do anything if it means not going to jail. You know that."

"You're the best," he said.

"Should I go back to using my real name, too?"

"Misty's not your real name?"

"Oh, come on. Half the girls in the porn business go by Misty. Misty Stacks, Misty Love, Misty Mountains, Misty Haze. I thought everyone and his half brother knew that. My real name's Patty Driver. It's on my driver's license. Misty can be gone tomorrow."

"Then make her disappear." To the others he said, "If you have questions about what I just told you, ask them now."

His crew acted cool with the deal. He suddenly felt flat-out exhausted, and dropped into a chair. Without thinking, he picked up a half-eaten slice from a plate and took a bite out of it. He chewed mechanically and felt himself start to unwind.

"You're leaving out the good part," Pepper said. "When do we go back to Galaxy and get our score? I've got places to go and things to do with that money."

"We have to wait awhile. I know it's a drag, but there's nothing we can do about it."

"How long?"

"Three months. Maybe longer."

His crew let out a collective groan. He wanted to tell them there was nothing wrong with delayed gratification but didn't think they'd appreciate the sermon. One by one, they drifted out of the kitchen into different parts of the house.

Except for Misty. She'd run with Billy long enough to know that he would want to hear how her little adventure had gone.

"Any problems hiding the score?" he asked.

"It went without a hitch. I rode the service elevator to the fourteenth floor, found the dirty coveralls in the storage closet, and threw them on," she said. "I walked past a couple of workers in the hall, and they didn't pay me any attention. I went to room 1412 like you said and stashed the money orders behind the AC duct in the open closet wall. It took two minutes, tops."

"Did anyone talk to you?"

"No. You're going to find this is funny, but I've been wanting to get a face-lift for years."

"But you've got a beautiful face."

"Some guy put the blow job movies I did on a free porn website, and there's no way I can get them down. My face is out there, if you know what I mean."

"So this is a good thing."

"Yeah. I'm ready for a change."

She left the kitchen and he finished eating the slice. In a few days, room 1412 would be finished, the closet wall sealed up. When the time was right, he'd make a reservation at the hotel and ask for that suite, telling the reservationist it was his lucky number. Gamblers were by nature a superstitious group, and his request would not draw scrutiny.

He'd check into the hotel under a false name. In his luggage would be an electric saw. The morning of his departure, he'd play loud music in the suite and cut a hole in the closet wall. The money orders would go into a piece of luggage, which a bellman would remove from the room and put in Billy's car. This method of taking stolen money out of a casino wasn't new; casino employees had been using it for years to rip off their employers and supplement their 401(k)s.

He got pumped just thinking about it.

- - -

He went to say good-bye to his crew. It was going to be a while before they hooked up again, and he wanted to look each of them in the eye and make sure they were okay with cutting up the score later on. Last thing he needed was for one of them to get sore and start shooting their mouth off. Misty and Pepper were in the study huddled in front of the computer, checking out the before and after photos of face-lifts on a plastic surgeon's splashy website, Pepper saying, "You're going to look ten years younger, girl. Think of all the rich men you'll meet." Misty laughed mischievously under her breath.

"I've got to blow. Call me if anything comes up, or you want to talk," Billy said.

"You going to stay in town?" Misty asked.

"I'm taking a friend to LA. I might hang there awhile."

"The plastic surgeon I'm thinking of using is in LA. Maybe we can get together while I'm recuperating, go hang out at Disneyland or something."

"That would be a blast. Let's do it."

They said their good-byes. Pepper walked with him into the hallway.

"Hey, Billy, do you think I could get a face-lift, too?" Pepper asked. "I was in those movies with Misty. It would let us both make a clean break, if you know what I mean."

He couldn't say no without hurting Pepper's feelings. In the kitchen he gave her two more stacks from the strongbox. She squealed with delight and kissed him.

Next stop was the garage, where Gabe and Travis were preparing to move the bulky Italian press and spark-erosion machine that the fake chips had been manufactured on.

"I'm out of here. Are you guys good with everything?" Billy asked.

"I'm good," Travis said.

"Same here," Gabe said.

He asked them how they planned to spend the time away from the casinos.

"Hanging out with my family, doing crap around the house, working on my dice switch," Travis said. "You won't recognize it the next time I move."

"You going to videotape yourself?" Billy asked.

"I was planning on it," Travis said.

"Practice keeping your thumb still."

"I'll do that."

"How about you?" Billy asked Gabe.

"I'm going to drive down to San Diego to see my ex and the girls," Gabe said. "I texted her this morning, and she seemed okay with it. I was hoping to shower her with money, you know, just to show her I wasn't the biggest loser that ever lived, but I think it's better that I don't. I'll send her some later."

"I hope it goes okay," he said.

"Me, too. Look, Billy, I've got to get something off my chest. I've had it up to my eyeballs with Cory and Morris. We all make mistakes, but those two . . . no."

"Anything in particular bothering you?"

"Yeah. Cory came into the casino without his disguise. When I asked him why, he said he forgot to put it on."

"Was that his excuse? Jesus."

"You know about it, then."

"It came up during my chat with the gaming board. How about you?"

"I feel the same way," Travis said. "They're going to ruin us one day if we're not careful."

"Had enough, huh?" Billy said.

Both men said they'd had.

- - -

He found Cory and Morris in the backyard smoking a joint so fat it could have passed as a small cigar. Seeing Billy come out the back door, Cory ground the joint into the grass while his partner kept the last puff trapped in his lungs. Billy had told them they were not allowed to get high during a job, yet they'd kept right on doing it. Their stupidity was making his decision a lot easier.

"Get over here. Both of you," he said.

They shuffled over, embarrassed. There was no reason to beat around the bush, so he laid into them. "You guys have been fucking up a lot lately. First at the golf course, then Cory forgets to put on his disguise when you parked the rental behind the casino. The gaming board made you. It's a miracle I got you off. You could have screwed the whole thing up."

They hung their heads in shame. Morris let the smoke go and started hacking.

"We'll make it up to you," Cory promised.

"Yeah, we'll do you right," Morris said.

"It's too late for that. I'm cutting you both loose. You'll get your money when we cut up the score, and that's it. No more jobs. You're done."

"You're not going to give us another chance?" Cory asked.

Billy shook his head and thought they might cry. He went inside without saying good-bye, grabbed the strongbox off the kitchen table, and headed out the front door. As he placed the strongbox in the trunk, they came up from behind.

"Quit following me," he said.

"Come on, Billy, we've been loyal," Cory said.

"Soldiers to the end," Morris said.

"You want my advice? Go back to college and get degrees in hospitality management. It's all you're good for."

"No, Billy," they both said.

"Or slinging drinks in a bar. You could do that. I let you join my crew, teach you everything I know, and what do I get in return? A bunch of high school fucking jive artists who can't remember to put on their fucking disguises before they walk into a joint. You're both a disgrace. Now get out of my way before I run you over, which is what I want to do right now."

They jumped onto the grass next to the curb. Billy got in and fired up the engine. His heart was beating out of control, his hands shaking on the wheel. He didn't need this, and he shot them an angry look through the passenger window. They took it the wrong way and brought their faces up to the glass, thinking he was going to give them another chance to make things right again.

He sped away, refusing to look back.

SIXTY-FIVE

His heart was still pounding as he pulled into the parking lot of Ly's motel. He'd had members of his crew leave before, usually for personal reasons, but he'd never had to fire anyone. Cutting Cory and Morris loose was tearing him apart, and he didn't know why.

He rapped softly on the door to Ly's room. He'd promised to drive Ly to LA and didn't see any reason to wait. He needed to get her out of Vegas before the gaming board ran her down and held her feet to the fire.

"Go away, or I'll call the cops," a woman that wasn't Ly said through the door.

He backed away from the door, knowing he was being watched through the peephole.

"Sorry."

He walked around the building and entered the tiny office that served as registration. The young Latina working the desk was the same one who'd checked him in, a tough little number with lots of makeup. She unplugged herself from an iPod and arched her eyebrows.

"Have you seen my friend? She isn't answering her door."

"Your Asian friend checked out," the Latina said.

Ly didn't have enough money to buy a bus ticket, and Billy wondered where she'd gone.

"Did she say where she was going?"

"I don't like to get involved with people's business," the Latina said, "but since you paid for her room, I'll tell you. Your friend met a guy in the restaurant, a software salesman out of Reno. He stays here a lot. Your friend left with him."

"You don't say. Decent guy?"

"The women seem to like him."

That solved that problem. He started to back out of the office. The Latina wasn't done with him. "You had another visitor. She's still here."

"Who's that?"

The Latina said, "Try the pool," and plugged herself back in.

He walked around the building to a metal gate that required a room key for entrance, and hopped over it. The pool was deserted except for a beautiful woman sound asleep in a lounge chair. As he drew closer, the breath caught in his throat. It was Mags.

A tired smile formed at the corners of his mouth. He'd wanted to strangle her a few days ago, but those feelings had faded away. She'd stepped up to the plate when it counted, and shown her true colors. And when she'd gotten sprung out of jail, she'd run straight to him.

His smile grew. He realized that it had all been worth it—the beatings, getting thrown in jail, the whole nine yards. He'd do it again if it meant Maggie Flynn would be waiting for him when it was all over. If that wasn't a definition of a fool in love, he didn't know what was.

"Hey."

Her eyes snapped open. She stood up slowly, uncertain of where they stood.

"I never thought you'd come," she said.

"I was tying up some loose ends. How'd you find me?"

"I asked your lawyer after he bailed me out of jail. He said a friend of yours was holed up here, that you might come by."

"My friend split."

"So I heard. God, do you smell rank. You need a good bath."

It sounded like an invitation. He didn't know what to say, and just stared.

"I rented a room. Want to see it?"

They showered together, soaping down each other's bodies beneath the steaming spray. His body was tense and it took a while before he relaxed. He'd been in some tight spots, but nothing like what he'd just gone through. For the next few hours he was going to pretend that it had never happened and that the brutal memories banging around in his head weren't real.

They toweled each other off. She led him into the bedroom while holding his prick. She was in control, and he was more than willing to be her slave. She told him to lose the bedspread, and he whisked it away like a nightclub magician and threw it on the floor.

She clicked her fingers and pointed at the bed. He lay down obediently, and she mounted him. He had imagined this moment so many times that he didn't think it would live up to his expectations. Dreams rarely did.

He was wrong. Being inside her was heaven, and the room started to move as if they were having an earthquake. Shutting his eyes, he thought about the lengths they'd traveled to reach this cheap motel room. The odds of them connecting had to be a trillion-to-one. If that wasn't fate, he didn't know what was.

Done, he took several exhilarating breaths.

"Want to do it again?" she asked.

- - -

Early the next morning, his Droid started making rude noises. Caller ID said it was Cory, king of the fuckups. Mags was out like a light, and he slid out of bed and took the call in the john.

"What do you want?"

"Hey, Billy, me and Morris just wanted to say hi, see how things are going," Cory said. Everything's cool here. No gaming board at the doorstep, ha-ha."

"Hi, Billy," came Morris's voice in the background.

"What do you *want*?"

"We've been working on this cool scam with a hotel concierge," Cory said. "We need someone with experience to make the play, so we called you. We won't let you down this time, and that's a promise from both of us."

Scams involving a hotel's concierge were the bread and butter of many hustlers' existence. The suckers were usually rich suckers with supersized egos and zero common sense. They took their beatings in stride, and their checks never bounced. He realized he wanted to hear what Cory and Morris had cooked up.

"Lay it on me."

"You want to hear the scam? Really?"

"Yeah, and it's the only reason. Start talking."

"Okay. You're going to love this. This software king from Silicon Valley flies into Vegas each month to host a private poker game at the Palms. Fifty-thousand-dollar buy-in, winner take all. The sucker brings five of his buddies with him and has the hotel concierge invite a local player to round out the field. Now, here's the good part. The sucker's afraid of getting cheated, so he buys the cards for the game from the hotel gift shop. Morris bribed the manager of the gift shop, and we stacked the shelves with a hundred decks of marked cards. The sucker will be bringing marked cards to his own game, and he won't even know it."

"What marking system did you use?"

"We juiced them. Just throw your eyes out of focus, and the marks pop out."

"Juiced them how?"

"We used aniline dye mixed with pure grain alcohol and applied it to the borders with an airbrush. We cut glycerin into the mix to help bring back the shine after the dye was applied to the card. It was a lot of work, but the payoff will be huge."

"Were you smoking dope when you did it?"

"No way, we're off the dope. We learned our lesson."

"You still haven't explained the play."

"Morris is buddies with the concierge at the Palms," Cory said, his voice growing excited. "The concierge will front for you and get you into the game. You know the rest. We'll go fifty-fifty with you, after we pay off the concierge. The sucker is flying in Tuesday night. So what do you say? Are you in?"

Marking cards was an art *and* a science. If the marks were too strong, they could be seen under a bright light, exposing the scam to everyone at the table. Knowing Cory and Morris, they probably hadn't let all of the marked decks dry properly, and a couple decks in the Palms gift shop had too much dye on them. If by chance the Silicon Valley sucker purchased a bad deck and spotted the not-so-invisible marks, he and his pals would put two and two together and know that the stranger in the game was at fault and throw Billy off the balcony.

"You must be out of your fucking mind," he said.

"Why? What did we do wrong?" Cory choked on the words.

"Figure it out for yourselves."

He ended the call and slipped back into bed. The sheets were still warm, and he snuggled up next to Mags and heard her murmur.

"Who was that?" she asked.

"No one important," he said.

SIXTY-SIX

They ate a late breakfast in the hotel coffee shop and decided it might be a good idea if they both left town for a while.

"Where do you have in mind?" he asked.

"LA. I've always wanted to visit there," Mags said.

"You've never been to LA? It's my favorite town next to this one."

"Where should we stay?"

"Venice. The beach scene is really cool."

They used his Droid to find a boutique hotel in Venice called the Erwin. Mags dug the decor, and he booked a partial ocean view that set him back six hundred bucks. Normally, he'd never spend that much, but Mags had given him what he wanted, and he felt whole again.

His Droid was making noises again. He checked it in the parking lot. His attorney had sent him a text. *Desert Springs Medical Center, ICU, #224*. He had one last unfinished piece of business to attend to, and he took Koval north until he reached East Flamingo and hung a right.

"This isn't the way to the freeway," Mags said.

"I need to see a sick friend of mine," he said.

"I thought you were taking me to Venice to fuck my brains out."

He stared at the road. She was trying to control him, show him who was boss. He guessed it was to be expected. "I'll make it up to you. Promise."

"You'd better," she said.

The hospital appeared in the windshield, and he flipped on his indicator.

- - -

Desert Springs Hospital Medical Center was known for its trauma unit. Entering through the sliding glass doors, he detoured at the gift shop and bought a basket filled with purple carnations and white daisy pompons before taking the elevator to the ICU unit on the second floor.

Room 224 was at the end of a hallway and was distinguished by a large gathering of visitors outside its door. It was the Gypsy wedding party, now attired in street clothes.

Seeing Billy approach, one of the clan broke free and came forward. It was the best man who'd asked Billy to take the group's picture. The best man was in his late twenties with fierce eyes and had the take-charge attitude of being next in line to inherit the throne.

"Excuse me," he said, "but I think you have the wrong room."

"I was there yesterday. I came by to see how he was doing," Billy said.

The best man grew flustered. "You're the guy who stopped to help. You saved my father's life. The doctors said he would have bled to death if not for you."

"I'm glad he pulled through. You mind if I say hello?"

"He's resting right now. I'll be sure to tell him you asked about him."

The best man tried to take the get-well basket from Billy's hands. Billy kept his grip on the handle. The best man's eyes narrowed, his radar now on full alert.

"I need to speak to your father," Billy said.

"I just told you—"

"I think he wants to talk to me. Tell him that I'm here."

"What is this about? Who are you?"

"Just tell him I'm here. I'll be at the nurse's station."

- - -

In hindsight, Billy knew he should never have asked dear old Papa where he'd stashed the earth magnet. The old guy had probably spent the night sweating through his hospital sheets, convinced Billy was going to turn his family over to the gaming board. Nothing could have been further from the truth, but how was dear old Papa to know that?

The truth be known, Billy admired the old guy for making such a gutsy play. Certain makes of slot machines had a flaw buried within their design. Many cheaters knew about this flaw but hadn't found a way to exploit it. The old guy *had* found a way, and gone and done it.

Every slot machine had a memory chip called an EPROM, which generated millions of numbers per second, making each play truly random. EPROM chips of inferior design could be scammed using a DEPROM software program, which added a lengthy code to the EPROM chip that tricked the machine into paying a jackpot. The additional code contained the usual rows of ones, zeros, and letters and appeared normal when inspected.

The hard part was adding the code to the machine. While hiding behind the bride's gown, Papa had silenced the Money Vault machine's internal antitheft alarm with the earth magnet, then opened the machine with a skeleton key. Using a handheld computer loaded with the DEPROM program, he'd added the code to the EPROM chip and rigged the machine.

The jackpot would be stolen later by a claimer. Claimers were female, often a schoolteacher or dental hygienist with a squeaky-clean background. The claimer would play the Money Vault machine using a specific sequence of coins. This sequence would trigger the additional code to assign a line of jackpot symbols to the game, and pay a jackpot.

The claimer's cut was 5 percent. Not a bad payday for an hour's work.

And I was there to see it, Billy thought.

- - -

The best man approached the nurse's station and motioned with his hand. Billy followed him down the hall. The gathering at the door parted, all eyes on the stranger. The room was a single. Papa sat upright in bed with a pillow behind his head, surfing the hospital's measly choice of cable channels. For an old codger he was plenty vain, his face freshly shaven and his hair neatly parted. Two of his daughters were also in the room. He spoke under his breath, and they departed.

"You, too," Papa said.

"I need to stay with you, Pop," his son said.

"This man is our friend. I'll be fine."

"How do you know he's our friend?"

"Listen to what I say to you, and no back talk. Do you understand?"

"Yes, Pop. I'll be out in the hall if you need me."

"I'm not going to need you. Scram."

The best man reluctantly left the room. Papa pointed at the chairs. Billy sat, thrilled at the idea of spending time alone with him. The TV hanging over the bed went dark.

"You're a cheater, aren't you?" the older man said.

"Guilty as charged," he said.

"When you made the crack about the earth magnet, I figured it was just a matter of time before the gaming board arrested me. When they didn't come, I knew otherwise. What's your name?"

"Billy Cunningham."

"Mine's Victor. Nice to meet you, Billy."

"Same here. I've heard about your family for years. I didn't think we'd meet while I was doing a job, but I guess that stuff happens sometimes."

"You were ripping them off, too? That's funny. So what can I do for you?"

"I wanted to warn you. The gaming board is after me, and they're going to be scrutinizing the casino's surveillance tapes for the next several weeks. They might get suspicious if you win that jackpot too soon, if you know what I mean."

"You think I should wait awhile before I send in the claimer?"

"I would."

"How long?"

"A couple of months, just to be on the safe side."

"You're a stand-up guy for coming here to tell me. Let's have a drink."

Victor produced a worn silver flask from beneath the sheets. Billy went to the bathroom and grabbed two paper cups into which Victor poured a liberal amount of whiskey. They saluted each other's health and knocked back the drinks. Billy winced. It was like licking a nine-volt battery.

"So tell me, how'd you know we pulled a slot scam?" Victor asked. "Don't tell me one of my kids screwed up. It's always something with them."

"I actually figured it out on my own," he said.

"No kidding. You must be a smart son of a bitch."

"Sometimes." He paused. "Do your kids screw up a lot?"

"All the time. I train them the best I can, but they never get things right. On top of that, they're always bickering with each other, causing me grief. Sometimes I think I'm running a babysitting service. It's all I can do not to wring their necks."

His problems sounded no different than those Billy had experienced with his crew, which he found surprising. Victor had been cheating casinos a lot longer than Billy had.

"Have you ever gotten rid of one of them?" he asked.

Victor blinked, not understanding.

"One of your kids."

"Have I ever gotten rid of one of my kids?"

"For screwing up a job."

"Of course not."

"Why not? If they're causing problems, isn't that the smart thing to do?"

"Trust me, I've thought about replacing my kids with outsiders plenty of times. It would make dealing with day-to-day problems a hell of a lot easier. But at the end of the day, one thing always stopped me."

"What's that?"

"You can't buy loyalty."

The words cut straight to the heart. Billy took the flask out of Victor's hand and poured himself another drink. It didn't burn nearly as badly the second time around.

"I know it's none of my business, but what were you doing?" the head of the Gypsies asked. "Blackjack, craps? Or was it something else?"

"We made a run at the cage."

"Wow. That hasn't been done in a long time. Did you pull it off?"

"Yes, sir."

"You must have some crew. You got a cell phone?"

"Sure."

"I'll give you my number. Next time you're in Sacramento, give me a call. I'd like to get together with you, hash around some ideas. I've got some scams that require two crews working in tandem. I haven't tried them because I don't trust nobody. But you're different. I could work with you. And from the sounds of it, your crew isn't bad, either."

He would have crawled on his belly through cracked glass to spend an hour with Victor Boswell, just to hear the stories. Taking out his Droid, he hit the icon where his contact information was stored. His hand was shaking, and he hoped Victor didn't notice.

"Ready when you are," he said.

SIXTY-SEVEN

The sun was doing a slow Hollywood fade when Billy and Mags arrived at Hotel Erwin. It was a funky spot, with wall-sized graffiti in the valet area and colorful surfboards in the lobby. They went to the rooftop lounge, where they enjoyed a glass of champagne while listening to a DJ.

"You sure know how to treat a girl right," Mags said.

"I told you I'd make it up to you, didn't I? Want more champagne?"

"Actually, I had something else in mind."

Their suite had a spectacular ocean view and a firm king bed. When they were done, he called room service and ordered one of everything off the limited menu. She dug that and rested her head against his chest. It felt perfect, and he wondered if he was dreaming.

"So when do I start?" she asked.

The question knocked him sideways.

"With my crew?" he asked, just to be sure.

"Yeah. That was our deal, and I'm holding you to it."

"You'd go back into the casinos, after what happened?"

"You think I'm scared of the gaming board? Screw 'em."

It was crazy talk, and he wondered if it was the booze. The gaming board was going to make sure Mags never cheated another casino. Her face and characteristics would be sent to every gambling establishment from here to Atlantic City, and they'd spot her before she placed her first bet. Her grifting days were finished.

"You're sure about this?" he asked.

"Damn straight." She lifted her head and looked him in the eye. "So what's my role?"

"I haven't thought that far ahead."

"So start thinking." She hopped out of bed and went to the mini-bar. "Like a scotch?"

"Sure. Straight up."

He sat up in bed and watched her fix their drinks in the nude. Normally, it would have turned him on. But he was seeing her differently now, and it scared him. She wasn't being rational. She *couldn't* go back into a casino ever again.

She joined him, and they clinked glasses.

"Here's to running together," she said.

"You're sure about this?" he said.

"Why do you keep saying that? Of course I'm sure. I've been grifting since I was a kid. What the hell else am I going to do? Work the register at Mickey D's?"

He took a swallow of his drink. She was on a suicide run, the blinders on so tight that she couldn't see the forest for the trees. If she wanted to kill herself, fine, that was up to her. But he wasn't going to let her take him and his crew down as well.

He decided to give her one more chance.

"You should take some time off first," he suggested. "Go back east, see your kid. It would be good for you."

"You sound like you're trying to get rid of me."

"You need to clear your head. You've been through a lot."

"My head is plenty clear. I want to run with your crew."

"You want me to set up a meeting, make introductions?"

"Is that how it works?"

"Yeah. Like introducing a new dog to the pack."

"See where I fit in the pecking order."

"Something like that."

"I can dig that. Set it up."

It was turning into a bad dream. Mags was a liability and always would be. He wondered why he hadn't seen it before, and realized he'd been blinded by his feelings.

He downed the rest of his scotch. She did the same.

"Want another?" he asked.

"That would be great. So, am I in?" she asked.

"You're in. Let's celebrate."

He got her good and loaded. She started slurring her speech and soon was fast asleep. He put on his clothes and went downstairs to the valet area. His car came up. He popped the trunk and opened the strongbox. Two stacks were left. It was all the money he had in the world. He peeled off two hundreds for himself and could not help but laugh. It was the same amount he'd arrived in Vegas with, ten years ago.

He returned to the suite and put the stacks on the empty pillow so it would be the first thing she saw upon awakening. He stole a last look before walking out the door, made a mental picture so he wouldn't forget. It would be a long time before he fell this hard again.

He thought about kissing her but decided it was a bad idea.

- - -

With the sultry voice of his GPS to guide him, he drove east on Pacific to Neilson Way, went right on Olympic Boulevard, and a quarter mile later was greeted by the sign for I-10 East. Traffic was flowing, and he lowered his window and let the wind dry the stinging tears from his eyes.

He told himself he'd get over it, but he knew that was a lie. He'd never gotten over his mother going to prison or his old man checking out, the losses gnawing away at his insides like slow-moving cancers, and he didn't think it would be any different this time around.

Soon he was on I-15 North. It was a straight 208-mile shot into downtown Vegas. He put his foot to the pedal and started to race. Eighty, ninety, then a hundred miles per hour, the houses and buildings falling away until he was in the desert, the car practically driving itself.

He tried to take his mind off Mags and thought about Victor Boswell instead. When he'd told Victor he'd figured out their scam, Victor had asked if one of his kids had screwed up, as if it was a common occurrence. Yet Victor wouldn't think of replacing them. Victor's family was devoted to him, and he was devoted to them, and that was why the Gypsies had lasted so long.

There was a lesson there. At the end of the day, it was about family, and watching each other's backs, and sharing the good times. Maybe that was why he was hurting. Losing Mags was hard, but losing two members of his crew was worse.

He pulled off on the shoulder and made a call on his Droid.

"Billy?" Cory asked breathlessly.

"You guys still up?"

"Just watching a movie on Netflix."

"Hey, Billy," Morris said in the background.

"Some of those marked decks in the Palms gift shop are bad," he said. "When I taught you how to use juice, I left out the most important part."

"You did? What's that?"

"After you apply the marks, use a blow-dryer to dry the cards. Set the dryer on low, and gently pass it over the cards. That way, the marks will never show."

"Are you saying we need to replace all the cards?"

"That's exactly what I'm saying."

"We can do that. Do you want in?"

Knowing Cory and Morris, they hadn't thought the scam out, and it was a risk. But what scam didn't have risk? It really didn't matter. The siren's song was calling to him, just like it had so many countless times before. He needed to hustle again and stuff his pockets with other people's money. But most importantly, he needed to run with his crew. Without them, there was only so much stealing he could do.

"I'm in," he said.

ACKNOWLEDGMENTS

The author wishes to thank the following people for their generous contributions to this book. Andy Vita and my wife, Laura, who helped me with the early drafts. Kjersti Egerdahl and Kevin Smith, whose contributions and editorial suggestions are worth far more than a simple line of thanks. The crew of cheaters I met in Las Vegas in 2008 who agreed to let me tell their story. And a very special thanks to Stephen Roberts, who made me sit down and watch an old French movie with subtitles called *Bob le flambeur,* which inspired me to write this book.

ABOUT THE AUTHOR

Photo © 2007 Robert Allen Sargent

James Swain has been writing most of his life and has worked as a magazine editor, screenwriter, and novelist. He is the national bestselling author of seventeen mystery novels. His books have been translated into many languages and have been chosen as Mysteries of the Year by *Publishers Weekly* and *Kirkus Reviews*. Swain has received a Florida Book Award for fiction, and in 2006, he was awarded France's prestigious Prix Calibre .38 for Best American Crime Writing. When he isn't writing, he enjoys researching casino scams and cons, a subject on which he's considered an expert.